For a Father's Pride

Diane Allen was born in Leeds, but raised at her family's farm deep in the Yorkshire Dales. After working as a glass engraver, raising a family and looking after an ill father, she found her true niche in life, joining a large-print publishing firm in 1990. Having risen through the firm, she is now the general manager and has recently been made Honorary Vice President of the Romantic Novelists' Association.

Diane and her husband Ronnie live in Long Preston, in the Yorkshire Dales, and have two children and four beautiful grandchildren.

By Diane Allen

For the Sake of Her Family
For a Mother's Sins
For a Father's Pride

DIANE ALLEN

For a Father's Pride

PAN BOOKS

First published 2014 by Macmillan

This edition published 2014 by Pan Books
an imprint of Pan Macmillan
20 New Wharf Road, London N1 9RR
Associated companies throughout the world
www.panmacmillan.com

ISBN 978-1-5098-9550-2

A CIP catalogue record for this book is available from the British Library.

Typeset by Ellipsis Digital Limited, Glasgow
Printed and bound by CPI Group (UK) Ltd, Croydon, CR0 4YY

Dedicated to the memory
of Shirley Monks.

A true friend.
I miss you, lass . . .

I wish to acknowledge my thanks to Roy Sedgwick, of Cowgill, an ex-signalman on the Settle-to-Carlisle Railway. His knowledge of the line gave me inspiration and guidance for this book. I am also grateful for the use of information from *Memory Lane, Leeds*, Volume 1, published by the *Yorkshire Evening Post*, with its valuable insight into Victorian Leeds.

1

Grisedale, Yorkshire Dales, 1872

The sun shone through the chapel window, the shimmering rays dancing and playing around the young couple who were taking their vows of marriage, quietly and with reverence.

Daisy Fraser watched with damp eyes as her older sister, Kitty, let her new husband tenderly slip the ring onto her finger and then kiss her gently on the cheek. She was torn between jealousy, regret and anger at herself. She should have told her sister who she was marrying: what a rat Clifford was, and that he was only after their father's money. Clifford Middleton – there he stood, the dark-haired and handsome heir to Grouse Hall, Grisedale, marrying the baker's oldest daughter, who came into the marriage with a handsome dowry. But it was young Daisy who knew what he was really like. She quickly swept away an escaping tear that was falling down her cheek. Her mother noticed, squeezed her hand and whispered, 'Never mind, dear, your day will come,' not realizing that her daughter wasn't crying out of regret.

Daisy gave a false smile. She had tossed and turned for nights, wondering whether to tell her sister, but the wedding plans had been well under way. And how could she spoil Kitty's wedding day with the most disastrous news you could hear coming from the lips of your sweet younger sister? Daisy had always lusted after Clifford. She knew he was a good-for-nothing, but his father was wealthy, he dressed in the sharpest suits and he always had a twinkle in his eye and a smile for the ladies – everything that young Daisy, at sixteen, had admired. But it had been Kitty's hand he'd asked for in marriage this spring, and Daisy had been broken-hearted at the fact that Clifford had never given her a second glance.

That was until Kitty and their mother had gone to Sedbergh for some supplies for the wedding breakfast. Daisy had been in the house alone; her father had been delivering bread over in the nearby valley of Uldale, and she'd been left to tidy up and prepare the spare room for the guests who would soon be arriving. She'd turned round quickly, sensing someone in the room with her, to find Clifford leaning against the doorway smiling at her. She could still hear his soothing, dark voice and see the way he looked commandingly at her. She could remember how he said that he was being a fool and was marrying the wrong sister, and that he would rather have Daisy's brains than Kitty's beauty. She could remember how he'd wooed her and made her feel special, saying that at sixteen she was nearly a woman – and would she like to know what it felt like to be a true woman?

Colour rose in her cheeks as she thought of the moment when he carried her into her mother and father's bedroom, pulling up her skirts and kissing her tenderly, making her feel like a grown woman, and secretly satisfied that Clifford was showing her the lover she could be. He unbuttoned his trousers, but it was then that she'd come to her senses and pleaded with him not to go any further – to no avail. She'd pounded her fists on his chest and screamed in his ear, as he grinned wickedly at her while unbuttoning his trousers. Daisy winced aloud as he entered her, frightened but too scared to shout any more, as he roughly covered her mouth with his foul-smelling hands. He kissed her roughly, biting and scratching her, as each thrust became harder and deeper. Never had she been touched and used like that before. It was painful, and her legs and body ached. Finally he'd rolled off her, exhausted, and Daisy had lain next to him nearly in tears, realizing what she had done, overcome with pain and shame after the agony and heat of the moment had passed. She had allowed her future brother-in-law to go where no honourable gent would even mention, let alone touch – losing her virginity to a cad, someone who had no respect for her or her sister.

She'd watched as Clifford had buttoned up his trousers and grinned before saying, 'Two sisters in one day – one with money and the other without. Still, you were a good ride, Miss Fraser.' And she remembered sobbing into her mother's bedding as she pulled her skirts down, feeling used and filthy. She'd stayed in her parents' room until she heard him go down the stairs and slam the front door, and then she'd stood, with his seed running down her legs. She remembered the rush she had made to the kitchen, to wash him away; how she'd trembled with the jug full of cold water and the cloth, washing her private parts and getting rid of the smell that he'd left behind, before her parents returned.

'Daisy, are you all right, you look quite flushed? Don't they make such a beautiful couple? Kitty has done so well for herself. To think my daughter is going to be the mistress of Grouse Hall – I just can't believe it.' Martha Fraser was pink with excitement, but at the same time concerned about her younger daughter's reaction to the wedding. 'Now, we must find you a young man, perhaps a farmer's son. Or Luke Allen has a good-looking lad – perhaps you should go into Hawes one day. Two bakeries together, now that would be something!'

'Mother, I don't aim to marry. Besides, who'd have me? Compared to Kitty, I'm plain and ordinary: too short, too plump, with mousy brown hair. We are like chalk and cheese.' Daisy came back from her thoughts quickly.

'Nonsense, you'll grow into a fine woman. You are still young, my dear. Plenty of time to look around and find the right man – at least another five years. You don't want to be sitting on the shelf when you are over

4

twenty, though, my dear.' Martha giggled and rushed out into the aisle as the young couple made their way down the steps, stopping at the pews of their parents.

'Mrs Fraser, you look beautiful. Why, I know now where Kitty gets her looks from – they always say "Like mother, like daughter".' Clifford Middleton kissed his mother-in-law's hand, making her go a darker shade of pink with his comments.

'Now, Clifford, words are a fine thing, but you'd better look after my daughter. She's precious to me; both of them are.' Tom Fraser pulled Kitty close to him and shook Clifford's hand, little knowing that he was shaking the hand of the man who had taken advantage of his younger daughter.

'Of course I will, Mr Fraser. I love your Kitty and hope to make her a good husband, and I'll treat Daisy like the sister I never had.' Clifford smiled like a wily fox, nearly snarling at the sight of Daisy.

'Good man – you're welcome to our family. As long as you do right by us, we'll be right by you.' Tom slapped Clifford on the back and walked up the aisle, past the few guests and relations that had been invited.

Daisy dallied at the back of the group. She didn't want to go near her new brother-in-law; in fact, she would have done anything not to have been at the wedding. But now she knew that worse was to come, as the wedding breakfast was to be held at Grouse Hall. How dare Clifford say he would treat her like a sister? You definitely didn't take your sister to bed.

'Come on, everybody, the carriages await. My father

will make everyone welcome at our home. Please don't be alarmed by the way he looks – he can understand every word you say. I'm afraid that his stroke has left him unable to speak, and his face is slightly lopsided, but behind the mask is a brain that still works.' Clifford ushered everyone into the carriages, including his blushing bride, who hung on his every word and smiled as her loving husband held out his hand to assist her.

Everyone knew that old Middleton was on his way out. He'd had a stroke a few years ago, losing his speech, but had managed to retain control by writing everything down for people to read. He'd lost his wife in childbirth, when she had tried to give him another heir; both mother and baby had died, leaving a distraught ten-year-old Clifford and a grieving husband. Since then Clifford had been brought up by a housekeeper, and his father had slowly slipped into becoming the old man he now was. Soon Grouse Hall would be Clifford's, along with the four hundred acres of land and two farm cottages that were tenanted. Clifford Middleton was a good catch for anyone who could put up with his wild ways.

'What's up, Daisy, you've got a face on you that could turn milk sour?' Tom Fraser looked at his younger daughter. 'It's a wedding, not a funeral, we've been to, and you're about to fill your belly at someone else's expense, so make the most of it.' Her father scowled at Daisy. She was his favourite, a clever lass, but far too sombre and deep-thinking sometimes. He worried that her thoughts were sometimes too deep for her own good.

'I don't like Clifford. I don't want to go and see his home, or his old father.' Daisy could have cried, but she had to keep her secret.

'Well, you were all over him the other day – tha changes with the wind, lass. I thought you liked him. Or is it, happen, a bit of jealousy creeping in?' Tom made light of her mood.

'I don't think he's right for our Kitty.' Daisy had to say it.

'Hush, child. Course he's right for Kitty – she loves him.' Martha Fraser urged her outspoken daughter to be quiet.

'Too bloody right. He's right for our Kitty. He has plenty of brass and plenty of land, which is what a father likes to hear, so you'll keep your mouth shut and make best of it.' Tom Fraser's mood changed quickly. He'd worked hard to find his daughter a good man, and it had cost him a pretty penny. He'd made sure Kitty had been seen in all the right places and in all the society papers, just for her to catch the eye of Clifford Middleton: the catch of the Dales. He wasn't going to hear any different. 'It'll be finding somebody for you that we'll have bother with now, and you don't have the looks of your sister.'

'Father, watch what you say.' Martha scowled at him as the carriage turned up the driveway of Grouse Hall.

*

The long, low house of Grouse Hall stood in front of them. The limestone from which it was built looked grey and dark in the dimming light, and Daisy couldn't help but notice that the windows and doors could do with a lick of paint. It was set high on the fellside of Grisedale and had wild rushes and rough fell-grass growing around it. What had been garden walls was now rubble, and nature had taken over, making its own display of wild brambles and ragged robin, which gently bobbed its frayed petals in the breeze.

Martha Fraser held her husband's hand as he helped her out of the carriage, not quite believing this was the place where her daughter was going to live. She had understood, by the way Clifford dressed and spoke, that it was a grand hall he lived in, as the name had suggested. But this was nothing more than a rambling, neglected farmhouse. She scowled at her husband. He'd known all along what the house looked like, so why hadn't he said?

Tom whispered to her, noting her disappointment, 'Don't judge a book by its cover, Martha; he's got brass in the bank.' She held his hand and smiled at the two rather grubby servants who were standing at the gate, waiting to greet their new mistress and her family.

Daisy, left to her own devices, climbed out of the carriage unaided and stood and watched as the servants bobbed and curtsied. Then she watched as they scrambled back into the house while Clifford urged them to go about their work. With tears nearly welling up in her eyes yet again, she watched as Clifford swept Kitty off her feet and carried her over the threshold of Grouse

Hall, laughing and screaming, with her family and guests cheering them on. The marriage was a farce. Were they all blind, and could they not see that Clifford's twinkling eyes and easy charm were just a pretence and that he would never be faithful to her sister? She stood for a second by the rundown garden wall, admiring the view of the dale and trying to block her ill feelings from spoiling her sister's wedding day. She watched as a nesting curlew circled overhead, crying its familiar call, before landing down in the valley bottom below. She wished she could join it and not have to attend the wedding breakfast; anything was better than having to look into the dark eyes of her brother-in-law.

She felt a hand on her shoulder.

'Now, little sister, when were you thinking of joining us? Kitty is asking for you.' Clifford's grip was like a vice on her shoulder.

She shrugged her shoulder from him to loosen his grip, and walked down the path to the porch and entrance to the hall, but he caught her just as she was about to enter.

'Don't you ever say a word about what happened the other day, or I'll make life hell for your sister and ruin your father, do you hear me? After all, you were nearly begging me for it,' Clifford snarled, holding Daisy's wrist tightly, before releasing it as one of the wedding guests strolled by the doorway.

'I'll not say anything, but you be kind to our Kitty, for she loves you.' Daisy turned her back on Clifford and entered the low, beamed home of the Middletons.

She stared at the shape of Tobias Middleton, sitting in his chair watching the wedding-party visitors come and go around him, grunting his greetings to them. She couldn't help but feel a little sorry for him, as his son completely ignored him, choosing to flirt and chat with his new in-laws and relations. She watched Tobias for a while as he tried to converse with people and then looked lost, as people gave up being polite once they couldn't understand him. She felt a bit like old Tobias herself – out of place and an outcast – and decided to sit next to him. He grunted his greeting as she introduced herself. He smiled a slow smile and took a chalk board and some chalk from next to him, before starting to write a few words very shakily. Daisy picked up the board and scrutinized it as he pushed her arm, urging her to read what was written on it. The writing was hardly legible, due to his shaky hand, but she could just make out the word 'BASTARD' written in the centre. Her face must have given her thoughts away, as the old man nudged her and pointed at his only son. She didn't reply, but Tobias Middleton nodded his head in agreement as if he knew her thoughts.

On seeing the old man laughing with Daisy, Clifford raced across the room. 'Now, Father, what are you up to? Time for your midday nap, I think. I'll call Violet, to take you into the other room.' But the old man was too fast for him, and his written thoughts about his son were quickly erased by a wipe of his jacket sleeve. Tobias grunted his objections and flayed his arms in protest. 'Now, Father, stop it, or else I'll have to tie you in your bed. You will go in the other room, for you are disturbing the guests. Violet, take him away.' Clifford raised his voice, shouting at the small dark-haired maid who cowered as she wheeled the old man out of the room. 'Sorry, everyone, my father gets a bit excited if he sees too many people. Time for him to have a nap.' Clifford calmed his agitated audience and gave a long, dark stare at Daisy.

'Poor Clifford, it must be an awful strain on him, looking after his father in such a state. He must be a saint. The dirty old man – did you see him dribbling? I couldn't believe it when you sat next to him, Daisy. Surely you have more pride?' Martha Fraser lifted her teacup to her lips, curling her small finger like royalty, as she sat next to her daughter.

Daisy looked at her. Why did her mother put on airs and graces, and think that she was better than Tobias? They were bakers, for God's sake, in the middle of the Dales – nothing special, just ordinary folk like the Middletons.

The wedding breakfast seemed to go on for an age, but at last the sun was disappearing over Baugh Fell, and with that came the announcement from Tom Fraser that tomorrow was another working day and that a baker rose early to make his money. Daisy was thankful, but held Kitty tight as she bade her farewell at the ramshackle garden gate.

'You take care; you know where home is, and that I love you.' Daisy squeezed her radiant sister tightly, tears filling her eyes as she held her hand. They weren't the closest of sisters, but she did love Kitty, and the guilt that Daisy was feeling was beginning to gnaw away at her as she bade her sister farewell.

'Don't be silly, little sis. Clifford will take care of me now, but I will miss you all.' Kitty grabbed the arm of her new husband and blew her younger sister a kiss, as Daisy climbed into the carriage that trundled down the rough path back up to the head of Grisedale.

Daisy sat quietly in the carriage, listening to her mother making plans for Kitty's future family and hoping that she'd soon be a grandmother. Daisy could think of nothing worse than her sister giving birth to children by the bastard she now knew Clifford to be, and prayed that her sister would be safe with the letch.

2

Two months had passed since the wedding and now life was back to the everyday running of the small but busy business at Mill Race. Daisy stood at the back door of the bakery. Both ovens were filled with loaves of bread, and she was about to start on the pastries and cakes. Her father had baked the first batch of bread and had long since left the small, hot bakehouse, striding out across the fell and walking up the so-called 'Coal Road' to the open-cast mine set between Garsdale and Dentdale. There he traded his freshly baked bread, cheese and ham from his own butchered pigs. The money was good, and an extra income for the family, which made the hard slog of the walk worthwhile.

This was Daisy's only chance to take a few minutes out from her day, and from helping her family. Her mother was milking in the dairy, and the house and bakery were empty apart from her. It was still only 6 a.m., but she felt as if she had been up for an age. She'd tossed and turned all night in her bed, while a silent niggle played on her mind. She'd missed her monthly, for the first time since she'd started being a woman, and now she was beginning to worry. She might only be sixteen but, having been brought up in the country, she knew all too well what happened when opposite sexes were put together. She prayed that the one fateful time, eight long weeks ago now, when Clifford Middleton had raped her he'd not left her with child. The consequences would be devastating to her family, especially for Kitty. She had heard Clifford and Kitty talk of the family they planned, and for Daisy to be bearing his child would ruin their plans and cast dark shadows over both families.

Fighting back welling tears, she sniffed and wiped her nose with the back of her hand. There was no need to cry yet – she might just be late. After all she'd been helping her father a lot more than usual, and she was probably just tired. With brighter thoughts in her head now, she smiled as she watched a mother blue-tit bring her new family to the back door of the bakehouse to look for crumbs. The little chicks were not yet showing their full colour, with the odd fluffy feather looking out of place.

'There you go, Mum: a few crumbs for your brood; you've got a right handful there.' Daisy threw a handful of bread from the pine kitchen table and stood back as the mother bird and her brood tiptoed nearer, pecking delicately at the crumbs and then flying into a nearby honeysuckle bush.

'Talking to yourself, Daisy? Is that second batch of bread out yet, and have you started those apple pies, ready for the market in the morning?' Martha Fraser shouted out the orders as she quietly entered the room and poured the day's milk through muslin, to catch any dirt that might be in it, then stood at the sink of the bakery.

'They need another minute or two.' Daisy turned and started to rub the fats for the pastry into the flour, without thinking; she'd been baking since she was barely able to talk, and it was second nature to her. She looked at her mother. Dare she say anything to her, while they were alone? Dare she speak of things that were private and usually went undiscussed in the Fraser household?

'I'm not going to the market with you tomorrow. Kitty has sent word she wants to see me, so perhaps it's good news.' Martha scrubbed the bread board, before sighing and looking longingly out of the kitchen window. 'You never know, there may be a baby on the way, but it's early days yet. Still, I live in hope.' She carried on cleaning her dairy utensils without turning to look at Daisy. 'You'll have to go with your father tomorrow. You can drop me off on the way down to Sedbergh with the horse and cart.'

Daisy patted the pastry dough hard, the flour rising into a fine cloud as she let it fall from the huge earthenware bowl. It was no good – she couldn't keep her worries to herself any longer. She let out a sob as the pastry hit the pine table, her hands caked with sticky pastry.

'Daisy, what on earth is wrong with you? You've

been acting strange since Kitty's wedding. You shouldn't be so jealous of your sister – someone will come along for you.' Martha stopped her scouring and looked across at her daughter, who was clearly upset. 'Now come on, let's get this bread out of the ovens, before your father gets back.' She looked at her younger daughter. She found it hard to talk to Daisy, for she wasn't as open-hearted as her firstborn, and showing emotion towards her was difficult.

'Mam, I need to talk. I need to talk now, before my father comes back.' Daisy pleaded with her eyes.

'Well, I'm listening. Get on with it!' Martha opened the big oven doors and pulled the first few loaves of bread out, nearly burning her fingers as she placed them on the shelves to cool.

'I'm late, Mam. You know – it's what we don't talk about.' Daisy sobbed, not daring to look at her mother.

'Aye, lass, you're young; you'll just be settling down into your stride. That'll be nothing to worry about – you've not been with a fella, so you'll be fine.' Martha sighed and pulled the last batch of bread out of the oven, patting the bottom of it to test it, not bothering even to look at Daisy's face. 'I was all over the place when I was your age.' She placed the bread on the shelf, then turned to look at her daughter, whose fretful face told her everything.

Daisy's face was red with tears and betrayed her anxiety.

'You've not, have you, Daisy – you've not been with a man? Your father will kill you, and me, if you have.

16

He'll make our lives hell, you know that?' Martha felt sick. She knew the answer already. She'd had a sulky daughter for the last eight weeks, now that she thought about it. It made sense, what with Daisy's moods and the odd comment when she'd mentioned wanting to be a grandmother. Martha felt herself flush from head to toe with fear at how her husband would react. She knew Tom Fraser would never handle the shame of his youngest, most precious daughter being with child. Daisy was his favourite, and the apple of his eye. He boasted about her to friends, saying that Kitty was bonny, but Daisy had the brains. Martha knew he'd never be able to handle it. Sex outside marriage was not even thought about, let alone practised. In fact anything in that department was simply not talked about, full stop.

'I'm sorry, Mam, I couldn't stop him. He'd done it before I knew, and besides, I couldn't say no to Clifford.' Daisy thought her heart was going to burst; the sobs filled her throat, and she felt sick as she tried to explain. 'I'm sorry, Mum, I'm sorry. I know he's Kitty's . . . I couldn't stop him.' The words tumbled out of her mouth between breaths.

'Clifford! You mean, Kitty's Clifford? Bloody hell, lass. This gets worse by the second. Oh my God, the shame! Your father will go mad, and Kitty's trying for a bairn and having no luck. And there you are, pregnant by him. It couldn't get much worse! We're ruined, that's what we are.' Martha sat down at the table and watched her bawling daughter. 'Shut your mouth, girl! You fluttered your eyelashes at him all the time he was

17

courting Kitty – well, you've certainly got what you deserved.'

Martha's face was flushed with anger and embarrassment, and with fear at having to tell her husband. She quickly gave a glance out of the window as she heard the noise of the garden gate.

'Get yourself out of here. Your father's coming up the path – I'll have to choose my moment to tell him.' Martha knocked Daisy out of the way and started to roll the pastry. Daisy ran out of the back door. It was one thing telling her mother, but quite another telling her father. He loved her dearly, but he ruled the family with a rod of iron.

She ran up through the yard. The family's goose gave its alarm call as she sped through the yard and up the outside steps that led to the tack room and the storage room for flour and seasonal fruit. There she threw herself onto a pile of hessian sacks and sobbed to herself. She wanted to die. Even worse, she wished the baby inside her would die. She curled up and rocked her body. What was she to do? She had nowhere to go. Nobody would give a pregnant lass house-room; not even the workhouse would want her. The cat that had been asleep in the window stretched its back and yawned, showing all its discoloured teeth, before walking casually across to her and winding its body round her arms, nudging its head against hers. Daisy pulled it towards her and held the furry, purring body close, stroking the cat's chin, as it appreciated being loved.

'Smoky, what am I going to do? I wish I could die.'

Tears poured down on the grey fur of the cat as it purred its sympathy. 'I wish I'd never set eyes on Clifford Middleton. Look what he's done to me!'

'Have you made sure we have everything?' Tom Fraser looked at his youngest lass as he checked that the harness was tight. 'You look pasty this morning – what's wrong with you?' He stood tall and proud at the side of his horse, watching his daughter as she finished loading the cart for Sedbergh. He was a tall man of six foot or more, clean-shaven, with wisps of white hair showing from below his chequered cap. He talked as straight as a clean-living man should, and his clear blue eyes never missed a thing.

'I'm all right, Father.' Daisy couldn't look at him. She knew the shame he was going to feel and was dreading the consequences. She knew that Tom was usually a calm man, but she'd also seen him in a rage, when he'd taken on the world and won.

'Tell your mother we're ready. I don't know what's wrong with you womenfolk this morning. I can't make head nor tail of her, either. I swear she never slept a wink last night.'

The journey down to Sedbergh was silent. Martha Fraser sat nervously next to her husband, her head spinning with the knowledge that Daisy's predicament could not be kept hidden forever and that she would have to tell him sooner or later. The big question was whether she would tell Tom who the father was? It would mean shame for Kitty, and she dreaded to think what her husband would do to Clifford Middleton. Soon they were at the end of the lane leading to Grouse Hall. Tom pulled on the horse's reins and brought them to a halt.

'I can take you all the way up, if you want. We are in good time.' Tom lifted his wife down from the buckboard.

'No, get on your way. The earlier you are, the more trade you'll get. Besides, it'll do me good to stretch my legs.' Martha gave Daisy a nervous glance as she picked her skirts up and made her way along the dusty path.

Daisy felt her stomach churn. She was alone with her father, and all morning she'd felt sick with worry: had her mother said anything? She couldn't have done, for he was acting too normal.

'Tha's quiet, lass, what's up?' Tom looked at his youngest. She was dark and plain, but her heart was true. Not as flighty as her sister, and a better baker he'd never known; his business would be in good hands, if it were left to her. With a bit of luck he could do that. Clifford Middleton had enough brass for Kitty and any family that she might have with him. He patted Daisy's hand and smiled at her. She looked worried and had made herself scarce all day yesterday, for some reason. Perhaps she'd fallen out with her mother. 'Never mind, keep it to yourself. I don't want to know what you women get up to.' He grinned and pushed his team into a trot.

Daisy kept silent on her trip down the dale. It was a beautiful late-spring day, without a cloud in the sky. The rolling fells of the Howgills looked like velvet, as the valley opened out to reveal the small village of Sedbergh. She wished her mind was as calm as the day; it was a-swim with worry at the thought of her predicament. They entered the village to the usual greetings and pulled up in the historic market place, her father quickly setting out their wares, leaving Daisy to sell them while he stabled the horses and talked to his fellow traders and friends. Business went well. The Frasers had a good reputation for tasty bread and satisfying food, and by lunchtime their stall was nearly empty. Daisy enjoyed the banter; trading was all about making friends and hearing the gossip – and how much your skills were valued. It had helped settle her nerves for a few hours, and she smiled as her father praised her way with the customers. She loved him dearly; she felt closer to her father than her mother. He was quiet and steady, unlike her mother, who continually wanted a better life and was never satisfied.

'Away, lass, let's get back home.' Tom folded up the wooden stall onto the back of the cart and turned to look at his daughter. 'Tha looks white, are you sure you're all right?'

'I'm fine, just a little tired. We were up early this morning.' In truth, Daisy felt sick. She could feel a wave of nausea coming over her, and her head was light and her body wanted to give in. She heard her father's voice getting fainter as she tried to pull herself up onto the cart's seat; the blood rushed to her head, making her feel dizzy, before she collapsed and fainted in front of the market crowd.

'Out the way – make way, my lass is ill.' Tom parted the concerned crowd and lifted his daughter's head. 'Aye, Daisy, what's wrong? You've looked bad for weeks.' He held her tight, while someone passed him a drink of water from the nearby fountain to revive her. Daisy spluttered as he forced the water into her mouth. 'There, lass, don't move. I'll lie you down in the back of the cart and then I'll take you up to the doctor.' Tom put his strong arm around his daughter in an attempt to pick her up.

'No, no.' Daisy, her head spinning, struggled to come to her senses. 'I'm just tired, I'm fine.' She grabbed her father's arm and eased herself up onto her legs, still feeling queasy. 'See, I'm grand.'

'Tha doesn't look too grand to me.' Tom helped his daughter to the cart, assuring the gathering crowd they were all right and that they could all go about their own business. He didn't like folk knowing their business.

'I'm fine.' Daisy sat next to her father, feeling shaky and guilty. She knew he was going to have to be told shortly, because this was just the start of her pregnancy and she couldn't fain being tired forever.

Tom looked at his pale daughter and whipped his horses into action. He'd have words with Martha when he got home; she'd happen get to the bottom of it. Perhaps they'd been working her too hard since Kitty left.

*

22

Daisy lay in her bed cocooned by the warm feather mattress. Her heart was beating fast as she listened to her father going through his nightly ritual: the back door bolt being slammed, the grandfather clock's chain being wound slowly and carefully until the weight was at the top of the mechanism, the door of the case being carefully closed afterwards. The things she heard every night of her life, but never feeling the way she did tonight. She counted his steps in her mind. The third step always creaked and then she watched for the candlelight to pass her closed doorway. She listened through the age-old walls, too thick to hear normal conversation, but too thin to keep out the raised voices tonight. Daisy screwed her eyes tightly shut, hating the noises from her parents' room. She knew her mother was telling her father about her. Her father's voice rose with anger, and her mother was screaming at him. Daisy had broken his heart, and she knew it. The rumble of angry voices went on for hours and she cried lonely tears as she tried to sleep, eventually pulling her pillow over her head to cut out the noise. She hated the baby she was carrying; she hated Clifford Middleton; and most of all she hated herself for being so shallow with her affections.

When the early-morning light broke through Daisy's bedroom window she shook herself from sleep, but immediately the despair of the previous evening swamped her again as soon as her senses awoke. Did she dare enter the bakery and act normally, or should she stay in her room? She walked across the bare floorboards and poured cold water from the wash jug into the matching bowl, freshening her face. She felt drained as she pulled on her skirts while sitting on the edge of her bed, lingering there, not wanting to confront her parents.

'You needn't bother coming down today. Your father doesn't want to see you. I've to lock you in your room, because he'll not be responsible for his actions.' Martha Fraser stood in the doorway. She was quiet – too quiet for her nature.

Daisy hid her head in her hands, before raising her tear-filled eyes to look at her mother. 'What's he like, Mam? He's not going to cause bother for our Kitty, is he?'

'Nay, he'll not be bothering them. I didn't tell him who'd fathered your bastard bairn, and it's enough that we've one daughter in disgrace, without having two in bother. You'll not say a word to him about Clifford either, else by God I'll kill you and the baby myself.' Martha looked dark and forbidding. 'I'll fetch you something to eat later, when I've time. I'm doing two folks' work this morning, thanks to you.'

With that she slammed the bedroom door shut, turning the heavy iron key in the lock and leaving a heartbroken Daisy sobbing on her bed.

3

'By God, tha will tell who the bastard is!' Tom Fraser came down hard with the leather of his belt across Daisy's buttocks. 'No matter how far gone tha is, I'll belt tha every day till tha tells me his name!'

Daisy had been enduring the near-daily belting for the last six months, but still she'd not told her father who was responsible for her plight. She'd lived in her bedroom, locked away from the rest of the world in squalor, her hair cut as short as a man's and her diet consisting mostly of bread and milk, due to the shame of her father, and with her mother not lifting a finger to help her. Kitty had been told that she'd left home to work in Bradford, not suspecting for one minute the life that her younger sister was living.

Daisy held onto her round belly. The baby had been moving lately and she knew it was nearly her time. Another thrash and he'd be finished for the night – he usually only hit her three times. What had happened to the father she loved and the mother who had protected her? She didn't deserve all this, for the sake of being young and foolish. For the third time the air rushed by the belt and the leather cut into her skin. Daisy held her breath. She would not tell him Clifford's name. Another crack came down on her, this time even fiercer.

'You'll bloody tell me tonight, if I've to kill you.' Tom Fraser had lost control of his temper and the belt came down fast and sharp on Daisy's buttocks.

She screamed in pain and clung onto her unborn baby.

'Tell me – bloody well tell me – who the bastard is.' Tom was sweating and swearing as he lashed out with his belt. He'd rather lose both daughter and baby than have another man get the better of him.

Daisy screamed in pain, begging him to stop, as she feared for herself and her unborn child.

'I'll not stop, lass, until I get a name.'

Another thrash came down and, as the leather cut deep, Daisy yelled out 'Clifford Middleton', in desperation for her life and that of her unborn child. 'Clifford Middleton did this to me – our Kitty's husband!'

She lay uneasily on her bed, sobbing and beside herself with despair that her secret was now out. Her buttocks throbbed with the numerous lashings, and her baby kicked in protest. She buried her head in the pillows, not daring to look at her father.

Tom froze in disbelief and anger. That charmer, Clifford – he'd welcomed him into his family with open arms. He quickly regained his wits. 'When this bastard baby is born, you both get the hell out of my house. You've let me down, Daisy. You could have had all this,

26

but no, you've brought me shame. You've lain with your bloody sister's husband – have you no pride, lass? Your sister, for the Lord's sake. He's a red-blooded man, tha shouldn't have encouraged him with your flirty ways. A man can't help himself. Well, you had your pleasure, now tha must pay.'

Tom Fraser buckled his belt tight around his trousers and stood, red-faced, in the bedroom doorway. He brushed his white hair back through his fingers and sighed, slamming the door and turning the key. Once outside, he swore to himself. The bloody bastard, he'd make Clifford pay and all. He'd not let Clifford forget for one minute the day he'd had his way with his youngest.

Daisy listened to his footsteps going down the stairs. Her body was rigid. She girdled her stomach, feeling the baby kick. Her skin was raw and she saw blood on her fingers as she felt the welts on her backside. Well, her secret was out – whatever her father did with it was up to him. She prayed he'd say nothing, for Kitty's sake.

The baby gave another kick, reminding her of its presence. Her mother had already told her that there was going to be no one to help with the birth. Old Mrs Dinsdale from the row of houses called The Street in Garsdale wasn't going to be called to assist. Her gnarled old hand had brought many a baby into the world, and she was well respected by all the women in the dale. A tear fell down Daisy's cheek. What was she to do? Thrown out with a baby to care for, where would she go? She looked at her bedroom curtains and at the disused bacon hook that was screwed into the bedroom beams, from years past. Despair flooded over her – there was nothing else left to do. She'd hang herself; after all, neither of them was wanted. It would be the best end to a bastard baby and a ruined woman.

She wiped her tears away, her heart beating fast and her thoughts running away with her. She rose from her bed and pulled up the woven-rush chair to the window. The shutters had been nailed up months ago, blocking her beloved view of the fell leading up to the Quaker meeting house and the rolling hills beyond. She reached up to untie the cord that held the dusty faded curtains, her fingers fumbling with the knot that she remembered tying when she had been given the bedroom a few years before, when she was young and trouble-free. Tears streamed down her face as she choked with fear and hurt – nobody wanted her, it was for the best – and her legs wobbled like jelly when the chair tipped slightly as she reached too far. One last tug and the curtains would be loose. Daisy balanced on the very edge of the chair, leaning on the wall as she tugged, and shaking as she checked that the knot she had tied was tight. The next thing she knew, the chair had tipped from under her and she had banged her head on the edge of her dresser as she hit the floor.

She lay there, dizzy and dazed, tears pouring from her eyes and the torn curtains around her. Then the pain started, a gut-wrenchingly sharp pain, making Daisy cry out in a scream. Her skirts were wet and the pain kept pounding. She dragged herself up, pulling her body across to her bed while the jabbing pains kept her bent double. She slumped on the bed. The baby was coming – she knew the baby was coming – and she needed her mother. She let out another cry and lay on her bed, legs apart and with perspiration dripping from her brow. She raised her head as she heard her mother turn the key in her bedroom door. She was so thankful Martha had heard her cries.

She carried a bowl of hot water and looked sombre as she bent down and regarded her daughter giving birth. She should have got Mrs Dinsdale to help her. First births were dangerous, and she knew that because she'd lost her first. 'Be brave, Daisy, grit your teeth – it'll soon be over. Thank God your father's not here. He's flown out of the house like the Devil himself.' She looked at her daughter, who was in pain and frightened, and noticed the torn curtains and chair next to the window, guessing what she had been up to. Her heart melted for a moment.

Daisy let out a scream and gripped her mother's hand. The baby was coming fast, brought on by the shock of Daisy's thrashing and the fall from the chair. She put her finger in her mouth and bit on it hard, to stop her screams, as her mother looked at the progress of her birth. Never had she endured so much pain, and yet in some dales women had a baby each year. How did they endure it? Another wave of pain hit her and her mother shouted at her to push.

'It's here, Daisy, I can see its head. Another push and

you're done.' Martha Fraser wiped her forehead. Thank God Tom had left the house, for he'd not have put up with the noise.

With the next big push the baby was out in the world. Its wrinkled red body lay still on the bed, showing no sign of breathing. Martha picked up the baby boy and cleared his airway, slapping his bottom. There was no response or movement. The wrinkles on his tiny face didn't move, and the angry little hands remained closed tight. Martha cut his umbilical cord and wrapped the little body in a blanket that she had brought with her.

'What's wrong, Mam? Why is it not crying, Mam – tell me, is it dead?' Daisy pleaded. She was exhausted and fretful for her baby. She hadn't wanted it, in fact she'd wished it dead over the months, but now she felt responsible for the child that she had brought into the world.

'I'm sorry, Daisy. Happen it's for the best – he'd only have brought shame to us.'

'It's a boy! I've had a little boy, let me look.' Daisy tried to sit up, but cried out in pain.

'Lie still. You've to lose your afterbirth yet, and it's best you don't see him.' Martha picked up the baby in the blanket and began to leave the room. 'I'll be back in a minute.'

'Don't leave me, Mam, don't leave me!' She was exhausted, and heartbroken at her loss.

'I'll be back. You'll want a change of clothes and a wash-down, when you've lost all.' Martha walked out through the door with the bundle under her arm. She cradled the stillborn baby in her arms, tears falling as she made her way down the stairs to the kitchen. Poor baby – he had done nothing wrong; he just hadn't been wanted. She placed him next to the sink and unwrapped the blanket slowly. The child was still warm; he was a good size, with a tuft of black hair, bless him. At least she could wash him before burying him in the orchard, in an unmarked grave, unbeknown to anyone other than herself and Tom.

She filled the sink with warm water and picked the baby up, gently placing him in the water and washing him gently. Did he move? Had she imagined it? No, there it was again. His arm moved and his mouth began to make movements, his little eyes screwed up, wrinkling at the warmth of the water. He was alive! He made a silent cry and opened his dark eyes, staring at the woman who had nearly buried him.

'By God, man, if tha doesn't make this right, I'll ruin you. I'll tell every dealer – every farmer for miles around – what an underhand bastard you are! Your reputation will be ruined.' Tom Fraser held Clifford Middleton by the throat, at the side of Grouse Hall.

Clifford grinned at the old man, whom he was finding surprisingly strong for his age. 'You can't hurt me. She was asking for it, your precious Daisy, not like her useless sister – Kitty's never going to give me an heir; useless in bed, she is. Tell whoever you want. Money talks, and it won't be long before all this farm is mine, and then I'm off.' Clifford grinned at the angry old man.

Tom Fraser lifted his free hand and made a fist, ready to come down hard onto the grinning face, but stopping inches from his nose. 'You've no scruples, have you, you bastard? By God, I should make you greet your maker. But I can't, for you're my daughter's husband, and father to the baby that will soon be in the world. You want an heir? Well, you've got one. When that baby is born, you'll take it into your house and bring it up as your own. You'll not tell Kitty where it's come from – you can have found it, or taken pity on a penniless woman in need. But if you ever tell her the truth while your father's alive, I'll get his solicitor to witness what I tell him; and by God, if that baby lives, he'll make it the rightful heir of Grouse Hall. Everyone knows there's no love lost between you both. In fact, to keep your father's life safe, I'll see my solicitor in the morning and tell him of our conversation tonight.' Tom watched as the grin disappeared from the cocky Clifford.

'You bastard, let me go.' Clifford gripped Tom's arm and wrenched it off him. 'I don't want to keep the runt. You wouldn't dare say a word to my father.'

'Try me!' Tom walked away from Clifford's side and made steps towards the garden gate.

'Wait, you old bastard! Send word when the runt's born, and I'll take it in.' Clifford thought quickly of all the debts he was amassing in the Dales. He couldn't live without his father's inheritance.

'Right, I'll send word. It'll not be bloody long now, by the looks of her, so you'd better get ready. Tell our Kitty I'll see her on market day. I'm in no mood to talk to her tonight.' Tom reached over and took the reins of his horse, which had been waiting patiently, and rose up into the saddle. 'This is a gentleman's agreement. Not that you are any gentleman, sir!' He whipped his horse and rode down the road into the dusk, his hatred for the man he thought no gentleman growing with every yard towards home that he galloped.

Martha Fraser looked at the baby, now wrapped tightly in a blanket. She'd not yet told Daisy of his miraculous recovery. She held him close to her: this was her grandchild, her blood. A tear dropped on the baby's head. She held the perfect little hand and gazed at the angry red face.

'She's had it, then?'

Martha jumped in fright, for she'd not heard Tom enter the kitchen.

'Aye, she's had a rough time, but we've got a grandson – look at him.' She held the baby up for Tom to see.

'I don't want to look at that bastard.' Tom turned his head.

Martha knew better than to push it – he'd come round. 'I'll go and tell Daisy he's alive, and give him to her.' She rose from her chair, ignoring Tom's hard words.

'She thinks he's dead?'

'Aye, he didn't breathe for a good few minutes – not until I washed him, for what I thought was his burial.' Martha smiled at the little face.

'Well, tell her no different, because the baby goes to Grouse Hall in the morning. His father is going to have him, and our Kitty will never know he's her sister's. Now take him out of my sight. I can't abide to think of how he got brought into the world.'

'And Daisy?' Martha looked at her husband.

'I'll give her till the end of the week, and then she goes. Every time I look at her I think of what she's done to this family. She's nothing but a whore!' Tom's face turned red, remembering the smiles he'd seen Daisy give to Clifford Middleton and her near-tears at Kitty's wedding. 'She's no daughter of mine, and she's not welcome under my roof.'

The wind howled and the rain lashed down on the silent couple huddled on the seat of the cart. The horse's harness jangled and shook, as it pulled the cart of misery up the steep hill-climb out of Widdale and onto the rough moorland of Dent Head, the horse's head bent lowly, as if in shame itself, as it used each muscle on the steep fell-climb. Tom Fraser had said nothing as his wife had helped Daisy up beside him; he'd seen the tears in his wife's eyes and heard her sobs from under her shawl. It was no good – his mind was made up. The lass had to find her own way in the world. She was no longer welcome under his roof, and he'd not go back on his word.

He'd not said anything when Martha had forced a florin into Daisy's hand; after all, he'd have to be Christian about it, and make sure she didn't starve until she found work. Daisy had said nothing, cringing from her father's hand as he tried to help her up to her seat next to him. All the trust had been beaten out of her, and where there had been love in her eyes for her father there now burned hate. Not a word had been spoken since leaving Grisedale at first light. The horse and cart made their way out of Grisedale up the broader sweep of Garsdale, skirting through the sleeping village of Appersett, over the bridge and up the gillside road to Widdale and Dent Head. It was there that Tom was going to abandon Daisy; she could make her own mind up about where to go from there. She could either turn right down into Dent or go on to Ingleton, or even further if she'd a notion. The horse eased itself back into an easier stride as the summit of Widdale was reached and they steadily pulled the cart past the dwelling place of Dent Head. The house looked in darkness as the mist and rain tried to envelop it in nature's cloak.

'Right, down you get. This is far enough – tha'll not be walking back home in a hurry.' Tom pulled on the horse's reins and put the brake on.

Daisy pulled her cloak's hood back and removed the sacking that had been giving her a bit of protection from the elements. She looked around her at the bleak setting: the mists shifting and banking around the looming fells, and the rushes bent double in the wind and rain. She was used to Grisedale looking like this on a wild day, but she always knew there was a warm, dry home waiting for her. Today she was on her own against the elements, with no home and no one to love her. But no matter how wild the weather was, she would not attempt to walk home, so her father needn't be afeared of that.

Tom never stirred from his cart as his daughter climbed down onto the cobbled road. He watched her for a minute as she looked around her, deciding where to go. His heart hurt as he saw her take the first few steps down the road to Ingleton, never once looking back at him, but his pride forbade him to stop her, beg her forgiveness and take her home. He clicked his tongue and pulled at the reins, turning the horse and cart homewards on the road. A tear filled the big man's eyes and a silent prayer was said for his daughter's safety, before he whipped the horse into a trot to take them quickly down the dale and home. Tom hoped that the sooner he was away from Daisy, the quicker he could forget, although he secretly knew that would never happen.

Daisy heard her father click the horse into action. A wave of panic came over her. Had she been that bad – should she ask for his forgiveness and beg to go home? Her heart beat fast and she felt sick. No! There was nothing at home for her: just a dead baby buried in the orchard, a baby she'd never seen, and an unloving family. She'd make her own way in the world. She wrapped her cloak and shawl around her and set off down the dale. Somewhere out there would be a new life. She'd find a job and earn her own living, and Grisedale and the lecherous Clifford Middleton would be forgotten.

4

The rain came down and the wind was so fierce it nearly blew the weak Daisy off her feet. She stumbled down the twisting downhill road to the village of Ingleton, looking only forward, to the great looming sight of Whernside Fell and a brief glimpse of the Ribble valley, with the sleeping lion of Ingleborough Fell in her midst. Occasionally in the wind she could hear what sounded like the noise of thunder and wondered what it could be. This was new land to her. Although not really far from home, she was only used to her own patch and had never travelled more than the five miles to Sedbergh and Hawes on market day.

Feeling weary, she stopped for a moment under the seeping eaves of a gamekeeper's small shooting lodge by the side of the swelling river. Dare she knock on the door? Walking quietly around the low building, she noticed that it looked empty, as she peered through the windows. She knocked on the door, quietly at first, but then more noisily. All she wanted was a moment away from the lashing rain. No answer came, so she tried the door. It was locked – there would be no sanctuary here. She stood in the doorway and watched the peat-filled pools at her feet, the wind making ripples on them and shaking the purple heather that covered the wild moorland. She'd have to move on, for it would soon be dusk and she didn't want to be on the fell alone. She'd not seen a soul since her father had left her. Nobody would even send their dog out on a day like this. Her body was aching and her stomach felt empty as she rounded the bend. The sound of singing and of men laughing came from a rough-looking building set just below a well-built square grey house by the side of the road. She quickly went down the bank and looked in through the window.

'Now then, little 'un, looking for a bed for the night? Tha can share mine.' A huge man burst out laughing, showing his badly blackened teeth as he patted her on the back. He'd come from nowhere and was now urging Daisy inside, to what she knew to be a drinking hole, full of the roughest men she had ever seen.

'No, leave me be – let me go.' Daisy pulled her arm out of the grasp of the huge beast of a man and turned to flee, only to bump into his weasel-like mate.

'Now, you can't turn Jake down. He's a one with the women.'

Daisy shrieked, as the smaller of the two grabbed her arm.

Jake growled at his mate, 'Let her go. She's nobbut a young lass – there's nowt on her. She'd not keep me warm on a night like this.' Then he grabbed his mate, nearly throwing him into the foul-smelling drinking den, leaving Daisy shaking with fear.

She composed herself quickly and walked back up to the main road, making a note of the name on the house: GEARSTONES LODGE. If she was ever offered work there, she'd certainly not accept; it wasn't for the likes of her. In the distance she could hear the sound of pickaxes and men's voices in the wind and, when the fog and mists permitted, she could make out the shape of huts and a strange structure that spanned the Dales. She wondered what it could be. It was a strange place, and she'd be glad to get off the wild moorland road. She walked on, the rain seeping to her skin, making her shiver and feel feverish. It had only been a few days since she'd given birth, and she was exhausted. As she neared the outskirts of what looked like a hut settlement, an old woman came out of one of the cabins.

Daisy ran and caught her arm to ask her where she was.

'Tha's at Ribblehead, lass, or Batty Green as we call it. Come to help build the railway, have you? Wildest spot you could have picked. Today's like a summer's day; wait until a December's day, when it's a blizzard and you can't see your hand in front of your face.' She laughed and shook her head, before scurrying off like a busy hedgehog.

So that was what the noise had been: it was the railway! She'd heard it was being built. The farmers at the market last spring had been full of their land being bought up. Now it was here. Soon it would plough through the fells up to Garsdale, and even as far as the Scottish borders.

Daisy stood in the rain and looked around her. What a rough spot – how could folk live like this? She might have little money, no home and no work, but she couldn't stay here; these were not her sort of people. She trudged along a quagmire of a road with huts on either side, reaching a signpost that said 'Horton-in-Ribblesdale 8 miles' and, in the other direction, 'Ingleton 5 miles'. That was where she'd go to: Ingleton. There'd be plenty of work there for a decently brought-up lass. But for now she just needed to get herself there before nightfall. She'd get there and find a lodging that would take her in, for the florin that her mother had given her, and then in the morning she'd seek employment.

With renewed determination, she kept walking past the working navvies with horses and carts laden with tunnel waste, the loose women shouting at the men, some with babies on their arms, trying to vie for their attentions. All of them were standing out in the wild, unforgiving weather, desperate to make a living. Daisy shook her head. This was certainly not the place for her. She trudged on up the road to Ingleton, past one stone-built building called the Welcome Inn. The candles were already lit and she could see a young woman with long auburn hair serving behind the bar. She peered in through the window, looking at the navvies drinking and smoking, playing cards and joking with the woman.

It was all alien to her; she'd never been in a place like this, and it made her feel vulnerable and uncomfortable when she heard the rowdy laughter of the residents.

'Now then, little woman, what you doing, looking through my windows? Are you wanting a bed for the night?'

A sandy-haired man looked kindly at Daisy, as she glanced fearfully at him.

'It's all right. I don't bite, not like some of 'em around here.' He grinned. 'It's getting a bit late in the day for somebody your age to be wandering this road.'

'I'm on my way to Ingleton, after work. I was only looking in to see what the inside was like.' Daisy hesitated to provide any information about herself. She was vulnerable, and she knew it.

'Our lad's looking for help. You look a likely lass – are you any good at cooking?'

The man looked Daisy up and down, noticing her shivering and shaking in the fine drizzle that had been falling all day.

'It'll save you walking further, and he's only just up the road. I'll take you in the trap. He and Jenny will look after you well – he's good-natured, is our Mike.'

'Aye, I can cook. My father was a baker, and I'm not too proud to clean and do other jobs.' Daisy blushed. Perhaps she needn't walk any further. Rest would be a godsend, as she was sure her legs were getting weaker by the second.

'Right, wait here then, and I'll get Bess and the trap.' And with that her rescuer disappeared, only to return a few minutes later with a horse and trap pointing in the direction from which she had just walked.

Daisy felt so weary that she could feel tears bubbling beneath the surface, as she babbled to John on the journey down the rough track. He kept flicking the reins, listening to her talking and encouraging information out of her, while he urged his horse forward to where they were bound.

After fifteen minutes the horse and cart pulled up outside Gearstones Lodge, the place she had passed, where she had nearly been molested by the unruly navvies. Daisy let out a gasp of horror.

'Right, here we are. I'll just give our Mike a shout. He's a good lad, and he and his wife, Jenny, will look after you.'

The light from the alehouse wasn't strong enough to show the horror on Daisy's face, but John read her thoughts.

'Don't worry, lass. I'll not leave you with the navvies. I'll make sure they have a room for you in their house. That drinking hole's not fit for a young lass's ears.'

Daisy sat, shivering, on the buckboard as John talked to what she took to be his brother, Mike. The golden haze of an oil lamp silhouetted both brothers while they discussed her.

'Get yourself down, then. Our lad says you can willingly have the job. They are run off their feet and need another pair of hands desperately. Besides, I've told him

43

you look no more than a sparrow and will cause him no bother.' John held his hand out, as Daisy shook with cold and hunger.

She took hold of John's hand, alighted from the cart in as ladylike a fashion as she could, and thanked her rescuer as she followed his brother across the yard and into the grand house that was obviously his home. As she did so, her heart thumped: what was she letting herself in for? She didn't know this family; they could do anything with her, and nobody would know of her plight. She'd heard of women being used by men and then being found dead in a dark place. Overcome with fear and fatigue, she felt her legs folding under her as she entered the huge Gearstones house.

'Sit down here, lass, you look shattered.' Mike, the owner, looked at the frail form before him. 'I'll get Jenny, my wife, to bring you something to eat, and then I think the best thing for you this night is to get you to bed.'

He left Daisy sitting in the hallway, shivering and looking anxiously around her.

'Now then, lady, our Mike tells me you're after a job, but not until you've had a good night's sleep and something in your belly.' Jenny Pratt eyed the shivering young lass in front of her. 'Come on up these stairs. We've a spare bed you can have tonight, and I'll come up with some supper once you've got out of those sodden clothes.'

Daisy looked at the woman who was giving her orders. She'd never know how grateful Daisy was to have a roof over her head and some food in her belly.

She dutifully followed her up the stairs, to safety and warmth.

Daisy lay in the bed. It was early morning, and for once she felt warm and comfortable, lying on a feather mattress in a sparse but spotless room. Jenny Pratt had lent her a nightgown, realizing that Daisy had no belongings with her. Daisy had been horrified when she had walked in unannounced with it, to find her naked. The scars from her father's beatings were still visible to her new employer, and the woman hadn't been able to disguise the look of horror on her face.

Daisy looked around the bedroom now. There were heavy drapes at the windows, but they were not drawn and she could make out the misty shape of the great fell of Whernside in the distance. The walls were bare and whitewashed and, besides the bed and chair, there was a marble washstand in the room and a matching mahogany wardrobe. Outside she could hear the noise of people shouting and wagons rolling, and curiosity overcame her as her senses returned. She slowly raised herself to the edge of the bed. Her legs shook, but she was determined to look out of the window and see what was happening outside.

She raised herself up, holding onto the brass bedstead, before walking the few steps to the window. She held onto the sides of the window for support as she looked out upon the sight. Directly below her was a cobbled yard, with barrels stacked in one corner and a horse eating contentedly at its feed. But it was the sight further afield that caught Daisy's breath: a mass of raggle-taggle huts that surrounded the massive construction being built across the boggy valley bottom. She remembered passing it yesterday. It was the place that the old woman had told her was Batty Green. Then she remembered: she was in Gearstones Lodge, the place she'd vowed to stay clear of.

She had to leave; she couldn't stay here, not in this godforsaken place. She'd thank the Pratts, pay them part of her florin and then be on her way. Tears filled her eyes as she thought of the last few months – of her baby dead in the orchard; of her parents acting so heartlessly; and of the life she had, prior to the day she was raped by Clifford Middleton. She was ashamed of herself and felt worthless, and now she was in a strange bed in what seemed to be the roughest part of the district that she could have found. She muffled her tears and then the warmth of the bed and her exhaustion won again, and she found herself dozing back to sleep.

It was a restless sleep, full of bad memories, but her strength was returning and she awoke to the smell of fresh bread and a noise from the rooms below. She reached over to her clothes and looked into her apron's pocket for the florin that her mother had given her. She'd pay and thank these good people for her night's sleep, and then be on her way. Panic overcame her as her hand searched fervently for the florin, which was no longer in her pocket. She must have dropped it when she nearly fell – she couldn't remember. Perhaps the people who owned Gearstones had robbed her in the night. But that couldn't be, for they had all seemed so kind. Daisy felt sick as she grabbed the handrail at the top of the grand stairs and heard voices rising from the hallway below.

'Is your new help not up yet? Poor Ivy, she's moaning a bucketful. She thought she could have some time off today.'

'The poor lass – she's been belted to within an inch of her life, Mike. Wherever she was going, she's made the right decision.' The soft voice of Jenny Pratt filled the room.

Daisy stood for a while listening to the couple talking about her.

'Didn't John know where she came from? Poor bugger. If someone had treated me like that, I'd have left home and all.' Jenny stood in the hallway with her hands on her hips.

'He said she babbled on, but he couldn't make out half of what she said. He thought it had been her father who had belted her. It's a funny carry-on. Anyway, I'll have to go – our lad's waiting for me.'

Daisy watched as Mike kissed his wife on the cheek before leaving, Jenny shaking her head as he slammed the door. Suddenly catching a glimpse of Daisy's shadow, Jenny looked up towards her.

'Aye, pet, I didn't see you there. Now come down and through to the kitchen, and get some porridge. You look as if you could do with something in you.' Jenny cast an eye over the scrawny shape cowering on the stairs.

Daisy climbed slowly downstairs, following Jenny through the hallway to the kitchen. There she pulled up a kitchen chair, with tears welling in her eyes, while Jenny instructed her cook to rewarm the porridge pan for her guest. Daisy looked at Jenny, noting that she was a good-looking woman, but she'd never heard a woman talk like that before. She couldn't help think that her mother would have had nothing to do with Jenny – 'common as muck' would have been Martha's opinion. The cook, with a mob-cap on her head, smiled shyly as she spooned warm porridge into a dish and quickly put it in front of Daisy, before bobbing her curtsy and knowingly leaving her mistress and Daisy alone.

Jenny watched silently as she ate the porridge, her fingers playing with her wedding ring on her thin white finger.

'Now, by the looks of you, you've been through the mill, my lass. That's why I've let you have a lie-in. But if you are to work for me, I expect an honest day's work. I can't offer you much pay, but you can have a roof over your head and a full belly, and a bit of time off when we aren't busy. I don't expect you to work in the alehouse and lodgings; they'd eat alive a bit of a thing like you.' Jenny stopped and looked at the young lass sitting across from her.

'I'm sorry I can't pay for your hospitality last night, and if you are sure you'd like me to work for you, then I'll do my best.' Daisy's voice caught in her throat as she welled up with embarrassment at the sight she must have presented, and the fact that she had no alternative but to take the job that was being offered.

'Aye, well, we'll give it a go.' Jenny rose from the table, yelling for the cook. She came running in, on her mistress's beckoning. 'Ivy, this is . . . er . . . What did you say your name was?' Jenny looked at Daisy, thinking just how little she knew about the young ward she had taken on.

'It's Daisy, Daisy Fraser.'

'Aye, well, Daisy, this is Ivy. She's a good lass, knows my kitchen and house like the back of her hand. She'll keep you right.'

Ivy blushed and then smiled at Daisy.

'Ivy, you show her all we do today. And then tomorrow, miss, I expect you to give Ivy a lie-in in the morning. She hasn't had one of those since the day she started with us. Does that sound all right to you?'

Daisy nodded while Ivy answered, 'Yes, Mrs Pratt.' She bobbed a curtsy and then waited for Daisy to join her in the doorway.

'And, Ivy, find Daisy a change of clothes. She looks like a scarecrow.'

Daisy blushed. She knew she appeared unkempt, but hadn't realized quite how bad she looked.

'Go on, get yourself smartened up, and then make a start with Ivy. God knows I've enough on, with that baby of mine – just listen to him holler!' Jenny stopped talking as the baby's wails could be heard echoing around the house. 'He never stops, he's always hungry.' She sighed.

Daisy didn't know what to say when she heard the baby crying. She hadn't realized there was a baby in the house, and it made her want to cry; hearing his bawling reminded her of her own lost child. But she had nowhere else to go, and now she realized there were worse places to be than Gearstones.

'What's wrong? Are you not happy with that arrangement?' Jenny looked perplexed as she watched a cloud appear on Daisy's face.

Daisy lowered her head and a teardrop fell as she nodded, too choked to answer.

'Good. Now for God's sake, smile, lass. You'll be all right with us, won't she, Ivy?'

'Yes, Mrs Pratt. We'll look after you.' Ivy smiled and urged Daisy to join her.

Daisy lay on her bed later that afternoon. It had been a full day, one of eye-opening events. Her head buzzed with thoughts: had she done right, accepting a position at Gearstones? Only time would tell, but now all she wanted was a good sleep. As she closed her eyes, she noticed the glint of her lost florin underneath the washstand. She smiled; she thought she'd lost it on her way to Gearstones, or that someone here had stolen it from her. Now she had a roof over her head, a florin in her pocket and a new family. Who could want for more?

5

As Bob Lambert squeezed Daisy's hand tightly, she couldn't believe how the three years at Gearstones had flown. Both of them stood in awe as the steam engine blew its whistle and chuffed its way over the huge viaduct that stood towering above them. The steam from its pistons twisted and curled down the great arches, and the coal smoke assaulted their nostrils.

The year was 1875 and the magnificent Settle-to-Carlisle line was now officially open. It had been a fair day, a band had played, and Daisy had been run off her feet cooking and cleaning at Gearstones. Everyone had been celebrating; the beer had flown, speeches had been made, and children had laughed and played around people's feet as the line that had cost so many lives had been opened. Daisy couldn't help but remember the day when she had arrived, half-dead and completely ashamed of her young life, at Gearstones Lodge, near Batty Green. It had been three years since that wild, wet night – three years that had changed her life and opened her eyes to the world outside her cushioned family life in Grisedale. She'd learned not to judge people by the way they looked; that no matter how penniless they were, or what people's worries at Batty Green and nearby Ribblehead were, they would stand by her and their own. That was until drink sometimes got the better of them. Even then, after a night in the cells at Ingleton or a hard fist flattening them, they would shake hands and get on with it, because everyone depended on the next person to survive. Life was tough here, and that was a fact. If you didn't have the support of your next-door neighbour, you'd not last long in this wild desolate place.

'Penny for them.' Bob spoke softly as he watched Daisy look around her and smile.

'Sorry, my love. I was just thinking of the day I came here.' She patted her sweetheart's hand. Bob was a good man. No matter what anyone said, the age difference didn't matter to her. He might be in his fifties, but he was a caring man who never asked about her past and, most importantly of all, he was dependable.

'Aye, well, I know nowt about that – you never say anything about then – but I know it's been a grand day today, and I've got the bonniest lass in the dale on my arm. I've a bit of news and all, and a question. But I don't want to spoil our day by saying something daft, so I don't know if I dare ask it.' He squeezed Daisy's hand even tighter, before curling his long grey hair behind his ears and running his hands down the length of his sideburns.

'You never say anything daft, my dear, and you

certainly couldn't spoil this day.' Daisy smiled at her beau. She'd known him for over a year now and she felt comfortable in his presence – the only man she had felt easy with since Clifford Middleton's assault on her.

'Well, it's like this. I've been offered a job at Blea Moor signal box. They are moving me from Horton, and I can have the house there that goes with the job.' Bob paused, looking at Daisy's face.

'That's good news, Bob. You will be nearer, and you can get out of that rented room that you hate.' Daisy twiddled the ribbon under her best hat and smiled at the serious-faced Bob.

'Aye, it's good news. But what they said was that they preferred me not to be single. What they think I'm going to get up to at my age, I don't know! But I was thinking: we've been walking out for some time, and I know you are only young, and that I'm an old man and folk talk about us, making out I'm a cradle-snatcher.' Bob hung his head as Daisy smiled shyly. He blushed and stammered, before blurting out his intentions. 'Damn it, Daisy, what I'm trying to say is: will you marry me?' He stood back in amazement at his outburst.

Daisy looked at him, her mouth open. 'Oh, Bob!'

'I know – I'm stupid to even think it. You deserve much better than me; you've got all your life in front of you.' Bob shook his head and looked up again at the massive granite arches, to hide the feelings that were written all over his face.

'It's the suddenness, stupid. You took me by surprise. How could anyone want me?' Daisy's eyes filled with tears. 'I don't know: what do I say?' She pulled on his hand and did a little jig, assessing her feelings and what she should say. 'But, yes; my answer is yes . . . Of course it's yes! And I'll be the perfect wife and I'll always be there for you, no matter what anyone says about the age difference.'

Bob lifted Daisy off her feet and swung her round like a twirling roundabout, her skirts billowing in the wind as they hugged and hugged again.

'I'll always be there for you, Daisy. I'll never let you down, and you'll want for nothing, my love. You've made this old bachelor a very happy man.' He squeezed her tightly and grinned, because he'd got his woman.

Daisy hummed and sang under her breath all the way back to her room at Gearstones, giving the drinkers standing outside the alehouse a more than generous welcome, before going inside to the main house and climbing the stairs to flop onto her bed. She was to be married – and have a house of her own – with a man she knew would look after her and treat her right. She lay on the metal-sprung bed that creaked at every turn, and looked around the room that had been her home for the three years that she had been at Gearstones Lodge.

They had been good years, full to the brim with events, despite there being illness, poverty and despair as navvies lost their lives building the iron rail-line through the Dales. But along with the bad times came hope and friendship, especially the friendship and support that the Pratt family had shown her. She remembered the morning she'd crept downstairs to witness Jenny and Mike talking about her, and how she had thought how crude and rough Jenny was. In fact she'd been just the opposite, and had shown Daisy nothing but kindness. A pang of guilt washed over her. She'd have to tell Jenny of her plans to marry Bob. Once she was married she'd have her own house to run, and she wouldn't have time to work at Gearstones Lodge. Her place was by her man's side, attending to his every need in the square-built house that she knew to be the signalman's, across the track from the signal box at Blea Moor. She wouldn't be on her own, as there were two small cottages for the plate-layers and their families nearby, and she knew both families well. Thoughts about planning her wedding dress, and decorating her house, danced around her head as she tossed and turned. She tried hard to find sleep, knowing that she had to be awake early because it was Ivy's day off and she was the cook in the morning.

Morning came all too soon, as the grey fingers of dawn crept into Daisy's bedroom. She felt tired and didn't want to go down to the kitchen and start her usual routine. She eased her body out of bed and smiled again at the thought of marrying Bob, then splashed her face in cold water from the ewer on her washstand. Pulling back the curtains, she let the morning's weak light in and gazed at the flanks of Whernside. The huge mountain outline was crisp and sharp in the morning's light, but soon she'd be waking up in her own home directly under its menacing scars, then making breakfast for her man and cleaning the house. She'd never thought that day would come.

The warmth from the kitchen met her as she crept downstairs and set about the business of lighting the oven. The previous day's embers were still glowing slightly as she laid new kindling and punched the bellows, to get a good roar from the flames. The lodge was quiet – not a sound was to be heard. It would be like that for some time yet, and Daisy appreciated the time to herself. She'd loved this kitchen, and the hours she'd spent in it since her arrival that stormy night. Her thoughts often wandered back to her home – back to the days when her father had been her best friend and protector – and then her thoughts clouded as she thought about the way he had treated her when he'd found her with child. The beatings and cruelty that he and her mother had shown, and the death of the baby, had left her feeling bereaved of a family's love, and it was at quiet times like these that she cast her mind back to those terrible days. She brushed a tear from her eye as she pounded the dough; it was no good dwelling on the past. It was time to look to the future.

'Morning, Daisy. Mmm . . . that bread smells good. And just listen to that.' Jenny joined Daisy in the kitchen, still trying to pin her hair in place as she bent down to smell the newly baked bread.

'Here, let me.' Daisy wiped her hands and helped Jenny place her pins in her bun on the back of her head.

'Listen to what?' she enquired, as she deftly placed the hair pins in place.

'Exactly – peace! Would you believe it? Jonathan is worn out from going rabbiting with his father, and baby Ben is dead to the world. Though what a difference in babies: Ben is so good, compared to Jonathan, who was Satan, I'm sure.'

'He was a handful, I'll grant you that, but never Satan.' Daisy smiled as she poured Jenny a cup of tea.

Jenny drank deeply and smiled. 'What would I do, without you and Ivy? Two young boys take some looking after, and then there are all the lodgings to keep an eye on. At least, since the navvies have moved on, our rooms are let to respectable workmen. But still, they take some upkeep.'

'I'm sure you'd manage without either one of us. You can turn your hand to most things. I sometimes think it was out of pity that you kept me on.' Daisy tested the water, for she wanted to know how much Jenny relied on her. She was dreading having to tell her that she was going to be married and leave Gearstones Lodge.

'Nonsense! I knew you'd be the wonderful cook that you are. Poor Ivy is sometimes quite jealous of your skills. She should know that I'd never see her out of a job, as she's a distant relation, but it's your cooking that the lodgers always ask for.'

Daisy hesitated. 'Oh! You might as well know, because I can't keep my news a secret any longer.' She clattered the spoon into her mixing bowl and slumped into a chair. 'Bob will not be able to keep it to himself, anyway.' She looked sheepishly at Jenny. 'Bob and I are to be married. He's got the signalman's house at Blea Moor, and we are to live there.' She waited for Jenny's response.

'Oh, Daisy, that's lovely news. There's me, blurting on about how we can't do without you, and all along you knew you wanted to tell me this. Congratulations, my love, you'll make him a happy man. He's a bit steady, but he's a good 'un, and there's not many of them about.' Jenny rushed over and hugged Daisy. 'We'll have to make a special day for you. By heck, I'd better order some more ale. And of course you'll have the reception here!' She chuckled.

'Trouble is, Jenny, I will be leaving Gearstones Lodge. I'll need to look after my man.' Daisy looked serious.

'Aye, well, we'll cross that bridge when we come to it. Now, when have you set your wedding for?' Jenny tried to skirt around Daisy's departure.

'We are going to see the vicar today, after dinner time, so I'll know more then.' She was surprised that Jenny was taking it all in her stride and felt that a weight had been lifted. 'Don't worry. I'll stay as long as you want me – that is, until you get a replacement – because I know you are run off your feet with the bairns, and the number of guests you have lodging. I'm only living up the line, after all.'

'Well, we'll make it a wedding to remember. I'll go upstairs and get dressed and tell Mike the news. He'll be so happy for you.' Jenny smiled before climbing back up the stairs. Unbeknown to Daisy, she shook her head in disbelief when she was halfway up. Daisy was marrying a man more than twice her age. A pretty young thing like Daisy should have a handsome lad on her arm. Still, if Bob made her happy, that was all that mattered. You could tell that he adored her. Perhaps young men weren't for Daisy; it took all sorts to make a world, and perhaps she felt safe with Bob. She'd try and get Daisy to stay on as her cook, just for a little while after she was wed, in the hope that she would soon find out what a lonely life it would be up at Blea Moor signal box, just running a house for an ageing husband.

'Well, that's settled then: three weeks on Saturday.' Bob held Daisy tight. 'Are you happy with that, my love?'

'Yes, of course I am. It means our wedding can be a quiet affair. That's what I wanted. I've no family, and I'm not one for fuss.' Daisy smiled and gazed into her beloved's eyes. All she wanted was her man.

'I'll be good to you, my love, and you'll want for nothing. I know I'm no millionaire, but we'll be happy, I swear.'

'I know, my darling.' Daisy held Bob's hand tight as they walked along the path that led to their new home at Blea Moor. The signal box and the railway cottages stood proud of the railway line. Around them lay the wide-open spaces of fell-land, with the wild red- and orange-coloured moorland grasses blowing in the summer breeze. It was a bleak place; even now, towards the end of summer, the wind had a sharp nip to it, just to remind people of the harshness of the fells. The huge, dark chasm of Blea Moor tunnel loomed further down the track, the brickwork around it coloured red from the iron ore that dripped and seeped in the fell-waters and drained down into the stone-covered track.

'So, this is it – this is our home, Daisy my dear.' Bob paused outside the garden gate that formed the entrance to the small garden, stocked lovingly with pansies and marigolds, plants hardy enough to survive the harsh climate that surrounded the squarely built house. 'I think you know our neighbours, the Ivesons and the Sunters. Both families are good folk.' Bob waved to a woman with ragged children around her feet as she stood outside the doorway of the plate-layers' cottages. 'And this is the signal box. Do you want to look inside? Bert won't mind.'

Daisy looked across at the white-painted signal box and up at the clear windows, through which she could see the gleaming brass-topped levers of the signals and the round face of the signal box's clock. It was an integral part of the smooth running of the railway. The figure of Bert waved his hand at her, as she gazed up at the smoke rising from the signal box's small stove. She waved back and smiled.

'I'd rather look around the house, if you don't mind?' Daisy peered through the windows of her new home, trying to look into the rooms inside.

'I haven't got the key yet. Next week, the gaffer said, but you can see from outside how big the house is. It's big enough to hold us two, and perhaps some family, Daisy. What do you say? A little girl and a boy would make us complete. I'd love a lad, just to show him how to do things and to know he's mine.' Bob blushed. He'd never broached the subject before.

'We'll see. I think we should be on our own for a while – not rush into family, not yet.' Daisy's voice went cold. She couldn't possibly think about children yet, and the one thing she had been dreading was the thought of sex. So far Bob had been nothing but honourable, but she knew that, once married, he would expect things of her. The memory of Clifford's rape came rushing back to her, and she shuddered as she recalled his hands wandering over her body. She didn't know how she would manage it, but there was no way she could ever have Bob touching her as Clifford had. He would have to be content with friendship – that had been part of his attraction from the start. She'd watched Lizzie, John's stepdaughter from Gearstones Lodge, and her beau, Dan, fondling and playing around, and had decided a long time ago that it was not for her; she needed friendship, not lust. Nothing good came of lust!

'Daisy, are you listening to me? Bert's put the kettle on in the box, he's made us a brew. Now watch out as you cross the line.' Bob pulled on Daisy's hand as he made his way across the ballast and the train track. 'Watch your skirt don't get caught in the points. We don't want you splattered by the mail train that's nearly due.'

Daisy picked her way carefully across the track, lifting

61

up her long skirts and taking note of the wires and points along the track, before following her husband-to-be up the steps to the signal box. It was quite cosy inside. The kettle was boiling on a small coal stove, and she was immediately made welcome by the beaming red face of Bert, as he shook her hand.

'What are all these levers for?' Daisy looked at the handles. There were some pointing up and others down, in preparation for the passing trains.

Bert grinned. 'Aye, lass, these are for the signals, and these are for the points, so that I can put the trains on the right track. But don't ask me – your fella here will tell you all. He's the man for the job.' Bert patted Bob on his back and grinned as he passed Daisy a steaming brew in an enamel cup.

'This lever sends trains up to Leeds and London, and this one's for the track down to Carlisle.' Bob's voice was full of pride.

'But surely it's up to Carlisle and down to Leeds, from where we are?' asked Daisy, showing interest in the work of her husband-to-be.

'No, it's up to the city of London, and down to the country – the opposite to what you think. That's what we've been taught.'

'That's not right at all.' Daisy laughed as she took a swig of her tea. Just then a bell on the cabin wall rang.

'That'll be the four-fifteen,' Bert announced, as the train set about making its way down the line.

'See, my love. I'm only just over the other side of

the track from you – never too far from your side.' Bob squeezed Daisy's hand.

'Now then, you lovebirds, you are going to make an old man blush.' Bert winked as he pulled the lever back into place, as the steaming engine and its carriages rattled past the signal box. The smell and smoke from the engine filled the box as the driver blew the whistle to show his thanks.

'Ta for showing Daisy the box, Bert. We'd better go now; don't want to get you into bother, because I know visitors in the box are against the rules.'

'Aye well, good luck with your wedding. You make a grand pair.' Bert shook Daisy's hand as she turned at the top of the stairs leading down to the track.

'He's a good man, is Bert. Comes from Settle, loves his job. Even when he's not working, he tries to travel on a train anywhere in the country. Other day he said he'd gone to Blackpool, and stopped in one of those cheap boarding houses on the Golden Mile that they advertise on the station posters. Imagine Blackpool! They say it's the place to go to at the moment. I can just see Bert in a bathing costume, dipping his toe in the Irish Sea.'

Both Daisy and Bob laughed at the thought of the rotund Bert with bathing trunks on.

'He says he's going to go to London one day, on the train. Imagine going to London – by, that's a long way, and a different world from here.' Bob went quiet, imagining the bustling streets of London and his mate Bert walking them.

The courting couple walked hand-in-hand along the path leading back to Gearstones Lodge. The wind gently blew the smell of peat over their faces, and the slight warmth of the setting sun glowed on their skin and on the flanks of the three great peaks of Whernside, Ingleborough and Pen-y-ghent, making them look like sleeping golden lions. Daisy had been trying to pluck up the courage all day to tell Bob her news.

'Bob, my love, you know that when we are married I said I'd give over working at Gearstones Lodge? Well, I'm in a bit of a spot. I can't let Jenny down completely. She'd be lost without me. Would you mind if I stayed working for her, just for perhaps one or two days a week? She's so busy. Just until she's found someone to replace me?' Daisy knew she should show some commitment to Jenny, for it had been her who had saved her on that terrible night. 'Please say you understand. I can't leave Jenny in the lurch.' She looked up into Bob's eyes, sensing that they seemed troubled.

'I thought you were only going to look after me when we got married, and that Gearstones Lodge was going to be a thing of the past. That Jenny owes you, lass – she's not paid you a penny since you first stopped there.' Bob scowled.

'But I've bed and board for nothing. If she hadn't taken me in that night, I don't know where I'd have been by now. It would just be for a week or two after we wed, and then Jenny will have to find someone else.' Daisy stood on her toes and kissed him gently on the cheek.

'Well, make sure that it is. A woman's place is in her home, looking after her man, not flaunting herself about in them lodgings.' Bob's voice was cold and matched the look in his steely eyes.

Daisy was taken aback by his harsh words. Bob was usually gentle, and had never once voiced his opinion about her working for Jenny. The walk back home was done in silence, with only the sound of the resting lapwings and curlews. The goodnight kiss outside Daisy's door was cold and reserved. For a moment she wondered if she was doing the right thing. She'd learned to be independent since being thrown out of her family, and now she was going to have to become a wife, doing what her husband bade her.

'Oh, Daisy, you look beautiful. When I saw it in Tenby's store in Bradford, I had to have it for you. And don't say a word. I could hardly deny you a dress, for all you have done for me over the past few years.' Jenny stood back and admired the blushing Daisy. 'Bob will just want to eat you, looking like that. I hope he's got a decent bed in that house of his, because he'll be using it tonight!' Jenny laughed a crude chuckle, and Daisy's complexion reddened to the same colour as the roses that she held in her hand.

'I don't know how to thank you, Jenny.' Daisy ran her hand down the frills and lace that adorned her wedding dress.

'Well, we couldn't have you marrying in that dull stripy thing you were starching the other day. Good

Lord, lass, this is your day to shine.' Jenny put her hands on her hips and grinned. 'Mike's downstairs. He's decorated two traps and is waiting to take you to the church. The girls have set the drawing room for your wedding breakfast, so the day's yours and Bob's, my girl. So try and look like you'll enjoy it.'

Daisy smiled and thought about the small Dales church at Chapel-le-Dale and of the vicar who was waiting for them. She was worried about the dress, but that was not her main concern. She was beginning to have her doubts about the marriage. In fact, if she could, she would have run and hidden somewhere – anywhere – nobody could ever find her. Since the day they had set their wedding date, and the walk back from the visit to the signal box, Bob had become more interested in keeping her at home and becoming a mother to the family he had secretly dreamed of for years, it would seem. Daisy was beginning to feel smothered by his demands. The wedding night she was dreading, for she knew Bob would expect her to be his, and more besides, and she feared his advances. A tear started to fall silently down her cheeks, and her hands trembled as she held the rose bouquet, watching a petal fall to the ground. She couldn't help but think she was like that petal: falling and alone, without support of others from this day onwards. A married woman who had to do her husband's bidding. And if he wanted a family, then she would have to give him some, even if she couldn't abide the thought of holding a baby.

'Daisy, love, why the tears?' Jenny looked at the

woman she had come to think of as a younger sister and squeezed her arm tightly.

'Just sad to leave here – you've been so good to me.' Daisy wiped away the telltale signs of unhappiness.

'Not nerves, then? Everyone gets them.' Jenny fussed around her and then turned to look in the dresser's mirror, at her own finely placed hat, its feathers drooping over one of her eyes.

'No, it's not nerves. I'm just . . .' Daisy looked at the puzzled face, not wanting to tell her secrets.

'Let's go then. Mike's waited long enough. The horses will be getting impatient.'

Daisy sniffed hard and pulled herself together. After today she would be Mrs Lambert – for better or for worse, for richer or for poorer – and she would have to be dutiful to her husband, no matter what he asked. No respectable woman could want more than that, and it was time to value what she had and not complain.

'That's my girl – go and get him! Even the sun's come out for you.' Jenny pulled back the lace curtains and knocked on the window, to let Mike know that the bridal party was on its way. She kissed Daisy on the cheek and whispered, 'Be happy', before Daisy descended Gearstones' grand stairway.

'Goodbye, room. I've been happy here.' Daisy gave her home of the last few years a quick glance before following Jenny. Even though she knew she'd be back in the kitchen during the following days, things were going to change from the next hour onwards. She would no longer be free to do as she pleased, and she hadn't realized how precious her freedom had been. Her thoughts were also with her parents. They wouldn't know that on this day she was getting married, that she was to start married life without their blessing. A tear filled her eye as she remembered Kitty's wedding day and the fuss that had surrounded it. She had no kin to walk her down the aisle, and no dowry. Still, what did it matter? She'd the Pratts as a good substitute for family, and a husband waiting for her. She steadied her nerves, wiping the tear away, and smiled. No good dwelling on the past. Today was her wedding day – a fresh start.

'Come on, lady, your carriage awaits.' Mike held out his hand and helped Daisy up the steps into the trap.

It was quiet on the road outside. Gone were the navvies' huts and the makeshift hospital; gone the sound of hammers hitting the hard granite rock and the noise of workers that there had been in months past. Instead there was the solitary cry of a curlew circling the lonely fell, looking for its mate. The huge twenty-four-arched viaduct spanning the dale disappeared within the bowels of Whernside. Things were changing. Daisy was to be married and would make Blea Moor her home.

'Come on, lass, let's do it.' Mike patted her hand and then jollied the horses into motion. He was going to miss the quiet Daisy, but she was marrying what he thought a good man, and that was all that mattered.

Daisy stepped down from the trap and entered the small Dales church on Mike's arm. The ancient arch of the church doorway was decorated with nodding dog-daisies entwined with the blue of cranesbill, brightening the ancient stonework in honour of the marriage. In the ray of light amid the darkness of the small church a smiling Bob turned, as the organ started playing the wedding march. Daisy noticed his face cloud over slightly as he looked at the dress she was wearing, but thought no more of it, as the vicar sped through the wedding vows, with Bob dutifully repeating the vows after Daisy until the vicar finally declared them husband and wife in a gusty finish. Bob gripped her arm tightly as she walked down the aisle, smiling at people.

'Where did you get that hideous dress? It looks like a cheap whore's,' he whispered, while smiling at the few guests who had witnessed the wedding.

'Jenny . . .' Daisy tried to speak.

'Should have known. You get it off as soon as we are home, and I never want to see it again,' muttered Bob under his breath, before shaking John's hand and accepting his good wishes. He pulled Daisy to one side, out of earshot of the guests. 'You're my wife, and you'll dress like a railwayman's wife from now on, not like some tart.'

Daisy could feel the tears welling up inside her. What had happened to the sweet Bob she had known? Was this how he was going to treat her, now that she was his wife? He held his hand out and helped Daisy into the trap, not saying a word to her.

All through the wedding breakfast Bob kept looking at Daisy and her dress. Never had he seen such a waste of frills and lace. He loved his Daisy plain and pure;

she didn't need the flounces of a town girl. Good manners demanded that he comment to Jenny on how lovely the wedding breakfast was, only for him to curse her under his breath for being so over-the-top with her elaboration on what should have been a simple Dales wedding, whispering to Daisy that there had been no need for anything so decadent, and that it was all too vulgar for his taste.

Daisy was exhausted with anxiety by the time they left for their new home. Bob strode out along the fell track yards ahead of her, urging her onwards as she tried to catch him up in her petite wedding boots, which seemed to catch in every strand of heather.

'You can take them disgusting rags off now. Every man was looking at you, dressed like that. I couldn't believe it. I love you in plain, simple clothes; there was no need to dress like them at Gearstones. I love you for you, not your finery.' Bob slammed the front door of their new home behind them.

'I was the bride, Bob – that's why.' Daisy pulled her tightly laced boots off her aching feet. 'Everyone admires the bride. That's all they were doing. Besides, I've only got eyes for you.' She snivelled as her fingers trembled, undoing the beautiful buttons of her tight-fitting bodice. She finally stood in her bloomers and corset on the cold stone flags of the kitchen, while Bob paced the floor, running his hands through his grey hair.

'I thought you were different from other women. I thought you were sensible and would make a good wife. And now you want to keep working. I love you for how sweet and innocent you are, and today is tarnished by them at Gearstones making us out to be something we aren't, and asking you to work, when I want you at home with me.' Bob was nearly in tears, as he held his head in his hands over the kitchen table.

'All I want is you, Bob. I love you. This dress and the fancy wedding breakfast mean nothing to me. It's you I love, and if you want me not to work, then I'll tell Jenny in the morning. Don't let's argue on our wedding day,' Daisy sobbed.

'I love you, Daisy. I'm sorry, but I'm an old-fashioned man, with old-fashioned ideas. I want roses round this cottage's door, and three or four children for when I grow old, to look after me.' Bob reached for Daisy's hand and smiled as she came near him.

'You know I love you, Bob. My heart's yours, but perhaps I'm not ready for children, not yet.'

Daisy cringed as Bob ran his hand over her buttocks and his grip tightened on her firmly laced waist. Her thoughts went back to Clifford, and the rape she had endured at his hands.

'Listen to us arguing. Come here and sit on my knee, and make me a happy man. It's time to stop talking. Come and do what a newly married couple are supposed to do. We've both waited long enough; we've hidden our passions well, but our argument will be all the sweeter, if we make up by making love. Children will come, my love, and you may not want them now, but you'll grow to love them once they are in your arms.' Bob pulled Daisy down to him and kissed her hard on

71

the lips, while his free hand felt its way down the front of her bodice, squeezing her pert breast.

'No, Bob, I can't do it this way. I'll not have you treat me this way. We need to talk. I don't want children. In fact I don't want sex – never, ever! I hate a man's hand touching me. I'm sorry. I love you, but I can't have children. I won't have children, not with you or anyone.'

Daisy pulled herself away and stood defiantly in her undergarments, her face red and determined.

'What sort of wife are you to me? You show me up, by wanting to work; you won't lie with me; and now you are telling me you won't bear me children? Perhaps we shouldn't have got married today. Perhaps I've been an old fool, and I should have listened to my mother. She told me I was too old to wed.'

'Perhaps you should have listened to your mother. I don't think we should have married, if all you want of me is sex, and for me to be tied down with a baby every year. That's not for me. And I'm away to my bed now, and you needn't follow.'

Daisy gathered up her dress and decided to climb the stairs to their bedroom. There she changed into her nightdress and lay in the new marital bed. She waited, fretting about the tempestuous Bob. So his mother had told him not to marry; perhaps she had been telling Bob what to expect from his new bride, and Daisy was not fitting into his mother's expectations of a perfect wife. She waited for Bob's footsteps to mount the stairs. She didn't want him to touch her, but with the temper he was in, she thought it better just to lie there and take whatever she was given. She felt tears welling up to the surface again; this was not what a wedding night should be like. Although she had not been looking forward to this moment, she had hoped he'd be kind and caring, if there was to be any lovemaking, but now she was alone.

She lay in the darkness, with the ticking of the clock passing the seconds, the minutes and then the hours. She couldn't hear Bob. He wasn't making a sound downstairs – he must be sitting sulking. Well, let him sulk, she thought, as her fear turned to anger with the passing of the hours. He'd ruined her day and shown his true colours. The cloak of sleep eventually got the better of her, although thoughts of a raging Bob clouded her dreams.

Dawn came quickly, and Daisy rose from her sleep to find the other side of her bed cold and empty. A late-summer mist hung around the house and trailed along the valley bottom, following the course of the river. The windows were cold and covered with condensation from the difference in temperature inside and out. She wiped a clear round on the wet window and noted that, once the mists cleared, it would be a fine day. She could tell that by the bit of blue sky that fleetingly made an appearance through the white cloud. She pulled her now long brown hair from behind her shoulders to the side of her face and, after using the chamber pot, quietly made her way down the stairs to the kitchen and living room.

The clock's constant tick was the only noise, until suddenly the clatter of an early-morning train rattled past the house, making Daisy jump as her unclad feet hit the cold stone-flagged floor of the kitchen. The rocking chair was empty, and the grey embers of the fire were the only sign that someone had been in the kitchen the previous evening. Daisy pulled the green chenille curtain back. It divided the kitchen from the living room. The week before she had lovingly sewn the tassels that now hung from it, as she'd looked forward to seeing it hanging in their new home. She fastened it back with the hook that retained it, and shivered in the morning's light.

'Bob, I'm sorry. I shouldn't have listened to Jenny. You are right. I should never have worn that dress – it wasn't me. And as for children, we can have as many as you like, my love.' Daisy spotted Bob's hand over-hanging the red padded sofa that had been placed in the living room in front of the marble fireplace.

There was no reply.

'I'm sorry, really I am.' She thought it better to submit to his feelings before approaching him.

There was still no reply, and his arm did not move or flinch.

'Bob, you are just being stupid and stubborn now.' Daisy could feel her temper rising as she walked towards him. 'It was only a dress!' She stood opposite him. He wasn't moving. His mouth was open and his head was on one side, his body lifeless and still. He looked ashen and his hair was grey, and Daisy suddenly realized how old he looked, before she let out a scream like a banshee.

Her groom was dead. He was dead in his chair. He'd never made it to bed because he was cold like the grave, leaving her alone in the world again!

Her scream echoed around the small settlement of Blea Moor, making Bert abandon the signal box and the womenfolk from the Iveson and Sunter households knock on the door and shout their concerns. Hearing Daisy weeping, they entered the clean, new marital home to find her on her knees, holding the dead man's hand, constantly muttering that she was sorry, between her sobs.

'Aye, lass, sit over there. Let me see if I can get a pulse.' Bert urged Sally Sunter to sit Daisy down in a chair, while he ran his fingers down Bob's neck, and felt his wrist, looking for a pulse. He shook his head, as Sally consoled Daisy. Betsy Iveson shooed her children out of the kitchen, their curiosity having got the better of them, as she did the only thing she could to help: lighting the fire and putting the kettle on to boil.

'So you came down and found him here? Did he never come to bed last night?' Bert scratched his head, with his cap in his hand, and looked at the heartbroken Daisy.

Daisy shook her head between sobs. 'We had a row, and I went to bed without him. I was so upset I cried myself to sleep. And the next thing I knew it was morning, and he'd never come to bed,' she wailed, as Sally put her arm around her.

'He was an ill man. He were taking pills for his heart, but bloody hell – I didn't think he was that poorly.

Betsy, can you go to Gearstones Lodge and tell them what's happened and that we need the doctor from Ingleton. I'll have to get back in the box, else we will have more than one death on our hands.'

Bert hit his cap on the side of his leg, in defeat of death, and let out a long sigh.

'By, it's a hard one on thee, lass; you've not been married twenty-four hours. Sometimes you wonder if there is a God up there. He's a bloody joker, if there is. I'll miss Bob, he was a good man; always the same, no matter what his worries. Look after her, Sally. I'll come back across – I'll send word to Horton and Dent on what's happened, and get someone to relieve me of my shift.' Bert patted Daisy's shoulder as he left the grieving house. He'd always known that Bob wasn't that strong, but fate was cruel. That poor young lass: bride-to-be one day, and widow the next.

'Oh, Daisy, my love, what are we to do?' Jenny put her arm around the small frame of her good friend and employee, as the undertaker placed Bob in his coffin. 'You'll come back and stop with us tonight? You can't stay here, with a corpse in the house, on your own.'

'No, I can't face the lodge tonight. I'm his wife – I belong here with him. I let him down, with my pride and my stubborn ways. I'll not leave him now.' Daisy dabbed her eyes with her hankie. 'Besides, I'll have to write and tell his mother. She needs to know – give her a chance to be at his funeral, if not at his wedding.' Daisy breathed in deeply, thinking of the woman whom she now knew had partly ruled Bob's life and had refused to see her son wed.

'Don't let her upset you. She sounds like an old dragon to me. She's the one to blame for his death, if anyone – telling her son that he wouldn't be happy wed. I think you are well out of it, my lass, and the sooner you get back to working for me, the better. Put all this behind you and get on with your life.'

Daisy looked at Jenny. Sometimes she was so uncaring it was unbelievable – her business being the only thing that mattered in her life.

'I don't know what I'll do. I need time.' Daisy looked at Bob laid out in his coffin. He'd raised his voice in life, but never his hand, and he definitely wouldn't be doing so in death. She'd stay with him; the Sunters and the Ivesons were next door and they were good folk, just as Bob had said.

'Well, no doubt you'll suit yourself.' Jenny pulled her hat on and stood in the doorway, waiting for a reply.

'I'm all right. I'll be fine – stop worrying. I'll be back with you once the funeral's over; after all, I'll need the money. Is my room still vacant? The railway bosses will not want me to stop here, after I've buried Bob.'

'Buried Bob' – the words seemed unreal to Daisy, yet they were coming out of her mouth, just as the words 'I do' had done the previous day.

'Aye, it's all yours, lass, for as long as you want it. I'll welcome an extra pair of hands again.' Jenny fumbled with her gloves, quickly reminding herself how lucky she was to have a husband – unlike Daisy.

Daisy closed the door behind Jenny. At last she was on her own. The evening's shadows were beginning to close in, and she lit the paraffin lamps for light and comfort and stoked the fire's embers into life. She walked into the living room and peered into the open coffin where Bob lay. His face looked more relaxed, and some of his age seemed to have disappeared with his death. The doctor had confirmed it was a massive heart-attack that had taken him and that Bob had, as Bert said, been taking pills for his heart for years. Why hadn't Bob told her? But then, would it have made any difference? She'd still have married him.

She kissed him gently on the brow and a tear trickled down her cheek. It had been stupid to argue over a dress. She hadn't even liked it, but Jenny had insisted that she wore it. And, as Bob had said, children would have come, with the love of a good marriage. She should not have been so stupid, and should have driven thoughts of the callous Clifford from her head. She stood transfixed at the side of the cheap coffin, before turning to the small desk, which held paper and envelopes along with a new wedding certificate and a death certificate. She'd write to Bob's mother – a woman she had never met, but had grown to hate in the last few hours. What she would write she didn't quite know. How did you tell someone her son was dead, the day after his wedding? Whatever she wrote, this woman was going to hate her, because it would be her – Daisy – whom she would forever blame for her son's death.

Daisy wrote a few words, trying to convey her sympathies, but at the same time relay in her correspondence her own heartbroken feelings. She knew the blame would be laid at her door, and that her own feelings would be overlooked by Bob's mother. She sealed the envelope. Tomorrow it would be delivered, and by Wednesday his mother would be arriving for the funeral. It would be then that she would face the wrath of the mother-in-law she had never met.

She lifted her flickering candle and went into the kitchen, because her stomach was complaining from a lack of food. She'd not eaten all day, and her legs felt weak. She snatched a piece of bread and cheese from the larder and dutifully chewed at them. The bread went round and round in her mouth, finally being washed down by a glass of milk. So this was her lot: a widow and not yet twenty, left with not a penny to her name and no roof over her head, after the funeral; reliant on Jenny's generosity, and stuck cooking and cleaning at Gearstones. She'd had all she had wanted the previous day, but hadn't had the sense to realize it.

She walked to the back door and opened it wide. Standing in the doorway, she smelled the moorland air. It was a mixture of dark, boggy peat and sweet moorland herbs, sharp with the threat of the coming autumn nights. She heard one of the Sunter bairns crying and watched the lamplight in the signal box – the relief signalman's shadow playing on the wall. It seemed like a lifetime since the wild night when she had knocked on the door of Gearstones Lodge. Perhaps it was time to move on. People would only show her pity now: the lass with no family; the lass who had lost her husband. She wanted to escape – have a new life somewhere nobody knew her or cared about her. She'd done it before, and now she'd do it again. She closed the door on the outside world and quietly mounted the stairs. Tomorrow was another day; time enough to think then. Now, exhausted, she was away to her bed.

The little dark-haired woman climbed down from the train. She was as round as she was tall and struggled with the step, as the stationmaster offered her assistance.

'Out of my way – I can manage without your help.' She walked along the platform, leaning heavily on an ebony stick, dressed in black from ankle to neckline and with a mood to match.

Daisy watched the woman struggling to walk, before she plucked up the courage to introduce herself. She walked over and offered her assistance. 'I'm Daisy, Bob's wife. I'm sorry it's been due to bad news that we have had to meet this way.' She offered the woman the use of her arm to lean on.

'Don't you touch me, you trollop! You've killed my Bob. My boy – he was well and happy until he met and married you. Now I'm burying him in this godforsaken hole away from his father's grave and mine, which I'll soon be in, because of you.' Her grey eyes were full of malice as she pulled her arm away from Daisy and walked, with the aid of her stick, through the station gates.

'But, Mrs Lambert . . .' Daisy pulled on her arm, tears in her eyes.

'Get off me! Don't touch me, don't talk to me. I'm nothing to do with you – never have been, never will be. Now, I'm off to bury my lad, when I can get into this blasted trap.' Bob's mother swore as the stable lad tried to give her a helping hand into the waiting trap, which was lined up behind the hearse that was carrying Bob's body.

Daisy put her head down and cried. She had known she would not get a warm welcome, but Mrs Lambert's words cut through to her soul. She'd loved her man, and today she was burying him, and she had no family in the whole wide world to turn to.

Railwaymen always stood together and supported their own, and it was no exception at Bob's funeral. Plate-layers, signalmen and station guards packed the tiny church and watched as Bob's mother and his widow jostled for position in the quiet church in the glen. The vicar's voice rang out clear and true, declaring his sorrow – and that of his parish – at the loss of someone so recently married, and saying that his heart went out to his young bride. Bob's mother tutted loudly enough for the entire congregation to hear, making clear her feelings. The body was carried out with reverence and laid to rest in the extended graveyard of St Leonard's. A bunch of dog-daisies and cranesbill was lovingly placed on the raw soil of the grave by Daisy.

'You needn't think you can get your hands on any of his money, you hussy!' Bob's mother spat as she walked away from the grave. 'I've got it saved safely, away from thieving hands like yours. Bob's been sending half his wage to me since he was a lad, and I'm not giving it to the likes of you. I know your sort – ten-a-penny in Leeds, you are.' She urged the stable lad to assist her again as she walked to the trap, not bothering to talk to anyone.

'I didn't know he had any savings – that wasn't why I married him.' Daisy shook with grief as the insults were thrown at her.

'Now look here, you. This lass loved your lad, although God knows why. She could have done a lot better, if you ask me. It wasn't about his money.' Jenny had seen and heard enough of this bitter woman.

'You're nothing but a trollop. I've heard all about you, and all. You came from nowt, with your fine airs and graces.' Bob's mother flung insults down from the trap, before yelling at the lad to whip the horses into action.

'Aye, piss off, you old bugger! I'll come down to your level – bugger off back to Leeds, where you belong,' shouted Jenny at the trap, as it started off over the bridge back up the lane to the station.

'Jenny, don't – she's not worth it. That's the last we will ever see of her. Leave her be. You can't blame her for thinking I killed her son.' Daisy pulled on Jenny's sleeve. 'I've had enough; I've got to move on. Bob's dead, I'm a widow, and there's nothing I can do about it.'

'All right, pet. But she was a right old bugger, and

she'd no right to talk to you like that.' Jenny smiled and put her arm round Daisy. 'Anyway, let's go and see your old fella off in style with a few drinks. Tea in your case of course, seeing as you don't drink, you funny bugger.'

Daisy smiled. Jenny was a rough one, but a better friend you couldn't have. She gave a long look at the gravediggers filling in the grave of her dead husband, then slipped her arm through Jenny's to walk with the rest of the mourners up to Gearstones Lodge. Her head was full of plans, but she was uncertain which way to go. For now, it was back to Jenny and her family, but in the coming days her plans for the future would have to be made.

6

Daisy looked at the bag of money in her hand. It contained four guineas, ten shillings and sixpence ha'penny. Along with Bob's last week's wages, she now had over five guineas. She'd never had that sort of money in her life.

'Thank you, Bert. Can you thank everyone for me. Folk have been so kind – they really shouldn't have given me all this.' Daisy wiped a tear away from her eye.

'Nay, lass, you're one of us, like Bob was. We stand by our own on this line. Everybody's put a bit in, no matter how small, because we knew how much Bob loved you, and he wouldn't want to see you go without.' Bert fumbled with his cap and looked round the empty railway house. 'Have you emptied the place then? I hear the new fella moves in tomorrow. Don't ken him – he's from out of Lancashire.'

'Yes, I've moved some of our furniture to Gearstones and left some in the house. I've no use for it.' Daisy looked around at the house that had been her home so briefly.

'Are you going back to work for Jenny then? I know she's missed you!' Bert had warmed to the idea of Daisy living nearby and being company for him, with Bob.

'I am for now, and then I don't know. I could do with a change, else I'm going to live here until I'm an old maid.' Daisy gazed down the valley.

'Old maid – tha's nowt but a spring chicken! Now if I was a day younger and not married to my Mary, I'd wed you and run away to Blackpool with you,' chuckled Bert. He had grown a bit sweet on Daisy.

'I'll never marry again, Bert, too much heartache. Now travel – that might be me. I'll have to see; you can always come back home, if you're not happy.' Daisy turned the lock of the door and hid the key under the flowerpot on the windowsill, as instructed by the stuffy landlord, for the new owner.

'"Never" is a bloody long time, but whatever you do, lass, I wish you luck. You take care, and may God be with you. If there's owt I can do for you, you let me know. I've friends from one end of the line to the other.' Bert winked and slowly crossed the track to the signal box.

The youngest of the Sunters came running up with a bunch of heather. 'Bye, Daisy. Mam says I've got to give you this white heather, for luck. We picked it from Dent Head this morning. Mam says she's sorry she couldn't give you any money, but she knows you'll understand, with all her mouths to feed.' The little girl wiped her nose on her tattered sleeve, before running back to the arms of her mother, who was standing watching at her doorway.

Daisy would miss living in the little community of Blea Moor. They were good folk and had made her welcome, in the brief time that she was with them. With a heavy heart she trudged down the track back to the twinkling lights of Gearstones Lodge. Jenny would be there, along with Mike and the two boys, at their home, she thought, but it wasn't *her* home. Her home was Grisedale – a place she hadn't thought of until she had scattered earth on Bob's coffin. The hurt caused by her family, and now the loss of her husband, overwhelmed her and made her want to run away from anyone who knew her. As she entered the door of the lodge, she knew she had to get away. And now, with those five guineas, she had the means. She'd wait just a few weeks until she felt more settled and then she'd start to look around for employment. Surely somebody, somewhere, would want her skills.

Jenny tied the ribbons of her hat under her chin and ushered her eldest boy into the back of the carriage that was waiting for them. 'Are you sure you aren't joining us, Daisy? It's not too late to change out of that drab black. You can't be in mourning forever, you know. Besides, you'd enjoy the picnic at Fox's Pulpit, and there will be some eligible young men. I know Robert Stanley is going to be there, for sure.' Jenny scowled at Daisy as she stood in the doorway, watching the picnic party depart.

'No, I'll not join you. It's too soon after losing my Bob, it wouldn't be right. And as for this black, I'm always going to wear it, just like our dear Queen does for her Albert.' Daisy was standing her ground. She didn't want to pretend to be happy. For the three weeks since Bob's funeral she'd put her efforts into cooking and baking, and making sure that all was running smoothly at Gearstones, but now she wanted to be on her own.

Jenny looked at Daisy. She was going to have to chivvy the lass along. She couldn't have her hanging about the place with a long face on her.

'Nonsense, you'll find another fella and be back to normal in no time. If you insist that you're not coming, then don't wait up. Make sure you keep an eye on the place. You know we are staying with the Staintons tonight, so lock up and we'll see you in the morning.' Jenny smoothed down her finery around her, before telling Mike to whip the team into action.

Daisy watched as they wandered up and over the moorland road towards the Dent Head turning. She couldn't believe Jenny – sometimes she showed no respect for other people's feelings. But now it was time to make good her plan. She quickly locked the door of the lodge behind her and climbed the stairs to her room. There she packed her few belongings into her carpet bag and carefully placed the lovingly handwritten note on the washstand. They'd understand that she needed a fresh start. She'd relied on Jenny and the comfort of Gearstones Lodge for long enough; her time was up. Now she'd have to hurry if she was to catch the eleven-thirty to Leeds.

Leeds – her heart missed a beat. The furthest she had ever been was Settle or Ingleton. But it was too late now to fret. She'd a train to catch and a new life waiting. She was off to Leeds, to seek employment as a cook in one of the great houses that were being built as fast as you could blink. Bert had told her of houses three storeys high, with parlours and drawing rooms where staff waited on the owners nearly day and night. And of how water was on tap in the kitchen and rooms were richly carpeted, displaying the best of furniture. It had been more than Daisy could have dreamed of, when Bert had been true to his word and had helped her secure a position with a friend he knew, who was about to set up in business. He was apparently a local chap from Skipton, and that was as much as Daisy knew. But Bert had assured her that he was a good family man and would treat her right, and that she could always come back to Jenny's, if it didn't suit her.

Daisy locked the huge wooden door of Gearstones Lodge behind her and placed the key through the newly acquired letter box. She was thankful Jenny had insisted that the door had one fitted a few months back, after she had caught the postman harassing Ivy in the kitchen. Daisy remembered the postman getting a good ear-bashing for his lustful antics, and that he was told in no uncertain manner that he was lucky he didn't get reported. The following day Mike had been made to fit a letter box. Bless Jenny – she had been a mother hen to both Daisy and Ivy alike, and she'd be missed, for her care. Daisy breathed in deeply, savouring the clean, peaty air; it would soon be replaced with the smoke and smells of the city. She picked up her carpet bag, along with her courage, and stepped out to catch her train, giving one last, loving look at the sweeping viaduct and the double-fronted inn that had formed such a part of her life. She only hoped she was doing the right thing, and that she wasn't running away yet again from her wounded feelings.

Daisy sat in her carriage studying the people seated opposite her. One was a sharply dressed businessman, obviously on his way to do business in Leeds or Bradford, perhaps to trade in wool or cotton. Daisy deduced wool, for his complexion was red and weathered as if he had walked many a mile to view sheep. Next to him sat a small, demure little woman with a natty hat on her head, who never dared look at anyone. Daisy thought she looked like a shy sparrow, her eyes never making contact with anyone. After sussing out her travel companions, Daisy gazed out of the train window, though the steam from the engine kept floating down, obscuring the view. The green fields of the Dales and the Ribble valley had long since gone, giving way to tall mill chimneys and the back-to-back terraces of town living. Daisy had never seen so many houses before and marvelled at how people lived in such cramped conditions. She was just admiring the winding canal, and the barges unloading at the wharfside, when the guard came by, shouting out, 'Next stop Shipley. Change there for Bradford, and then it is Leeds, our final stop.'

Daisy secured her hat, as the man in the suit rose to go to his destination. She clung to her bag. It was all she had in the world, and she was not going to let anyone part her from it. Town folk were different – you couldn't trust them. After meeting Bob's mother, she feared that Mrs Lambert might be making the same trip, on board the train bound for Leeds station. After all there couldn't be that many folk living in Leeds!

The train jolted to a halt and she could hear the great engine let off steam, as if exhausted. The salesman coughed apologetically as he pushed past her, in a hurry to go about his business, and the slight form of the woman rose and disappeared amid the engine's steam. Daisy stood in amazement, staring at the sheer number of trains standing at platforms and at all the people – they were like ants! Never had she seen so many people: women with hats, men in suits, children squabbling, plus trains blowing whistles and porters yelling. If this was Shipley, then what was Leeds going to be like?

'You all right, miss? Do you know where you are going?' The guard of the new train she had joined stopped for a moment as he slammed the carriage door shut. He couldn't help but notice that Daisy was all alone. He saw that she had a fresh-from-the-country look and knew that she might need his guidance.

'Er . . . I'm fine, I'm going to Leeds.' Daisy blushed. She felt like a very small fish in a very big pond, and she felt stupid at her reply. Of course he knew she was going to Leeds. She was sitting on the Leeds train, wasn't she?

'The train is just filling with water. We'll be on our way again shortly.' The guard pointed to the front of the crimson-coated engine with its block of carriages. 'Take care, miss, just be careful who you talk to.'

He started walking back down the train. He'd seen so many young women travelling from the Dales to Leeds to seek work in the mills. It was a shame they couldn't find work in their home towns. It was even worse when, on his walk back home of an evening, he met some of the same girls, touting for business as ladies of the night, down by the wharfside. He hoped the fresh-faced lass he'd just helped didn't go the same way. He couldn't help but notice that she was in mourning, other-wise he'd probably just have left her and not enquired about her welfare. Anyway he had enough of his own worries – she'd have to survive. Sink or swim, that's what she'd have to do.

To detract from the silence, Daisy unfolded the address that Bert had given her. He'd also told her to get some lodgings, just for the night, as soon as she arrived in Leeds, because his friend lived some way from the station and she wasn't expected until the following day. She looked at the address, trying to memorize it and picture her new place of employment:

Mr William Mattinson,
4 Newtown Terrace,
Leeds

91

She folded the address and placed it back in the safety of her bag. She couldn't thank Bert enough for his help. She sighed and leaned back in her seat, playing idly with the brooch that contained a lock of Bob's hair, in remembrance of him. A tear came to her eye as she remembered clipping it from his head before the coffin lid was closed down upon him. Poor Bob, he would never have been happy with her; perhaps it was for the best that their moments together had been fleeting. She closed her eyes, trying to block out thoughts of the funeral and the life she had just left. The slamming of the carriage door and the sudden jolt of the carriages made her come to her senses quickly.

'All right, lass? It's a foggy one out there, enough for old Nick to sneak up on ya wi'out you kenning.'

Daisy looked at the bubbly young woman who had joined her carriage, not quite understanding what she'd just said.

'Cat got ya tongue then? Or don't you talk to the likes of me?'

Daisy apologized quickly as she just made out the last few words.

'Nay, sorry, I didn't catch what you said.'

'Blimey, you're a right one to talk to. What's with the nay – ain't that what horses eat?'

Daisy went quiet.

'I'm only joking. You're from further up north, from them there Dales, eh? Well, keep your wits about you in Leeds, my girl. Don't let 'em know how green you are behind the ears, else your pocket will be picked, and we don't want you losing your possessions.'

Daisy gazed, fascinated by her new companion, and listening to every word she said. She quickly found out that she was called Susie.

'You could do with a bit of this on, girl. You look a bit peaky to say you've come from the country.' Susie hastily put rouge on her cheeks, aided by the dim gaslights, as the train pulled out of the station.

'Oh, I could never wear anything like that – it's not for me.' Daisy watched as Susie next applied an ample lashing of lipstick.

'You got to make the best of what you got, girl, and make the most of it while you can. I do!' Susie smacked her lips together and leaned over towards Daisy. 'All the world's a stage – and it's yours for the taking. Think on what I've said, for no one looks at a shrinking violet.' It was then, as she rearranged her drawstring bag containing all her potions and lotions, that she noticed by the train's dim light that Daisy was wearing black.

'I'm sorry, lass, I didn't notice you were in mourning. Lose anyone close, darling?' She hesitated for a moment.

'My husband. I lost my husband three weeks ago. I'm just getting over the funeral and realizing I'm a widow.' Daisy could feel a lump in her throat as the word 'husband' caught in her mouth.

'Oh, doll, I'm sorry. There's me telling you to paint yourself up, and there's you grieving. I just don't know when to shut my mouth, that's my problem.' Susie leaned over and took hold of Daisy's hand. 'Tell me all about it; we've a while before we get into Leeds.'

Daisy looked at her companion. It was the first time anyone had shown her any concern since the funeral. Life had needed to carry on as usual at Gearstones Lodge, and there was no time to feel maudlin. There had been meals to prepare and rooms to clean, and no one had time to listen to a simpering cook. Death was an everyday fact, and you just knew to get on with your lot. Now it was like unleashing a flood barrier, as Daisy told this complete stranger the story of the last few months and why she was on the train.

'Well, girl, I don't speak ill of the dead, but perhaps it was a blessing. He'd a' been a sod to live with, and his mother . . . You see, that's why I play the stage. I don't want to be pinned down by anyone.' Susie sat back into the shadows of the carriage.

'Are you on the stage? You keep saying you are.' It was Daisy's turn to ask the questions.

'Isn't everyone, darling? Aren't we all on the stage of life? Some, perhaps, are in the spotlight more than others. Now tell me, where are you stopping tonight, and do you know where you're going in the morning?'

'Nay, I've no idea where I'll rest my head tonight. I nearly turned back just before you got on the train, because I suddenly realized how foolish I'd been.' Daisy was feeling vulnerable and silly, for already she realized that she had underestimated the size of Leeds and the number of people who lived there. What on earth was she thinking of?

'Have you any money? Because, girl, I'll get you into lodgings tonight, and I know my plot fairly well. I'll point you in the right direction for your job. And for the Lord's sake, drop the "nay" if you're going to make it here. You don't want folk thinking you are off the first train from up north, in no-man's-land.'

'It's not up north, it's down, if you work on t' railway.' Daisy quickly remembered what Bert had said in the signal box that day, which seemed so long ago. 'And I'm not changing how I talk for anyone.'

'You talk daft. North's up. You'll soon change your twang anyway, when you've been with us a while. Now, am I to sort you some lodgings?'

'If you can. I'll stand on my own two feet tomorrow. I'll find my way to my new employer in the morning.'

'Going into service ain't my idea of a job, but as long as you're happy.'

Susie stood up as the train jolted over the many track points and swayed back and forward, making her adjust her balance. Steam entered the coach as she pulled on the leather strap to open the window. She then leaned out to open the door as it slowed down alongside the platform.

'Come on, girl, look sharp. It's a walk down the platform.'

First, Daisy put her head out of the doorway and looked around her. It was early evening, but the station was beginning to be lit by an amber glow from the gaslights that illuminated the great glass-roofed station. She stepped out of the train and stopped at the edge of the steps, her mouth open. All those platforms, all those people, and they were walking so fast, with tiny steps, not the big long strides of home, but small, quick movements. She looked at the flower-sellers and paper-boys yelling their trade, and yet it was nearly the end of the day. Horses and carts were being filled from goods trains as they stood, still steaming, with water dripping onto their huge axels and pistons, while letters were being unloaded in mail bags. She'd never seen such a busy place.

'Come on. I ain't got all night. I've got to earn a living, as well you know.' Susie pulled Daisy by the shoulder and linked arms with her, bustling her and her carpet bag down the platform and out of the busy station onto the streets of Leeds.

Outside, horses and cabs were waiting for any passengers who needed their assistance, the horses chomping at the bit, their harnesses jangling. A man shouted down from his seat. 'Evening, Susie, can I take you anywhere tonight?'

'Nah, not tonight, Harry. Keeping it local!'

Daisy was quickly escorted along the side of the huge, noisy station and down a wide cobbled street with warehouses and offices all crammed next to each other. She looked up at the street name: Water Street. It was apt, as it ran parallel to the canal. Daisy wondered which had come first, the buildings or the canal? She remembered all the navvies on the railway talking about their time building the canals before joining the railways. The canal was bustling with barges, and with men loading and offloading goods. Wives were cursing their men, as every so often a salute to Susie was shouted from a grinning husband. Susie herself seemed oblivious to their shouts, and carried on nearly dragging Daisy to her destination.

They finally stopped halfway down Water Street, outside a squat building with small stained-glass windows and a low doorway. The door creaked when Susie opened it.

'Evening, Susie. Usual, is it?' A small, chubby man with whiskers as white as snow, and hair to match, smiled at them both. 'I don't know your friend. Are you not going to introduce us?'

'You've twisted my arm. I'll have a gin. This is Daisy. What do you want, lass?'

'Er . . . I don't – I don't drink.' Daisy was busy looking round the smoke-filled room. It was full of people playing cards, smoking pipes or reading newspapers. In the darkness of two corners of the room there were what Daisy took to be courting couples, apart from the fact that she thought they were being a bit too free and easy with their actions towards one another. However, Daisy noted that they were all well dressed and didn't show the slightest bit of interest in the two new customers who had just entered.

'Daisy, is it? And you don't drink? Well, there's a first for my little club. I take it you are from up north, by that accent – just come off the train?'

He poured Susie a large gin into a highly decorated glass and winked at her.

'Nah, don't you be thinking anything like that, Mr Trotter. I know what you are thinking, by that wink. But Daisy is looking for gainful employment in service. She's an excellent cook and is going to a job at Newtown Terrace tomorrow. She just needs a roof over her head for tonight, and I'm sure you can oblige.' Susie swigged the gin back in one. 'She's got money, and I'll vouch for her.'

Daisy smiled. She didn't know what the wink meant, but obviously Susie had put him right.

'I see. Well, I have a spare room. It's sixpence for the night. I will tell you my rules: no pissing the bed and definitely no fleas, and payment up front. Oh, and if you entertain, keep the noise down – it puts other customers off.' He put his gin pitcher down sharply on the table and waited for a response.

Daisy was taken aback by the sharpness of his attitude. She wasn't likely to entertain anyone, or wet the bed and have fleas; and the less said about them, the better. She pulled her purse out of her bag and quickly gave him sixpence.

He grasped it tightly and then leaned towards a shelf to place a candle in a candlestick, which he lit by holding it to an already burning candle on one of the tables.

'Well, if you don't drink, I'll show you to your room.' He grinned and turned round quickly. 'Will you be wanting some supper? I've some nice cold mutton and pickles. They're only tuppence. You can eat them in your room.'

'That would be grand – and a glass of milk, if you'd

be so kind.' Daisy dug in her purse again and paid him for her supper.

'My privilege! Any friend of Susie's is welcome under my roof. She surprises me every day, does our Susie.' Ebenezer Trotter grinned at Susie as he guarded the candle from the draught. The door opened yet again, to a courting couple who were laughing loudly in each other's company. 'This way, Daisy. Will I be seeing you later, Susie, or will you be elsewhere tonight?'

'I don't know about tonight. I might call by – it depends on how busy I am.' Susie stared hard at Ebenezer; she didn't want her game to be given away. 'You look after Daisy here. Make sure she's not disturbed, and point her in the right direction in the morning.' She turned to Daisy. 'You take care, girl. Keep your door closed tonight, and try and sleep. Ebenezer here will look after you. If you need me or get into bother, come down here. I'm always calling in and out of here of an evening. Just tell Ebenezer you need me, and he'll tell me.' With that, Susie gave Daisy a big hug and walked out into the night, leaving Daisy standing with Ebenezer in the middle of his so-called 'club'.

'This way then, Daisy.' Ebenezer led her through some unlit dark rooms and up three sets of creaking stairs, nearly to the attic rooms. There he took a set of keys that had jangled around his waist on the ascent up the stairs and unlocked a dark oak door, pushing it open for Daisy.

'You'll be all right in here, lass. It's one of my more quiet rooms – nobody comes up here much.' He held the candle and it flickered, showing the room to be decorated, but rather sparse. 'It's got all you want, and I'll send your supper up shortly. You can light the fire if you want, but that'll be another penny, and it's not that cold at this time of year.'

Daisy looked around the room. It would do for a night. Hopefully she'd be in work by tomorrow. 'Thank you, Mr Trotter, I'm most grateful for your hospitality.'

'You've paid me, girl, and Susie's vouched for you – that's all that matters.' The old man shuffled out and closed the door behind him, without saying anything more.

Daisy lit a further two candles and sat on the bed. It wasn't like home. There was no mountain air and no stars to see, just the heady bustle of people and horses in the streets. People didn't look at you; they were too busy going about their business. And she dreaded to think what it would be like in the morning, when Leeds was truly awake. What had she done? If it hadn't been for kind-hearted Susie, she would have been on the streets tonight. She couldn't help but think that Susie was an odd one. Daisy still didn't know what she did for a living, and yet everyone knew her.

A knock on her door brought her back from her thoughts as a small maid entered her room with a laid tray. She bobbed as she placed it next to Daisy.

'You saw me come in tonight with Susie?' Curiosity was getting the better of Daisy, and she wanted to find out why Susie was well known by everyone, so she asked the maid.

'Yes, ma'am, I saw you.' The maid blushed.

'Then tell me, what does Susie do that makes her so well known?' Daisy watched the maid's face.

'I don't know if I should say, ma'am. It's not my place, and besides she's a good customer here. Mr Trotter wouldn't be happy with me if he found out I'd told you.'

'You can tell me. I'll not say anything to Mr Trotter. Besides, Susie's been good to me and I'd like to thank her, when I can.' Daisy looked at the young maid, who appeared distinctly uncomfortable.

'Well, ma'am, I know her as Shipley Susie. Her patch is just behind Granary Wharf. She's a favourite with the gents, and she comes here most nights with her clients. Mr Trotter say's he's built his empire with her lying on her back – she's his favourite.'

Daisy looked at her in disbelief. Her new friend was a prostitute, a lady of the night, and she herself was sleeping in a brothel. Tomorrow she would have to leave. In fact, no matter how exhausted she was, she would leave by first light. She couldn't be seen leaving the doors of this establishment by anyone.

7

William Mattinson stood in the hallway of his home. His hands were shaking as he took in the news his brother had just told him. William's son James was fighting for his life, back at Skipton, at the home of his sister-in-law in Caroline Square. William's wife had been in such good spirits, wanting to show her widowed sister the new baby and for her to spend time with her mischievous nephew. When William had kissed his two-year-old sweetly on the cheek, along with the newly born Charles and his dear wife Angelina, James had seemed in such good health. A slight cough perhaps, but nothing that had concerned him. Now it seemed that James was on his deathbed, and it was only a matter of time until the inevitable happened.

William paced the hallway, looking at the newly papered walls and the carpet that had just been laid. He was starting to make money, but he'd give it all away for the life of his first son. He looked at his pocket-watch. Where was that bloody woman? He wished he had never listened to his old friend Bert Pritchard, but

Bert had assured him that a better cook he'd never set eyes on. She'd have to walk the streets if she didn't come within the next few minutes. William's main priority was to get to his son's bedside.

As if by surprise, the doorbell rang, nearly making William jump out of his skin. He'd wished for it so hard that it was a shock when it happened for real. He rushed to the door, opening it wide to find a dripping, bedraggled, thin woman, looking quite young in black attire, standing on his step. She held out her hand and muttered a few words of apology for her lateness.

'Come in, come in. I haven't time for your apologies or niceties. I've wasted enough of my time waiting of you. My son's ill – I'm away to Skipton to be with my family. The kitchen's downstairs – everything's there that you need. You'll find a room made up for you next to the kitchen. There isn't much natural light there, but it's warm. Now, if you'll excuse me, I'll be off. Don't know when we will be returning. My brother Jim will keep you informed, and if there is anything you need, he's at the grocer's just around the corner.'

Daisy watched as a very abrupt William Mattinson snatched an umbrella, to shield him from the inclement Yorkshire weather, and then slammed the door after himself, leaving her bemused. She hadn't had time to say how grateful she was to her new employer, or to tell him what she could do and, more importantly, to seek her instructions. Did he say that his son was ill in Skipton? He must be gravely ill for the poor man to behave in such a fashion, leaving a woman he didn't even know in charge of his house.

She took off her sodden topcoat and shook her head free of the dripping raindrops. She held her coat over her arm, not knowing where to place it. She lifted her drenched skirts and ventured up the dark hallway. There was a door to her left, and she opened it gingerly and looked into what seemed to be the family drawing room. A good leather settee and chairs took pride of place, with a piano next to the wall. Daisy noted that someone in her new family must be musical. The fireplace was in white marble, and upon it were figurines of young women leading mottled brown cows, surrounded by brightly coloured daisies; to either side of the fireplace were glistening candelabra. The clear-crystal glass caught the rain-filled light, making it shine like diamonds.

She closed the door behind her, careful not to catch the trailing leaves of an aspidistra plant that stood guard at the door, on a carved cane stand. A further door led to what seemed to be the family's main living area. There was a desk and chair, and an everyday table strewn with papers and invoices; a grandfather clock that ticked the time away happily; and two Windsor chairs by the side of an uncleared fire grate. So her new family had no servants other than herself, else all would have been tidy and the fire laid. Daisy put her coat over the back of one of the chairs and checked her hair in the mirror that hung next to the window. Then she looked out of the window. The rain was pouring, and it looked colder than the month would suggest. All she could see was an austere, walled back yard with an outside lavvy and coal shed. There were no flowers, just paving; and not a hint of the early September day that it was.

The stairs led both up and down, and Daisy decided to explore upstairs first, holding onto the curving mahogany handrail that led her to a master bedroom and two smaller bedrooms that were filled with children's toys. One had a bed in it and toy soldiers lined up, as if to attention at the presence of Daisy; the other bedroom contained just a small cot and not much else, apart from a cloth rabbit that looked at her helplessly from behind the cot's railings. Daisy picked up the floppy rabbit in her hands and shook it to make its head wobble and the small silver bell on the end of its ear rattle. Would her son have had one of these, if he had lived? She hugged it close to her body and then placed it back into the safety of the cot. The Mattinsons obviously had two very young children. Bert hadn't mentioned that – she might have thought twice about taking the position, if she'd known there were young children. Lately she had found herself feeling more and more uncomfortable in the presence of children. It hurt to think of the loss of her baby, and life had begun to teach her how unreasonably her parents had treated her and her child.

She closed the door silently, almost reverently, and made her way down two flights to the kitchen and the small room that was to be her home. To her delight, the kitchen had running water with a huge white pot-sink directly beneath the small window that let in light from the pavement above. There was even a built-in pot-boiler, so that she could heat water as and when she wanted. Such luxuries were unheard-of at Gearstones Lodge. But most of all her eye was taken by the fireplace. It was blackleaded, with an oven and a warming drawer at the top, and it proudly boasted on the fireback of being 'A YORKSHIRE RANGE'. Daisy just stared at it and thought of the things she could cook in the oven, and the pans she could put on the fire, on the trivets that dropped down for just such a purpose.

She stood and looked around at the china and the glasses that were in every cupboard. This was a different, finer world from the one at Batty Green. Finally she opened the door to what she had been told was to be her room. William Mattinson had been right – there wasn't a lot of natural light, but the room was clean, with a bed, a chest of drawers, a chair and a mirror. It would suffice. After all, most of her time would be spent in the kitchen. She sat on the edge of the bed and pushed her sodden shoes off, then folded the few clothes that she had brought with her away in the drawers, hiding what money she had left underneath her clothes. Well! Here she was in a fancy house in Leeds on her own, with no one to tell her what to do. Tomorrow she'd find William Mattinson's brother and establish how ill the boy was. But for now she'd just have a lie-down. She'd not slept last night, after finding out that her lodging was a brothel, and the hard street-walking had made her legs ache; the cobbled streets were not like the soft fells of home.

She lay on her single bed and closed her eyes. She could hear the trotting of horses and carts going by in the street above, and the laughter of children playing and their mother chastising them for making so much noise. She was a long way from home, but now all she wanted to do was sleep.

William rushed along the streets of Skipton to Caroline Square. He knew most of the people who lived in the area, from his old job of delivery boy for his uncle, who traded in groceries on Sheep Street. By the time he turned the corner into Caroline Square he knew that things were not good. People who would usually have said hello were going out of their way not to talk to him, crossing to the other side of the road so as not to show their sorrow to the unknowing father. The heavy velvet curtains were pulled closed at number 2 Caroline Square and, at the sight of the drawn curtains, William's heart broke. He pushed the garden gate open and turned the brass door handle as he entered the home of his grieving sister-in-law.

'William, my darling William, you are too late! Our angel, James, was taken from us this morning. The doctor could not save him; he could not fight the pneumonia that racked his little body.' Angelina sobbed and cried as William held her close to him.

'My love, I'm sorry. I tried to come earlier, but things got in the way. I'm sorry you have had to bear this grief without me by your side. Where is my little man? Let me see him.'

'He's in the front room, looking just as if he is asleep on the sofa. We've left him there until the undertaker comes later this afternoon. I nursed him there until his dying breaths. Oh, William, it was terrible – my first-born, my James.'

'Hush, my dear. Come, we will look at him together, and will say our farewells before he is touched by the hands of the undertaker.'

The heartbroken couple kissed the cold, white skin of their first child and sobbed together. The loss of a child was the greatest loss of all. Angelina's sister watched the couple as she nursed the month-old baby that Angelina had been so proud to show her, along with her two-year-old, the previous week. She shook her head in disbelief at the terrible death that had happened in her house. Smiling, she placed her finger in baby Charles's hand, and his fingers clutched tightly to hers as he gurgled contently, undeterred by the surrounding grief. 'God protect you, my little one. He has another angel this day.'

'Now there's a fine sight on a cold, wet day.'

Daisy turned round quickly as the man's voice startled her from cleaning up the ashes from the coal fire.

'A prettier ankle I've never seen.' The tall, well-dressed man grinned at her as she straightened her skirts and brushed her hands clean of the fire's dust, rising to her feet.

'If you are looking for Mr Mattinson, I'm afraid he's not here. And I'd like for you to note that I'm in mourning, and your comments are not becoming.' Daisy was both startled and annoyed that someone had walked into her new home without knocking on the door.

'That I know, my dear. I'm his brother, Jim. He's sent me round to make sure that you are holding the fort and haven't robbed him of the family silver, after his hasty departure yesterday.' Jim pulled up a chair next to the table and studied the slim-figured Daisy, before placing his bowler hat on the table. 'I'm afraid his son died yesterday, and he will be staying in Skipton for the next few days. The boy's to be buried at the church there. So you will be on your own for a while. That is, unless you want me for company?'

'I've not a problem with being on my own, sir. And I'm sorry to hear of the family's loss – it will be a hard one to bear.' Daisy stood and looked at Jim Mattinson. His face was round and his cheeks were red, and he had a playful glint in his eye as he stroked his sleek hair back into place.

'Aye, it's a sad do. He was a grand little lad, and Angelina must be heartbroken. Still, she's got the new baby to concentrate on – that must help a bit. You don't have to call me "sir". We don't stand on ceremony in this family. It's Jim, especially if you'll be cooking for our new venture. What do they call you anyway? Our lad never said, and I can't remember from the letter he showed me prior to your arrival.'

Daisy looked at Jim, who had started glancing

109

through the pile of papers that she had carefully stacked earlier on. 'I'm Daisy. You mentioned a new venture that I'm to cook for, but I've never been told anything about that. I thought I was here for the family.'

'Daisy, eh! Has our William not told you anything, the scatterbrain? But then again, forgive me; he did have other priorities yesterday. Well, let me tell you. He's bought himself a grocery shop – the one around the corner – which he's left me with for the next few days, as I'm his business partner. He intends to fill it with home-made delights. And you, my dear, are his secret weapon. From what his friend Bert has told him, you are a top cook – just what he has been looking for. A Dales lass who knows good food, and how to make it. Just like our dear aunt, who runs The Bull at Broughton, if you know it? A finer dining place you'll not find that side of Skipton.'

'I'd no idea – I've not been told. What does he expect of me?' Daisy didn't know what to think. 'I'm nobbut a straightforward cook, nothing fancy.'

'Well, that's just what he's wanting. Somebody who can make something from nothing. In fact the less, the better – after he's spent all his money on fancy surround-ings and playing the perfect father. He can make fun of my lifestyle, but at least I take pleasure in life. You see, my dear, we are like chalk and cheese. He'll tell you I'm the black sheep of the family and to stay away from me, so before he dirties my name, I'll tell you myself.' Jim picked up his bowler hat and fumbled with it, bal-ancing it on his knee and then looking up at Daisy.

110

'I don't think I need to know family matters, sir. I just came here to work.' Daisy felt uncomfortable with his admission of guilt. Besides, she would take as she found, and make up her own mind about things.

'I've told you before, Daisy – it's Jim. Now, how about you light that fire and put the kettle on? I'm fair parched.' Jim stood up and walked to the window. 'Just look at that bloody weather; it's always bloody raining in Leeds, and it's so grey. God, I wish I was back home in Skipton, just to look out on those open fells and breathe in the air. All you get here is a lungful of coal dust and smoke. Still, there are more attractions here, and I suppose you can't have everything. I suppose I'd better look through these papers while you get the kettle to boil. Someone's got to keep an eye on the coffers.'

Daisy busied herself lighting the fire and putting the kettle on. She tried not to look at Jim, even when he kept tutting at the paperwork he was working through. Earlier Daisy couldn't help but notice the number of unpaid bills that had been in the pile of papers, and even though she was no financier, she knew there was a lot of money owing. She made tea in one of the good china teapots that she had found in the beautiful china cabinet, then poured it into a cup for Jim, walking quietly around him so as not to disturb him.

'Just look at this! What does he want with all these lemons – the man's a fool. He's had to have them sent from Italy, and who's going to buy them? He's only trying to curry favour with his wife's family, by buying

111

the lemons from them.' He clasped the offending bill tightly in his hand and looked at Daisy. 'Are you not joining me? Get another cup and saucer, and sit down and tell me a bit about yourself.'

Daisy took another cup and saucer from the cabinet. Curiosity was getting the better of her now, and she wanted to know more about the family she had just joined. The cup rattled in the saucer and the tea slopped slightly as she stirred it. Her nerves were getting the better of her, but at the same time she had an urge to find out more about this forthright man sitting across from her. Besides, it sounded as if he missed the countryside, and that was a vote in his favour.

'So, Daisy petal, you lost your husband lately. I'm sorry for my careless words when I arrived. I should have known better. They must have been a shock. My brother let me read the letter that his friend Bert sent, so I do know a little about you. You must miss your husband, and coming to live with my brother must be a big move for you. Are you sure you've done the right thing? Town life is different from the country, you know. I still find it hard.' Jim placed his cup down, after taking a long sip from it, and looked at the still-young widow. She was quite pretty, in a plain way; her ice-blue eyes looked honest and true, her mousy brown hair seemed healthy and clean, and her face was openly kind.

'I had to get away – start a new life. I didn't want to stop at Gearstones Lodge for a minute longer, for there were too many memories.' Daisy took a sip of her tea and looked at one half of the partnership that she was obviously going to be answerable to. She plucked up the courage to ask him a question, as the conversation seemed to have been all one-way up to that minute. 'Is Mr Mattinson's wife Italian? And you – are you married?' Daisy quickly wished she had not been so forthright with her last question, because it was followed by a huge bellow of laughter.

'Me – married? Nobody in their right mind would have me, my dear. I look and perhaps touch a lot, my dear, but so far nobody has caught me. No, the life of my brother is not for me. And yes, my bloody stupid brother married an Italian from Skipton. Just to get his hands on some money, I must add. Both her uncle and her father own grocery stores, on Swadford Street and Sheep Street. They've even built their own houses, and now our Bill is following in their footsteps. But I'm not complaining. He's made me a partner – just as long as he keeps his head and doesn't run up too many bills, like this bloody pile on the table. Now, what are we going to do with five hundred bloody lemons, when they land down at the canal wharf? Any suggestions?'

Daisy was beginning to realize that there was no love lost between the two brothers and perhaps she had joined a family at war. She couldn't help but think that William Mattinson would not be happy about his brother airing his dirty washing in public, so she decided to be discreet. 'How about lemon cheese? It's a lovely preserve and keeps well, once potted. That would take a lot of the lemons, and you can charge a good price for it.'

'What the hell is lemon cheese? I've never heard of it, and it sounds revolting.' Jim pulled a face and leaned back in his chair. 'Still, we can try it. Come round to the shop for a lemon or two in the morning, and then surprise me with your concoction. If it gets rid of the bloody lemons, I'm willing to try it.'

'Lemon cheese is lemons that are grated and squeezed, with eggs and butter and sugar. You bring it to the boil and then, once it's thickened, you cool it down and pot it. Then you can spread it on bread and butter, or even in the middle of a cake, if you want.'

'Never heard of it. Doesn't sound that good to me, but we'll give it a try.'

'You'll like it – honest, you will. Everyone does.' Daisy laughed at his reaction. Lemon cheese had been a favourite for afternoon tea back home, so it was a sure bet and she knew it.

'Well, Daisy, that's why we took you on. We wanted some new ideas from a country lass – and a bonny one at that. You should laugh more; it brightens up your face.'

Daisy blushed. She hadn't been called bonny for a long time, and for a few moments she'd forgotten that she was a grieving widow. Oh, she'd have to watch Jim Mattinson. He was nothing more than a silver-tongued cad, and she'd seen plenty of them in her time.

'Thank you, Jim . . . I'll do the best I can for all the family.'

'I'm sure you will, Daisy petal. I'll see you in the morning and supply you with all that you want for the lemon cheese.' He grinned as he lifted his bowler hat onto his head. He'd taken a fancy to the little cook. She could be a bit of sport, widow or not.

8

Daisy didn't bother putting on her hat and coat. Unlike the previous few days, the sun was shining and the street felt warm as she closed the house door behind her. She walked down the few steps onto the street. Some children were playing hopscotch while their mothers talked to each other, one with a donkey-stone and scrubbing brush in her hand from cleaning her three steps. Both were busy with gossip as Daisy passed them; both watched and nodded as she walked quietly by them. She could hear one woman say, 'He's dead, you know?' and the other gasp, but neither approached Daisy to find out any more.

Daisy pulled her shawl around her and hurried along the sun-soaked pavement. She looked at the terraced row that she now regarded as her home. It was well built and she could tell the residents were proud of their homes, because the steps were scrubbed and the brass door knockers shone. It wasn't like some of the back-to-back mill homes she had walked past on the way to Newtown Terrace. There she had seen true hardship:

women standing in doorways, thin and lifeless with hungry bairns on their hips. Why anyone would want children if they couldn't feed them, she just didn't know. And how could they live with a sewer running past their front door? She might have had it rough, but never that bad – her pride had never abandoned her, if nothing else.

She turned the corner and arrived at Burley Road. This was a busier street with shops on either side and traders yelling as they sold their wares. It was quite a shock for Daisy. The greatest number of shops she had seen had been in Settle or Ingleton, both of which were small villages with as many shops as there were in the first few yards of Burley Road.

'Bunch of flowers, missus – here, sweet-smelling phlox, marigolds; they would look a picture, they would, in your home.' Daisy shook her head and declined the insistent flower seller. She'd little enough money on her without spending it on flowers, no matter how much they reminded her of home.

She wandered down the street, looking in the windows, amazed at the goods each shop was selling. There were haberdashers, butchers, dressmakers and cobblers, but the one that caught her eye most was the hat shop, where she gazed into the window, admiring the feathers and flowers that adorned the large, sweeping brims and the beautiful ribbons that tied them together.

'Daisy, Daisy, are you deaf? I've been calling you for the last ten minutes.' Jim Mattinson came running across the street, dodging a horse and trap just in time to grab her arm before she moved off. 'I should have known: women and hats, that's more important than anything else in the world!'

'I'm sorry, I've never seen anywhere as busy as this. I got delayed, and I couldn't help but admire this window.'

'Never mind that. We are over here. The signwriter's just finished our business sign. Come and tell me what you think of the lettering.' Jim grabbed her by the arm and propelled her across the street to stand outside the shop's doorway, above which was newly painted on light-green boarding the words:

W. & J. MATTINSON,
Purveyors of Fine Foods, Est. 1875

'Very good – it looks wonderful, you must be very proud.' Daisy smiled at the man beside her, who looked as excited as a five-year-old with a new toy.

'I just wish our William was here to see it. Him losing James has come at a bad time and taken a bit of the shine out of it, poor bugger.' Jim stood back and gazed quietly for a while before blowing his nose. 'You've come for those lemons. I've some in the back. I'm just stacking the shelves with dry goods. We had hoped to be open next week, but with the funeral, it will have to be delayed. William sent word this morning: the funeral is on Friday, so you've only another three days, and then William and Angelina will be back. I'll not be around on Thursday and Friday, so I don't know what to suggest you do. I'm not used to giving orders. William is the one for that. But tomorrow why don't you come down to the wharf with me? Those bloody lemons will need to be picked up, along with some fresh produce and other groceries. You could unpack them while we are away.'

Jim walked into the shop. The doorbell jangled as he opened the door and waited for Daisy to enter.

The air smelled of paint and fresh wood as Daisy walked across the threshold. A long counter stretched from one end of the shop to the other, and all the walls, except the window that was bare for a display, were covered with shelving. There were sets of drawers marked up with labels for tea, sugar, coffee, string, spices and dried fruit – anything and everything you could think of – and large bins for flour and oats, and delicate cake stands awaiting the cakes that would adorn them. Daisy gasped. It was going to be a beautiful shop, but so much work remained to be done – now she knew why she'd been employed. The Mattinson home would be run by the lady of the house, Angelina, and it was the business that needed her touch. The cakes, the jams, the pies and the cooked meats that would grace the shelves – that was what William Mattinson had taken her on for.

'What else do you need for this lemon cheese then?' Jim walked behind the counter and into a back room, his voice muffled as he produced four lemons from a straw-filled packing box.

Daisy followed him. 'Butter, eggs and sugar.' She watched as he opened the back door of the shop and crossed the yard to a little stone shed that obviously contained the perishable goods.

He came back carrying what she needed. 'Sugar is over there – help yourself. And here's a dozen eggs and a pound of butter. We keep everything like that over there in the shed, as it's cooler than in here. William's going to order the eggs and butter on his trips to Skipton, along with some of the milk, so we hope it's always going to be fresh. He's kept his farm contacts from when he worked as a delivery boy for his father-in-law. He's not daft that way. I just wish he'd watch the pennies.' Jim sighed as he passed Daisy a brown paper bag to put her sugar in.

'Aye, well, it's not for me to say, Jim, but I'm sure he knows what he's doing. He seems to have his head screwed on – look at what you've got so far.' Daisy filled her bag and looked at the worried man.

'Aye, but it's not all his money. Some of it is mine, and some of it is his father-in-law's. William's stopping me from living my life and doing what I want, and he's going to be beholden to his wife's family until he drops down dead. That's no way to be!'

Daisy looked round the shop. It was a grand place. She was sure William would make money and was determined to help both brothers do so, if only to put Jim's mind at rest.

'Right, lass, go and make me this so-called lemon cheese. I'll pick you up first thing in the morning, sample it for my breakfast and then take you to pick up our delivery on the canal wharf. Don't listen to me twaddle

120

on about my worries – it's not your concern. Besides, our William won't be suited with me telling you the affairs of the business, especially when he's told you absolutely nowt.' Jim's mood lightened as he placed his bowler on his head. 'Right now – bugger this place! I'm off to see a man about a dog.' He nearly pushed Daisy out of the shop as he firmly locked the doors behind them both. 'I'll be at your door at eight on the dot, and I look forward to sampling your fare.' He gave her a wicked wink and sauntered off, whistling his way down the street as if he hadn't a care in the world.

Daisy watched as Jim walked away. She couldn't help but think what a complex man he was. But then again, she hadn't really met his brother properly yet. Perhaps William would be even worse. It seemed that he definitely liked to spend other people's money.

The autumn sunshine flickered through the kitchen window as Daisy lifted the warm bread out of the oven of the Yorkshire range. It looked lovely and crusty and made the kitchen smell warm and homely – there was something about the smell of freshly cooked bread that made you feel content. She'd pulled the kettle to one side to take it off the boil and had set the table ready for her guest. She'd succumbed to the flower seller on her way home and had bought a fragrant bunch of sweet-peas, which were now taking pride of place, along with a beautifully presented pot of lemon cheese. There, she was ready now.

She'd tossed and turned all night, thinking about her

visitor and then the trip into the centre of Leeds. It was exciting, but more to the point, *he* was exciting! Jim was a different breed of man from the steady Dales men; he was sharp, witty and, most of all, he had elegant good looks. She stopped herself: how could she think like that, her a widow, with a husband barely cold in his grave? Perhaps Bob's mother had been right – perhaps she was a whore! Her face blushed as she checked herself in the mirror. She fanned herself with a towel to cool herself down. How stupid to feel that way over a man she hardly knew.

'Now then, Mrs Lambert, let's be trying this lemon cheese you've talked so much about.'

Daisy heard Jim's unforgettable voice coming down the stairs to the kitchen.

'My horse and cart's outside, ready for our trip, but before that I need something to eat. I'm bloody starving.' Jim Mattinson entered the kitchen and made himself at home at the kitchen table.

Daisy didn't turn round as she picked up the kettle, but asked him why he was using her formal name this morning.

'I got told last night, by some bloody bloke, that I'd no manners and that I didn't know my place, so I thought I'd better start afresh this morning.'

As Daisy turned round to look at Jim, she gasped. His face was battered, with a purple egg of a bruise over his left eye.

'What in the Lord's name have you been up to?' Her hand shook as she poured out the boiling water into the teapot. 'Have you seen anybody about them bruises? I hope the other fella came off worse?'

'Let's just say we had an argument over that dog I was telling you about. I didn't like the way the owner was treating it. And that's when I was told to know my place.' Jim took a long sip of the tea that Daisy put in front of him.

'Well, I hope it was worth it. I don't think I'd take a beating for the sake of a dog.' Daisy stood and looked at him. 'Put some butter on your bruise above your eye – it takes the swelling down. My mother swore by it.'

Jim grinned. 'Aye, the dog was terrible precious to me. Go on, Daisy, put some butter on the bruise for me. I've never heard that one before, but if you think it works, I'll try it. Can't go to the lad's funeral looking like a thug.'

Daisy hesitated. Putting butter on his face felt a bit too close for comfort, but she picked up the butter dish, stood close to him and smeared his bruise with a covering of grease. His hand went round her waist as she gently pressed and patted the edge of the bruise with the towel she had slung over her shoulder. He looked up into her eyes, and Daisy could feel her heart flutter as she met his stare. There was something about Jim that made her lose her inhibitions. She could almost hear herself shouting: *Hold me, love me. I don't care who or what you are.*

'You make a good nurse, Daisy. I'll let you know if it works.' Jim loosened his grip of her and the moment was gone. 'Now, let's try this lemon cheese, because my mouth's fair dribbling with the smell of that bread you've got there.'

'I hope you like it, I've never had any complaints, and it's easy to make. I don't know why you haven't had it before. All the farms up the Dales make it, and it costs nowt, because everyone has eggs and butter. When you are farmers, all you need to add are the lemons and sugar.' Daisy cut two large slices of her bread and spread it with lashings of butter, followed by a good covering of lemon cheese. She passed it to Jim on a plate and then sat down firmly and awaited his reaction.

'Bloody hell, lass, this is good. In fact I don't think I've had anything as nice for a bloody long time.' Jim wiped a dribble of escaped lemon cheese from his chin and tore another piece of bread off, before closing his eyes and eating it. 'We've got to have this in the shop – folk will love it. You've hit a winner with this, Daisy petal, and it gets rid of the lemon pile that we are about to pick up.'

'I'm glad you like it. It was always a favourite, along with my jams in the summer.' Daisy smiled.

'Aye, if you can make jam and bread like this, it will sell. Folk like good-quality stuff, but it's got to be priced right, and then we can attract everybody.' He finished the last bit of crust on his plate and lifted the jar of lemon cheese up to examine it. 'It needs to be packaged right, in jam jars with a little frilly top – like this one you've put on it – and a good label, something like:

MATTINSON'S LEMON CHEESE. Aye, damn it, that's what we'll call it. Does it keep?'

Daisy liked being told she was good at her job, even though Jim would put his name on her work.

'It keeps for a good while, if you seal the cheese from the air with some greaseproof paper. It will keep for weeks, if it's kept cold in a pantry.'

'Right, I'll order some jam jars and then we'll go into production. Bloody good job, lass. Now, come on, get your coat or shawl – or whatever you womenfolk wear – and join me up on the cart. I thought I might take you for a tour of the new town that's growing up around us. Things are changing so fast in Leeds that I can't keep up myself. Did you see that bloody great town hall they are building, and the Corn Exchange? That's what I really want to have a look at. All the traders are interested in that. Buildings are going up left, right and centre. There's some brass being spent in Leeds, lass, and it's all thanks to the mill owners and the investors. If I have my way, William and I will be joining them shortly.'

Daisy wrapped a shawl around herself and followed Jim out of the house. He offered her his hand as she climbed up next to him on the delivery cart, which now displayed the same lettering as that seen over the shop.

Jim clicked his tongue and the team set off, trundling over the cobbles. The children at the bottom of the street yelled and ran after the horse and cart until they could no longer keep up with it, their mothers shouting at them to return home before they got a good hiding.

Little was said as the couple swayed with the motion of the cart. Daisy was busy looking at the streets they were passing: hundreds and hundreds of back-to-back houses, built for the mill workers by the industrious mill owners.

'You want nowt with working in a mill, Daisy. It's long hours for bad pay, and you end with your lungs full of fluff or, even worse, lose a limb if your hand gets caught in the looms.' Jim watched her looking at the mill workers' houses and gazing up at the huge mills and their chimneys. 'Nowt but slave labour. How else do you think the owners can build the houses they live in?'

'I couldn't work in a mill. I can hear the noise of the looms from here. Anyway, I've got to see the sky and be outside – can't do with being cooped up like a bird. I'm already missing my fells and the wild winds that blow. I didn't realize the noise and smells of a city, and the number of people . . . How does everyone live on top of one another?'

'Well, they do, Daisy love. You just get used to it after a while, and it's adapt or die. They call it progress. Speaking of which, look: that's one of them new horse-drawn trams. It's the first time I've seen one. It's like a train that takes you around the streets on tracks, but it's pulled by horses. You get a ticket and just say where you want to go. They think of everything nowadays. That's the Corn Exchange. I see they've not quite finished it; they've built it round, so that the bidders and buyers can see everyone from the centre of it. Up there they are going to be building some fancy shopping arcades. I can just see you in another few years, Daisy, strolling around them with a man on your arm.'

'I'm not going to ever have another man, Jim Mattinson. I've decided fate told me not to bother with them, when my husband died on our wedding night.'

'Give over, Daisy. I saw you look at me when you put that butter on my bruise. If I'd kissed you, you wouldn't have complained.' Jim grinned at his passenger as they bumped down Water Street along the cobbles to the canal.

'I blinking well would, and you'd have got a slap, whether you're my employer or not,' Daisy blustered, but in truth she knew he was right. She went silent as they passed the place that she now knew to be a brothel, hoping that no one would notice her going past.

'A slap, eh! I'd have enjoyed that. I like my women feisty.' Jim grinned at his determined passenger. Somehow he knew that Mrs Lambert was not as holy as she was making out to be.

The conversation went silent again as the horse and cart made their way down to one of the warehouses at the bottom of Water Street. The canal was buzzing with barges being loaded with goods, and with goods being offloaded. Horses waited patiently while carts were filled with coal, cotton, wool and all manner of items.

'Just hold the reins for a minute, Daisy. I need to speak to Edgar from t' Yorkshire Glass Company. We want some jars for your cheese to go in, and he's reasonable with his bottles, so I might as well order them off him.' Jim jumped down from the cart and made his way to the canalside, where he shook the hand of a man who was watching a crate being loaded onto a barge. Daisy held tight to the reins, hoping the horses wouldn't be spooked by the noises all around them. She watched as Jim laughed and talked to the man. He certainly knew how to deal with people, and she smiled when they slapped one another on the back, obviously sharing a joke.

'Now then, I didn't expect to see you down here – bit out of your way for Newtown Terrace.'

Daisy nearly jumped out of her skin. She'd been so busy watching Jim that she hadn't seen Susie walk up next to the cart.

'I'm with that man. I've come to help him with some stuff for the new shop.' Daisy didn't want Jim to see her talking to Susie, who looked a little rough in the cold light of day.

'Him – you are with him? That vagabond! How come an innocent Dales lass is involved in that load of trouble?' Susie laughed and flung her hair back over her naked shoulders.

'I work for him, and he's not a vagabond, he's a respectable businessman.' Daisy was quick to defend her new employer.

'Is that what he tells you? I don't suppose he told you how he got that black eye last night?' Susie watched as Jim started to make his way to the cart.

'I think it was something to do with a dog – that's all I know.'

'Jim-fucking-Mattinson, you're calling me a dog now! You nearly killed us both, and now you're insulting me to this poor lass.' Susie walked up to Jim, her face hard, and hit him firmly on the chest with both fists.

'Wooh! I never called you a dog. I don't know where Daisy gets that from. Anyway I was doing you a favour, sticking up to that dwarf Ebenezer Trotter – he takes most of your earnings.'

'Aye, but he looks after me. I get fed and I've somewhere to go, rather than touting on a street corner. That is until you give your four penn'orth.'

Daisy listened to the two arguing, trying to butt in about her misunderstanding of 'something to do with a dog'.

'You can do better, Susie. You are a grand lass – you could get a good job, if you tidied yourself up a bit. You know I think the world of you. You've a heart as big as England. It's time to come off this dockside and do better for yourself.'

'So now I need to tidy myself up, do I? Funny how last night I was all right for you when I was flat on my back, thinking of England – because I need to, with the length of time you take to come. Funny that now, with Mrs Widow Weeds here, fresh from the country and all innocent, you're preaching to me better than the Lord himself! Next time you want a quick shag, find someone else and don't come looking for me, because unless you can keep your gob shut and realize that Ebenezer is part of the game and needs his cut, I don't want to know.'

129

'Susie, you know I love you. I just want something better for you. Susie, come on. Daisy didn't know what I was on about; she knew nothing.' Jim grabbed her arm as she picked up her skirts and stomped off.

She turned sharply. 'Jim Mattinson, you are such a bastard, but one day you'll be in real bother. You mix with the wrong sort, and you're not hard enough. There are men out there that'd slit your throat if you tried to stick up for me like you did last night. Be thankful it was just a candlestick he hit you with a few times. If his son from Bradford had been there, you'd be dead.' Her hand lingered in Jim's for as long as she dared, before she smiled slightly and walked off.

'By God, Daisy, that woman's lovely when she's angry. She makes the blood rise in my veins. It's just a shame she's a bloody tart.' Jim shook his head and grabbed the horse's reins, urging it on to the warehouse.

Daisy said nothing. She didn't quite know what to say, but she'd learned one thing: she'd never forget about going to see a man about a dog.

'Got woman trouble, Jim? It's not like you.' The warehouse man laughed and joked with Jim as they filled the cart with goods for the shop. Daisy listened, but didn't get down from the cart. She'd be a lady and wait patiently, like a proper woman should. Jim Mattinson was obviously one for the women, and she was not going to amuse him any more.

9

Daisy started unpacking the many boxes that Jim had unloaded from the cart. She was on her own, as it was the day of the funeral, and there was little else to do. The house was tidy and clean, and until she got her instructions from William she couldn't do much else. Her mind wandered to the scene that would be unfolding in the graveyard as the poor little lad was put to rest. His parents must be heartbroken; at least her son had never even breathed earthly air. To bring a child up to the age of two and then have his life snatched away must be one of the cruellest blows a parent could receive.

She shook her head as she undid the top of a wooden crate and started taking out the straw packing to reveal the contents. She gasped. Within the straw lay the most beautiful china she had ever seen: teapots and cups with matching saucers, cake stands and dinner plates. They would look beautiful displayed on one of the counters, to the first customers who arrived. She marvelled at the delicately painted designs, and carefully unwrapped each piece, placing it in a key position near the serving counter.

131

Jim had told her where to put the main bulk of the goods, but he'd not mentioned the china. But she could see that it would sell and would complement the cakes that could be placed upon it.

She stood back and looked at her handiwork. Most of the shelves were filled now: tea, sugar, tinned fruit, dried fruit, syrup and treacle, flour and salt. She'd been busy. She'd also made a display of a few of the fresh lemons, with a pot or two of her lemon cheese placed strategically among them, just to see if it would sell. Anything else would have to wait for William Mattinson's instructions. But yes, it was beginning to look like a real shop. Both brothers could be proud of themselves. She brushed away any straw that was left on the floor and tidied the boxes and packaging away, before locking the door. Tomorrow William and his family would return and it was then, she knew, that the proper work would begin.

'Ah, you never stand up to him, you stupid man. He comes to the funeral with a black eye and you just laugh. He disrespects my family, and yet he'd be nothing without us! I tell you, William, I've had enough.'

Daisy stood waiting at the door of number four for her new family to enter. She couldn't help but overhear Angelina talking in her Italian accent, and it was quite obvious who she was talking about. 'My father's right. You should buy him out. Father would give you the money. I don't know what your problem is.' She brushed past Daisy with the baby Charles in her arms, oblivious to Daisy's sharp curtsy, and carried on arguing as she mounted the stairs, while her husband William carried the bags from the horse and cab.

'Daisy, have you been all right? I'm sorry I left you in such disarray, but the circumstances didn't give me any choice.' William removed his hat and placed it on the hall stand as he gave his apologies to her.

'You and your family have my condolences, sir. I feel your loss. I didn't realize on my arrival that the child was so ill.'

'Nothing is worse than losing a child. But now, Daisy, you must know that we don't stand on ceremony. I'm William, and Jim has been telling me all about you, especially your lemon cheese – that will be a real winner for the shop. Let me get myself and my family settled back in the home, and then we can sit down and talk. I'm afraid Angelina has not returned home in the best of moods. Her grief is overwhelming her, and my brother and her do not see eye-to-eye.'

'William! William, come and put your son to bed, and stop wasting your time talking to that girl. Why we need her I don't know!' shouted Angelina from the top of the stairs

'Sorry. She'll calm down in another day or two. It's her Mediterranean temperament. I'm afraid she doesn't hold her tongue.' He walked to the bottom of the stairs and turned to say something.

'William!' The voice shouted again from above.

'I'll make some tea and cake and put it in the parlour.' Daisy smiled, recognizing a man under pressure.

William whispered 'Thank you' and went up the stairs to his wife and child.

Daisy went down to the kitchen and put the kettle on the range to boil, while she laid a tea tray with cups and saucers, then added slices of a newly baked lemon Victoria sandwich cake. She had spread her lemon cheese in the middle, and hoped that it would impress both William and his wife. She looked round the kitchen. Would this be her domain, or would Angelina expect to cook as well? If she did, Daisy could see that there would be sparks flying between them. Angelina had not exactly made her feel welcome. She poured the boiling water into the teapot and carried the tray into the parlour, setting it down on the newly polished table. Then she pulled the curtains on the encroaching night and lit the candles.

'William tells me you are a good cook.' Quietly Angelina viewed her new member of staff as Daisy brought light to the room. Angelina's black skirts rustled as she sat down at the table and her dark eyes watched Daisy's every move.

'I'd like to think I am, ma'am.' Daisy stood still as Angelina poured herself and an absent William a cup of tea.

'Did you make this cake? I have never seen that filling in it before. What is it?'

'It's called "lemon cheese", ma'am. It's made with fresh lemons and butter. Can I just say how sorry I was to hear of your loss?' Daisy watched as Angelina carefully crumbled off a piece of the cake and its filling and placed it delicately into her mouth.

'My child was ill. The good Lord decided it was his time, and we don't ask the reasoning of the Lord. I must grieve, but life must also go on, for the sake of others.' She took another mouthful. 'This is good; you'll be making it for the shop?'

'If everyone agrees.' Daisy smiled.

'They'll agree. I will see to that. I'm Angelina, but you call me Angi. We've got to work together, for the kitchen is only small, so none of this "ma'am" business. I'll look after the home; you look after the business. That way we won't fall out.' She looked straight at Daisy.

Daisy showed her relief and smiled.

'See, I'm not that bad – just like to put my menfolk in their place. I play on my hot temper, to get my way.' Angelina smiled. 'You've got to or, frankly, nothing would get done.'

Daisy smiled again, wondering just what sort of household she had entered.

'You and I will get on fine. Just don't let that Jim into my kitchen – he's no good, a *bastardo*!' Angelina's eyes flashed. 'Why my husband had to include him in the business, and give him the room above the shop, I don't know. He could rent it out and put a manager in there, then he would have more time for me and his family.' She sighed.

'Because he's my brother, my dear, and I promised my parents that I'd look after him. And I'm sure Daisy doesn't want to hear – or, indeed, care – about our personal affairs.' William entered the room after obviously hearing part of the conversation, sitting down opposite his wife.

'Tuh! I give up . . . I sometimes think Jim means more to you than anything or anyone else in your life. But you know how I feel.' Angelina's eyes flashed as she showed her displeasure.

'Enough! Tomorrow I will go to the shop with Daisy and see what she suggests that we could produce here in our kitchen. If this cake is anything to go by, then my old friend Bert has done us a huge favour by sending you our way.' William smiled at Daisy. 'The house looks clean and tidy. Thank you for keeping on top of everything while we were away.'

'The house is my doing, along with my children. I'm mistress of this house.' Angelina rose from her chair and stamped her authority by banging on the table.

'My dear, I know you are. I'm just thanking Daisy for the last few days. Believe me, Daisy is going to be busy. For a start, I need a few batches of this lemon cheese. It will definitely sell, along with the cake, and I'm sure there will be other preserves and pickles, biscuits and fancies that could adorn our shelves. Now do you want our venture to make money or not? Because that is why she is here – not to take over your household.'

'The cake and spread are good. I'm sorry, Daisy. I'm tired – the journey and our loss have taken it out of me. Forgive this crazy Italian lady.' Angelina grabbed

Daisy's hand and patted it. 'We will be a winning firm, with you helping. I'm away to my bed. Baby Charles will need a feed through the night and I need my rest.'

Daisy watched as Angelina walked gracefully up the stairs, leaving her with William, who was still eating her cake.

'Tell me what ingredients are in your lemon cheese and cake, and then I can cost them and tell you if we can afford to supply our customers. Write them down for me, along with some more ideas. I don't want bread – there's a newfangled factory down the road that's just started baking bread, so we can't compete. And I've promised our neighbour, the butcher, that we won't deal in meat. There's only so much money to go around; it's no good standing on someone else's toes. But owt else you can think of: put it down, and I'll see if we can sell it.' William looked at her over the top of his teacup. 'Sit down, lass, I don't bite. Bert tells me you helped run Gearstones Lodge with one hand tied behind your back, so there must be more about you than meets the eye.'

Daisy blushed as she pulled up the chair to the table. 'I learned to cook just after I learned to walk. I had to, for our family to survive.'

'And where are they now, and what were you doing at Gearstones?' William wanted to know a bit more about his new employee.

'I don't know – my father chucked me out when I was nobbut sixteen, and I was fortunate enough for Jenny to give me a roof over my head.' Daisy tried to shun eye contact, for she didn't want William to see the hurt she still felt when talking about her family.

'I think it was Jenny that was the fortunate one, from what I hear. And what happened to your husband? Bert said he died of a heart attack.'

'That he did, on our wedding night.' Daisy could have felt sorry for herself at that point. She felt her chin begin to wobble with pent-up grief, but she bit her lip and smiled. 'And then I decided to make a new life for myself, by coming here.'

'Well, Daisy Lambert, you did right. Tomorrow, with the aid of my useless brother, we will sort out what food we need and what's going to be our leading brand. I hear Jim has already laid claim to the lemon cheese by calling it "Mattinson's Lemon Cheese". He's ordered the jam jars and even got the printer to make us labels to put on them. God knows how much of our hard-earned money he's already spent.'

Daisy grinned. 'He was saying the same about you and the stockpile of lemons.'

'He was now, was he? Well, I just have to keep the family happy, and he's just a playboy. And no doubt you'll have found that out by now, because he just can't help himself in front of a young woman.'

Daisy chuckled and put her head down.

'I bloody well knew it! You can't leave him for more than five minutes. Angelina was right, he is a liability.'

From the top of the stairs a voice shouted down, 'I know I'm right. I'm always right, but nobody bloody listens.'

William and Daisy just smiled. They had the feeling they were going to make a good team.

'So that's it then. We'll try the lemon cheese, marmalade, onion chutney, Victoria sandwich cake, fruit scones and, on the insistence of Jim here, Kiss-Me Cake, which says everything about bloody Jim. Now the jams and pickles are no bother – you can make big batches as and when we want them – but the fresh stuff will have to be made daily.'

'Don't worry. I'll get up early in the morning, light the fire and bake them before Angelina needs the oven and range. I prefer to be on my own. The other things I can cook on the range, when it's not needed by her.' Daisy had thought long and hard about how to work the kitchen space, and getting up early in a morning was no hardship to her. Besides, the less time she had around the baby, Charles, the more comfortable she would feel. So she was thankful that most mornings her baking would be done early, and she could escape to the shop, out of the way of Angelina and her baby.

'Right, Jim, take Daisy back home with these jam jars and labels. Let's get the first batches made. Load up the lemons, oranges, onions and whatever else Daisy wants, and then come back here. I need to go over the accounts with you.' William strode around his shop, checking the shelves and that everything was accounted for.

'"Jim, do this; Jim do that." I am your partner, you know. And you needn't check the accounts. I did them while you were away. Who ordered all that bloody china anyway? How are we going to sell that in a grocer's shop?'

'That's exactly why I have to check the accounts. And Angelina ordered the china; she thought it would attract some different customers.' William slammed the shop's receipts onto the counter. 'If you don't bloody like it, you know what to do.'

'I suppose she got it through her bloody family, did she? Has she got relations in the Potteries now?'

Daisy watched the feuding brothers. If this partnership was going to work, they were going to have to stop fighting one another.

'Oh, just get out! Go and help Daisy peel her onions and lemons, and don't bother coming back until you can be civil. You owe a lot to Angelina, and her father. Like the roof over your head, and part of the profits we are about to make.' William brushed his hair back through his fingers; he'd had enough of his surly brother since his return. He wasn't sure which, but Jim either had money troubles or woman troubles – it was always one or the other when his younger brother was in one of his moods.

'Don't worry. I'm off. I'd rather be around a woman's skirts than stop in this spot.' Jim lifted a bag of lemons in one hand and a bag of onions in the other and slammed the door, with its tinkling bell, behind him.

'I'm sorry, Daisy, you'll have to get used to our hot tempers, if you are to work with us. He'll be loading the cart up around the back, out of the cold store. If he goes home, try and keep him out of Angelina's way. I wouldn't want to come home to a bloodbath.'

'I'll try. It's strange to think you are brothers, for you are like chalk and cheese, if you don't mind me saying. He means well, you know. He does think a lot of you.'

'Aye, well, he's a funny bloody way of showing it.'

Daisy worked her way through the bag of onions, peeling and chopping them at the kitchen table of number four. Her eyes streamed with tears as she put them into the huge jam pan, which was going to sweat them down into chutney, once placed on the fire. She added the vinegar, sugar and spices, then placed the pan on the fire, before sitting down at the table.

'Jesus, Daisy, I'm going to stink of onions, and that bloody vinegar is making my eyes sting! Women are going to smell me before I get anywhere near them.' Jim took a long draw on his cigarette.

'Then you'd best get back to help your brother.' Daisy couldn't stop herself – the words came tumbling out, partly because she was beginning to realize that Jim was a leech on the Mattinson business, not contributing much except for his gift of the gab and a bit of artistic flair, when he bothered.

'Phew! But I'm not doing that. I've other things to do tonight, and I've a bit of my own business to sort out.' Jim leaned back and sniggered. 'Make us a drink of tea, Daisy petal, I'm fair parched. It's the smell of your bloody onions.'

141

'I can't put the kettle on – there's no room, with the jam pan taking up the fire. Besides, Angelina will soon be back. She's taken baby Charles out on a walk in his new perambulator. She'll not take kindly to you being here in her kitchen.'

'Bloody Italian witch! She's altered our Bill. All he thinks about is making money. The trouble is, he puts it all back into the business, instead of having a life with it.' Jim got up and flicked his cigarette stub into the fire. 'I'm off. I'll leave you to your onions – and you'll never get another fella smelling like that.' He grinned back at Daisy just before he ran up the stairs to the hallway and out of the front door.

Daisy heard the door slam as she stirred the simmering onions. Jim was right. She wouldn't get another fella, smelling and looking like she did, but she didn't care. She was happy as she was, cooking in the kitchen and making food for people to enjoy.

'You shouldn't let him talk to you like that. I heard him. I was up in the parlour.' Angelina stood at the kitchen doorway.

'I didn't know you were back, I didn't hear you come in.' Daisy blushed.

'Charles is asleep in his perambulator in the back yard. The fresh air will do him good, so I came to sit and have some time to myself. So, Jim thinks I'm an Italian witch – that's what my darling brother-in-law sees me as. I could have come down and said what I thought of him, but there are other ways of dealing

142

with ignoramuses, and he will find out one day exactly what I am.'

'I'm sure he didn't mean it. He says a lot of things without thinking.' Daisy didn't like Angelina's tone of voice. She seemed distant as she looked into the simmering pan of chutney.

'Your loyalty is to be commended, but he is no good. He will be the death of my family, and the business, if he's not stopped. What is this you're making it? It smells foul.'

'It's onion chutney. You eat it with cooked meat, and I'm labelling the jars ready to put the chutney in. It doesn't take long to cook, and I've opened the windows down here to let the smell out.' Daisy picked up one of the labelled jars to show Angelina.

'Mmm . . . "Mattinson's Onion Relish". Does my husband approve?' Daisy nodded. 'He knows what you English like to eat. He cannot stand garlic, you know – I cannot understand why!' She put the jar down and smiled at Daisy.

'I can't say I enjoy it, either. I've never cooked with it much.' Daisy hated garlic, but didn't dare say that there was no room for it in her cooking.

'I will give you a recipe for a sauce with garlic in, and we'll see what we can do. Perhaps we could call that "Petronelli's Tomato Sauce", in honour of my father. He's a great man.'

'We could certainly try.' Daisy smiled. She'd say anything to keep Angelina amused and in the good mood she was currently in.

'I'll speak to William tonight, then let you know. We'll sort something out.' Angelina smiled. 'I'll go and bring Charles back in. The moist evening air is coming in, and it might do him some harm. Plus it's nearly time for his feed. Will you be finished in time for me to prepare our supper? William will want something on his return from the shop. He will be a happy man tonight, with the grand opening tomorrow. He has put so much into the venture, and I am so proud of him.'

'Yes, don't worry. I'll have this cleared away within the hour.' Daisy's head was a-flutter. Two women in one kitchen was never going to work, and it was going to get even worse once the shop opened.

'Take care, Jimbo my love.' Susie pulled her skirts down and tied her corset, as Jim buttoned up his breeches.

'Ah, don't you worry about me, lass, I can look after myself. But it's a bugger when I've got to get my oats up some back alleyway, like a bloody dog. Next time you come to me.' He shoved a sovereign in between Susie's breasts, his fingers lingering there as he did so.

'There'll not be a next time, if you don't watch out. Old Trotter's still on the lookout for you, you mark my words.' Susie slapped his hand and tossed back her hair.

'Ah, stupid old git! This is Jim Mattinson, and tomorrow I open my own shop with my brother. I tell you, lass, there will be no catching us. We'll have a chain of them all across Leeds. Then will you marry me and become respectable?'

'Marry you and become respectable? Jim Mattinson,

144

you are not the marrying kind! And well you know it. Now bugger off, before you are found down here on Water Street, and let a poor lass make a living.'

Susie wrapped her shawl around her shoulders, ran her fingers down Jim's face and kissed him gently, before wandering out of the shadows onto the wharf edge. She looked quickly back at Jim as he disappeared into the night. She loved that man, but she was right: he wasn't the marrying kind. In fact his sort were ten-a-penny.

10

Daisy's face was flushed. She'd been up since five o'clock, baking cakes, potting lemon cheese and putting the finishing touches to all the things that were needed. She looked round the kitchen. She'd tidied up as she went along, and so everything should be in place for Angelina when she came to make breakfast. Now all she had to do was wait for Jim to come with the cart to pick her up.

She heard the faint cries of baby Charles demanding his morning feed. Soon William would be appearing, no doubt excited about the first day of opening his shop. He'd paid a young lad a farthing or two to deliver flyers around the surrounding streets, so a good turnout was expected. Daisy slumped down at the kitchen table. She was tired already, and she'd forgotten about all the early mornings that a baker had to do. When she had been mixing the scone mix in the dim lamplight of the early morning, her thoughts had wandered to home. Were her parents still alive? Was Kitty still happily married, or had Clifford eventually shown his true colours?

She had remembered the cool autumn mornings, with the dawn rising over Grisedale; the autumn mists following the bubbling stream down the dale; and the spiders' webs embroidered with dewdrops as they shimmered in the honeysuckle around the kitchen door. What a young foolish thing she had been, headstrong and jealous of her older sister. Her father had been right: she had led Clifford Middleton on; but not enough to have done what he did. He was a *bastardo*, as Angelino said.

A loud, heavy knock on the front door made her rouse herself from her thoughts of youth. She threw off her apron and ran up the steps from the kitchen to the hallway. The knocker banged again.

'I'm coming, Jim. Hold your horses – these legs will only go so fast.' Daisy pulled back the bolts on the door and opened it wide, ready for Jim to enter and collect the goods to be loaded onto the cart.

'Morning, miss. Is this the home of a William Mattinson?' A grim-looking man stood on the doorstep, dressed in the uniform of the Yorkshire Constabulary.

Daisy was taken aback. This was the newly formed police force for Leeds. Something must be wrong. 'Er, yes, it is.'

'Would you mind getting him for me, miss?' The constable put his foot in the doorway, making his presence felt.

'Yes, yes, of course.' Daisy turned round.

'No need to, Daisy. I'm here.' William rushed down

to the bottom of the stairs, tucking in his shirt as he reached them. 'What can I do for you, Officer?'

'I think we should talk in private, sir, if you don't mind.' The constable entered the hallway.

'Of course, of course. Please come in – come into the parlour. Daisy, could you make me some tea? Officer, would you like a cup, and perhaps a slice of toast?'

'That would be most welcome, sir. Thank you, miss.'

Daisy knew there was something drastically wrong as she boiled the kettle on the range and toasted some slices of bread over the red coals with her toasting fork. She hurriedly laid the tea tray and buttered the toast, before quickly carrying the tray upstairs and knocking on the parlour door. The room was quiet. William seemed to have aged twenty years in the last five minutes.

'It's all right, Officer. Daisy is part of my household.' William put his head in his hands and then ushered Daisy in, to offer the policeman some refreshment.

'Sorry, miss, but James Mattinson was found by The Cut this morning, by one of the wharf hands. He's only just alive and in St Mary's Infirmary, in a sorry state. Someone has tried to kill him.'

'The Cut?' Daisy gasped. Where was The Cut, and who would do such a thing? Poor Jim – he was a monkey, but he didn't deserve to be beaten nearly to death.

'The canal, miss, down on Water Street. We think he'd been drinking, but we can't be sure. He's not a pleasant sight, and we can hardly make out what he's saying.'

'Officer, there's no need for details. Once my wife joins us, I'd prefer for you not to tell her the lurid situation. We've recently lost a baby and her nerves will not stand it. Daisy, are you all right? I know he was with you in the kitchen yesterday. Did he say where he was going last night, or if he was going to meet someone?' William paced the floor while the officer tucked into the cooling toast.

Daisy felt her legs trembling and sat down on one of the velvet-upholstered chairs. She remembered Jim's laughter at her at the bottom of the stairs, and teasing her about smelling of onions, and the cheeky grin he had given her. 'No, he didn't say where he was going. I couldn't make him a cup of tea because I was making chutney at the time, and he was sick of the smell. I should have made him a drink.' She covered her eyes with her hands. ' I can't believe he's fighting for his life.'

'I can.' Angelina entered the room. 'He always lives life to the full – he's a Jack-the-lad. Is that what you English say?'

'And you are?' The constable looked at Angelina, taking in that he had entered a house already in mourning and that both women were in black.

'She's my wife, Officer. If you can take me to see James, I'd be grateful. Are you sure it's my brother you've found? I can't believe someone would attempt to kill him.'

'Oh aye, we are certain, sir. He'd one of your bills in his inside pocket, and Ebenezer Trotter recognized him. He was apparently a customer of his at the knocking

149

shop. Sorry, ladies.' The constable coughed. 'I'll take you to the hospital now. If he's conscious I'm sure he'll be pleased to see you.'

'I'll come with you now, Officer. My younger brother means everything to me.' William went into the hallway and grabbed his hat and coat.

'But the shop, William. It's your opening day – what about the customers?' It would appear that Angelina was more concerned about the business than about the nearly dead Jim.

'Bugger the shop, woman! This is my brother, and he's dying in St Mary's. I need to see him and make sure he'll live.' William shoved his arms into his coat and put on his bowler hat.

Daisy watched the face of Angelina and the hurt of William. 'I'll open the shop. I can manage it on my own. I used to help my father with his market stall. If you can carry some things round for me and open up the shop, I'll manage. You can't let folk down on your opening day. Jim wouldn't want it.' Daisy looked determined – there was no way she would accept a refusal.

William hesitated. 'Are you sure? You've worked a full day already.'

'I'm sure, I just can't carry all that I've made. Can someone help me get it there?'

'I'll help, lass. It's on the way to the hospital anyway. Give us what you want us to carry.' The constable shoved the last piece of toast into his mouth and waited for his instructions.

'She'll manage – she's a strong woman.' Angelina

wasn't going to waste one working day worrying about her wayward brother-in-law. In fact she wasn't going to worry about him full stop. She was glad he was going to be out of the picture for a while; it would prove what her husband could do, on his own two feet.

A procession of a police constable, a woman in mourning and a distraught businessman, laden with filled jam jars and baked goods, made their way through the still-sleepy streets of Leeds. This was not the opening day the Mattinson brothers had foreseen. Daisy looked up at the sign above the shop's doorway as William unlocked the door, and remembered the cheeky grin of Jim as he proudly showed her the wording of the sign. Bless him, she thought. She hoped with all her heart that he would be all right, for she had secretly fallen in love with Jim's cheeky ways. But she also knew it was like playing with dynamite, if she got too close.

'I'll just go up to his rooms and see if he's left any clues about what he was doing down at the canal. Although, if you don't mind me saying, sir, we all know the attractions on Water Street for the single man.' The constable unloaded his arms of baskets and jars and waited for William to show him the way up to Jim's rooms.

'Of course. Here, let me show you the way, though I dread to think what state his rooms are in.' William opened the door behind the counter that led up to Jim's rooms and the two of them went up the stairs.

Daisy listened to the voices from up above as she

arranged her jars of pickles and jams and displayed the baked goods, checking that there was enough cash in the till for change, before William left. Already there were people starting to shop further down the street. It would only be a matter of time before they expected the new shop to be open. Daisy closed her eyes and tried not to see the cheeky face of Jim, as she remembered him grinning at her from behind the counter. She couldn't believe it; it seemed to her that any man she took a fancy to died, got beaten within an inch of his life or was an out-and-out cad. There was something about Jim Mattinson, and she couldn't stop a tear falling down her cheek as she thought of him fighting for his life in a hospital bed. She wiped it quickly away; she wasn't going to show her feelings to William and the constable. Jim would be soon be back, calling her 'Daisy petal', before she knew it.

'There's nothing there, sir, to make me suspicious. I think he's just been set upon. He'd no brass in his pocket, so it's a case of robbery.' The policeman blew his nose on a grey-coloured hankie and shoved it back into his trouser pocket, before viewing the cakes Daisy had put out. 'Nice-looking shop, sir. I'll look in from time to time, see how you are doing.'

'Thank you, Officer. Daisy, are you all right? Everything's priced, there's change in the till, and I'll be back as soon as I can. I seem to be making a habit of throwing you in at the deep end.' William gave her a wan smile, before gesturing the policeman out the back door of the shop. The last thing customers wanted to see, on opening a new shop, was a peeler walking out of it.

Daisy watched the minute-hand on the wall clock ticking slowly around to exactly nine o'clock – time to open up. She tidied her hair, smoothed her apron down and breathed in deeply as she opened the doors to the crowd that had gathered. Let the trade begin, she thought. She didn't know how she'd manage, but somehow she damn well would.

William watched his brother as he struggled to draw breath. His head was battered and bruised, with hardly a clean place of skin on view, while his arm was in a sling, with splints holding his broken bones in place.

'Aye, Jim, who's done this to you? I bet you've been messing with something, or someone, you shouldn't.' William sighed and banged his bowler on his knee. His younger brother was always getting into scrapes, and it was always him who picked up the pieces. 'Our father would play hell with you, if he could see you. Why can't you keep out of bother?' William squirmed on the edge of the hard chair that he was sitting on, as he dropped his head in desperation.

'He'd play hell with you, and all,' came the faint reply from a conscious Jim, along with a faint smile, followed by a spluttering fit.

'Nurse! Nurse, he's coming round. Quick! My brother's awake.' William bent over Jim as he whispered more words.

'You can't get rid of me that easily.' He smiled a weak smile and reached out for his brother's hand.

'Shush, our Jim! Just keep your strength.' William watched as the nurse cleared the blood-spattered saliva that was blocking Jim's airway, while he held his brother's hand tightly. 'Who did this to you, our Jim?'

'I fell.' It was a weak answer, before Jim drifted back into a deep sleep.

'I think you'd better leave now, Mr Mattinson. Your brother needs his sleep. Come back in the morning.' The nurse smiled as she indicated the exit to William.

William stole a quick look at his sleeping brother. Jim was lucky he wasn't a lifeless corpse lying out in the cold grey morgue of the police station. The morgue and station had only recently opened, and the people of Leeds were grateful for the new force. The city had grown so quickly and needed a stabilizing police force to bring it to heel. He had heard rumours of gangs of thieves and their honey-traps, set up to trick prey like his brother, hiding in the sprawling dark and dank city streets of Leeds. He shook his head, trying to quell dark thoughts about the corruption, prostitution and gaming in many of Leeds's back streets, especially on Water Street, where the prick-pinchers made their living and where Jim had been found.

William took a deep inhalation of breath as he made his way out of the hospital. The air outside was relatively clean, compared to the smell of ether and opium used by the hospital. He felt guilty, thinking of the times he'd fallen out with his brother of late, and regretted the row they had the previous evening. There was a gnawing worry as he walked away from the hospital. Jim did like a drink, but he'd never seen him drunk in his life; he always drank at the Three Bells – his local – with his cronies, while enjoying a game of cards. He hadn't tripped, so someone must have hammered him to within an inch of his life. Jim had obviously been womanizing, probably with someone else's woman, and had been caught. Whatever he had been doing, William found himself whispering, 'Please, God, let him live' under his breath.

Daisy looked around the shop. It was the first time she had been able to have a breather all day. Trade had been brisk, groceries had been bought, and she was especially pleased that her baking and preserves had nearly sold out. The trouble was that she'd have to do it all again in the morning. She hoped William would be able to hold the fort at the shop on his own tomorrow. The poor man had looked heartbroken at the news of his brother. But she couldn't understand the reaction of Angelina – it was as if she didn't care. She knew there was no love lost between her and Jim, but she could have shown a bit more understanding for her husband.

The shop bell rang, bringing Daisy back from her thoughts.

'Afternoon, ma'am. Can I help you?' Daisy smiled at the well-dressed lady who had just entered the shop.

'Yes, perhaps you can. My housekeeper purchased

some of your goods this morning, one of which I've never sampled before. I believe it's called "lemon cheese"? I'd like to place a regular weekly order, for it to be delivered to my home.'

'Of course, ma'am. How many jars would you like, and is there anything else I can help you with?'

'I've written a list that my housekeeper tells me you can supply. I'd like to set up an account in my name, which is Lady Amelia Hall of Rothwell Manor, Leeds. I must admit, from what I saw of the produce she bought, your standard is very high. My cook and housekeeper will be recommending you.'

'Thank you, ma'am.' Daisy was proud of her cooking skills and was glad the shop was going to benefit from them, but she was beginning to wish it was *her* name on the label of the preserves. After all, it was her recipe. However, she knew it was the Mattinsons who were investing their money, and she was only a woman in a man's world. But one day she hoped things would be different.

Taking a glove off her lily-white hand, Lady Amelia picked up one of the china dishes. 'This is beautiful china. Where has this come from, do you know?' She studied the potter's mark on a dish, turning it gently in her hands.

'I think Mrs Mattinson had it imported from Italy. I'm afraid, other than that, I don't know.'

'I'll take it. Have your delivery boy bring it to me, along with the first week's order.'

'All of it? I'm afraid I don't know its cost.' Daisy's

face must have shown her amazement at this woman's wealth.

'It's of little consequence. It's too beautiful not to be in my home. I expect all the pieces to be supplied in perfect shape – no chips or breakages.' She replaced the glove on her elegant hand. 'Tell your boy that I want him to deliver on Tuesday next week. And no ringing the front doorbell; all deliveries to the back door.' She smiled. 'Good day.'

Daisy sighed as she closed the door behind her. She'd never talked to a lady before. She didn't know who the delivery boy was going to be, but she was sure William would sort something out – that order was too good to miss out on. Daisy leaned on the shop counter. She was exhausted. It was now nearly four o'clock and there was no sign of William. She'd give it another hour, and then she'd lock up. She slipped off her shoes and rubbed her aching feet, taking her eye off the counter for a minute until she heard the doorbell ringing. She raised her head, to see a weary William entering the shop. He looked round at his new empire. The stock needed replenishing, the floor needed sweeping – and there was his assistant in her stockinged feet.

'Just look at it! One day without Jim and the place has gone to the dogs, and you are serving with nothing on your feet. I can't do this without him – he's always there. He's a pain-in-the-arse perhaps, but he is my little brother.' William collapsed on top of the counter, his head in his hands.

'I'm sorry, William . . . If there's something more I

can do?' Daisy pushed her shoes back on her feet and walked over to the door, turning the Open sign over and bolting the door. 'Here, sit on the stool, and I'll restock the shelves and sweep the floor, ready for the morning.' She knew how William felt. She knew what it was like for your world to fall apart. 'How did you find him? How's Jim?'

'He regained consciousness while I was there, and then fell back into a deep sleep. He managed to tell me that he fell, which I don't believe for a moment. I just can't understand why he was at Water Street at that time of night. He never drank down there. All right, he probably sowed a few oats with the whores when he was younger, but even then he knew always to be careful.'

Daisy stacked the empty shelves. William covered his face with his hands and sobbed.

She put down the items she was stacking and gently put her arm around her employer. 'He's a strong young man. He'll pull round, and he'll be back bossing us all around before we know it.' She patted William gently and looked at the hurt in his eyes as he lifted his head.

He smiled through the tears. 'You're right, Daisy. He'll be all right. Us Mattinsons don't give in easily.'

'He's a character, our Mr Jim, but he wouldn't want to see you like this. And besides, you should see the takings in the till and the orders for delivery. If we can manage them, and it carries on like this, you'll both be millionaires.' Daisy tried to lighten William's mood. 'And we've sold all the china to a Lady Amelia, nonetheless, along with a weekly order.'

'You've done well, lass. Tomorrow we'll put up an advert for an apprentice. Some young lad will want a job – he can do the donkey work and leave the rest to us. Talking about donkeys, I'm guessing the horse hasn't been fed. I'd better see to it, and then we'll call it a day here?' William pulled himself together as he counted the day's takings.

'Oh my God, I've forgotten the poor creature.' Daisy was horrified. She would never have forgotten the horse in the old days.

'Never mind, Daisy. He'll appreciate his food more, for going hungry. I'm sure it won't be the first time. Our Jim is always forgetting the poor bloody thing. You sweep the floor, and then we'll go home. I want to tell Angelina that Jim's talked to me and, hopefully, is going to be fine.'

11

Daisy looked at the scrawny, filthy young lad who stood in front of her. He clenched his crumpled-up cap in his hands and lowered his eyes to the ground, as Daisy viewed him from top to bottom.

'And Mr Mattinson said you'd to ask for me?' She stood with her hands on her hips.

'Yes, miss. He said I'd to make myself known to the woman behind the counter, and that you'd know what to do with me. And then he said to tell you he will be along shortly, and that things are not as bad as they seem.' The young lad looked up for a second, then thought better of it as Daisy just shook her head.

'He did, did he? Well, we can't have you working in here looking like that, can we? When was the last time you had a bath? I've seen tatties growing in less muck than is on you.'

'I had one at Christmas, miss. Me mam made all eight of us line up for the tin bath round at my grandma's.'

'Christmas! That was nearly ten months ago. And

there's eight of you? Where do you fit into the family? Are you the youngest?'

'No, miss, I'm the oldest. Our Tim's the youngest, he's just started crawling. Me mam say's he's driving her mad – all he does is bawl all the time.'

'So, Freddie – it is Freddie, isn't it? I think the first thing we'll do is give your face and hands a wash. That'd be a good start. Then I can see what we have got to work with. There's a cold tap in the outhouse, with some carbolic soap next to it. Go and give yourself a good scrub – make sure you get behind those ears. And then I'll see what we can do.'

'Yes, miss.' Freddie's face said it all. He was obviously averse to soap and water.

Daisy showed him where the outhouse was and left him to it. Eight children and he was the oldest – he only looked thirteen, or less. That was nearly one a year. What on earth was his mother thinking of? Daisy thought that if it was her, she'd have told her husband to chop the offending article off; or she would be kicking him out of bed, to get his pleasure elsewhere.

Freddie came back into the shop and looked at the dragon who had told him to have a wash.

'Well, let's have a look at those hands.'

Freddie held out his hands for inspection.

'Not bad. They'll get cleaner, the more washes they have. Let's have a look behind those ears.' Daisy looked behind his ears and ran her hands through his short-cut hair. 'Well, at least you've no nits. Sit down and I'll give you something to eat and drink.'

His eyes lit up as Daisy poured him a glass of milk and cut him a slice of cake, which she gave to him. He immediately wolfed it down as if he'd never been fed before.

'Where do you live, Freddie?'

'On Armley Road, miss.'

'In that terrace near the prison?'

'Yes, miss. We can hear the prisoners yelling some nights.'

Daisy shook her head. That was one of the worst housing districts in Leeds. The conditions were squalid, and even in her short time in Leeds she'd heard of Armley Road. 'Call me Mrs Lambert. And here, have another piece of cake.' Her heart was melting for this little vagabond, and the least she could do was make sure his belly was full before he went home. 'I tell you what, Freddie. Can you give our horse in the stable behind a good grooming and give him his feed for the evening?'

'Oh aye, Mrs Lambert, I ken horses. I help my uncle, and he's a rag-and-bone man. I go all over Leeds with him. I'll look after the horse – what's its name? I love horses. My mother says I'll make a good jockey, on account of being so scrawny.' Freddie had come out of his shell at the mention of a horse.

Now Daisy knew that she was looking at their new delivery boy. Freddie knew Leeds, he knew horses and he had quite a bonny face when it was clean. Above all, his mother needed the few shillings the lad would earn, to keep the family fed. There was some sense in William taking him on.

'He's called Ginger, on account on him being a reddish colour – when he's clean, that is. He's got a good temperament. Now, off you go. Get him fed and watered before Mr Mattinson comes back, and I'll give you threepence to take home with you.'

Daisy watched as the young lad picked up the currycomb and brush and stroked the horse's withers to gain its confidence. He'd be all right, would young Freddie. She'd make sure of that.

Jim had missed Daisy's company for the last few days and was anxious to find out about his replacement.

'I hear we've taken on a young lad, Daisy. Am I that dispensable that a young back-street urchin has taken my place?' He winced as he reached for a piece of the toffee that Daisy had lovingly made and brought to him. 'These bloody ribs are killing me.' He lay back on the bed with a flop, while the piece of toffee turned round in his mouth. 'This is bloody good – another seller for the shop, lass.'

'Never mind my toffee. Yes, we've taken on Freddie, and a right grand lad he's turning out to be. Old Ginger's never been so well looked after. Anyway, this fall: was it anything to do with a dog? I rather think it happened where that stray you've got your eye on hangs out?'

'Don't know what you're on about.' Jim looked at Daisy through swollen, bruised eyes, hardly able to make out her features.

'Well, the dog came by the shop the other day – name of Susie. She was asking after you and wanted me to pass on her "bestest wishes", I think she said. I told her that you were mending, but probably wouldn't be making it down to Water Street for a while.' Daisy smiled.

'She did, did she? Tell her, if you see her again, that I'm fine. And tell her to watch out for herself. That Ebenezer is a bastard. He'd see her dead in The Cut, just like me, if she wasn't making him money.'

'I thought it was a fall?' Daisy grinned. 'And Angelina sends her love. William is right under the cosh, now you are out of action. Me too, come to that.'

'Just you watch Angelina. She's a spiteful cow, too. Jealousy is her best friend, and her father . . . Well, he just thinks he can buy everything – bloody Itai.' Jim winced again as he moved.

'I'm going to leave you in peace now. You look worn out, but at least you're back in the land of the living – and back to calling everyone names. I agree with you about Angelina. I don't know how we'll fare in the coming weeks, but we'll see.' Daisy rose from her hospital chair and looked down at the sorry state of Jim Mattinson.

'Give us a kiss, Daisy petal. I might be dead tomorrow. Give me something to remember you by.' Jim reached out his hand, only to wince again.

She bent down and kissed him on the brow, on the only unbruised piece of skin there was.

'I meant on the lips. How can I survive with just that?'

'You'll live. They don't call me "Shipley Susie".' Daisy grinned at him. She was thankful Jim was recovering, because life at the terrace was dull when he was not around. And he was right: Angelina had no love for anyone but herself and her family.

The autumn wind blew as Daisy made her way to open up the shop. The leaves fell down onto the grey pavements; their year was done, but they would appear anew in the spring, carrying on the circle of life.

'Oi, Daisy, wait a minute!'

She turned quickly. Susie was rushing towards her from behind.

'I know you won't want to talk to me, lass, and I shouldn't be here, but I just wanted to know how Jimbo is doing? I know I shouldn't, but I love that man. There aren't many gentlemen left in the world, and he is one, when he wants to be. Plus he's better than the bloody foreigners his brother married into.'

'He's fine, Susie. Go and see him: he's on ward ten at St Mary's, and it would make his day.'

'Nah, they'll not let me in. They know who I am, and what I do. Just you tell him to look after himself.' She wrapped her shawl around her as the wind blew stronger.

'He said the same about you. Told me to tell you to keep away from Ebenezer. Jim said he was a bad lot.' Daisy smiled at Susie.

'I know, but a girl has to make a living. You're not getting me in the workhouse – I'd sooner starve on the streets.' Susie's mood dropped, before she bounced back. 'Give him my love, and I pray to the Lord to keep him safe. And you too, darling. It's a hard world, without a doubt.'

'I will, Susie. Keep calling by and I'll pass your messages on. He'll be glad to hear from you.'

'I will, darling, I will. But think of your reputation – you don't want to be seen with me.' And, with that, Susie picked up her skirts and almost ran back down the cobbled street.

Daisy felt sorry for Susie. She had a heart of gold and she obviously loved Jim. But at the same time there was a little pang of jealousy in Daisy's heart. Susie wasn't the only one who had feelings for the lovable rogue; and hers were growing by the day.

That night Daisy tossed and turned in her bed, thinking about Angelina and the hateful words she had been saying about her brother-in-law. At one time she had actually heard her say to William that perhaps it would have been better if Jim had died. To her, the business was everything. And if anyone got in the way of the Petronellis' fortune, they weren't worth bothering with.

Next week Jim would be home in his own rooms above the shop. However, Angelina could only see the time that was to be wasted looking after him, until his strength returned. Her words were sharp and hurtful. How true what Susie had said when Daisy arrived in

Leeds: you had to keep your wits about you, else you could be dead. She'd have to watch herself with Angelina; she was obviously one to keep sweet, or you'd risk your life.

'I've been thinking.' Angelina watched as Daisy bottled the latest batch of lemon cheese. 'If you gave me the recipe for lemon cheese, I could make it and place it in jam jars for you. Then you don't have to work such long hours. You look tired, Daisy. My husband shouldn't ask so much of you.' She smiled a sickly smile that Daisy had come to realize Angelina hid behind, when she was plotting something.

'I don't mind being busy. It stops me from thinking. I'm my own worst enemy when I think. It's like my father used to say: "The Devil makes work for idle hands."' The words spilled out of Daisy's mouth without her thinking.

'Your father? You've never talked of your family before. Are they still alive?'

'I don't know, we lost touch some time ago.' Daisy didn't look up, but concentrated on tying the gingham fabric lid onto the jar – the one people had come to expect.

'That's sad. Family is so important; it comes before everything else, and there is honour to be had with a good family. Will you give me the recipe? It is the least I can do. Besides, baby Charles is such a good baby, I need something to keep me occupied. I'll mention it to William – I'm sure he will agree. After all, he was just

167

saying what a good salesperson you are, and that young Freddie has taken a great liking to you. It would be better if you worked behind the counter, once you have baked the cakes that are needed.' Angelina smiled and walked gracefully out of the kitchen, leaving Daisy secretly fuming.

It was her recipe, not Angelina's. She fumbled with the string's knot as she tied and sealed the last jar of lemon cheese. She glared at the label on the jar that said 'Mattinson's Lemon Cheese. Made in Leeds'. Too bloody right Angelina could have the recipe. Why should she herself flog her guts out, just for the jar to carry the word 'Mattinson's' on it? Besides, Angelina would soon tire, when she'd stood over the brass jam pan for an afternoon or two, nearly burning her arms and making red blotches appear with the heat. Anyway, with Christmas just around the corner, Daisy had another recipe idea that would sell just as well as lemon cheese. She'd like to see Angelina make Christmas mincemeat – that would be far too complicated for a woman like her.

'So we are all in agreement. Angelina will make the lemon cheese and the marmalade, while you, Daisy, will bake the fresh cakes that we need first thing in the morning, then come and help me in the shop and keep an eye on our Jim, just until young Freddie has finished his delivery round. I think this will work out well. It gives you a little spare time, Daisy, and gives Angelina her kitchen back during daylight hours. And it gives me time to train young Freddie, so that he can eventually

168

learn a trade. Plus, our Jim has someone to hand, just until he gets back on his feet.'

William Mattinson was laying down his law. He had had enough of warring women in his house, and this was the way forward.

Angelina smiled. 'This is fair, my dear husband, and I am grateful that Daisy has been gracious enough to give me both recipes. I will not let either of you down, especially when our sales have been so high. Who would have thought that a small fortune could be made from a simple country recipe.'

If looks could have killed, Angelina deserved to be dead, as Daisy gave her a long, hard stare. The cheeky bitch: *a simple country recipe*. If it was that simple, why hadn't she thought of it?

'And the Christmas mincemeat?' Daisy turned and looked at William.

'Make me a dozen jars and we'll see how it goes. It's a bit too early to take on another product just yet. Let folk get used to what we've got, and then we'll push it more. Plus, our Jim will always be yelling for something. I'll be glad when he's back on his feet.' William scratched his head. He'd just freed up some time for Daisy to call her own, and now she was trying to fill it by looking after Jim and making mincemeat. She was an odd woman – never happier than when she was run off her feet.

Daisy nodded graciously. She'd have given up on her request to sell mincemeat in the shop if it had meant not looking after Jim. But, on his return, Daisy wanted to be with him as much as possible, just to look into his smiling eyes and let him tease her. It had been a long time since she had felt like this, a long time indeed. As her obsession clouded her thoughts, memories of Clifford Middleton arose, taking the shine off her feelings.

'Bloody hell, the place has gone to the dogs without me!' Jim Mattinson hopped on his crutch through the shop doorway and glanced around, while his brother propped the door wide open for him. 'What's this stuff here? Another of your concoctions, I take it? Eh, I like the little bags of toffee. I bet they are going down a treat.'

'Get yourself up them stairs, our Jim, you're blocking the doorway.' William urged his brother forward as a bustling shopper tried to get past.

'Aye, can't get in the way of a sale. What would Angelina say?' Jim walked to the back of the counter and gave Daisy a peck on the cheek, making her blush.

'You're back then.' She smiled.

'Oh God, yes, he's back. He didn't stop moaning the whole way here.' William sighed.

'Aye, I'm back, lass, and I hear you are to be my nurse. You must be mad, trusting me in a bed.' Jim winked as the customer left in disgust.

'Enough! Get yourself up them stairs, and stop embarrassing Daisy and frightening our customers away.' William was running out of patience with his free-talking brother.

'All right, I'm off. See you later, Daisy petal.' Jim winked as he hobbled up the stairs.

Daisy blushed. She was glad he was back. Looking after his every need would be no problem at all.

Freddie appeared, red and flushed in the face, just as Jim was making his way up the stairs. 'Is that him then?' he asked. 'Is that the boss's brother?' He placed his delivery basket on the counter.

'Aye, that's Jim.' Daisy smiled and polished the already spotless china on display, thinking of the cheekiness of Jim Mattinson.

'Well, he's made you blush; there must be something about him. Do you fancy him, Mrs Lambert?' Freddie smiled with his head on one side.

'Don't you be so cheeky. And get on with your orders.' Daisy flicked her duster at the young lad's ear, before swirling her skirts around her ankles and humming to herself as she made herself busy arranging the window display.

Freddie grinned as he filled his basket with the next goods to be delivered. It was lovely to see Daisy happy. She had been kind to him, and she didn't have to answer his question – the pink of her cheeks told him all he needed to know.

The autumn days lengthened and, before anyone knew it, the long winter nights were upon everyone and the run-up to Christmas had begun. The streets of Leeds and Kirkstall were grey and weary, as if weighed down by the year's age. Before daylight, the knocker-uppers could be heard coughing loudly, long before their early-morning tap on the terraced bedroom windows. The smog and grime in the air were awful, but life in the city had to go on.

Daisy wrapped her shawl around her. This was her first winter in Leeds and she didn't appreciate the heavy, smoky air that clung around the streets, making its way into people's lungs, causing them to wheeze and cough and gasp for breath. She hurried quickly along the dark street, her baked goods in one hand and the keys for the shop in the other. Only the workers were out at this time of the day, and in the dim gas-light she could make out the small form of Freddie waiting in the shop's doorway. He was a good lad, was Freddie, and he was turning out to be an asset to the shop. William Mattinson had bought him a respectable uniform, along with a thick winter coat and cap, and he'd scrubbed up well. He might have come from a rough part of town, but he'd obviously been taught some manners, and Daisy had grown fond of the 'li'l fella', as she called him.

'Morning, Freddie. It's a miserable morning, but the sun might break through later on.' She smiled and turned the key in the lock. The shop bell tinkled as she opened the door.

'It is, Mrs Lambert. I can hardly see my hand in front of my face, and I hope old Ginge doesn't mind this weather, because we've a few deliveries to make this morning.' Freddie followed in her footsteps and waited until Daisy put on her serving apron behind the counter.

'You and that horse – he's had a new lease of life since you started to look after him. I think he's fed far too well. Have you had owt to eat this morning, or is your belly empty? I bet I can guess: you slipped out of the house while everyone else was asleep?' Daisy lit the small coal fire that kept the shop warm and put the blackened kettle on to boil. 'We'll have a brew, before I get started with the orders and you see to Ginger. And I suppose I can spare a penny or two for a currant bun from the baker's, if you want to run and get one for us to share. He'll be open. Tell him I'll know if it's fresh or if it's yesterday's. He'll only laugh, the old devil; he knows better than to give me his leftovers,' chuckled Daisy. She got on well with the baker and his wife, who worked further down the street, though she knew he tried to get rid of what he had left from the previous day on unsuspecting customers. Daisy dropped a couple of pennies into Freddie's hands and he beamed up at her. His eyes were full of gratitude and it melted her heart. He was a grand lad, and she didn't mind sharing her meagre wage on a bun in the morning to fill his hungry belly. 'Go on then, be off! And then we'll have to make a start on the day.'

'Right away, missus. I'll be back in a crack.' Freddie turned on his heels, leaving Daisy grinning as she fed the fire a few more lumps of coal to warm the freezing shop. She could hear footsteps up above her, suggesting that Jim was stirring from his sleep. His strength was returning, and it wouldn't be long before life was back to normal and the two brothers would be arguing about expenses and which goods to buy. As she brushed the hearth she could hear the familiar creak on the bottom step of the stairs. 'Morning, sleepyhead. Another few days and you can be lighting the fire, and then I can look forward to a warm place of work.' She didn't look round, thinking it could only be Jim making his way down the stairs.

'I don't think so, lovey. I've only been visiting, and you didn't see me here. Don't tell Jim's brother, nor that vixen, his wife.' Susie grinned as she tidied her hair. 'My man needed some extra loving, and he can't come to me, so I came to him.'

Daisy blushed as Susie looked around the shop.

'He's definitely on the mend. He's got his strength back – he kept us entertained all night, did my Jim. He's got a good little business here, ain't he? Must be worth a bob or two, not that it matters to me. I'd love him, no matter what.'

'Yes, yes, he's got a good business head; both brothers have.' Daisy felt a pang of jealousy and anger sweep over her. Susie had spent all night next to the man Daisy now knew she was in love with. The man she would do anything for, if only he asked.

'Ah well, pet, I'm off. Things to do, people to see. Remember – not a word!' Susie smiled as she let herself out of the shop, the bell tinkling louder than usual as she closed the door behind her. Her cheap perfume filled the shop and reminded Daisy that she was just a plain Dales lass, with no townie ways.

'Who's that, Mrs Lambert?' Freddie came rushing in with two warm buns clutched tightly in his hands.

'That is Susie. She's a friend of Mr Jim's.' Daisy brushed away the lone tear that had escaped from the corner of her eye.

'He must keep funny friends, 'cause she looks like a tart to me.' Freddie munched into his bun as Daisy made him a pot of tea.

'Quiet, Freddie, or Mr Jim will hear you. Pretend you never saw her coming out of the shop this morning.'

'So, I was right. She *is* a tart. We have them at the end of our street. My mam says to keep clear of 'em.'

'Well, you keep listening to your mam and you'll not go far wrong,' Daisy growled.

Susie might be a tart, but she held Jim's heart – and that, Daisy knew, she could never have.

12

'I love an English Christmas, but this year I am so tired. With the baby, the house and the business, I didn't realize this lemon cheese and marmalade took so long to make, and that you were going to make so much of it. Every day your orders grow. Something is going to have to be done.' Angelina was complaining to William over their evening meal.

'Well, my dear, you were so quick to take the making of it off Daisy. I must admit I was surprised, because you have enough on your plate, with the house and our dear Charles.' William pushed his dessert dish to one side and helped himself to a grape or two from the fruit display in the middle of the table, spitting the seeds out onto his dish.

'I had to take it off her. She was getting all the glory – our rough northern servant – and I didn't want her forgetting her place. I'm the lady of the house, and it is my family's money that keeps us afloat.' Angelina scowled at her husband.

'Aye, and it's her recipe that's making our fortune at

the moment. I can't believe that bloody lemon cheese could be so popular, *and* her mincemeat is selling. I don't think she was so pleased when we called it "Mrs Mattinson's Mincemeat", but I'll raise her pay or find something to appease her, once we close for Christmas Day. I suppose she'll be off back to the Dales for a day or two. I know her father won't have her back, but she'll not want to be with us.' William leaned back and lit his usual after-meal cigar.

'She has no family, or at least she's lost contact with them. She told me so, some weeks ago, so who is she supposed to go to?' Angelina sipped her tea. 'I don't want her staying with us. It's a family time, and Daisy is not family. Anyway my papa is coming to stay, and what will he think of her!'

'Angelina, you are the most unchristian person I have ever known. The poor woman has no family, she is making you a small fortune working all the hours we could possibly ask of her, and yet you won't share your Christmas with her.' William scowled at his hoity-toity wife.

'At Christmas, William, I need my kitchen to myself – and she'll be there. Besides, I could do with her room for my father to stay in. Can she not go somewhere? Suggest something to her, for I need my house back!' Angelina slammed her napkin down and stared at her husband.

'I don't know what you expect me to do, but I'll think about it. Where is she tonight anyway? She can't hear us, can she?' William didn't want to offend Daisy, for he'd grown to depend on her, and he knew his wife was just wanting her own way.

'She's visiting friends. I think it's the baker, Fergus, and his wife Mary. She said she was having supper and a game of cards with them, and that I hadn't to worry if she was late back. As if she thinks I'd care! As long as she's out of my kitchen, I'm not bothered where she is.'

'The bakers – I don't know how she got friendly with them. You don't think she's off to work for them? My God, I hope not. She could take everything with her. We'd have nothing to sell in the shop!' William looked worried.

'Daisy, Daisy, Daisy . . . It's all I bloody hear.' Angelina started rattling Italian swear-words at her husband, as her temper got the better of her. 'I want her out – out by Christmas Day – so that the house is my own!'

The drawing-room door slammed, leaving William with an uncleared dining table and an extremely agitated wife. If his ears didn't deceive him, he had a yowling baby, too. He could do without this in the run-up to Christmas.

William watched Daisy as she displayed her latest product of mincemeat in the shop window. It was selling well, especially as she was telling people how to make mince pies and mincemeat crumble. She had an everyday knack with folk, and she worked like a trooper. His old friend Bert, from up the dale, had certainly done him a favour when he had sent Daisy his way. But the thought of her getting too friendly with the baker and his wife was beginning to worry William, and he'd thought long and hard about how he could keep both of his women happy.

'Are you not going home for Christmas, Daisy? You've got three days off – I'm closing the shop for three days. Angelina has her father coming to stay, so we will all be at home.'

'No, this is my home now, William, but I understand. I'll find somewhere to go, if I'm going to be in the way.' Daisy's face dropped. She'd known this was coming. Angelina had not exactly been subtle with her hints of late. Daisy had thought of visiting Jenny Pratt, but she'd left so slyly, without so much as a by-your-leave; besides, she wasn't family and they probably had long since forgotten about her.

'Come on, our William, you can't throw Daisy out at Christmas!' Jim looked up from his calculations. His health was improving day by day, and he was now keeping the books and stock in order.

'Well, it's Angelina: she wants the kitchen to herself. She likes to impress her father. I'll see what I can do.' William looked worried. Yet again he was stuck in the middle of the two women.

'I understand, don't worry.' Daisy smiled, but underneath she was fretting. She had nowhere to go, and Christmas would soon be upon her.

'You'd better look after our Daisy, brother – we owe

her a lot,' Jim whispered to William, as the brothers showed an interest in the figures they were discussing. 'Don't let Angelina boss you around his time.'

'I'll see, but you know what she's like.' William glared at his younger brother. Jim had no idea what it was like to be married. 'Why don't you give Daisy *your* rooms. I'm sure you've somewhere to go – after all, you've plenty of admirers.'

'I know you're being sarcastic, but I might just do that. Nearly dying gives you a whole new outlook on life.' Jim slammed his books shut. 'Daisy petal, stay in my rooms over Christmas. I've other plans,' he shouted over to her, after she finished serving the latest customer.

'I can't do that. Where would you go?'

'Never mind about me. I've something to do over Christmas – something I should have done a long time ago.'

'Don't be hasty, our Jim. I'll sort it with Angelina.' William looked as startled as Daisy.

'Aye, and pigs can fly! It's all right, I've made my mind up. Daisy, go no further. My rooms are yours over Christmas.' And with that, Jim left the two of them searching for words as he climbed the stairs to his rooms.

A tear filled Daisy's eye. She'd heard all the arguments – it was only a terraced house they were living in and its walls were thin. She'd also heard Angelina being sick in the morning, a sure sign of things to come. With a new baby on the way, things were only going to get worse.

*

180

'And you're going to stop over the shop at Christmas!' Freddie looked at her in dismay as he listened to Daisy's new living arrangements, and looked around the room that was now a mixture of Daisy's meagre belongings and Master Jim's.

'That's right, just until Mr Petronelli returns home.' Daisy smiled at the young lad.

'My mam says a woman needs her own space, and sometimes she just wishes my father would bugger off. Like he's not with us a lot of the time, but he always turns up when he's run out of brass.' Freddie stopped for a breather and looked round the room.

'What's your father do, Freddie?' Daisy couldn't help but smile, thinking that she bet his mother wished his father would bugger off – to get away from his obviously lustful arms.

'He works down on t' canal wharf, loading and unloading stuff, when he can be bothered. He sometimes brings us all sorts of stuff. He even brought me a thing called a "banana" t'other day. I'd never seen anything like it before in my life. It was a funny yellow thing that you peel and then eat. I didn't like it. The trouble is, he trades what he gets for drink money, and then we don't see him for days, until somebody sobers him up or he limps home penniless. I don't know why my mam puts up with him. We can manage. I give her all I make and she takes in washing, and our Annie will soon be old enough to go into service.'

Daisy listened to the young lad. He talked more like the man of the house than his years suggested. Poor lad, he's had it hard, she thought. 'Well, here's a sixpence for helping me with my move. Don't spend it all at once.' Daisy took the small silver coin out of her meagre savings and thought it was money well spent. Freddie had worked hard, and now he could have a treat.

'Oh ta, Mrs Lambert. I'll get me mam summat special for Christmas. My uncle's coming around with a broiler hen for Christmas dinner. He pulled its neck last night and plucked it, so we've something good to eat. I can't wait!'

Daisy looked at young Freddie's eyes twinkling as he thought about eating the aged hen. 'I tell you what, Freddie. Take this cake. I've just made it. I was trying the oven out and it's not good enough for the shop.' There was nothing wrong with it, in fact it was a perfectly good Victoria sandwich cake. 'Here, take care with it. Tell your mam it's a present from me, and have a good Christmas.' She wrapped it up in one of the 'Mattinson' bags and patted him on the back. 'Now go on, get yourself home and have a good Christmas. And don't lose that sixpence.'

She watched him run down the stairs and heard the back door slam. She shook her head. She must be going soft in her old age, but she had almost everything, and the lad had hardly anything. The only thing Daisy didn't have was the love of Jim, and she knew she'd never have that. Especially when he had disappeared without telling anyone where he was going over the Christmas period, leaving everyone worrying about what he was up to.

*

'Oh, Papa, that is fantastic news, isn't it, William? William, thank Papa. Just think what you can do now.'

William looked at the pompous Italian sitting on the other side of his Christmas dinner table. He didn't want to thank him; he didn't want to be any deeper in debt to his father-in-law.

'William, say something!' Angelina flashed her dark eyes at him.

'Thank you, sir. That is indeed generous.'

'It is nothing. I couldn't have my daughter slaving in a kitchen, making jams and jellies. Besides, think of the sales you will now have, with a factory of your own. You can distribute this, er . . . lemon cheese, all over the country, not just in Leeds. Use my contacts. People won't say no when they realize who you are.' Franco Petronelli took a long drink of his red wine and looked satisfied.

'I've also got some good news, Papa. I think William will already have guessed, but I wanted to tell my two favourite men together.' Angelina paused and blushed. 'We are to be parents again. I am with child, so there's even more reason for the factory.'

'*Bellissima* – God be praised, a new grandchild. You do your father proud.' Franco walked around to Angelina and hugged her. 'A new baby *and* a new business – who could want for more, William?' Franco laughed and his round belly shook with mirth. 'I wish your mother was still alive, to see how well our family is doing. My two strong boys with two shops each; our eldest daughter well catered for, even with her husband dead; and now you and William in business, with more grandchildren on the way. What more could a man wish for?' Franco lit a cigar and patted William on the back. 'We need a talk, man-to-man. Angelina, you understand. Leave us to talk, for there are some things William needs to know.' Franco's face went serious and he sat back down at the table, pouring himself a port.

William scowled at his wife. He had suspected her news, for he'd witnessed her sickness and knew the signs, but he was peeved that she had not told him first. He could never compete with her father. In fact he had a feeling that, compared to her father, every man would always be inferior, so strong was her love for him.

'Of course, Papa. William, are you not pleased? You haven't said anything.' Angelina's eyes glanced at the troubled look on her husband's face.

'Of course I'm pleased, my dear. It will be a play-mate for Charles. I had suspected it, my dear, for you have been a little off-colour in the mornings.' William smiled. A new baby in the family he would welcome, but his father-in-law's interference in his business he might not, depending on the terms.

'Then I'll leave you two men to it, and I'll go and play with baby Charles. He's been so good, and slept while we had our dinner in peace. I'm sure he's an angel really – he's no bother at all.'

Angelina swept out of the room and left the two men smoking and talking over their cigars and port. Her plan had worked: she'd got her father to push

William that little bit further into the family firm, and now they were properly in business. A factory making that blessed woman's recipe. She hated the sight of Daisy Lambert, but her culinary skills were going to make them rich. Anyway, she'd devised a plan to get rid of her. She was going to do it after Christmas. That stupid Jim had scuppered her hope that, once Daisy had returned home, she might have stayed there. But now she'd deal with Daisy herself, for there was only room for one woman in the Mattinson family. Still, the stupid bitch was going to make her – Angelina – a woman of substance, and her family envied. She hummed a song as she climbed the stairs. This was going to be a Christmas Day to remember.

'Aye, Mary, that was a grand dinner. The goose was so tender, and that plum pudding was so light. I'm fair full. I don't think I'll ever move again.' Daisy sat in front of the fire with her good friends, Fergus and Mary McGregor.

'Well, it was nice to have a bit of company on Christmas Day. It's usually just me and the old fella.' Mary grinned, her cheeks glowing red in the light of the glowing fire.

'Less of the "old fella", for you're no spring chicken yourself,' laughed Fergus. 'But aye, it's good to have a bit of company and a bit of fresh news. I'm right glad you'll be living over the shop, albeit just until after Christmas. You'll be glad of a bit of time away from that Italian woman – her family has a reputation for getting what they want, no matter how they get it.' Fergus emptied his clay pipe into the fire and refilled it, lighting it while looking slyly at Daisy.

'I'm not keen on her, and I'm glad I'm away from Newtown Terrace. Angelina has a fearful temper, but I shouldn't speak ill of her. I've a roof over my head, a full belly and a job – I've been a lot worse off in the past.' Daisy twiddled her thumbs and decided not to say much more, else she'd not be able to stop herself.

'Well, you watch yourself, lass, because from what I hear, if you stand in the way of the old father, you end up the worse for it. And we can't be having that.' Fergus took a long draw on his pipe and stared into the fire.

'She knows she's got to look after me, for the sake of the shop, and William's and Jim's profits, so don't fret.'

'Aye, well, you just take care of yourself. Keep making them money, and don't mention being friends with us, or else she'll put two and two together and get half-a-dozen. Keep yourself to yourself, lass, and keep 'em happy, and you'll be there as long as you are useful. But mark my words, one day they'll not want you – they are that sort.'

Daisy knew what Fergus said was true, but she hoped that day was a long time off. She liked working for the Mattinson brothers, and tended to forget that the Petronelli family was the backer of the enterprise.

Soon the group of friends found themselves going

silent, basking in the warmth and their full stomachs, and feeling content with one another's company. That night they were in good health and good spirits, with a day without work to look forward to.

13

The blushing couple looked at one another with love in their eyes, as the announcement was made. The atmosphere in Newtown Terrace's drawing room was heavy with the weight of jealousy and hatred, as Angelina refused to look at the besotted bride-to-be. Susie showed off the gaudy engagement ring upon her long, thin finger, and Angelina glared at William, not saying a word about the latest member of the family, her face belying her thoughts.

'Innit lovely. I love him so much. I came to my senses when I nearly lost him last year. What idiot would turn a man down like my Jimmy?' Susie giggled and clung to Jim's arm.

'Who indeed?' William Mattinson looked at his younger brother and at the common whore he knew to be 'Shipley Susie'.

'And where do you think you are both going to live?' asked Angelina. 'You can hardly live above the shop. There isn't room to turn around in that poky place.'

'Now, sister-in-law, stop fretting. We've just come

back from looking at some new houses they are building at a place called Roundhay Park on the other side of Leeds. From what my brother tells me, we'll be able to afford a spot like that, now that your father's making us go into full-scale production.' Jim couldn't stop himself – Angelina's face was a picture, and he loved rubbing her nose in it.

'Tah. Exactly – it is my father you should be thanking, you and your common whore, you *bastardo*!'

'Oi! Who do you think you are calling a "common whore"? I'm respectable, me. I know only gentlemen!' Susie glared at her sister-in-law-to-be. She wasn't going to let the Italian bitch get the better of her.

'Stop it! I'm sure you'll be moving as well. We may well both be millionaires in another few years. Now, where's Daisy? She's not at the shop. We called there, as I wanted her to be the first to know, but there was only young Freddie serving.' Jim Mattinson looked questioningly at his brother.

'She's downstairs, in her bed. After she came back from your rooms in the New Year, she took sick. She's been ailing for a week or two now.' William bowed his head.

'Has she seen the doctor? What's wrong with her?' Jim fretted for the health of Daisy. 'I've never known Daisy complain or be ill before.'

'Of course we have. You may think we don't care, but we do!' Angelina glared at Jim. 'The doctor says the air in the town does not suit her country lungs, and has advised her to return home. She wrote to her sister last week, asking her if she may return to live with them.'

'But she hates her family – she'd never do that!' Jim shook his head in disbelief.

'Go and see for yourself. Both of you go down and see her, and tell her your news. I'm sure Daisy will be glad to hear you are to be married.'

Angelina smiled a cunning smile, knowing full well that the imminent marriage of Jim to Susie would be the final straw in the downfall of Daisy. Her plan was working even better than she had expected. No one had suspected her of adding a little grain of arsenic, now and then, to Daisy's meals, making her so ill that she was no use to the business. Now, the marriage of Jim to Susie would definitely break her heart. She'd seen how the stupid girl had been enthralled with her brother-in-law. This, combined with Daisy's culinary talents, meant that Angelina had to get rid of her. Daisy threat-ened her position, and no one could be allowed to do that!

'Susie, wait here. I'll go down and see Daisy. I need to break the news of our marriage myself.' Jim loos-ened his starched collar. Unusually, he felt slightly nervous, because he knew that Daisy had feelings for him and he didn't want to make things awkward between them.

'Yes, Susie, you sit next to me. Tell me about your-self, and what you can bring to the business. We will need a cleaner, I suppose,' Angelina smirked.

'You fucking bitch! I'll give you "cleaner",' Susie let rip.

'Ladies, I'll not have this kind of conflict under my roof. Angelina, mind your manners. And, Susie, don't use language from the gutter, if you want to be part of the family.'

William nodded to his brother to indicate that everything was under control and he should go and see Daisy.

Daisy lay looking grey and limp on her bed in the basement bedroom. Beads of perspiration stood out on her brow, and there was a bucket of bile by the side of her bed.

'Daisy petal, my love, you look ill. What have you done to yourself? Don't tell me you are lovesick for me, darling. You should have known I'd come back.'

'I . . . I don't know what's wrong with me. The doctor says it's the town's smog and I'm not used to it, but that shouldn't make me sick.' Daisy slowly lifted herself up on the pillows and smiled at Jim.

'You're in a right state, lass. I'll get you the doctor again, and see what he says. Don't worry about the bill – I'll pay.'

'No, it's all right, Jim. I'm going home to Garsdale on Friday. I'm going back to my sister's house. Her reply to my letter arrived this morning.' Daisy pulled the scribbled note written by her sister Kitty from underneath her pillow. 'She says someone will pick me up from the last train to call at Garsdale station, and then they'll take me back to Grouse Hall. I don't want to go – I don't want to face my family – but if I stay here I'm going to die.' She fought for her breath between the sobs and tears.

'Ah, Daisy lass, you're not fit to go anywhere. Stop with me until your strength returns. I can't bear to see you so ill.'

'No, Jim, I'm going. If I'm dying, I don't want to be buried in Kirkstall cemetery. At least let me lie with open skies above me, and the curlews calling over my head.' Daisy spluttered and coughed.

'All right, lass. Then I'll take you to the station. I can even go with you to Garsdale, if you want – make sure you get there safely, get myself some lodgings, and then come back on the train in the morning?'

'We'll see. I might be feeling stronger by Friday.' Daisy reached for Jim's hand and squeezed it lightly, before closing her eyes to sleep.

'I'll leave you for now, Daisy petal. Now you get yourself better, and I'll pick you up on Friday morning.' Jim felt a tear come to his eye. Would she be in the land of the living by Friday? She looked like the living dead now. He kissed her on the brow, and as he did so he smelled the breath on her lips. He knew that smell – he'd come across it at the apothecary's! What was it? He knew he'd smelled it before; perhaps it was the potion the doctor had given her to keep her drowsy.

Jim climbed the stairs from Daisy's bedroom with a heavy heart.

'Well, Jimbo, did you tell her? I bet she was excited at our good news.' Susie giggled.

192

'I didn't tell her anything, Susie. By the looks of her, we'll be lucky if she's here in the morning. What has the doctor given her? There's a smell on her breath, and it's horrible.'

'Ah, she's been given some potions by the doctor. She'll be fine. I'll go down and give her some soup, and make sure she's all right, when you've gone,' cried Angelina.

'Well, we owe that lass nearly everything. She thinks she's dying and, because of that, she's going home on Friday to her sister in Garsdale. She'd never do that if she was well.' Jim glared at Angelina, who seemed to be taking Daisy's decline very lightly.

'I'll feed her and sit with her until Friday, if you'll hold the fort at the shop, Jim. It was me who took her the reply from her sister this afternoon, and I was shocked when I saw how poorly she is. Angelina has not let me near her all this last week, in case it was infectious.' William looked straight at his brother, so that Jim knew he was giving him his word.

'She's a good 'un, is Daisy. She must know she's really ill, if she's going home. I remember when I first met her, she was green as the grass, bless her, and heart-broken as well. What that father did to her is beyond belief.' Susie sniffed into her new lace handkerchief before stuffing it down between her breasts.

'I'll make sure she gets no worse. If she does, I'll take her to the hospital. I'll sit with her, once you've all gone, and try to get her to eat a little. I'll nurse her back to health myself.' William stood up and put his hands behind his back as he looked out of the window.

'And what about Charles and me?' Angelina snapped.

'What about you and Charles? You are both perfectly well. Daisy needs me more than you.'

'Daisy, Daisy . . . always bloody Daisy. I hate her.'

'Perhaps that's the problem, my dear. And that is why I'm going to watch over her until she is fit to get on that train on Friday.'

The penny had dropped. Angelina's hatred of Daisy was killing her, and the safest place for her – no matter how terrible – was back home with her sister. And William was going to make sure she got there.

Daisy climbed the stairs, shaking slightly. It was the first time she had ventured from her bedroom for nearly a fortnight and her legs were very weak. William smiled as she took his hand and led her into the drawing room. 'There, I knew you could make it.'

'I'm still shaky and out of breath.' Daisy slumped into the chair that he quickly placed underneath her.

'Yes, but another day will make all the difference, and by Friday you'll be dancing to the station.' William smiled.

'I don't know about that. I've nothing much to dance to the station about. But I can't stay here, if the smog makes me this ill. I hadn't kept in touch with my sister until now – we were never that close. Now I realize that she is kind, and she assures me that my brother-in-law, Clifford, has changed. She also told me my mother died last year. Seemingly she had been ill with small-pox and there was nothing they could do for her.' Daisy hung her head. There may not have been much love lost between her and her mother, but there was still a deep feeling of losing something precious – something that could never be replaced. 'As long as I'm able to pull my weight, I'll be welcome there.' Daisy gasped for breath, before coughing.

'I'm sorry to hear your mother's died. That must hurt. You only get one mother. That's it – get all the badness out of your lungs, clear your system and then you'll be fine.' William passed his handkerchief to Daisy. 'Are you sure you will be all right back home? What about your father?'

'Kitty wrote to me about him also. My father is in Lancaster Moor Asylum. He lost his mind after my mother's death. So it seems I have only my sister left in the world. I feel responsible, in a way, for their down-fall, for I wasn't the best of daughters.' Daisy played with her handkerchief. She felt like crying her heart out. Over the years she had tried hard to hate her parents, but no matter what they had done to her, the bond was still there, and she still remembered her father's love for her. 'It will be strange returning home, but you can't run forever. And your family doesn't need me now. You will do well with your new factory.'

'Daisy, I want to thank you, while we are alone.' William knelt down beside her and took her hand.

'Tah! Isn't this sweet: my husband holding the

servant's hand. You are nothing but trouble to me, Daisy.' Angelina had crept silently into the room.

'It isn't what you think, Angelina, and well you know it. I was just thanking Daisy for all her help. You know we owe her a lot.' William rose to his feet.

'Well, it doesn't matter. She goes home on Friday, Jim marries his whore and we get on with our lives. Without her!' Angelina turned and stormed upstairs to Charles, who was peeking through the banister, watching the scene.

'Jim is to marry?' Daisy was shocked to hear the words.

'Yes, he's marrying his Susie. God knows why. He should be content just going to her for her services. But no, not our Jim; he's trying to make her into a lady.' William sighed.

'He loves her – that's all that matters – and she has a good heart. They will be happy.' Daisy felt as if her own heart would break. She'd held onto the idea of Jim being in love with her, and now it was shattered.

'He'll be telling you all about his plans when he takes you on the train. They've even been looking at moving into one of the new houses being built at Roundhay.'

'I'm sure they'll be happy together. Now, I hope you don't mind, but I'm going back to my bed. I'm feeling unwell.' Daisy could not hold back the tears any longer and wanted to shed them in the privacy of her room.

'Of course, Daisy. And take no notice of Angelina. She's hot-headed and doesn't mean what she says.'

William supported Daisy's arm as they went downstairs to her room.

'She does mean it, William, and that is why I'm leaving, while I still can.' Daisy sat on the edge of the bed.

William didn't reply. They both knew how close to death Daisy had been, in Angelina's hands, but neither dared say it.

14

'Now, are you sure you're strong enough to travel on the train alone?' Jim passed Daisy her battered carpet-bag and watched her struggle with the weight of it as she opened the carriage door. 'I'd feel better coming on the train with you, just to make sure there is someone there to meet you.' He fussed around her, feeling guilty that she would not have any of his help.

'I'm fine. Kitty says there is a man meeting me at the station to take me straight to Grouse Hall. Get yourself back to Susie, William and the shop.' Daisy knew she was being sharp with Jim, but she felt hurt and betrayed.

'Daisy, you know I think a lot of you, don't you? But Susie and I go back a long way. I couldn't believe she said "yes" when I asked her to marry me – she'd knocked me back so many times.' Jim looked pleadingly into her eyes, before taking Daisy's hand to help her into the carriage.

'I know, and I hope you'll both be happy. Watch your money, that's all I'm going to say, and don't let

Angelina get the better of you.' Daisy could feel the tears building in her eyes as the guard shouted, 'All aboard.' 'Take care, Jim, I hope life treats you well.'

'Take care, Daisy petal. I'll always remember you. I'll write.' He kissed her gently on the cheek and watched as her frail form mounted the train's steps and pulled the carriage door to.

Daisy waved and wiped a tear from her cheek as the train started to pull away from the station. She watched the figure of Jim through the smoke of the engine until she could barely make out his form. She loved that man. It didn't matter about William, Angelina and the new factory, and the shop to which she had contributed. It was Jim she would miss, but now she wondered what the future would hold for her? Under the same roof as Clifford, she'd lock her bedroom door for sure, and she hoped with all her heart that he'd changed, now that he was a married man.

She placed her belongings on the luggage rack above her head and sat down into the depths of the carriage seat. She'd not been on a train since her first arrival in Leeds and she was amazed by the changes. The station had grown, and buildings had sprung up alongside the canal and wharfsides. She sighed as the train built up steam, leaving the expanding city. So much had changed in such little time: houses had been built, the smoking chimneys of factories littered the skyline, and people were constantly in a hurry. Perhaps it was right that she was leaving this life behind – it had caused her a lot of worry and stress, and now she was going back to the area she had loved while growing up, and to a slower pace of life.

The train pulled up at Bingley and she smiled at the newly built rows of workers' homes that ran down to the line. Albert Street, Emily Street, Charlotte Street: all good, solid Victorian names. Bless the Queen, she was a good woman. The beautiful newly built town of Saltaire came next; Titus Salt was a man to be reckoned with, a man from ordinary roots, but now with a town named after him. He was a good man, though, looking after all his workers, with houses built for them according to their status in his weaving business. The great cotton mill's looms and shuttles could be heard sweeping back and forth as the train drew in at the station, even though the windows and doors of the train were closed. Daisy remembered Jim's words on her first trip into the centre of Leeds with him: 'You want nowt with working in a mill, Daisy.' And now she knew he had been right; she'd seen too many lasses with fingers – or worse – missing, from the flying shuttles, and women coughing their lungs up from the cotton fibres embedded in them. It was nowt of a life, and she knew that now.

At Skipton station she was joined by a small, bony woman who looked at her with curiosity when she entered her carriage. Daisy smiled and wished her a good afternoon.

'Aye, I don't know about that, lass. It looks like rain to me, and I've to walk home yet, when I get off this train. It's a good four miles from the station to Dent –

why they built it there I'll never know.' The straight-talking woman looked at her and smiled.

'Have you been shopping in Skipton?' Daisy decided to make conversation. Even though she had noticed a lack of bags, she thought it was polite to show interest and she didn't think her knowledge of why Dent station had been built, following the land's natural contours, would be of interest to her new companion.

'I'm off back to Dent. I've just been to Skipton to see my brother. He's been poorly this last week or two, had a terrible cough. We thought we were going to lose him at one time – like it would have given us a bit of trade if he had snuffed it.' The woman's face remained straight as she spoke.

'Trade?' Daisy asked, puzzled by the hard-natured woman who sat across from her.

'Aye, we are undertakers in Dent, but we never make much money in summer. It's winter that kills the old ones off. Last winter we had a funeral nearly every week – my Ernie was fair rubbing his hands. There's nowt like a good covering of snow to make the spirits low, and then they just start dropping.'

'I'm off to Garsdale, to my sister's.' Daisy decided to change the subject as the train clattered through the next station. She was watching exactly where she was on the line, for she wanted to watch out of the window once she reached Ribblehead, just to remind her of her past life there.

'Are you? Whereabouts does she live? I know some folk in Garsdale.' The woman peered at her with inquisitive eyes, making Daisy feel as if she had suddenly become prey for an undertaker's coffin.

'I'm off to Grouse Hall. My sister and her husband, Clifford Middleton, live there. It's just above the turning for Grisedale.' Daisy watched the woman's face as she was weighing up whether she knew the family.

'Clifford Middleton, now let me think.' The woman sat back and pondered, and then, as if a light had gone on in her brain, she shouted. 'Oh! I know him. His wife's mother died last year. They used to be bakers who came into Sedbergh on market day, until the old fella went mad. He's a bit of a bugger, is that Clifford – got a bit of a reputation.' And then she realized what she had said and noted Daisy's flushes. 'I'm sorry, lass, I didn't mean to upset you, and my mouth runs away with me sometimes. I was sorry to hear about your mother. I didn't realize they had another lass.'

'I've been away for a while.' Daisy decided not to say any more to the gossiping woman. Not only had she tittle-tattled about Daisy's immediate family, but she had rekindled her fears about Clifford. Why had she written to Kitty begging to come and live with her? She should have waited until she felt stronger and then found her own way in the world. She had the skills to look after herself, and there were plenty of grand houses needing cooks in Leeds.

Daisy looked out of the window as the train drew out of Settle station. Now that she knew the lie of the land, she recognized the sweeping hills and the drystone walls and her heart beat faster as she realized she was nearly home. At the same time, a dread from her past filled her.

Hilda Batty watched as Daisy stood and opened the train's window. Daisy turned her back on her new companion and breathed in the sharp Dales air as it filled the carriage. Even though the air was infused with smoke from the train engine, she knew she was back home. The station at Horton in Ribblesdale was immaculate as they pulled into it. The flowerbeds were filled with the delicate, nodding heads of hundreds of snowdrops, and the name of the station had been spelled out in whitewashed stones. She smiled as she looked up at the peak of Pen-y-ghent. How she'd missed her fells and dales. She stood watching the limestone walls go rushing past, nearly catching her breath as the train rounded the corner onto the straight length into Ribblehead station. She felt a tear nearly coming to her eye as she saw the road that she had walked down, half-dead and broken-hearted, a few years ago. It was the station to which she'd run away from Gearstones Lodge, and where she had courted Bob.

The stationmaster blew his whistle and the train rattled over the road bridge, with the Welcome Inn looking like a doll's house below. Then the train travelled over the mighty viaduct, the small moorland road running like a length of string under the huge arches. Daisy looked out over the wild moorland, remembering all the navvies she had served, with their toothless grins as they tucked into her meals, and the thanks she had received when their stomachs had been filled. Passing the signal box and Blea Moor cottages, her heart ached. So many hopes for a better life had been planned there, all broken on that fateful night when Bob had died. She said a silent prayer for him, before sitting down across from her fellow traveller.

'Aye, lass, tha looks proper white, are you all right?'

'I'm fine, just looking out at the view before we go into the tunnel.' Daisy wasn't going to tell her anything about her past.

'It's a fair height up, that viaduct. I wouldn't like to stand on the top of it – I'd be fair dizzy.' The old woman looked out into the blackness of Blea Moor tunnel. 'Just shut the window. The smoke's coming in, and it's bad for me lungs.'

Daisy rose and closed the window, breathing in the familiar fumes of coal dust and the smell of the many trains that had passed through the tunnel since it was built. She smiled. Memories were short, and people forgot; already the navvies buried in Chapel-le-Dale and Cowgill churchyard had been forgotten. She'd not forget them. They had made her what she was – a strong person. And now she was back.

'I always think this dale is my favourite. Though I would, as I was born here. But you've got to go a long way before you see anything as bonny as this view.' Her companion looked out of the carriage window at the green valley of Cowgill, which led to Dent. 'You either live on the sunny side or the money side, say the locals. Well, we're here; this is Dent. Looks like I'll have to walk home. Ernie isn't here for me.' She sighed. 'And it's beginning to snow! Well, it's been nice meeting you. I hope all goes well for you, and forgive me for being an old gossip.'

'Thank you.' Daisy gritted her teeth. She was glad to see the back of the nattering old woman, as she slammed the carriage door behind her. She was thankful that the carriage was empty again as the train made its way from Dent station through the darkness of Rise Hill tunnel. Her stomach churned with fear and apprehension as it pushed its way through a blizzard-clouded cutting and out into Garsdale.

She looked down the dale, through the falling snow, remembering which family lived in which house, and then looked up to the winding road that led to Grisedale. The lamps were being lit, and Daisy remembered the homeliness of the families behind the burning lamps; the nights when she and her sister and parents had dined and shared their lives with the neighbours and friends.

Daisy couldn't help but think that it was a pity Kitty and Clifford had never been blessed with children. Kitty would have been the perfect mother. She had always had more patience than Daisy, and had always entertained the babies and toddlers who had visited their home. Now that she was returning, what would she find? Could things ever be the same, and would Clifford still be the bastard she knew him to be?

The snow whipped around her as she climbed down from the train and made her way down the steep hill, towards a standing horse and cart on which an elderly man sat. He had a sack-cloth covering his shoulders.

'I'm Daisy Lambert. Thank you for meeting me. I hope it's not too much trouble.' Daisy waited for an answer from the scruffy-looking man, but instead she saw a gobful of saliva and tobacco being spat out at the side of the cart, and heard a slap of the reins on the horse's flanks as she climbed into the back of the rough cart without a helping hand.

The horse trotted along the road and out of the station yard, past the row of railway workers' houses and down the steep hill to the valley below. The pastures on either side of the winding hill road were being covered quickly with the fast-falling snow, and Daisy shivered and wrapped a filthy horse-blanket around her, from the back of the cart, to keep warm. She was already feeling weak, the journey having exhausted her, after nearly being at death's door just a few days ago. The snow and cold crept into her bones as the snowflakes settled on her hair and eyelashes, cold and wet, clinging until they melted with a frozen drip. She slid up to the back of the cart and wrapped whatever else she could find around herself. She'd forgotten how cold it was out in the bleak countryside of Garsdale, compared to the sheltered streets of Leeds and Kirkstall.

She felt every bump of the road and sighed with relief and anguish that they had started to climb the rough path to Grouse Hall. She'd not been back there since Kitty's wedding day and knew she had a lot to explain, but she would have to play the whole situation by ear. How much, or how little, did Kitty know? What had her parents said about her disappearance from home?

The horse and cart pulled up outside the long, dark shape of Grouse Hall. A dim lamp shone in the window of what she knew to be the parlour. It flickered for a moment and then disappeared as Daisy climbed out of the cart, her whole body shaking with the cold.

'Thank you,' she said to the old man who had driven her down the dale. 'Are you not coming in to warm yourself?'

Another spit of tobacco and saliva was the answer, and then a few words. 'Nay, you'll not get me in there, no matter how cold the weather is. It'll be worse in there.'

He turned the horses round with another flick of his reins and made his way back down the track, leaving Daisy standing in the snow with her meagre possessions.

She looked around her, hardly able to make out the shape of the opposite valley sides, and then at the long, dark, gloomy house of Grouse Hall. Oh well, she'd have to make the best of it and face what was to be. She picked up her belongings and made her way down the flagged path to the porchway. The previously broken gate and crumbling walls of the garden had now all but disappeared, telling Daisy that there hadn't been much money or love spent on the Middleton family home. She stepped up into the dry limestone porch and felt sick as she reached for the brass door knocker, which was in the shape of a fox's head. The last thing she wanted was for Clifford to greet her. She couldn't face him – not yet; not until she knew how much Kitty knew of her family's actions.

The door opened and a flickering oil lamp lit up the face of its holder.

'So, you've had to come home then. After all your selfish trailings, you've had to bury your pride and be looked after by your kin.'

Daisy recognized the voice immediately – it was her sister Kitty's. But where was the rosy-cheeked, beautiful blonde woman she had left behind on that wedding day? Even by the light of the dim lantern, she could see how gaunt Kitty was. And why did she have an almost venomous tone to her voice? Daisy had always loved Kitty deeply, and in years past her sister would never have accused her of being selfish or proud.

'Kitty, it is so good to see you again. I'm in your debt for letting me come and stay with you.' Daisy wanted to hug her sister, but she sensed things had changed between them, even though her letter had been warm and had welcomed Daisy with open arms into her household.

'Aye, well, put the wood in t' hole. I'm not keeping this door open for ever and letting this winter weather in.' She closed the door against the winter chill.

Daisy picked up her bags quickly and followed Kitty into the darkness of Grouse Hall. She was shown the way by the rustling skirts of her sister and the dim golden light of her oil lamp.

'You needn't think I've made you any supper – we're not made of money, like the posh family you've come from, so I hope you've eaten.' Kitty turned and looked at her younger sister. She hated Daisy for leaving her in the dale with a husband who treated her as little more than a slut, and with parents who had wanted constant attention, while Daisy herself had the life of a free spirit, going where she wanted and with whom she wanted, only returning home when she thought she was ill and near death. 'When you wrote, I thought you were nearly on your deathbed, but you look well enough to me.'

'I've eaten earlier in the day, so it's no problem, Kitty dear. I'm feeling a lot better now. William sat beside me day and night for a week, nursing me back to health. I still feel weak, but I don't think I'm on my deathbed any more.' Daisy felt she wasn't wanted, and yet Kitty's letter had not come across like that.

'William? Who's William, and why couldn't you stay with him?' Kitty hovered with the lamp. The way it shone made her face look like a phantom.

'He was my boss, and was married with a wife and family. A better man you could not find this side of Leeds.'

'So you were his strumpet who got in the way – that's why you are back to us with your tail between your legs.' Kitty turned and looked at her younger sister.

'No, Kitty, it's not like that. I was genuinely ill. I nearly died, and probably would have done, if he had let his wife continue looking after me. I swear I think she poisoned me!' Daisy had not said it out loud before, but now that she was away from the Middleton household she dared to.

209

'Well, you keep your eyes to yourself while you are under this roof. I remember that you used to flutter your eyelashes at Clifford before we were married. No self-respecting sister would keep away from her newly wed sister for months, then run away from home because she was jealous.' Kitty spat out the words as she mounted the creaking stairs up to the bedrooms. 'You're in Clifford's father's bedroom. He died while you were sulking over my marriage.' She turned the key in the lock and bade Daisy enter the cold, unwelcoming room.

'Kitty, I'm sorry. It's true that I made eyes at Clifford, but I was young and foolish then. I'd never come between you and your husband. But you've been told wrongly about me sulking, and why I left Grisedale – please believe me. One day I'll be able to tell you, but not now.' Daisy didn't know if she was thankful her sister didn't know the truth, but at the same time her parents had made up a complete pack of lies to cover her true plight.

'I'll think what I want. Why should our parents lie to me?' Kitty bent and lit a small piece of candle that stood in a square brass candlestick by the side of the bed. 'Don't burn it long. This'll have to last you all week, for we aren't made of money. And lock your door. Clifford will be back later tonight, providing the snow stops falling, and he'll have his hunting mates with him, who can get a bit rowdy.'

Daisy stood by the side of the bed watching her sister disappear with the lamp.

'Oh and, Daisy, Clifford likes his breakfast as soon

210

as it's light. You might as well earn your keep while you are under our roof.' And with that she left, leaving her sister alone in the dim room.

Sitting on the edge of her bed, Daisy looked around her. The small stub of candle flickered and danced as a draught from the rotten window blew across the room. It was freezing, and the room smelled damp and fusty. The covers on the bed felt damp, and the fire in the fireplace was not lit; nothing made Daisy feel welcome. The one good thing was that Kitty was definitely oblivious as to why she had left home. Perhaps it was best that she left Kitty thinking it had been jealousy that had caused her to leave. Her sister would soon see how Daisy felt about the dastardly Clifford – there would be no love lost there.

She picked up the candle and stared out of the window. She could see nothing but the occasional solitary snowflake that flickered down too near to the window to survive, and her own ghostly reflection in the glass. She was tired and hungry. She'd lied to her sister; she'd not eaten since early morning, and now the hunger, cold and tiredness were getting the better of her. She moved across to the door and locked it; the last thing she wanted was Clifford entering her room in the middle of the night.

She shivered; it was too cold to undress, and so she wrapped her cloak around her and climbed into bed. Lying there, she wondered if the bed had been changed since old Middleton had died – from the smell of it, she doubted it. She shivered again and pulled the covers tightly around her. Why had she come home? Things were worse here than anything she'd put up with in Leeds. If she'd kept her distance from Angelina, she would have survived. The little bit of warmth from the covers gradually made her dozy and soon she felt her eyes closing. Perhaps in the light of day things would look better.

Voices from the room below made Daisy wake suddenly. It was not yet light, and she stared into the darkness as she heard a man laugh loudly from the room below her.

'Come on, Middleton, you know we know your hand. Put it down and let's get it over and done with, so that we can be away before the cock cries.' The deep, booming voice of a man she was not familiar with could be heard above the rest.

Then she heard her brother-in-law's voice and it made her shiver. She had not heard it since that fateful wedding day.

'Damn you, Oversby. I'm sure these cards are fixed. How else do you keep winning?' She heard Clifford Middleton's chair scrape across the stone flags as he rose in frustration. 'You'll have to wait for your brass – all I've got is on the table. I'll make it right on market day at Hawes, come Tuesday.'

'Aye, and I'm the Devil himself. How many times have I heard that from you? If you haven't the brass, don't play. You never learn, do you?'

A third voice could be heard. 'Let's away, Josh, it's

212

bloody freezing in here and it's still blowing a blizzard. I'm away to my bed and my wife to warm me.'

'Middleton, I'll take three ewes in payment. Fetch them up to Yore House when this weather breaks. And make sure they're not geld. You owe me more than three barren sheep, and well you know it.'

Daisy listened as the two other card players mounted their horses outside her window. Clifford swore at their departure and kicked out at something in the kitchen, making it crash onto the floor. She heard his footsteps coming up the stairway along the landing, and stopping short before her doorway. The adjoining bedroom door creaked and slammed shut behind him, and then she heard him climb into bed and demand sex from her sister. As she heard the knocking of the bedstead against the crumbling walls, she knew Clifford Middleton had not changed his habits since she had been gone. Indeed, if anything he had become worse. The cries of her sister, and the fact that he was paying his debts with farm stock, told her all she needed to know: Clifford Middleton was still a complete bastard. How could she stay at the hellhole of Grouse Hall? But how could she leave her sister now? She must regain Kitty's trust and make her strong enough to leave Clifford.

15

In the cold light of dawn Daisy was still awake. As she had listened to Clifford and his lovemaking, the memories of the afternoon when she'd given herself so unwillingly had come flooding back to her. Never again, she knew better now.

She rose from her bed and looked around the room. It was sparse, and the walls that took the brunt of the north winds were green with mould, while the wall connected to the barn and cowshed was in need of pointing, with a crack that ran the full height of the wall. She ran her fingers down the rubble-filled crack. She could just about smell the hay in the barn over the damp of the room. It was a comforting smell, reminding her of summer days spent playing with her older sister in the hay fields of the dale; days when they had picked wild flowers and caught tiddlers in the River Clough, then returned home only when they were hungry or when the day was drawing to a close. Where had those days gone? They had been over all too soon, and the dark days of puberty had taken their place.

What a fool she had been. And how cruel her parents had been. She wasn't the first innocent lass to have a child out of wedlock, and she wouldn't be the last. The shame was Clifford's, and well she knew it. The unmarked grave under the apple tree back home was his doing, and she prayed to God that she'd never forget it. She shivered as she looked out of the window. The skies were grey, and the dale outside was covered with a white blanket of snow. It looked as if another blizzard was on its way. How different from the sheltered streets of Leeds. Her mind wandered back to the city: Freddie would be lighting the fire at the shop and grooming Ginger; Angelina the witch would be feeding her Charlie; and William would be getting ready for another day of business. And Jim? Oh! Would Jim be waking up in the arms of Susie? She guessed so and her heart felt heavy. How could she have been so daft as to have set her cap at that man. It seemed she'd not learned anything after all.

Fearing the wrath of her sister, she quietly unlocked her bedroom door, thanking the Lord that she had a key to secure it with. She hid it in her skirt pocket – at least she'd be safe at night. She made her way down the dark, creaking stairs. The handrail was nearly black with the age of the bog-oak from which it was carved, and it was as smooth as a baby's bottom with the passage of time and with the hands that had run back and forth over it. It came to an end in two snarling carved lions on either side of the stairway, showing that Grouse Hall had been a residence of some importance in years past.

Now it was just a farmhouse, in need of drastic attention to stop the wind blowing through the cracks and the damp seeping into its occupants' bones.

The hallway was flagged with sandstone flags that had been rubbed smooth with the century's passage of feet, and the walls were panelled in the same bog-oak as the staircase, making it dark, with the only light coming in from an arched window at the end of the passage. In the heavy, grey light of the winter's morning Daisy felt her way along the edge of a wooden settle that was the only piece of furniture in the hallway. She knew where the kitchen was, from previous visits, and made for the last door along the passage. Passing the door where the early-morning card game had taken place, she noted the empty beer flagons and the chair that had obviously been in the way of Clifford's temper.

The kitchen was pitch-black when she entered. The wooden shutters blocked any light from entering, except for the thinnest sliver of grey light that picked up dust particles playing and dancing for Daisy's amusement. She made for the huge oak door and pulled the heavy bolt back, throwing the door open to the morning's light. She shivered in the cold blast of January's morning air. It was fresh as the ice that covered the horse-trough and it hurt her lungs as she breathed in deeply. How she'd missed the sight that lay in front of her: the glisten of frost on snow-covered grass, and the shimmering rolling dale, broken up only by a wooded copse and the straight lines of the slave-built drystone walls. She was home. How she'd missed it. She hadn't realized until now, but her heart had yearned to come home, while her head had been content with her city life.

A tear fell from her eye as she thought of her dead mother, and of her father locked in the newly built lunatic asylum at Lancaster, caged up like an animal. Did he deserve that? Had she driven him insane? God only knew. She turned, quickly brushing away the tear, and made to open one of the latched shutters, before closing the door behind her. The kitchen filled with light as both windows let in the grey illumination. Daisy looked around the kitchen. It was tidy; at least her sister kept a clean kitchen. The huge pine table was scrubbed as white as bone, and the oak dresser was adorned with good willow-patterned china, with the dainty, patterned brass handles of the drawers gleaming in the morning light. The huge lintel of the fireplace was adorned with two Staffordshire figures and above them hung two rifles.

Daisy turned as she heard what she took to be a dog scratching in its basket under the table. It took her by surprise, as she stood in silence. The blanket under which it lay moved and wriggled for a minute, and then went silent as the animal went back to sleep. Daisy riddled the dying embers of the previous evening's fire and added some of the twigs that were stacked at the fireside, blowing gently to allow the growing flames to catch hold of the bone-dry kindling. Soon the twigs were crackling and the flames dancing, sprite-like, as Daisy added some coal and logs to the newly lit fire. The warmth brought the room to life and she stood in front of the welcoming heat. It was the first time she had been warm since her journey on the train, and she was going to give herself a minute or two of pleasure to get warm before preparing the breakfast that her sister was expecting.

She looked over at the dog basket, as the covers moved and a tuft of black hair appeared over the side. It was no dog – dogs didn't have that length of hair, nor did they have ankles and feet. Granted they were filthy, but they definitely belonged to a child. Daisy was horrified. It was a child asleep underneath the kitchen table, not a dog! She dropped her skirts to her ankles, her legs now nice and warm, as she moved towards the stirring bundle. She bent down slowly and pulled the filthy cover back from around the child's head. A pair of bright-blue eyes looked back at her from under a mop of jet-black hair, and the child flinched as Daisy stroked its hair. Whether it was a boy or girl Daisy could not tell; the only thing she did know was that the child was terrified.

She spoke softly. 'I'll not hurt you, little one. What are you doing here? Have you no home?' Thoughts of her lost baby filled Daisy's head, and her mothering instincts took over as she looked at the waif.

The child looked at her, not daring to speak, and flinched as Daisy ran her fingers through its matted hair and around its chin, whimpering in fear of being chastised.

'Shush, little one, I'll not hurt you. Come and sit by the fire and get warm. You must be cold, for there isn't much warmth in that old blanket.' Daisy shook her head. How could her sister treat a child like this? It wasn't Kitty's, she knew that. Kitty had said in her letter that they were childless, and had complained that God had not had the grace to make her a mother. So why was the child being treated like a dog, and to whom did it belong?

The child shook its head and Daisy held out her hand, coaxing it to come out of the crate that was obviously where it slept. 'I'll go and fill the kettle and, while I'm not looking, you go and sit in that chair and warm your toes.' She smiled and walked over for the kettle that was hanging over the open fire. She pretended not to watch as she filled it from the kitchen pump and the child made a dash to the fireside. It was a boy. He looked about four, or five at the most, and was almost skeletal. He had only the flimsiest of rags covering his bones. Daisy smiled as she hung the kettle back over the flames to boil. The child didn't look up and Daisy didn't say anything. She just hummed a tune as she went into the pantry to see what could be made for breakfast. She returned with a full milk jug and an earthenware jar filled with oats.

'Would you like some milk and then some porridge, when I've made it?'

The boy shook his head, but she could tell there was hunger in his eyes, and she took no notice as she poured him a cup full of milk and pressed it into his small hands.

'Drink – it'll do you good.' Daisy watched as the

219

little boy lifted the mug to his lips and, without saying a word, drank the milk as if he'd never before been given anything like it in his life. 'There, you see, that will do you good. And later I'll give you some porridge. Now what's your name, little one, and where do you come from?'

'His name is Tobias, but we all know him as "Bastard", and that is what you will call him.' Clifford Middleton stood in the doorway to the hall, watching Daisy with the child. 'You'll not feed him, or keep him warm, or mollycoddle him, while I am around. I cannot abide the sight of the child.'

Tobias ran as fast as quicksilver to his hiding place below the blanket under the table. His eyes pleaded at Daisy to keep quiet and not to make trouble, as he did so.

'That's it, Bastard, know your place,' Clifford boomed at the scared child as he walked over to Daisy. 'So, you've had to come running back to your sister for help. Well, you can thank me for giving you a roof over your head. If you are to stop here, you've to pay your way, so you can forget some of the extravagant town ways that you'll have got used to.'

'I thank you for letting me stay with my sister, Clifford, and I hope to pull my weight while I am a guest at your house.' Daisy was not going to be belittled by the raging Clifford, and she'd start as she meant to go on.

Clifford stared at her. 'And I've not forgotten our transgression, the day before I married Kitty. I want it never to be mentioned. Kitty has never known about it and there is no reason for her to know now. Nothing became of our bonding, do you understand? The child was born dead, and that was an end to it. I have no feelings for you now, and never will have, so you need not worry that I'll be diverting my attentions your way.' He stood firm, holding the back of the Windsor chair in which the child had sat, while he waited for a response.

'I have no cause to come between you and my sister. And, as you say, the child we made between us was born dead, so we have no ties. All it brought was grief and pain, so I am happy to move on. There is no need to mention it again.' Daisy felt her legs go weak. She was no longer the besotted teenager, but she was still aware of her brother-in-law's temper. But she would stand her ground; he'd no longer use her and treat her like dirt.

'Now that I've made that clear, make me a drink of tea. My mouth is parched and my head feels like a sledgehammer has hit it.' Clifford sat in the chair next to the fire.

Daisy dared to look at him while she carried the singing kettle from the fire. He had aged; his dark hair was showing tinges of grey at his temples, but his high cheekbones still made him a handsome man. The women of the district must still consider him a catch – that was, until they visited Grouse Hall and saw the conditions in which he really lived.

'Damn these boots! Come here, woman, and pull

them on for me. My fingers have rheumatics, and I have no feeling in them in this cold weather.' Clifford cursed as the leather riding boot fell to the floor.

Daisy placed his cup of tea down by the side of the fire and bent down beside Clifford, her eyes avoiding his. She pulled up his holey socks and pushed his boots onto his feet. He pressed hard onto her thighs, nearly bringing tears to her eyes as he pushed them into the boots. She raised her eyes to his and could see that he was enjoying giving her pain.

'Just where I like my women – grovelling on the ground for me,' he sniggered.

'I'm sure you could have pulled them on yourself.' Daisy rose from her knees and pulled her skirt into place.

'Didn't you enjoy helping me, Daisy? Not to worry. Tomorrow I'll get Bastard to help me. He never complains.' Clifford took a gulp of his tea and stood up. He already knew that Daisy would protect the brat and was taking delight in making her worry for his safety. 'Tell that lazy wife of mine I've some business to attend to, and that she'll have to milk the cow. I'll be back later in the day. I'm sure you will both have plenty to talk about.' Clifford grinned.

Daisy noticed the laughter lines around his mouth and the glint in his eye, which she had once admired. Now she noticed how cruel he looked. How could she have fallen for such a shallow, bullying man she didn't know. Nothing meant anything to him.

Clifford grabbed a piece of stale bread from the dairy,

put his cloak on from behind the door and stepped out into the white countryside. The sound of his horse neighing could be heard as he shouted at it to make speed, despite the covering of snow. Daisy slumped into the chair next to the fire. Why had she returned to this hellhole and this devil of a man? She put her head in her hands and despaired.

'Don't worry, miss, he's always like that in the morning.' Tobias had crept out from his hiding place and was tapping Daisy on the shoulder. 'You get used to him. I just keep out of his way.'

Daisy raised her head and looked at the little boy who was more concerned for her than for himself, and she smiled at him. 'Come here. Has anybody given you one of these?' She threw her arms around the little waif and squeezed him tight. How he had survived at Grouse Hall, she didn't know. But from now onwards she would try and protect him.

'I don't know, miss. I can't remember being squeezed like you're doing.'

'Well, Tobias, as long as I'm here I'll give you one of these every morning, along with some breakfast, before anyone else is awake. Is that all right? But you keep it our secret, mind!'

'I will, I think, like a squeeze every day.'

Daisy ruffled his filthy hair and stirred the porridge that she had placed over the fire. 'Well, seeing as His Nibs has gone without any breakfast in him, you'd better have some porridge in that stomach of yours.' Daisy spooned a dishful of porridge out for Tobias and watched him eat it, after she'd added sugar and cold milk to cool it. She'd left Freddie behind in Leeds, but now she had gained Tobias. Tobias was going to be her reason to stay at Grouse Hall; she could not abide a child being ill-treated.

'This porridge should be half milk, half water, and there's too much salt in it.' Kitty sat across from her sister, scraping her earthenware bowl clean of the porridge she had just eaten two helpings of. 'And the fires are too high. Are you trying to keep the entire dale warm?'

Daisy looked across at her complaining sister. In the cold light of day she could now see what four years of marriage to Clifford had done to her. The blushing bride had turned into a wrinkled, grey woman who did nothing but complain. The tables had turned; Daisy was now the one with the bloom in her cheeks and a shine in her hair. Even after her recent illness she looked healthier than her sister.

'Whatever you say, Kitty. I'll make it with less milk tomorrow. Wasn't it nice getting up to a warm kitchen? Didn't it remind you of when we were little and used to sneak down to the warmth of the bakery and be treated to the first two buns of our dad's batch?'

'I don't remember anything like that. I only remember being clouted around the ear for getting in the way. You were always the favourite – the one our father favoured.' Kitty scowled at her sister. 'You could never do anything

224

wrong. That's why my mother died of a broken heart when you left.'

'Don't be stupid – it was you they favoured; you they thought the world of. They even fixed you up with Clifford to make sure you had a secure future. I've never seen my parents happier than on the day you walked down the aisle with him on your arm.' Daisy couldn't believe her ears. Kitty jealous of her – it was ridiculous, if only her sister knew what she'd been through. Her mother had died of smallpox, not a broken heart, and even though Martha had treated her badly, the thought of her being so ill had tugged on Daisy's heart strings, especially knowing that she had not been there to help her. She realized that she had grown up a lot since those days locked in her own bedroom, and that hating her mother and father was wrong. Now she knew how heartbroken they had been over her pregnancy. Her mother had been a good woman – always fair, always there to kiss her better – and Daisy should have been there to tell her how much she loved her, when she was dying.

'Fixed me up with Clifford! He raped me on our wedding night – there was no love shown at all, that night and every night for a month, and after. He was desperate for a son to show to his father before he died. And then, when I didn't deliver, he slept with every woman in the dale. I was ashamed of myself; I couldn't hold my head up anywhere we went, because I knew everyone was talking about us.'

'Oh, Kitty, I thought you were happy, that you'd got your man and the home you'd always wanted.'

'What I wanted! What I wanted was to do what you did: leave the dale and make a life for myself, not be pawned off in a deal between families.' Kitty slammed her spoon down, her eyes filling with tears. 'Then the final insult came when, one night, he brought Tobias home – or "Bastard" as he calls him now. He tried to tell me that he'd found him nearly dead in a ditch, but I knew it was the baby of one of his whores. He thought he would be bringing me comfort. The only comfort I got was when the child was asleep and I prayed for the Lord to take him, instead of me having to see his face every day.' Kitty sobbed, her face reddening and her chest heaving. She'd shut up her feelings for years, with no one to talk to, and now they were rushing out like pent-up demons.

'Shush, Kitty, think of the child. He shouldn't be hearing such talk. It's a wicked thing you say. He is innocent in all this – it's his parents who are to blame.' Daisy reached out for her sister's hand and squeezed it tight.

'Oh! He's heard worse – things a child's eyes and ears should never see or hear. Clifford has made sure of that. He takes delight in abusing the child; you see how he sleeps, like a dog under the table, fed only on leftovers. He'd have been better off dead years ago, but he is a determined soul, I give him that,' Kitty sobbed.

'Well, I'm here now. We will be stronger together.

We'll stand up to Clifford, now that I know your true feelings, and I'm sorry if I've caused you any pain.' Daisy looked across at her sister. She couldn't let Kitty know her own story: what her parents had really done to her, and the death of her baby. Daisy decided not to tell her sister about her marriage to Bob, and simply told her about seeking service in the Mattinson household. She thought the less she told her sister about her true life, the better it would be all round. They both needed a roof over their heads, so they both had to play Clifford's game and hope that none of their true feelings were found out. She told Kitty about the wicked Angelina and her downtrodden husband, and about Jim and his decision to marry Susie.

'I think it was the decision of Jim to marry Susie that really brought you home, not your illness, sister.' Kitty held Daisy's hand. 'I know that look in your eye – you used to look at Clifford the same way, and I used to get jealous.'

'I did not. He was yours, and all the world knew it.' Daisy blushed.

'Happen not. But I'm right about this Jim. Even though we've been apart a while, I can still tell when you have a soft spot for a man.' Kitty sniffed and rose from the table.

'He is a good man. He used to call me "Daisy petal" and make me laugh.'

'There are some good men out there, I'm sure, but the tarts always seem to win them. One day it will be your turn, Daisy petal,' laughed Kitty.

'It doesn't quite have the same ring to it!' Daisy hugged her sister. 'We'll stand strong; we've got each other now.'

'Aye, happen so. Only time will tell.'

16

'Two bloody women in the house and I still don't get my bloody dinner on time, you useless bitches.' Clifford sat, cursing, at the table. 'And where's the bastard at? Where have you put his bed?'

'Daisy thought he'd be better in the barn above the cow. It's colder there and he's out of your eyesight, Husband. Out of sight, out of mind – isn't that what they say?' Kitty poured her agitated husband a drink, and urged Daisy on to make haste with the dinner.

'I thought he smelled, and that you wouldn't want him under your feet.' Daisy smiled at Clifford as she poured the mutton stew into a bowl, urging him to get some bread to go with his meal. 'Besides, I've taught him to milk the cow – he's nearer the job there, and it's no good having a dog and barking yourself, as the expression goes.'

'Uhh! Never thought of that. Perhaps I should have married you instead of that useless bugger.' Clifford grunted and slurped the potato and mutton down his chin. The grease dribbled onto the collar of his clean, white shirt.

Daisy and Kitty looked at one another; they'd take the insults thrown at them as long as it gave one or the other peace.

'I've Oversby and his friends coming over tonight. He owes me in cards, but I don't want you womenfolk around. You'll only turn their heads and give me bad luck. Get yourselves to bed and out of the way, once you've laid out something for us to eat.'

Kitty looked at Daisy. Both of them knew that meant a night of rowdy gaming and bawdy songs and, for Kitty, a loveless session of sex.

'They must be keen on their cards, coming in this weather,' said Daisy innocently, knowing full well the conversation she had overheard.

'Aye, the weather's cold enough to freeze the balls off a brass monkey all right, but a game of cards lifts the spirits. And besides, we have hunt business to talk about, so mind you stay out of the way.' Clifford spat out a piece of neckbone from his stew before continuing to eat.

Kitty bade Daisy join her in the pantry. 'Take Tobias into your room tonight. They sometimes have sport with him, and I wouldn't want to see him hurt.'

She walked back into the kitchen. Standing with her hands on her hips, she said, 'There's some cold meats, bread and cheese in the pantry for your guests. When are you likely to be going to Hawes or Sedbergh? We could do with some supplies.' She was worried that the flour barrel was getting low and the sugar block was disappearing.

'When I've some brass, which – if I'm lucky – will be tonight. I'll show that bastard Oversby that I can play cards.' Clifford grunted.

'Well, I hope you win, else it's going to be meagre pickings until spring.'

Daisy didn't want him to win, for his ego would be unbearable, but at the same time the larder was empty. If it came to it, she'd spend some of her savings. After all she did have a roof over her head.

'Light me the fire in the parlour before you're away to your bed. It's too cold to be in that back room without some warmth. You can lay the food out on the dresser in there and all – save my legs. As you say, why do it yourself when you've a dog to do it.'

Daisy looked at the fire crackling in the grate and pulled the curtains around the oil lamp that was burning brightly in the window. She'd laid the food out, and now she'd wait on Clifford's guests before sneaking down the stairs for Tobias, to hide him in her room.

'Well, he's kept *you* quiet, the old dog.' A portly grey-haired man pushed open the door and grinned at Daisy. 'You must be that plain skinny sister that was at the wedding. You've certainly filled out now. Middleton said you were staying, but he didn't say how much you'd changed.'

Daisy curtsied. She recognized the voice – it was Joshua Oversby from Yore House. As he'd said, he had been at Kitty and Clifford's wedding; a little slimmer then and a little younger, but he'd been loud then, as he still was now. She should have recognized his voice on the first night she had heard it, but it had been buried in memories of the past. She knew him of old to be a big landowner with influence in the dale, but he was also known to either mend or break people with his contacts. She blushed as her skirts brushed beside him, in her hurry to leave the gambling den.

Oversby's hand reached out and grabbed her arm. 'What's the rush? We could have a little drink and a conversation together, that would be most agreeable.' His ruddy cheeks wobbled as he smiled at the blushing Daisy.

'I'm afraid my sister awaits – she is in need of me.' Daisy tried to pull her arm away from the grip of his thick, sausage-like fingers.

'Not half as in need as I am. I could do with a kiss from them red lips – it's a while since I bedded a woman.' Oversby pulled her close, his face inches from hers, so close that she could smell on his breath the onions he'd had for his supper.

'Let her go, you animal. You've come to play cards, not shag my sister-in-law. Seek your sport elsewhere tonight.' Clifford entered the room unexpectedly and glared at Oversby.

'I see how it is. Tired of the wife, so now you're bedding her sister. Two women under one roof – I've got to give you credit, Middleton, you live a full life.' Oversby let go of Daisy's arm and patted her on her bottom. 'It'll have to be the urchin afterwards that gives me my pleasure. Where is the little bastard? You've moved him from under the kitchen table.'

Daisy turned. 'You leave that li'l child alone.' She'd have hit him if she'd had the strength to hurt him.

'Whoa! A woman with spirit. By God, Middleton, you are blessed. Perhaps not with brass, but with plenty of other pleasures.'

'Shut up, Oversby! Daisy, go to your room and lock it, and then I don't have to make excuses for my so-called friends.' Clifford scowled and poured a drink for his visitor as the third member of the party arrived.

'By gum, we've had some sport already, Isaac. Middleton's got himself a mistress under the same roof as his wife. You must just have passed the pretty bitch.'

'Shut your mouth, Oversby. You don't know what you are saying.'

Daisy could hear Clifford's voice as she climbed the stairs. Joshua Oversby was revolting. She prayed she'd get to Tobias safely and that, once inside her room, they'd both be safe. She sat on her bed and listened to the low rumble of voices below her for what seemed to be an age. It was pitch-black outside and her stub of candle flickered in the draught from the window. Time to pick up her courage.

She unlocked her bedroom door and crept along the landing and down the dark stairs, along the passageway, glancing only once at the three men playing cards, smoking and drinking. She ran across the cold kitchen flags, with the dying embers of the fire as her only light, and unbolted the back door into the cold night's air. She quickly made her way into the adjoining barn by the light of the full moon.

'Tobias, Tobias, it's me, Daisy. Come here, I need you,' she whispered and jumped slightly as the cow in the byre acknowledged her presence with a steady low moo. Then she heard a movement above the hayloft and heard Tobias coming to her. 'Tonight you sleep in my room – it'll be warmer there.' The little boy nodded his head and clung to Daisy as they crept back into the house like mice, up the stairs to Daisy's room, locking the door safely behind them.

'Do you know that man, the one who tethered his horse in the barn tonight?'

'Yes, I don't like him,' Tobias whispered. 'He makes me do things I don't like to do.'

'Shh . . . You don't have to tell me. He'll not be doing that again. I'm here now, and I'll look after you.' Daisy sat on the bed and cuddled him. How could anyone treat a child so? Even Freddie back in Leeds had not been abused; he may have had a hard life, but he was loved. 'Come on, Tobias, jump into my bed and we'll keep one another warm. It'll be a treat for both of us.' Daisy pulled the little urchin towards her, putting her arm around him as she pulled the covers over them. She watched as his eyes slowly closed. Did his mother ever think of him? Who was she, and where was she now? She would be his mother tonight; and tonight he would sleep safely in her bed.

*

234

Daisy awoke with a start, the sound of raised voices from outside her window making her lie there in fright.

'Damn it, Middleton, where is the little brat you promised me?'

'Get yourself home – you're waking the whole household.' Clifford Middleton swayed uneasily at the garden gate as he watched his wife come to the window with a lit lantern to see what all the commotion was. He didn't agree with Joshua's fascination with young boys, but he'd no option but to go along with him. He needed his credit; and besides, he'd no feelings for the boy.

'Aye, come on, Josh. Have your way another night. I'm away to my bed.' Isaac was already mounted on his horse, and it was getting frisky with the noise.

'If he's hiding in that barn, I want him found.' Oversby staggered over to the mounting blocks at the side of the barn and sat down firmly on them. He felt sick; he'd eaten too much and had definitely drunk too much.

'Get on your horse, and we'll come back another night. Remember we've a hunt meeting tomorrow, so you need a clear head.' Isaac grabbed hold of the reins of Oversby's horse and pulled it in front of Joshua, to enable him to mount.

'The little bastard – he's hiding.' Oversby climbed the steps and slouched on his horse's withers, before climbing onto its back.

'Thank God for that! See you tomorrow, Middleton – if he makes it back,' Isaac shouted as he steadily paced out of the yard of Grouse Hall, with Joshua Oversby dutifully following.

Clifford raised his lit lantern in acknowledgement and watched the drunken pair make their way into the darkness of the night. He was wondering the same as Oversby: where was the little bastard? He'd go and have a look for him – he must be hiding in the barn. Clifford waved his lantern around the cow and horses that were standing quietly there, wondering why their night was being disturbed. He looked up towards the hayloft and stumbled between the animals, tripping over the cobbled byres and landing in the warm, soft hay. 'Come here, you bastard, where are you?' He lifted the lantern and looked around him. His head was spinning and his eyes felt heavy; the warmth of the animals and hay was making him sleepy. 'Don't worry – I'll find you. And when I do . . . I'll get you, I'll get you tomorrow.' Clifford yawned and felt his eyes closing and his head dropping onto his chest. It was time to sleep.

Daisy had lain still until she had heard the noise of Oversby and his sidekick leaving, and then she lay waiting for the noise of Clifford climbing the stairs. She stared into the darkness, listening to every noise that the night made and to the soft breathing of the little boy lying next to her. The night was silent – not even the hoot of a hunting owl could be heard. Suddenly her senses were awoken; there was a smell of smoke filling the room. She rushed from her bed and lit her bedside candle. Looking around the room, she saw that smoke was seeping through the gap in the wall from the barn.

She grabbed her dressing gown and shook the sleeping Tobias awake.

'Quick, Tobias, quick! The barn is on fire – we must save the animals.' Daisy unlocked her door and hammered on Kitty's bedroom. 'Kitty, come quickly. The barn's on fire. Is Clifford in bed with you?'

Kitty opened the door almost immediately. 'No, he never came to bed. Where is he?' Both women and the boy ran down the stairs, gathering bowls, buckets and pitchers from the kitchen as they flew out into the yard and round to the barn.

Flames were just starting to lick at the doorway, and the sound of horses and cows going mad with fear filled the air. Daisy drenched herself with icy water from the horse-trough, not even feeling the cold as she rushed into the fire-filled barn to release the terrified animals. She threw the bucket of water she was carrying at the heart of the fire as she quickly untied the cow and horses, which didn't need the encouraging slap across their flanks to tell them to get out of the blazing barn. Kitty and Tobias rushed back and forth from the trough with buckets of water, while Daisy caught her breath after being in the smoked-filled building.

Daisy gulped. 'Clifford's in there. I'll have to go back and save him – he's out cold.' She coughed and bent double, trying to get her breath.

'Leave him – we are better off without him.' Kitty stood for a minute with her bucket full, not daring to think about the words she had just said.

'I can't. He's Tobias's father – he can't be all bad.'

Daisy watched Kitty as she struggled with her thoughts. 'Come on, Kitty. I might be a bit dim, but I'm not blind: Tobias is the spitting image of Clifford – anyone can see that.' She turned and ran back into the barn, then grabbed hold of Clifford's legs and tried to pull him, but he was too solid. She turned around to see Kitty standing behind her. Kitty grabbed Clifford's other foot and together they pulled him out of the barn onto the cobbles.

'He's a heavy bastard!' puffed Kitty. 'Leave him, but let's save the barn. If he lives, he lives; but I need my home.' The three of them paused for a second, looking at the body of Clifford, whose left arm and hand were badly burned, before getting back to saving the barn. Clifford was nothing to any of them, but they needed a roof over their heads.

Bucket after bucket was thrown at the devouring fire. The two women and Tobias were exhausted, but by the light of day they had saved the barn and their home. The last few dying wisps of smoke rose into the air as Kitty, Daisy and Tobias gathered around Clifford while he moaned in pain and spluttered for breath.

'He's alive then. I hope he's grateful to us for saving him.' Kitty looked down at her husband, unimpressed that he was still in the land of the living.

'I suppose we'd better get him into bed and comfortable. Should we send for the doctor from Hawes?' Daisy looked at her sister.

'I've no money. Do you want to waste *your* brass on him?' Kitty looked at her sister.

'Just bed it is then. Grab his shoulder – we should be able to manage him between us.' Exhausted, Daisy bent down and, with Kitty and Tobias, dragged Clifford up and into the spare bedroom of Grouse Hall, as he screamed in pain. All three looked at the man they hated, useless and bedridden. Now who had the upper hand? He'd dance to their tune for a while – that is, if he lived!

The tin bath in front of the kitchen fire was filled with steaming hot water, as both sisters took it in turns to clean their smoke-covered bodies and change into clean clothes.

Daisy towelled her hair dry while Kitty sat next to the open fire. 'Your turn, Tobias. Strip off out of them rags. I've found you a vest and shirt out of the bedding box from upstairs – they'll do until we can get you something better.'

'I'll drown in there.' Tobias looked at the half-filled bath and the block of carbolic soap waiting to scrub him clean. He'd never had a bath before.

'Nonsense! Come on, get in.' Daisy grabbed his arm and pulled the loose-fitting rags over his head. She stopped for a second, catching her breath – Tobias's body was a mass of bruises – and then glared at Kitty.

'I didn't know, Daisy. Honestly, I didn't know he'd been hit that hard.' Kitty was taken aback at the sight of the whippet-thin lad and his bruises.

'Come on, Tobias, in you pop. Let's get you clean, and we'll cut this mop of hair afterwards. It is hard to tell if you're a boy or a girl. And tonight, Tobias, you'll eat at the table with us. Won't he, Kitty?'

'I suppose so – just this once.'

Daisy rolled up her sleeves and washed the lad gently with a flannel and the soap. She doubted if his skin had ever seen the light of day, as she gently scrubbed the dirt of years off his little body. Then, tipping his head back, she washed his long, black hair – the hair that told everyone that he was Clifford's son. She rubbed him dry and dressed him in an adult's shirt and vest that she'd found in the bedding box next to her bed, tying it around his waist with string and folding the sleeves up to his wrists.

'There, at least you look clean. Now sit up here and let's tackle this hair.' Tobias sat still on the kitchen chair while Daisy clipped his hair short and even, the locks falling down onto the floor all around him. She stood back and admired her work. 'Quite the young gent, Master Tobias.' She smiled as the young boy looked at his reflection in the dirty bath water. 'Let's keep you that way.'

Daisy looked at her sister. She was weak, but she should have stood up to that bully, Clifford. No one should have let a child be treated like that.

17

The snow had melted and, although it was only mid-February, the weather was quite mild. Daisy looked at the horse that she had harnessed to the trap. She hoped she'd strapped it in correctly; it was a long time since she'd harnessed a horse, but they were nearly out of food.

'Are you sure you dare go into Hawes? It's a long way to go on your own.' Kitty stood at the rundown garden gate, watching her sister tighten the horse's girth and check the harnessing.

'I'm not on my own. Tobias is coming with me, and he needs some shoes.' Daisy climbed up into the trap and sat next to the little lad, who was beaming from ear to ear. 'Besides, if I don't, what are we going to eat? And I need some ointment for Clifford from the apothecary's, to ease his pain a little.'

Daisy flicked the reins and clicked her tongue and the horse stirred into action. She swayed with the action of the gig, as the pair of them set off down the twisting track onto the road to Hawes. She looked at her sore red hands; they were no longer the hands of a cook and soft-skinned shop assistant. She let the horse take a bit of slack; it obviously knew the way well. It had been a hard four weeks since the barn had burned and Clifford had been bedridden, leaving the running of Grouse Hall and its livestock to her and Kitty. She'd fed the sheep throughout the cold snap, milked the cow, cleaned out the badly damaged barn and been nurse-maid to the complaining Clifford when necessary. She hadn't had time to think of her past life in Leeds or to write a letter, until last night, and that was another reason to go to Hawes, to post it to the Mattinson family and tell them her news.

She'd sat and thought a long time before putting the words together. To say it was heavily edited would be telling a lie – it was barely telling the truth at all. All the negatives had not been touched upon, and the positives at Grouse Hall had been exaggerated out of all proportion. She didn't want the Middletons to worry about her situation. Besides, it was looking brighter, now that Clifford was off the scene for a while. He seemed to have found a streak of humility since his accident, and Kitty and her sister were beginning to pull as a team, even though Kitty still could have a nasty tongue in her head, when it came to Tobias.

'All right, Tobias?' Daisy looked at the young lad, who was speechless and quiet. He looked quite re-spectable now. She'd cut the old shirt down to size and had made him a little suit out of what she had found in the bedding box. The clothes must have been old

Tobias Middleton's when he was alive, so it seemed appropriate that the lad was wearing his cast-offs. All that was missing now were shoes.

'I'm all right. I've never been this far down the dale.' Tobias's mouth was wide open as he gazed all around him.

'That's the railway.' Daisy pointed out the railway track that ran all the way down the dale. 'I came back from Leeds on a train. It's like a big carriage on metal wheels, and the engine at the front puffs out steam, making it run along the track.' Daisy tried to explain to the little boy, as his eyes widened in disbelief. 'We might see one, if we are lucky. I'll stop at the viaduct at Dandry Mire. I can spare a minute or two to watch for a train.' She smiled as Tobias asked her what a viaduct was. There was so much that the little soul didn't know.

She pulled the horse up at the side of the road and looked across at the viaduct. It was short and stumpy, compared with the towering viaduct at Ribblehead. They sat in silence as they waited for the train. The smell of peat bog was on the air, sharp and clear, a mixed smell of heather and wild moorland grasses combined with the rich red peat of the fells. Daisy breathed it in; she loved the smell, and the cool northerly wind that was blowing and the snow-capped high fells. She sat back and closed her eyes for a second or two. Nowhere could compare to home, and she was glad to be back.

'Shhh . . . Tobias, can you hear that? Listen.' Both of them listened carefully as a train could be heard shunting down the line. 'That's it blowing its whistle to warn people it's coming along the line. It must not be stopping at the junction.'

Tobias watched as the engine and goods carriages shunted down the track and across the viaduct. Steam billowed from its funnel as it pulled its heavy load along the long drag – a name that the railway men gave to the hardest piece of the Settle-to-Carlisle railway line.

'It's like a monster – look at all that steam!' Tobias watched until it disappeared into the Ais Gill cutting, the last wisp of steam floating down in front of him.

'One day, Tobias, I'll take you for a ride on one. You'll enjoy it.' Daisy laughed as the little boy's bottom lip trembled as the train was lost to the surrounding hills.

'I'd like that, I think. It might eat me, though.' He looked sombre.

'It won't eat you, Tobias. It just eats coal, like we put on the fire – that's what makes it work and it's where the steam comes from.' Daisy smiled as she whipped the horse into motion. 'Right, let's get to Hawes and get some shopping done.'

It was market day in Hawes. The centre was full of farmers and their stock, and rushing housewives who were chatting with neighbours and market traders. Nobody looked at the young woman and small child as they tied the horse up outside the grocery shop run by Luke Allen. Tobias clung to Daisy's skirts as she handed her list of groceries across to the lad she knew to be Luke's son. Her memory flashed back to the time when her mother had said they would be a good match. She might have been right, for he was a good-looking man.

'Are you waiting for this?' He looked up from the long list, and Daisy noticed his soft brown eyes.

'No, I've some shoes to order for the lad.' Daisy nearly tripped over her words, looking at the handsome man in front of her.

'Have you an account?'

'Well, I think he will have, but I don't suppose there will be any credit on it.' Daisy thought that if Clifford had any credit, she'd use it. Otherwise she would pay and be done with it. 'I'm stopping at Grouse Hall – it'll be under Clifford Middleton?' She watched as he opened his account book and then closed it sharply at the mention of Clifford's name.

'You're right – he ran out of credit a long time ago, and my father's been chasing him for what he owes for months. Now, what am I going to do with this order? Have you money to pay for it?' A long sigh came out of the mouth of Samuel Allen as he waited for an answer.

'I've money. Tot it up quickly and let me know what I owe for today's shop, and I'll try and bring some to knock off his slate next time.' Daisy felt embarrassed as Samuel pencilled in the prices next to the goods. The farmers' wives were whispering behind her back. This was the one they'd heard Joshua Oversby talking about – the tart – and they started talking loudly about the young lad who was with her. She was Clifford

Middleton's floozy, but who was the father of the child, and where had he come from?

'It'll be two guineas for all this. Do you want me to put it in your cart?' Sam looked up at the embarrassed young woman, noticing a flush in her cheeks.

'I've only come in the trap – will it fit in that?' Daisy felt stupid, for she'd never thought about how to get all the flour, sugar and other goods home and knew there was not enough room for her, Tobias and the groceries. She opened her purse and passed him two guineas out of her earnings from the Mattinsons.

An even longer sigh was expelled by Sam. 'I'm going down to Sedbergh tomorrow. Do you want me to deliver it?' He looked up at the eavesdropping customers, who were all pretending to be interested in anything but the young woman who was staying at Grouse Hall.

'Would you? That would be a grand help. I'm sorry – I never thought of getting it home. I was too worried that I wouldn't be able to handle the horse and trap. It's been a long time since I've driven a horse.' Daisy put her arm around Tobias, who was feeling claustrophobic by now, with all the curious womenfolk around.

'I'll do that – be with you about twelvish.' Sam looked at Daisy. Now he knew who she was, but by, she was a bonny woman. It was a pity she was Clifford Middleton's floozy. Hawes had been full of the gossip spread by Joshua Oversby, and of the sisters sharing Clifford.

Daisy smiled and put an arm around Tobias, guiding him through a sea of skirts towards the doorway. She held her head up high as she heard one of the mouthy women say loudly, 'I don't know how she dare show her face. And look at the child – he's no shoes on his feet.'

Daisy pulled Tobias close to her and turned around.

'I'm not deaf, or daft. I am Kitty Middleton's sister, Daisy. I've come back home because I've been ill. I have no man in my life and, contrary to Joshua Oversby's gossip, I do not sleep with my sister's husband.' She felt the colour rising to her cheeks in anger. 'And I am about to buy Tobias some shoes, even though he's no kin to me. Is there anything else you need to know?' She stood at the doorway, looking at the aghast crowd and at the smiling face of Samuel Allen. Not a word was said as the shoppers decided they needed something urgently from the shelves.

'See you tomorrow, Daisy,' shouted Sam as the door closed behind her.

'You look happy this morning. What's wrong – did the chemist say yesterday that I'd not long to live?' Clifford growled and winced as Daisy rubbed some ointment on his arm and hands.

'There's nothing wrong with you but this arm, and it is mending, I can tell – the skin is finally knitting.' Daisy washed her hands in the bowl by the side of the bed and bandaged Clifford's arm. 'Another week or two and you can get back to work. Kitty and I are ready for a rest.'

'You mean you can't run this farm without me. Useless

bloody women!' Clifford grunted, then walked over to the window and looked out. 'Who's this bugger coming up the road?'

Daisy rushed over and looked out behind him.

'Oh, bugger! It's Luke Allen's lad – he'll be after some brass!' Clifford swore, knowing that the only visitors they ever got at Grouse Hall were after money that he owed them.

'He's delivering some groceries. How did you think we were going to live, on what was in the pantry?' Daisy wiped her hands on her skirts. 'I went and ordered some yesterday and paid, so it hasn't gone on your account. You've no credit anyway.'

She walked to the door, leaving Clifford watching Samuel Allen delivering goods from the back of his cart.

'I've put your order in the pantry. Your sister showed me where to put it.' Sam Allen looked at the woman who had stood her ground so well the previous day.

'Thank you. I'm grateful that you let me place an order and delivered it – you could have done neither, and I wouldn't have blamed you.' Daisy was going to be honest.

'Nay, I looked at that lad that was with you, and I couldn't have let him go hungry – he's like a whippet anyway. That reminds me: I took the liberty of picking these up from the cobbler's – I thought I'd save you the trip into Hawes. There was enough gossiping yesterday for one week.' Sam took a little pair of wooden and black-leather clogs from behind his back. 'I thought his feet would be frozen without them.' He smiled as he passed them across to Daisy.

She blushed as she took them from Sam. 'Thank you, that was kind of you. Can I make you a cup of tea and a sandwich for your bother?' She wanted him to stay. It was the first decent company she had met since she had come to Grouse Hall.

They heard a loud knocking on the floor rafters above, as Sam thought of a reply.

Kitty appeared in the doorway. 'That's Clifford with his walking stick – I'll go and see what he wants.' She decided to make herself scarce and to shut her impatient husband up, for she could see the looks that Sam Allen was giving her sister and decided to let nature take its course.

'I'll stop for a drink. Don't worry with the sandwich – I'll be fed down in Sedbergh.' Sam watched as Daisy lifted the kettle and poured the scalding water into the teapot. She was an attractive woman, but she'd got a wedding ring on her finger.

'Milk?' Daisy smiled and pulled up a chair across from Sam, who had made himself at home, sitting down at the table.

Sam nodded. 'Where's the lad at then? Don't put his new shoes on the table – it'll give you bad luck.' He moved the tiny pair of clogs off the table onto the floor.

'He's out in the barn. The cat's just had kittens and he's playing with them.'

Sam sipped his tea. 'Are you stopping here, or are

you returning to your husband before long? Tell me to mind my own business, but I couldn't help but notice the ring . . .'

'Oh, this! I sometimes I forget I have it on. My husband's been dead nearly five months now. We were only just married and he died on our wedding night. I don't know why I wear it – habit, I suppose.' Daisy sipped her tea slowly. 'And you – are you married, have any family?'

'No, my father keeps playing hell with me, says he'll have no one to leave the shop to, if I'm not careful.' Sam gulped his tea back. He'd found out what he wanted to know. Daisy at Grouse Hall was free of a husband. He'd deliver the groceries any time, to see the blush on those cheeks.

'Families – you can't do owt about them. Look at me here.' Daisy's heart fluttered as Sam rose from the table.

'Well, you know where I'm at, and I'll call in on my way down to Sedbergh. I go there every Wednesday. My father sells his bread there, and I go and pick him up.'

Daisy's eyes clouded over and her throat choked with tears. 'I used to go to Sedbergh market with my father – we used to go early on a morning and come back by dinnertime. It seems an age ago.'

'I remember him. My father took over his place in the market when he became ill. Is he still in the Moor?' Sam looked serious. He didn't know how to approach the fact that Tom Fraser was in the lunatic asylum at

Lancaster Moor. 'I'd forgotten you were his daughter. I'd better make sure our bread's all right, if you buy some.'

'Yes, he's still there. I don't think they'll ever let him out. I've not been to see him – we lost contact a long time ago. Don't worry about the bread. I make my own.' Daisy smiled.

'Well, we'll have to compare recipes.' Sam lingered next to the open door. 'See you shortly, Daisy.'

'Yes, see you soon.'

She watched him trundle down the track from Grouse Hall and wave as he reached the main road.

'He seems like a good match. Happen our mother was right about one thing,' whispered Kitty in her sister's ear.

'I don't know what you mean.' Daisy gazed after Sam. She wouldn't admit it, but perhaps Kitty was right.

18

'So, are you going to tell me about this lass?' Luke Allen looked at his son as he stacked the highest shelf in the grocery shop. It was Sunday morning and the shop was closed, so Luke thought it was as good a time as any to ask his son about the lass he'd been visiting.

'Why, who's been talking about me, and what's it got to do with them?' Sam blew the dust off the top of a tin of Lyle's Golden Syrup, placing it carefully back on the shelf, before climbing down the ladder. He wiped his hands on the cream shop apron and looked at his father.

'Well, let's just say the whole of Hawes has been telling me about my lad wandering down the road to Grouse Hall on a Wednesday, when I'm away at Sedbergh. And now you've taken to disappearing of a night, so it must be serious business.' Luke looked at his son. He wanted the best for him – not some woman without a penny to her name. He had a business to inherit, so he'd need a worker and someone with a business head.

'Well, you know damn well know who she is – she's

Tom Fraser's lass. And yes, I know Tom is in the lunatic asylum; and yes, I know Clifford Middleton is the bastard from hell and owes us money. But Daisy is different.'

Sam had known this was coming. Folk had been whispering behind his back for weeks. He was surprised that his father hadn't tackled him earlier.

'Aye, I ken her. She buggered off when she was only just old enough – broke her mother's heart and sent her father crackers. Not a good report, lad. And now, like you say, she's living with that bugger and her sister. You could do better than that.' Luke stamped down in front of him the paperweight that until then had been holding the weekly invoices in place on the counter, and looked at his son.

'She was thrown out by her father,' snapped Sam. He never argued with his father as a rule, but for Daisy he would.

'Aye, and why? That's what I want to know. She was the apple of his eye on market days. He'd come in here with her and she could do no wrong. And then all of a sudden, as soon as she got to a decent age, she was gone.'

'Well, I tell you what, Father – this will please you . . . You know those new brands of lemon cheese and onion relish that you are stocking? The ones from Mattinson Brothers of Leeds? Well, those are her recipes – she taught the brothers all they know. That's where she's been: cooking for Mattinson's in Leeds. She told me that the other night. Now think on that; she'd be an asset to the firm if I wed her.' The words were out before Sam could stop them. He'd no intention as yet of marrying anyone, but he was angry at being dictated to.

'Wed her? You'll do no such thing – over my dead body will you wed that lass. She's spinning you a yarn, my lad. She knows you are worth a bob or two, and she's plotting. Her father married her sister off to Middleton, thinking he'd money, but he soon found out different.' Luke slammed the glass paperweight down hard again, with the palm of his hand, nearly making it shatter.

'I'll do what I want, Father. I'm a grown man now, and I'll prove to you that she's not who you think she is.' Sam untied his apron and threw it down on the counter. 'You can stack your own bloody shelves. I've better things to do with my time.'

With that he made for the shop door, slamming it behind him. Luke stood for a moment, trying to calm his temper down, before going over to the shelf where the Mattinson's preserves had just been freshly stacked. He picked up a jar of lemon cheese. He'd got it in only last week. The firm was a fairly new one – Daisy couldn't have known that. He glanced at the label, looking carefully at the address, before unscrewing the lid and dipping his finger in the rich, yellow preserve. He licked it quickly as it spilt down his chin. By, it was good. If she could make him that, he could cut out the middle man: more profit for him. Perhaps he'd been hasty. He'd see what the lad did, and perhaps Daisy could make him a pot of lemon cheese, to prove she gave these Mattinson

Brothers the recipe. Aye, that's what he'd do. Perhaps the lad was not that daft after all; he'd get Sam to ask for a pot.

'Kitty, Kitty, whatever's the matter?' Daisy rushed to her sister's side. She'd heard the knock on the door, but hadn't bothered to come downstairs.

Clifford snatched the letter from his sobbing wife's hand and read it quickly:

> *Lancaster Moor Asylum*
> *Lancaster*
> *April 21st, 1876*
>
> *Dear Mrs Middleton,*
>
> *It is my sad duty to inform you that your father died late yesterday evening. He had been very disturbed of late and we had been struggling to control his moods. The nurse went into his room and found him hanging by the window from his sheets. I know this is distressing news for you and your family, but the sanatorium did all it could for this poor lost soul. It would seem that his demons got the better of him.*
>
> *He is to be buried in the hospital grounds, unless you would like to dispose of the body elsewhere. Please let me know of your wishes.*
>
> *Please accept our deepest sympathies.*
>
> *I am your obedient servant,*
>
> *Dr P. Snowdon*

'So, the old bugger's dead.' Clifford crinkled up the letter in his good hand. 'Best thing really – no life in that bloody spot; couldn't make head nor tail of nowt there.' He sat in the chair and poked the fire as he watched Daisy comfort Kitty between sobs. Tobias sat at the back of the room, not understanding what the wailing was all about and keeping out of the way of the now-recovered Clifford.

'He was my father.' Kitty lifted her head and looked at Clifford with swollen eyes.

Daisy didn't know what to feel. This was the man who had belted her to within an inch of her life, killing her baby and nearly making her take her own life. Yet she felt such a pain, as if part of her life had gone for-ever. He was her father. She remembered his sparkling blue eyes looking at her with love, and the times he had carried her on his shoulders when she was a child. She remembered how she had loved him; back then he had been everything to her. She hugged Kitty, but she couldn't cry; instead mixed-up memories of good and bad times ran through her head, playing with her feelings for the man she had once respected and loved. But she also remembered how she had felt when she had stood on the chair and contemplated ending her life. She never wanted to feel like that again.

'We'll let the hospital bury him there, to save money. Besides, I don't want to drive all the way from Lancaster with a dead man in the back of my cart – not with my bad hand. I wonder if he'd any brass, and if he'd made a will. That mill house up Grisedale is definitely his:

that'll be worth a bob or two, lass. Your old fella might have got us out of the mire, by dying.' Clifford felt more like himself for the first time in weeks. 'Bloody hell, I never thought of that. I'll go and see his solicitor in the morning. Good job the old bugger's dead – he's timed that just right.' Clifford poked the fire with vigour, thinking about the inheritance, as Kitty and Daisy looked on in disbelief at the cold-hearted bastard.

'What can I do for you, Mr Middleton?' Henry Winterskill looked Clifford Middleton up and down. He looked a mess. He'd heard that Clifford had been badly burned in an accident at the farm, but the man who used to think he was cock o' the midden looked a bit rough at the edges.

'My wife's father has died, and I wondered if he'd left a will?' Clifford hated Henry Winterskill. As well as being the local solicitor, he was on the local bench, and Clifford had been in front of him a time or two.

'Have you a death certificate?' Henry looked at him in the same way a fox looks at its kill.

'Nay, they haven't sent it yet. My missus wrote to say to bury him at Lancaster, and they'll send it then.' Clifford looked around the office: the walnut wall clock ticked steady time, the pendulum swinging the seconds away, as he hung on the next sentence to come out of Henry's mouth.

'Well, I can't do anything without it. I need proof of his death before I can do anything.'

Clifford couldn't hide his disappointment. 'But you've

got a will. He has made one? He has left some brass?'
He could feel the money in his pocket already.

'Yes, I have his will. However, when you do bring
the death certificate, bring your wife and her sister, as
it is of their concern, not yours. I believe Daisy is back
in the district and living with you?'

'Aye, she is, but he'll not have left her owt.' Clifford
was annoyed. Why did he want to do business with
women, especially with Daisy? Her father had hated
her by the time she'd left Grisedale in shame. But at
the same time he was secretly worried that bloody old
Fraser had named him as Bastard's father in his will
and had told the world that Daisy was the mother.
'There's nowt to upset my wife in his will, is there?'
Clifford looked at the slimy Henry Winterskill. How he
hated asking him that question.

'Are there any other factors or points you want me
to be aware of?' Henry loved having Clifford over a
barrel and watching him squirm, for he knew what a
horrible person he was. It would give him great satisfaction to read Tom Fraser's will out, just to watch
Clifford's face.

'No, no. I just thought, with having two daughters,
he might have done something daft.'

'Not at all, but they are both beneficiaries and, as
such, should be here to hear the will together.' Henry
rose and offered Clifford his hand. 'See you next Tuesday.
You should be in receipt of the death certificate by then.'

'Right, Tuesday it is.' Clifford let out a sigh of relief.

*

Outside, in the sharp April sunshine, Clifford looked at the market square of Hawes. He'd not been in town for such a long time. The Crown was thronged with customers. He put his hand in his pocket, pulling out a handful of silver and copper, perhaps just enough for an odd drink. He looked at his scarred red and twisted hand; he'd not attract many women with that by his side. Damn that lad – it was his entire fault; everything was the little bastard's fault. And now the women of the house were protecting him.

'Middleton – bloody hell, man, you're back in the land of the living.' Joshua Oversby slapped him across the back and shouted as Clifford entered the inn. 'Bad do about the hand, old chap. Still, you look as if you're still up for it.' Oversby screwed up his nose as he looked at Clifford's hand, making everyone else around him look at his disfigurement. 'You're just the man I want, when I think about it.'

'Why? Are you after some money? 'Cause if you are, you're out of luck. I've just enough on me to buy an odd drink, and that's my lot.' Clifford was mad with the loud-mouthed soak, for everyone had shied away from him, now they realized how bad his arm looked.

'Nay, nay, man. Let me buy you a drink, I've a proposal for you that'll get you in the good books of the hunt – you know how much they like their sport.' Oversby ordered the serving girl to bring them a gill each, and then he whispered his request in Clifford's ear.

*

259

'So, we've both to go down to the solicitor's on Tuesday?' Kitty and Daisy stood around Clifford Middleton as he ate his breakfast.

'Aye, that's what he said – he wants you both there, with the death certificate.' Clifford slurped down his porridge and wiped his chin with his sleeve. 'Where's that little bastard at? I've a job for him that's right up his street.'

'He's outside; just you let him be, he's all right where he's at.' Daisy jumped to Tobias's defence.

'Aye, well, there's a delivery coming from Oversby, and Bastard's going to look after it.'

'He's not going anywhere near that old letch – I'll not let him.' Daisy stared at Clifford.

'He'll be nowhere near him. Oversby's dug out some fox cubs from their den under Winder Fell and, instead of killing them, he wants someone to raise them. They'll be easy prey for the young hounds in the hunt this autumn. Some sport for our hunting friends.' Clifford grinned.

'You cruel bastards! Tell him to do his own dirty work – he knows he's not right. That's why he's got you rearing them.' Kitty picked Clifford's bowl up from under his nose and slammed it down in the stoneware sink. 'That's not sport, and you know it – they'll be like pets by the time they are released.'

'Hold your noise, woman! He's knocked some of what I owe him off my tab. I'll do owt to get him off my back.' Clifford scraped his chair back along the stone flags as he lost his temper. 'And you keep your mouth shut. I'll do what I want with the bastard.' His finger pointed directly at Daisy. 'You've interfered enough, while I've been in my bed, but I'm back now. And don't think I don't know about you and that simpering Sam Allen – you're the talk of Hawes.'

'It's nothing to do with you anyway – you don't own me. I've paid my way, and more besides, while you've been ill.' Daisy stood her ground. There was no way Clifford was going to go back to his bullying ways with her; he owed her his life.

'Why you . . . ' Clifford lifted his hand, stopping it an inch from Daisy's face.

'Go on then. That'll look good at the solicitor's.' Daisy glared at him without flinching. He was a bully, nothing more, and she was not going to be the dumbstruck, shaking wreck that he wanted her to be.

'So your father knows about me?' Daisy walked by Sam's side. They'd become close friends over the spring months and she found him easy to talk to.

'Aye, he tackled me in the shop on Sunday. You could say we had words.' Sam went quiet.

'Let me guess: he said I wasn't good enough for you, that you knew nothing about me and that I was only after your brass?' Daisy sat down next to the trickling stream, and picked and smelled a kingcup that was growing next to the bubbling beck.

Sam looked at Daisy. 'Summat like that.'

'It's only what my father would have said to me, if it had been the other way round. Besides, everybody knows everybody's business; and what they don't know, they make up. I'm the selfish sister who left her parents, and only came back when one was dead and the other as near as damn it.' Daisy dropped the kingcup and wiped her eyes.

'I'm sorry about your father – it must be hard.' Sam squeezed her hand.

'You know, I thought I wouldn't be bothered, but the more I think about him, the more I realize how much I loved him. With my mother it was different, for she always favoured my sister. But until I got older, I was always my father's favourite.'

'You did right to leave, Daisy. It wasn't your fault that you fell out, I'm sure he realized in the end.' Sam put his arm around her and held her tight. He wiped away the tear that ran down her cheek and looked into her hazel eyes. Dare he kiss her? He'd never tried to kiss her before. He reached down, closed his eyes and kissed her firmly on the lips, and then kissed her again and again. Daisy pushed him back gently, smiling. 'Sam, are you sure? This is beginning to be more than a friendship.' She had never felt this way before. Yes, there had been Jim; but this love was being returned, and this love had to be solid.

'I'm sure. I knew the moment you walked into the shop and stood your ground with the local gossips.' Sam twisted her fine brown hair around his fingers while she looked at him.

'All right, but we make it right with your father. I don't want to come between you two.' Daisy thought of her own family and felt guilty for not telling Sam the whole reason for her eviction from the family home. He must never know about Clifford and the dead baby. If he did find out, he might think her a loose woman and believe that the gossips in Hawes were right in their assumptions about her.

'That's an easy 'un, lass. Make him a pot of your lemon cheese – convince him that you worked for Mattinson's. He's never shut up about it since I told him; he's seeing pound signs in front of his eyes.' Sam lay back and laughed.

'Here I go again. Men only want me for my cooking skills,' laughed Daisy.

'Nay, I want more than that, lass.' Sam laughed and pulled her down beside him.

'Sam Allen, what would your father say?' Daisy smiled.

'*Remember to ask her for the bloody recipe.* That's what he'd say.'

19

'Firstly, may I give you my condolences on behalf of Winterskill & Winterskill. Your father was always an honourable, proud man, and we were glad to be of service to him when his days of health were better.' Henry Winterskill looked at the two sisters and at that rogue, Clifford.

'Here is the death certificate. He was buried in the Moor's cemetery on Friday.' Kitty passed across the certificate to Henry with a shaky hand.

'Mmm, yes – it all looks in order.' Henry opened the deceased man's files. 'Now, you must understand that your father was not a wealthy man. I believe he'd given you a healthy dowry before he was taken ill, Kitty, and then he had the expense of your mother's funeral just before he himself was admitted to the asylum. Then there was his expense—'

'How much did the old bugger leave?' Clifford could wait no longer.

Henry Winterskill coughed. 'Along with his house at Grisedale and his possessions, he left ten guineas, two shillings and tenpence in hard cash, which will just about cover my expenses.'

'Who gets the bloody house? At least we can sell it!' Clifford was desperate for money – he needed it.

'Mr Middleton, if you will keep interrupting, I shall have to ask you to leave. This is your wife's family affairs, not yours.' Henry leaned over the desk. 'The property at Grisedale is left to . . .'

The whole group held their breath as he double-checked the papers.

'The property is left to Daisy, on the understanding that she gives the grandfather clock and the oak dresser and its contents to her sister, Kitty, if Daisy is in agreement.' Henry smiled at the ashen-faced woman.

'Nooo! The bloody old bastard! What's he done that for, when he knew I needed the bloody money? It's me who's looked after his bloody daughter all these years.' Clifford lashed out with his walking stick, knocking the small side-table over in the immaculate office. 'The bastard!' He swore and stamped around the office, his stick hitting the side of his leg in anger.

'Sir, I don't like your manner. This is a will-reading and your temper does not befit the event.' Henry spoke sternly to the fuming Clifford, before giving his attention to Daisy.

'Congratulations, Daisy! I can give you the keys to the property.' He reached into his desk drawer and pulled out a bunch of keys that Daisy recognized from her childhood, and passed them to her.

She took them with a shaking hand, speechless that

her father had left the old home to her. He did love her after all. Her eyes filled with tears as she handled the keys of her family home, with visions of her father in all his moods playing in her mind.

'But what about us? The old bugger's left us nothing, except some worm-eaten furniture.' Clifford was furious, while Kitty just wept. She knew she had never been the favourite – her father had been quite blunt about that.

'You may not even receive that, if Daisy is not in agreement, may I remind you.' Henry reached yet again into Tom Fraser's file. 'I was also instructed to give you this, Daisy, on your father's death – to be opened when you felt the time was right.' He passed over a folded note, sealed to keep it private.

Daisy held it in her hand, looking at her father's handwriting on the letter. Her eyes filled with tears. She'd got her home back, and yet she'd never dreamed of having anything left to her by him.

'Go on – what are you waiting for? Open the letter. Perhaps he tells you where there's some money.' It was Kitty this time, still not believing that she had been left nothing but some furniture.

Clifford, on the other hand, said nothing. The contents of the letter could bring his life crashing down around him, if he'd been named and shamed.

Daisy looked at the letter and then at the solicitor. 'Don't feel pressured, my dear,' he said. 'Open it in your own time.'

She sniffed and then, with shaking hands, broke the seal and read the message:

Things will take a turn, my Daisy.
I'm sorry. Forgive me.

She held it in her shaking hands, her heart breaking. Her father had said he was sorry. That was all she had ever wanted to hear from her parents. All the years of heartache flooded out of her, as the realization that she possessed her own property and had gained her father's forgiveness sank in.

The letter dropped to the ground and Clifford snatched it up. He read it quickly and then passed it to Kitty, shaking his head as he handed it to her.

'Sorry! He's not half as bloody sorry as we are.' Clifford grabbed hold of Kitty's arm and pulled her out of the door and out of the building, leaving Daisy alone in the solicitor's room.

Henry smacked his lips together. 'Your father loved you, Daisy. He wanted to do right by you, for a past wrong. Leave Grouse Hall – your brother-in-law will never change his ways; even his own father was ashamed at the end of his days of the son he had bred. And, Daisy, think about what your father has left Kitty: the oak dresser and its contents. He was sure you'd remember what he was referring to.'

Daisy sniffed and rose from her chair. She felt uncomfortable, for she'd obviously been discussed and she was still ashamed of her past.

'Good luck, and if I can ever be of service, you know where I am. These, by the way, are yours. They are the deeds to your family home, which I believe is called

Mill Race.' He handed her a square walnut box that had always been kept in her father's oak desk. Until then, Daisy had always admired the precious box in her father's desk, but had never known what was locked inside it.

'Thank you. I don't know what to say.' Daisy smiled a weak smile and clutched the box to her.

'Go and be happy. That was what your father wanted.' Henry Winterskill shook her hand and showed her to the door. He felt warm inside – sometimes his job was worth doing.

Daisy lay in her bed. She listened to Tobias sleeping soundly on the mattress she'd placed for him in her room. He'd slept in her room ever since the barn had caught fire. She knew he was safe there, out of the clutches of Oversby, if not the insults of Clifford throughout the day. If she was to move into Mill Race, what would become of Tobias? He'd probably be treated like a dog again. But she couldn't take the lad with her, for he belonged with his father, no matter how badly Tobias would be treated by him.

The silence between Clifford and Kitty as she had climbed into the cart had been unbearable. She knew they had expected to receive money. In fact, the more she thought about the money her father had left, the more confused she was. He had always had a good head for figures and was never short of money, so leaving just ten guineas to his name made no sense. She tossed and turned, pulling the covers over her one way and then the other. Why had her father left her a house and her sister nothing, except the dresser and the clock? She remembered Henry Winterskill looking at her as he talked about the dresser and its contents, making sure she was aware of the contents in particular. But the dresser only held flour and spices – she'd seen her father at it nearly every day of his life, for it was an essential part of the family home. The furniture would be worthless now, with the length of time the house had been empty, and would be no good to anyone.

After breakfast she'd walk to Mill Race, confront her demons and visit the apple tree beneath which her child lay. That, she presumed, was why her father had left her the family home. While her mother and father had had Christian burials, her son lay unchristened and unwelcome in heaven, under the apple tree at Grisedale. It was over now – she had to forget it all. It was time to make a fresh start. She had a home, a good man on her arm, and perhaps she could make a living by supplying Luke Allen with preserves and baking, if she talked to Sam about it. But what would she do about Tobias? She'd grown fond of the boy, and he of her. It would break his heart to see her leave.

20

'Where's Clifford?' Daisy asked Kitty, who was giving her the cold shoulder as she cleared the breakfast pots away.

'He's gone to look at a lambing ewe up in the top pasture. He'll have to look after them, now that we are to live like paupers, with no inheritance.' Kitty glared at her sister as Daisy caught her arm.

'Kitty, it isn't my fault. It was our father's will. I didn't know about it.'

'What was he "sorry" for, and what "things will take a turn"? It was you who should have been sorry – jiggering off without a by-your-leave.' Kitty scowled at her sister.

'You've no idea what went on, Kitty, and I'm not about to tell you. I'm sorry you've had a hard life with Clifford, but that's not my fault. Father was as much to blame for your unhappiness as he was for mine. Parents shouldn't plot their children's lives. Anyway, you were as happy as could be on your wedding day.'

'That's what you thought. I felt like I'd been sold

off to the highest bidder.' Kitty slammed the clean pots down.

'Where's Tobias? I thought I'd take him with me to Grisedale and wander down the dale to see what the house is like now.' Daisy cut herself two slices of bread and put them in her pocket.

'That's it – rub my nose in it. The little bastard is with those fox cubs, probably getting covered with fleas.'

'Oh, Kitty, shut up! I can't help what's been done. I'll make sure your dresser and clock are still there.' Daisy walked out into the bright sunshine and around the back of the barn. She stood and watched the young lad playing with the fox cubs as if they were puppies. He'd be broken-hearted if the hunt group took them and the hounds tore them apart in the name of sport. Clifford Middleton was nothing more than a bastard himself, letting the boy get attached to the cubs.

Tobias suddenly cried out.

'Aye, watch your fingers! Their teeth are like razors. They are wild animals, you know.'

'Look at this one, Daisy. He likes his stomach being rubbed. Look at his feet kicking me.' Tobias giggled as he rubbed the cub's stomach.

'Put them back in the cage, Tobias. You mustn't get too attached – they're not ours. Feed them and then leave them,' said Daisy. 'Come with me, and we'll have a day away from here. Come and walk up the dale to where I was born. I've got dinner in my pocket.'

Tobias picked up the fox cub and slammed the cage door shut.

'Are we going to be away all day? What will Clifford say?' Tobias nodded his head at the house.

'Don't worry about him – he's all words. And you are with me. Come on, Tobias, race you down to the road.'

Daisy picked up her skirts and started to run, glancing around at Tobias, who was hot on her heels and soon overtook her. She laughed as her dress caught around her legs. She couldn't keep up with the young lad, and she knew it. She doubled up at the bottom of the field, out of breath and aching.

'You win. I'm too old to chase your young legs.' She held out her hand to Tobias, who took it quickly. 'Come on, we've to walk along the road for a little way up Garsdale, and then we'll walk up the lane to Grisedale and my old home of Mill Race.'

Tobias held her hand tightly. Since she'd come to Grouse Hall, Daisy had turned his life around, and he knew it. Her feelings were strong for the little lad, and she was growing fonder of him every day. He was such a loving little soul, when given the chance.

'It's a lovely day, Tobias – just feel that sunshine.' Daisy lifted her face up to the sun. 'Do you know your flower names? I was taught them as soon as I could walk.' She ran her hand through the hedgerow plants, stopping to smell the bluebells and primroses that filled the hedgerow along the roadside.

'Flowers have names? Don't be silly.' Tobias laughed.

'Yes, they do, just like you and me. This is a bluebell – that one's easy, because it's blue and shaped like

272

a bell; this little yellow one is a primrose; and this little one . . .' Daisy lifted the delicate little flower head. 'It's called a soldier's button, because – look, when you lift its head, it's like a soldier's button on his uniform. We'll play a game. It'll make the walk seem not as long. I'll ask you to find me a flower, and then you've to tell me its name.' Daisy smiled. This was how she'd learned the flower names, and it hadn't felt like learning when she'd done it with her mother.

Tobias kept running back and forward with different flowers. He was a quick learner and Daisy enjoyed teaching him. The walk felt like freedom, and she relished every moment. The day felt like a new start in her life, now that she had a home waiting for her.

After a while the flower game started to wear thin on Tobias.

'Come on, we'll play ducks and drakes down in the river, and then we'll get a move on.' Daisy scrambled down to the river bank with Tobias following her. 'What you need is a thin, flat stone that's really smooth. Then you hold it curled between your finger and thumb and throw it, so that it skims the water and bounces along the surface.' Daisy demonstrated, laughing as she counted the times the stone bounced along the river. Then Tobias tried, getting frustrated after the first time or two, and finally beaming when he managed to throw the stone successfully.

Daisy sat down by the bank, watching the little soul doing what a boy his age should be doing. She felt guilty about leaving him at Grouse Hall, but he wasn't her concern. She hadn't known he existed until she went to live there. The trouble was that he'd grown on her, and she felt responsible for him now. She looked around her. The new green leaves of late spring rustled in the wind, and their shadows played on the steady ripple of the River Clough. A dragonfly darted above the river and a trout jumped lazily, trying to catch its dinner, but missing.

'That was a three-er. Did you see that, Daisy?' Tobias ran across the riverside shingle.

'I did – you're getting good at this. If we've time on the way back we'll stop here again. Come on, let's go and see my new home.' Daisy patted down her skirts. They were damp from sitting on the mossy bank.

'Your new home,' said Tobias, sounding upset. 'You can't leave me. I don't want to be on my own again.' He pulled on her skirts with tears in his eyes.

'I haven't gone yet, my love. Besides, I'll make sure they treat you right after I've left. Now that you know where I live, you can always escape and come and see me.' Daisy bent down and wiped his tears away from his dark eyes. 'I promise you, Tobias, I'll not let them treat you like a dog again.' She didn't know how she was going to protect him, but she would. She could never live with herself if Tobias had to go back to the way he lived before.

The track up to the little dale of Grisedale was steep and windswept. The rough moorland grasses and sedges stung the legs of Tobias and Daisy, as she took them through the fields to her old home. Her heart beat faster with every bend they took, until down in the bottom of the valley she caught sight of the family home. She stood looking around her. She knew these fells like the back of her hand. She knew where the white heather for luck grew, where the curlew always nested, and where bilberries were to be found in autumn. This was home, whether she liked it or not. It pulled on her heart-strings and made her feel sick with sheer love for the place. And down there, in the bottom by the stream, was where she was born and raised to be a happy young woman, until that fateful day. She sighed and brushed a stray strand of her long brown hair from her eye, holding Tobias close to her by his shoulder.

'This is Mill Race, Tobias. This is my home.' Daisy held his hand tightly and strode down the fellside to it. She stood by the garden wall. Brambles and briars had taken over the square walled piece of land that used to be planted with cabbages, potatoes, carrots and what-ever other vegetables were needed to see them through the winter months. The gate was still standing, but the paint was cracked and dry, and it groaned as Daisy opened it. The path was lost under weeds, as Daisy and Tobias made for the front door. Light-blue paint was flaking from it, as Daisy pulled the large iron key from her pocket and turned it in the lock. She closed her eyes and pushed the door open, imagining that she was opening Pandora's box and that all the evils of the world would be released as she walked into the small, dark front room of Mill Race. A mouse scurried into the corner of the room, disturbed by Daisy and Tobias's entrance, and Daisy looked around her at what used to be her home. Everything was just as it had been, but covered with dust and cobwebs, and the mice had obviously made the horse-hair settee their home, with tufts of the filling strewn over the floor.

The grandfather clock that was to be Kitty's stood next to the doorway to the kitchen, and Daisy walked across the dusty floor to the kitchen and bakehouse. Memories flooded back to the morning when she had told her mother that she was pregnant, and she remembered the look Martha had given her, in disgust and panic, as she raced to get the baked bread out of the huge black Yorkshire range. She could hear her mother's voice nearly screaming at her, as it dawned on her that Daisy was with child.

She looked across at the long oak dresser along the kitchen wall. That was to be Kitty's as well, along with the contents. They were worth nothing, she realized, as she opened the top cupboard, blowing away the dust and cobwebs. All that was left now were mouse-droppings and chewed paper bags, with spiders hiding in the darkness. She pulled out one of the long middle drawers that ran down the centre of the ancient dresser. She hadn't appreciated how deep and wide the drawers were, and how heavy. Then she accidentally pulled out the drawer to its full length, making it fall onto the dusty floor. In the dim light of the kitchen she looked at the drawer – the last third of it was closed off with a wooden lid. She'd never noticed that before; she'd never pulled the drawers that far out, for the spices and other ingredients had always been at the front.

Tobias watched Daisy as she tried to lift the lid, but realized it was locked. But wait: she had a small key, along with the large iron house-keys in her pocket. She quickly pulled the key out and tried it in the lock. It fitted, and her heart beat fast as she turned it in the lock and pulled open the secret compartment. It was full to the brim with bank notes of all values. This was what her father had left Kitty – it wasn't the dresser that was of value; it was the contents. Daisy opened all four drawers and they all revealed the same secret compartment, with enough money to make her sister quite a wealthy woman. So, her father had done right by both his daughters: she had the house and Kitty had the money, but he'd left it in such a way that Clifford didn't need to know.

'Tobias, you've never seen all this money, do you understand? We've never found it, and we know nothing about it.' Daisy looked at the young boy's face as every drawer revealed a small fortune.

Tobias nodded his head. He'd do anything Daisy said.

'Come on, let's open this back door and let some light in.' She unbolted the back door and threw it open, to let the light spill into the kitchen. The honeysuckle that grew around the doorway bullied its way into the kitchen.

'Well, that's going to have to be cut back, Tobias. I think you've got me at Grouse Hall for a long time yet

– until I've tidied here up, anyway.' Daisy smiled. The next step was going to be hard, she thought, as she climbed up the back garden stairs into the sunshine and the orchard. The grass was knee-high as she stood quietly under the apple tree that had been growing there for decades. Under the soil lay her baby, buried and forgotten, rotted back to nature, without a mother's love. She brushed back a tear. She had to come back and live here to make sure that her bairn was not disturbed – her father had known that.

She watched as Tobias swung on one of the branches of the apple tree. Her baby lay dead under the soil, and another woman's baby was swinging in the tree, unloved and unwanted. How many other bastard children did Clifford Middleton have? And how ironic that his wife – her sister Kitty – couldn't bear him children? Nature had a funny way of getting even with folk.

Daisy's mind was racing as she lay in her bed that night. Her sister obviously didn't know that the dresser drawers contained money and thought she'd been left nothing.

What if she drip-fed it to Kitty, making her promise to keep Tobias out of harm's way, once she left Grouse Hall? That way Clifford wouldn't get his hands on it. It was quite obvious that her father hadn't wanted him to have the money. It would at least serve a good purpose then, and Clifford wouldn't get the chance to squander it all. Sisters should be closer than they had been, and as long as Kitty kept receiving her father's money, Daisy was fulfilling his wishes. That's what she'd do, then her conscience about the young lad would be clear.

'Some bloody father you had! You looked after your mother when she was ill, and all you get is a dresser that's got woodworm and a grandfather clock.' Clifford pushed the dresser onto the cart, swearing at the weight of it. 'Daisy got bloody everything, yet she's done nowt for it. And I hear she's worming her way into Luke Allen's family.' He leaned on the wheel of the cart and moaned to Kitty, as he watched Daisy lock the door of Mill Race behind her.

'She can't help it – my father was the one to blame. Besides, I'll be glad to get my house back to myself. The sooner she's out from under our feet, the better. A kitchen isn't made for two women.' Kitty was looking forward to her sister leaving, for Daisy was beginning to be the more dominant one, and she didn't like sharing the decision-making.

'Aye, and that bastard can stop being mollycoddled. He's turned into a baby since she came,' growled Clifford.

'I think we could turn him into a gentleman, Clifford, if we put our minds to it.' Kitty looked at her husband.

'And why the fuck would we do that? He's nowt to me.'

'Clifford, I've never said anything until now, but I believe him to be your son. Regardless of who or what his mother is, you should raise him properly.' Kitty felt the money in her apron pocket. She'd do as her sister asked, if the money kept coming – she was such a soft

279

lump, her Daisy. She always had been the softer one of the two of them as they grew up, always looking after a stray kitten or an orphaned chicken that used to beg at the kitchen door.

'He's not of my loins – not a weak, scrawny thing like that. You're soft in the head, woman. You can do as you please and think what you want, but keep him out of my way. Are you coming back home or are you walking?' Clifford's patience was running thin as he watched Daisy pick her way through the tall grasses of the garden. It should be his bloody house, not his sister-in-law's.

'Just be patient. I wanted to make sure I'd locked the door.' Daisy pulled herself up onto the cart next to her sister.

'Why? There's no bloody Crown Jewels in there, and we are miles from anywhere. This spot isn't exactly on the busiest highway.' Clifford climbed up next to the two women and clicked his tongue, setting his horse into action.

'God, he's sarcastic!' Daisy whispered to her sister.

'I might be bloody sarcastic, but I've got good hearing, and I can stop this cart and throw you out,' he growled.

'You can, but you won't. Otherwise, who would pay for next week's shopping?' Daisy knew she had the upper hand. Until the back-end lamb sales, Clifford's bank balance would look rather empty. His only income would be coming from the spare butter that Kitty churned each day, and from the eggs that were sold in Hawes each Tuesday.

'Phew, you are a bitch!' Clifford grimaced. But it was better that Daisy was paying their way than him having to borrow from Oversby. He'd grin and bear it for now.

21

'So you are the lass who's taken my lad's eye.' Luke Allen studied Daisy as she stood in front of him. She was all right, he thought. She had bonny eyes, but was a bit plain.

'It's nice to meet you, Mr Allen. Sam has talked so much about you.' Daisy knew she had to impress. The villagers' gossip was against her, and she had to sway his perception of her.

'Aye, well, he can talk a load of rubbish sometimes.'

'Oh, thanks, Father! How good of you to say so.' Sam's face reddened and he looked as if he was about to explode.

'It was all good, and not a load of rubbish at all. He was praising your business head, and saying you'd a sound eye for a new product.' Daisy tried to calm the troubled waters between father and son, as well as move the conversation in the direction she wanted.

'Aye, well, I like to think I have. What do you think of the shop? Our Sam says you've been in retail.' Luke stood with his back against the shop counter and weighed up the lass, who was fast with her compliments. He knew her sort: quick to please, but with no depth to her character, particularly as she'd left her parents. Dales lasses just didn't do that.

Sam looked at his father – he knew what he was up to. Luke was testing Daisy, and Sam knew it damn well.

'It's a grand shop, Mr Allen – full of everything you want. And you try new brands. Sam tells me you have started taking products from Mattinson's in Leeds. No doubt he's mentioned that I worked for them?' Daisy looked at him, knowing full well where the conversation was leading. Sam's father hadn't asked her to afternoon tea out of curiosity. It was because he wanted to know what she could do, and what he could get out of it.

'Aye, well, we try our best. Our lad did happen to mention that you worked for Mattinson's – said you were a bit of a cook. You must take after your father: he was a good baker. Not on the same scale as us, mind. I've four lads in my bakery up Gayle Lane. They start at three in the morning, and I've bread on the shelves by seven. Better bread you can't find this side of the Pennines. I'm usually sold out by dinner time.' Luke Allen put his thumbs in his waistcoat pockets as his chest filled with pride. 'Now, which products did you make these Mattinsons? Owt I should be knowing about?'

Luke's dark-brown eyes stared at her, as Daisy reeled off her duties at the shop and what recipes she had made and given the Mattinsons. She didn't want to sound as if she was bragging, but by the time she had finished telling him what she had done, it sounded rather good. It even impressed Daisy herself, let alone winning over old Luke Allen.

'See, Father, she's not just a pretty face.' Sam linked his arm into Daisy's. 'I told you she knew her stuff.'

'Aye, but the proof is in the pudding, lad. I tell you what, Daisy. You make me a pot of lemon cheese, and we'll see if we can come to an arrangement. If it's as good as that pot over there, tha can make it on a regular basis for this old duffer standing in front of you. And I'll pay you well.' Luke pointed to the shelf where Mattinson's Lemon Cheese stood.

'All right, I'll do that for you. Once I leave Grouse Hall I'll need to make myself some money, and it would be ideal to supply you with preserves – or whatever you want that I can make.' Daisy grinned. Her life was turning full circle, but this time for the better, with a family she could trust.

'You're leaving Grouse Hall! Where are you going?' Luke looked surprised.

'My father left me Mill Race in his will – my old home up in Grisedale. I got the key last week, so I'm moving back home, back where I belong. I thought Sam would have told you.'

'I never—' Sam didn't finish his sentence before his father butted in.

'Nay, he never told me that. So you own your own house and all?'

'Yes, and a little paddock where we used to keep a

pig, and an orchard. I wish I could thank my father, but I'm sure it's common knowledge that he died in the asylum and is buried there.' Daisy blushed.

'Aye, it was a sad do. You never know what's going to happen to you from one day to the next. Live each day as if it's your last – that's what I say, as you can probably tell, by this belly of mine.' He put his hands on his full belly while looking downcast, thinking about his rival, Tom Fraser. He'd been secretly happy when the old fella had gone mad; it had given him more trade. But to be buried without family around him, in the asylum's graveyard, was not to be wished on anybody. 'Anyway, enough! Come through to the back and meet Mary. She's made us a bite to eat. She's been fretting about meeting you all day; thinks you are going to pinch her lad from her. He's the apple of her eye, soft lad!'

'Father, I'm not soft. I'm my own man!' Sam looked annoyed.

'Aye, well, you are still in short trousers and always will be, as far as your mother is concerned.'

Luke led the way through a low white door at the back of the shop. 'Take no heed of this lot. This room doubles up as a storeroom. Mary keeps playing hell with me to tidy it up. But how can you, when stuff keeps coming and going all day?' He snaked his way through piles of boxes and cans, until they came to a second doorway and entered the living quarters of the Allens.

A round table was set with the best china on a white lace tablecloth, and four plush walnut chairs were positioned around the edge. A cake-stand stood proudly in the middle with a display of various home-made cakes, and elsewhere on the table were biscuits and fancies.

'Mary? Mary! Where are you, woman, you've got a visitor?' shouted Luke at the top of his voice.

Sam winked at Daisy, reassuring her that she'd be all right with his mother.

'I'm here – no need to shout, I was only in the scullery.' Mary Allen entered the room. She was tall and thin, her white hair placed on the top of her head in a bun, emphasizing her height. 'So you are the lass that my soft lad's smitten with. I keep telling him there's no match for a mother's love. We'll put up with our bairns, no matter what they do.'

Daisy felt uneasy. Had she fallen for another Bob? Was his mother going to dominate Sam's life? She felt herself blushing as Mary Allen's eyes looked her up and down.

'But you can't keep 'em tied to your apron strings all their lives. They'd have nobody when you've passed away, so you hope they make the right choice in women. Sit down here, and I'll make us a brew. I want to know a bit about you.'

'Mother, she's only come to tea. We aren't going to elope together next week.' Sam squeezed Daisy's hand tight as he pulled out a chair for her to sit on.

'I know how these things start. I only knew your father for six months and then we were wed. My mother nearly had a fit.' On her way to the kitchen Mary stopped in her tracks.

'Aye, but only because you were expect—'

'Father, hold your noise. There's no need for you to add your four penn'orth.' Mary stopped Luke sharply. 'The less said about that, the better. And let's not tempt fate – we'll have none of that yet.' She wagged her finger and aimed it at Sam, while glaring at Luke, who was tucking into a piece of shortbread.

Daisy sipped her tea as politely as she could. Mary had filled it to the brim, and her hand was shaking with nerves as she was cross-examined about her life, her hobbies and her appearance. Mary Allen wanted to know the far end of a fart, and where it had gone, over tea. And she wasn't going to rest until she knew everything there was to know about Daisy.

'And what made you leave home? I've heard various tales, but I want to hear it from you. You can't believe all you hear, I know that! You seemed such a close family, when you were with your father on market days in Hawes and Sedbergh.' Mary waited for Daisy's reply and looked at her as if she knew what she was going to say, making Daisy feel uncomfortable as the biggest lie of her life came out of her mouth.

'My mother's friend at Gearstones Lodge sent for me to help her with her lodging business and, as I'm sure you are aware, I met and fell in love with a signal-man while working there. Sadly he died on our wedding night, but I couldn't bear to come home – I didn't want everyone's pity. So I applied for a job with the Mattinson brothers, and that's where I was until I took ill and had to return home to my sister's.' Daisy couldn't look straight at Mary. She'd lied, but she didn't want her new life tainted by Clifford Middleton's act of selfishness.

'Did your mother not want you to come back home when she was dying? She was ill for some weeks, if I remember.'

'By that time I was in Leeds, and my father insisted that I stay there. He knew how good my job was, and how much the family depended on me.' Daisy carried on the lie, regretting every word that came out of her mouth.

'But you didn't even come to her funeral. I was there.' Mary wasn't finished. This lass was selfish. If her Sam were to marry her, then there'd be no help for her and Luke in their old age.

'Mother, give over,' Luke interrupted. 'It's like an inquisition – you're frightening her to death. Just look at how white she is! It makes no difference. Her folk thought a lot of her, and old Tom left her his house and the lot. She's a woman of substance, is our Daisy, and she's going to make me a pot of that lemon cheese. I've told her if it's as good as that Mattinson's stuff, I'll put an order in here and now.' Luke leaned back in his chair and grinned at Daisy.

Never had she been so thankful for an interruption. She'd hated lying to Mary Allen, but if she'd known the truth, she would never have Daisy in her house again.

'You're right. I just get carried away, but you only

want the best for your lad. One day you'll understand, when you've children of your own. I'll make a fresh pot.' Mary stood up with the teapot in her hand.

'Mother, I keep telling you: we are just good friends, so you needn't talk about family or weddings.' Sam smiled at Daisy.

'Aye, and I'm a monkey's uncle! No other lass has ever been invited to tea by you, or your father. And I've never seen a lad so smitten. Today I know I've lost my lad.' Mary filled up with tears and rushed into the kitchen, trying to hide her sobs.

'Aye, she always was over-emotional, was your mother. Take no notice of her – she'll come round. Anyway, lass, you've yet to convince me whether you're worthy to enter this family. Your pot of cheese will tell me that.' Luke laughed as he added, 'I'm only joking, lass.'

Daisy smiled at him, knowing full well that he wasn't joking. She was just another business deal, and her lemon cheese had better be up to scratch, if she was to catch her man.

Daisy stirred the thickening lemon cheese in the heavy brass jam-pan. The smell of lemon filled the kitchen of Grouse Hall and made it feel homely. Tobias watched as she judged whether or not it was ready to pot, and waited to run his fingers inside the pan that he'd been promised. Six warm jam jars were lined up on the scrubbed pine kitchen table, and Daisy carefully spooned the thick yellow mixture into each awaiting one, lovingly wiping the dribbles from the side of the jars, before putting them next to the open kitchen door to cool. She laughed at Tobias as he nearly burned his tongue in his eagerness to lick the remains of the lemon cheese from the pot.

'Watch what you're doing! Let it cool first, you greedy monkey.'

'I've never had anything like this – you've got to make it again.' Tobias grinned as a dribble of cheese went down his chin.

'Nay, there's no money at Grouse Hall for luxuries like lemons. I've only made this because Luke has given me the ingredients. Once I've got my own house tidy, I can make it again, and the stove at home is a lot better. If I can start selling this on a regular basis, I'll get some income coming in.' Daisy talked away to Tobias, even though he didn't understand half of what she was saying, and didn't care either, as he scraped the last dribbles of lemon cheese from the pan.

'Well, I'll just be bloody glad to get you out from under my feet.' Kitty entered the kitchen with a bucket of warm milk, fresh from the cow in the barn. 'You're filling this bugger's head with rubbish, and getting in my way. He's nobbut using you, is Luke Allen. He knows a good deal when he sees one. He always did try to undercut our father when he was alive, but you were too young to remember, and your head was always full of rubbish.'

'He's not a bad man. Anyway, that's how business works – you've got to be competitive, or else folk will 'go elsewhere. That is one thing I learned from my time in Leeds.'

'Leeds, Leeds. It's all you bloody talk about. But I notice they don't write back to you so quick. When will you get it into your head that you were their skivvy, and nothing else?' Kitty sighed at Daisy's thunderous face. 'Here, take this milk; skim the cream off, put it in the butter churn with the other cream I put in there last night, and make me some butter to take with you to Hawes. You're sitting nicely, with a paid house in place and a grand scheme, but we've still to make a living.'

'You've got Tobias's money. I promised to give you something every month towards his upkeep, and I'll be true to my word.' Daisy snatched the bucket from her sister.

'Aye, and that will only be a flash in the pan. You'll not be able to keep paying me when you're married to that simpering Sam. Besides, it's all going on Tobias: look how hungry he always is. Clifford will soon realize money is coming in from somewhere, other than us making it.'

Daisy glanced at young Tobias. He looked healthier now, and there was spare meat on his bones and more colour in his cheeks. 'You'll not say anything to Clifford, will you, Kitty? He can't go back to treating the lad like a dog, once I've left. And you'll make sure Tobias can sleep in my old room, not back under the table?'

'I'll not say anything, but you are simple in the head

to be wasting your hard-earned brass on his bastard, because that's what he is: a whore's bastard with no prospects, as you would say. Aye, he can sleep in your old room, but I expect under the table will be warmer in winter. At least he'd have the heat from the kitchen fire.'

Daisy knew her sister was right. The lad would never be accepted in society, but at least for a while she could see that he was fed. She skimmed the cream from the top of the milk and added it to the rest of the cream, before screwing down the metal lid that held the wooden panels and handle. She hated this job. Sometimes the cream would quickly turn into butter, and sometimes it could take up to an hour of turning the handle that rotated the wooden panels that battered the cream. Her arm would ache by the time it was made, and then she'd have to add salt to the separated butter and pat it into usable blocks with the butter-pats. Never mind. After she'd done this job, she was going to see Luke with the lemon cheese and, hopefully, some butter to sell him.

Kitty's words rang in her ears as she turned the handle of the butter churn. The truth hurt, but Kitty was right: the Mattinson brothers hadn't written to her since she had left – she had just been another worker to them. And yet she was sure Jim had thought something of her. She was just a bad judge of men – that was the top and bottom of it – and she only hoped she'd got it right with Sam.

22

The summer months were flying by. Daisy had never known the year pass so quickly. It had been a glorious summer, the sun had shone and she had been so busy. The house at Mill Race was now nearly ready to be moved into. The only room that had not been touched was Daisy's original bedroom, and she had not plucked up the courage to open the door and walk into what had been her jail for the term of her pregnancy. Today she stood on the landing with her hand on the door knob, willing herself to open the door. Today was the day she would step back into her bedroom.

'Hello, hello, anybody here?' A voice drifted up the stairs, just as Daisy was about to turn the door knob and enter.

She breathed a sigh of relief. She knew it was stupid, but she felt that once she opened that door, it would be like opening Pandora's box and all the evils of the world would come spilling out.

'I'm here – coming,' shouted Daisy, recognizing Sam's voice. She looked back at the door and then lifted up her skirts, before running down the stairs to Sam, who stood looking around the spotless kitchen.

'By heck, lass, this spot gets better every time I come. You couldn't live in a bonnier place. You've tidied the garden and all. I'm glad you've kept that old rambling rose around the door – it smells so bonny.'

'I'm shattered, Sam. I'm working here and working at Grouse Hall, and making your father various preserves. I've never been so busy in my whole life.' Daisy sat down in her father's old chair.

'Well today, my girl, make it a day off, because you're coming with me.' Sam grinned.

'No, I can't, really I can't. I haven't got time. I've got to tackle my old bedroom – it's the last room to be done, and then I can move in before the autumn. And, once that's sorted, I won't have much else to do.'

'I'm not taking "no" for an answer. I've to take this lemon cheese and bramble jelly to my father – he's got a stand at the Moorcock Show. So it's time you had a day off, for you've never stopped. Besides, I've some business to do there.' Sam picked up the jars full of preserve and put them into his basket, which was emblazoned with the name 'Luke Allen' on it. 'Come on, get your hat on and lock that door. We're off and no, I won't let you stay here.' Sam patted her bottom affectionately while Daisy tried to protest. 'Call it customer relations, because my father will be showing you off to everyone. He's over the moon with his sales.'

'But I've so . . .' Daisy didn't want to go, for she

knew all the locals from the surrounding Dales would be there.

'Get a move on. I'll be waiting in the trap. I'll treat you to a ride in the swing-boats.' Sam giggled like a small child.

'We are too old for the swing-boats – they are for children.' Daisy shook her head.

'You're never too old. I go on them every year.'

'Oh! So I'm not the first woman you've led astray on the swing-boats.' Daisy picked up her straw boater from the hat stand and secured it with a hat pin, while viewing herself in the coat-stand mirror and smiling at Sam's shocked face.

'I go on them with my mates. I've never been on with a woman.'

'Go on then. I suppose there will be plenty of wet days to tidy my bedroom out. I didn't want to do it anyway.' Daisy just hoped there would be nobody at the show from the farms around Gearstones Lodge. They were bound to recognize her – she hadn't changed that much. But, it was a day out with Sam, whom she now knew that she loved. Everything would be all right if she was with Sam Allen.

The road up to the Moorcock Show was busy with farmers and their wives herding sheep and carrying wares to sell, and with couples and children eager to get to the big show-field set in the bottom of Garsdale valley. It was the end of summer and almost the beginning of autumn, and it was time for Dales folk to show off their best sheep and sell surplus produce to add to their meagre living.

Sam waved and talked to nearly everyone they met. They all knew Sam Allen, for his father owned the main grocery shop in Hawes and was one to count as a friend. The men tipped their caps and bowlers, while the women looked at Daisy by his side and either smiled weakly or whispered behind gloved hands.

'Come on, lass, let's get this to Father and then we can have a look around. My mother's come to help, so I can have an hour or two off.' Sam climbed down from the trap and walked with the horse, guiding it through the crowds while Daisy held onto the basket of produce.

'Am I glad to see thee. I'm nearly out of bramble jelly, and my bread's almost all sold. I suppose when it's gone, it's gone, but I could do with another few loaves – nowt like making money when the sun's shining.' Luke wiped his brow as some more coins jingled into his hand.

'You want nothing with more bread – we've enough here. You don't half panic, Luke, just calm down. Hello, Daisy. Your lemon cheese, jam and jelly are selling well – we'll be needing more before the end of the week.' Mary smiled at Daisy, before serving the customers bustling around their stall.

'I'm going to tether the horse up, and then Mary and I are going to have a wander around. Is that all right, Father?' Sam looked back at Daisy, whose gaze was wandering. She was taking in all the people gathered at the show, along with the smells of cooking and the shouts of the stallholders, mixed with the bleats of the sheep being shown.

'Aye. Don't do anything I wouldn't do – that means tha can do owt tha likes.' Luke belly-laughed as Mary scolded him.

Sam put his arm through Daisy's and they meandered past the long skirts of farmers' wives and children running along with their fraught fathers. Daisy felt as if all eyes were on her, and that she was being talked about. Yet she knew it was her own mind playing tricks.

Sam leaned over a pen of Swaledale sheep and pretended to be judging them, until the dancing bear with its owner caught his eye and he dragged Daisy by the hand, to watch the poor creature doing its trick for the awestruck crowd. The bear teetered on a red drum and was made to stand on one leg, as the crowd clapped and applauded. Its eyes were full of fear and pain, and it was made to clap its paws together in recognition of the crowd.

'I don't like this, Sam. The poor creature's being whipped and prodded. Look at the heavy chain and muzzle on its mouth.'

'It's better having the muzzle on than taking a chunk out of us.' Sam smiled at Daisy.

'It would be better freed and taken back to the wild, where it came from.' Daisy closed her eyes as some children threw a stone at the poor creature, obviously leaving it in pain.

'Come on, Daisy, I'll take you to the swing-boats. The bear will be all right – it gets a rest between shows,

I'm sure.' Sam pulled her through the crowds until they came to the bright-red swing-boats. 'Here, mister, there's two of us.' He pulled out some coins and gave them to the man in charge of the swing-boats, before climbing into the bottom of the wooden gondola, holding onto the rope that made it swing as he helped Daisy into the other side of the boat. 'Here, Daisy, pull at the opposite time to me, and then we'll see how high we can go.'

The man in charge of the swings gave them a push and then they were off. The iron rods that held the boat in place groaned as the couple laughed and pulled on the rope, making the swing-boat go higher and higher in the air. 'Stop it, Sam, stop it! I'm worn out, I can't get my breath.' Daisy squealed as the boat lurched downwards again, and Sam grinned at her from high above. She really hadn't wanted to go on the swing-boats, but she had enjoyed every minute on the fair ride.

'All right, Daisy, we'll stop now.' Sam slowed his pulling on the rope and, with shaky legs, they both climbed out.

'I'd better put my hat on straight. I bet I look a right mess.' Daisy straightened her skirts and tucked a piece of stray hair back underneath her boater.

'You never look a mess to me, Daisy – you are always perfect to me.' Sam squeezed her hand. 'Come and sit down by the beck with me; let's have a bit of quiet time together.' His face looked serious as he held her hand tightly. They walked through the crowds to the edge of the field where the beck ran. There he took his jacket off and laid it on the dry grass of late summer. Both sat quietly, listening to the bubbling of the beck and the distant sounds of the fair.

'Daisy, since early spring I've begun to think more and more of you.' Sam held her hand. 'I've never felt like this before. My mother was right: this is serious, for me anyway. What I'm trying to say . . .' Sam put his fingers into his shirt pocket and pulled out a box. 'What I'm trying to say, Daisy, is: will you marry me?' Inside the box a delicate diamond engagement ring shone and glittered in the sunshine.

Daisy gazed in disbelief. She'd be lying if she said she hadn't thought about it, but it still came as a shock. And she knew her feelings for Sam were growing every day. Her heart missed a beat when he flashed his cheeky grin her way, and when his hand touched hers, it felt like being hit by a lightning bolt. She knew she loved him, but dare she marry him? It felt too good to be true. He was everything she had ever wanted, everything Bob had never been. Her eyes filled with tears.

'Daisy, say yes; come on, say yes. I've plenty of money, and the business will be mine after my father's day. I'm a good catch.' Sam's hand began to shake, as the ring within the box was not taken.

'Oh, Sam, I'm frightened. You don't really know me; there are things . . .' Daisy looked at him. She loved the lad – she couldn't say no.

'Will you be quiet. I've heard all the talk and I'm not bothered. I know you, and I want you to be my wife. Besides, what's my father going to do when he runs out of lemon cheese? He's cancelled his order with Mattinson's. Say yes, Daisy. I love you, and you know it.' Sam held out the ring, waiting for Daisy to slip it on her finger.

Through tear-filled eyes she nodded her head and held her shaking finger out. 'I love you too, Sam. I just hope you don't live to regret marrying me.'

'And why in the world would I ever regret marrying you. I know exactly what I'm getting: a grand Yorkshire lass, who's a better cook than my father. I win all round.'

Daisy smiled and gazed at the sparkling ring.

'I love you,' cried Sam, putting his arms around her and squeezing her tightly, before kissing her passionately on the lips, then on her neck and down to her breasts. 'I love you, Daisy, and I'll always be there for you.'

'I love you too, Sam. I'll not let you down.' She raised his head gently to look into his eyes. 'My mother always said we'd be a good match, but I never listened – that was before I knew you. But she was right for once, and you are everything I've ever wanted.' She kissed the smiling Sam and lay down by his side on his jacket.

Sam ran his hand up the inside of Daisy's leg, battling with her layers of skirt and petticoats while kissing her passionately. He placed his leg over her and whispered into her ear, 'Go on, Daisy, let me, you know you want to. And now we are engaged, it's all right.'

Daisy wanted to cry. She wanted to feel him within her, but her head was saying no. A ring meant nothing until you were married, but, God – she'd waited so long for Sam and her to be like this.

'Go on, Daisy.' Sam had his hands in her drawers, and every inch of her body was saying, *Please me – please me in a way I've never been pleased before.*

She nodded. She couldn't resist, and tears filled her eyes as Sam entered her, passionately stroking her hair, her face and her most intimate parts. So this was what proper sex and love were – not rough and hateful, but sensuous and pleasurable. The couple entwined their bodies, forgetting the fair and the people gathered there, enjoying the pleasure of one another until they were exhausted.

'I love you, Daisy. I just want to say that to you all the time – I can't help myself.' Sam lay on his back with Daisy next to him.

'Aye, I love you, but we shouldn't have done that, not really; not before we are married.' Daisy was starting to worry. Her passion had got the better of her, and now panic had set in.

'You'll be all right, lass; you'll be bloody unlucky if you are in the family way after having it just the once.' Sam sat up and buttoned his trousers and shook the grass seeds from off his shirt.

'I suppose so.' But all Daisy could think of was that it had only been the once with Clifford Middleton, and that had had a terrible outcome. She combed her hair through her fingers and fitted her displaced boater on her head.

'You'll be all right. Stop worrying; we are to be

married anyway.' Sam held his hand out to her and pulled her up from his jacket, which he shook and then put back on. 'Come on – they'll be missing us, so we'd better show our faces. And, Daisy, keep the ring and our engagement quiet today. I want to pick my time to tell my mother and father – they've enough on today.' Sam smiled as he linked his arm through Daisy's and started whistling.

'Of course, Sam. I understand.' Daisy looked at her fiancé. She'd made a terrible mistake, and she knew it. All she'd do now was worry whether or not she was pregnant. She'd been in that situation before and had not forgotten the anguish that went with it.

Daisy stood in her former bedroom's doorway. It had been a week since Sam's proposal. Looking around her old bedroom, it felt as if she had never been away. Her bed with its rotting, dusty covers stood in the centre of the room, along with the marble-topped washstand and chest of drawers. On top of them were Daisy's old toys: a rag doll that her mother had made her, and a tatty cloth cat that had once belonged to Kitty. She knew every inch, every crack of the room, and she hated it. It had been – and still was – a cell to her and, no matter how she cleaned it, it would always remind her of the guilt she'd carry with her all her life about her liaison with Clifford and subsequent conception.

She set to work, stripping the bed and folding up the ticking mattress into a roll. There were bloodstains on it – her bloodstains from childbirth. She pulled the whole lot down the stairs and out into the garden, putting it on top of an already-lit bonfire. There she watched it smoulder, slowly burning away the evidence of her guilt. Tomorrow she'd paint the walls of the bedroom and wash the floor and then, at the end of the month, she'd move into her new home – away from Clifford Middleton, her unsympathetic sister and Clifford's son – ready for a new life.

23

'You look surprised to see me.' Sam stood on the doorstep of Mill Race cottage. 'I went up to Grouse Hall, but they said you were here, getting ready to move in.'

'I haven't heard anything from you for weeks – not since Moorcock fair day. I thought you'd had enough of me.' Daisy rubbed her engagement ring on her finger. She was relieved to see Sam, but also annoyed, thinking the worst of him as the days passed and, with them, his integrity.

'What do you mean? You thought I'd have my wicked way with you and then leave you high and dry? Besides, Daisy, it's only been three weeks, and we've been busy. Hawes has been heaving this last week or two, with sheep and lamb sales. The Penny Garth holding pen has been full every day and, where there's sheep being sold, there's hungry farmers – and money to be made.' Sam rubbed his head with his cap and looked at Daisy's worried face. 'Anyway, I've come to pick up what you've made and take you to tea at home. With it being Sunday, and my father in a good mood with all the brass he's been making, it's as good a time as any to tell them our news.'

Daisy sighed with relief, and then panic set in. 'But I'm not even dressed right. I've got to do my hair, and my hands are a mess from scrubbing my bedroom floor with soda.' She gazed at her rough hands.

'Does it matter? You should see my mother. Some days she looks like something the cat's dragged in. It's a good day for telling them. Besides, my mother knows you are coming and she's guessed something's afoot. She keeps looking at me strangely and nearly crying.' Sam made his way into the parlour of Mill Race. 'Go on, get changed and tidy. If you must change, I'll wait for you here. You must have something fresh to put on here.'

He sat down on the reupholstered sofa, which had previously had mice nesting in it, and looked around him. She was a good home-maker, Daisy, and he'd done right asking her to marry him. Folk had told him all sorts: that she was after his money; that she shared Clifford Middleton with her sister; and that she cared for nobody. But none of them knew the real her – they'd just listened to the gossip spread by the evil Joshua Oversby at Yore House.

'Are you ready, lass? It'll be dark, if you don't hurry up.' Sam heard the floorboards above him creak. He put the waiting jars of preserves into his father's basket and placed it on the floor.

'I'm coming, I'm coming.' Daisy rushed down the

stairs, still pinning her hair tightly into place as she reached the bottom.

'Aye, tha looks bonny. There's a blush in your cheeks from rushing about.' Sam put his arm around her waist. 'Maybe we could have half an hour to ourselves? I bet your bed's comfy upstairs – should we try it out for size? Just to see if it's big enough for when we are married.'

'No, we will not, Sam Allen. Your mother's waiting for us, and I'm not being led astray again by your sweet talk.' Daisy kissed him on the lips and pushed him gently away as he tried to demand more from her.

'Bloody spoilsport. But you're right. Let's not put the cart before the horse, else me mother would never forgive me. God help me if I was to be a father before we were married. I take it we are all right, that way?' Sam nodded at her.

'Yes, you're all right, so stop bothering. But we are not tempting fate again, not until we are married. I did nothing but worry until I knew I was all right. That was why I was cool with you, turning up on my doorstep after weeks of no word. I thought you'd gone and left me.' Daisy blushed.

'I'd never do that – you know I wouldn't.' Sam squeezed her hand and lifted the basket from the floor as the couple made their way outside to the trap and to tea at Luke Allen's.

'I knew it, I just knew it. I could tell on Moorcock Show day that something had happened. There was that look in your eyes when you came back to us. I said to you, Father, didn't I?' Mary Allen sobbed into her hankie at the news of her son's engagement.

Daisy blushed at the thought of what had happened at the fair, grateful that Mary hadn't witnessed the unleashed sexual exploits of her son and soon-to-be daughter-in-law.

'Aye, Mother, you'd think it was a funeral, not an engagement. I'm right suited for you both. Couldn't be a more perfect match. You keep him on the straight and narrow now, Daisy, you promise me? He can be a bit of a bugger, can this one.' Luke Allen slapped his son on his shoulder. 'Time for a tipple, I think, Mother. Get the sherry out. That is, if you haven't used it all in the trifle. It was a bloody good one, by the way, lass.' Luke sat back in his chair. 'When are you thinking of getting married – have you set a date then?'

'Stop it, Father, give them time to think.' Mary passed over the sherry bottle from the sideboard and turned around for the small sherry glasses that were displayed on its shelves. She sniffed into her delicately embroidered handkerchief before passing everyone a glass.

'No, we haven't set a date. In fact, we have hardly talked about it since fair day; we haven't had time.' Sam looked at his parents: his father was taking the news well, but he knew his mother was going to give him a lecture about marrying below what she thought to be his status.

'Where are you thinking of living, lad? Here isn't

the place for you and Daisy; you'll want family, so you'll want a home of your own.' Luke sipped his sherry.

'I haven't thought about it. I suppose, if Daisy will let me, we'd be happy at Mill Race in Grisedale. It's a bonny little cottage, with a good kitchen and orchard, and a paddock big enough to keep a pig or two for bacon.' Sam smiled and squeezed Daisy's hand for a response.

Daisy nodded. 'Yes, that would be perfect. It would make me happy for us to stay there and raise a family.'

'Hush, now, there's no need to talk of family yet. I can't get it into my head that my son's getting married, let alone me becoming a grandmother. I'm not old enough, and are you sure you are both ready for this? Sam, you've never been with another woman – are you sure Daisy is the one for you?' Mary stared at Sam. Daisy was not good enough for her precious son, but then again, nobody could look after him like she did. She wouldn't let him go without a fight.

'Mother, you are upsetting Daisy and insulting me. I'm no longer your little boy.' Sam placed his sherry down sharply, nearly spilling the golden liquid on the white linen tablecloth.

'I think I'd better go. You need to talk to your family alone, Sam.' Daisy's cheeks were flushed and her legs shaky as she stood up from the tea table. 'I do love him, Mrs Allen, and I'll always be there for him, if that's what you are worried about.' She pushed her chair away and walked to the doorway.

'Don't be silly, Daisy – stop! My mother will never

be happy with whoever I marry, and I want to marry you.' Sam grabbed hold of her hand, pulling her back into the room.

'Aye, lass, tha's right with me. I can see it being a good marriage,' said Luke. 'In fact, I was going to give you a bit of a nest egg to start you off right. Maybe you've rushed it a bit, eh! Mother? Have a long engagement, and let your mother get used to the idea, Sam. Shall we say a spring wedding, if you are still hell-bent on getting wed?'

'Spring! That's ages off.' Sam raised his voice.

'I can wait until spring, Sam. What's six months, when we love one another like we do?' Daisy squeezed his arm. 'We'll do that, Mr Allen. I'd rather you all accepted me than we all sneak and plan behind one another's backs.' She aimed her words at Mary; Daisy knew she'd never win her over.

'Nay, lass, we'd never do that. Say it as it is, that's the best way. Give Mother here some time to get used to it, and then she'll be celebrating with the rest of us.'

Mary Allen said nothing. A lot could happen in six months, and it gave her time to turn her son's head away from the woman who was going to pinch him from her.

'Daisy, I'm sorry. Are you sure you are happy to wait that long?' Sam looked worried; he didn't want to lose the woman he loved.

'We'll still only have known one another a year, and some folk are engaged to be married for years, Sam. As long as it makes everybody happy.' Daisy's face belied her innermost feelings. She was disappointed, but she had time to win over Sam's mother before they wed.

'See, lad, happen your lass has got sense – it's no good rushing these things. I'll feel better about it when I know Daisy better. And I'm sure she thinks the same of me.' Mary smiled a dry smile and wiped her eyes, knowing that she'd won the battle this time.

'All right, we'll wait, but neither of us will be changing our minds. You can count on that.'

Daisy leaned on the garden gate of Grouse Hall. It was a quiet autumn day and the smell of decaying leaves and drying peat from the turfs cut for winter filled the air. Across on the surrounding fells the purple heather gave the hills a glorious hue, and the rowan tree at the bottom of the garden hung laden with red berries. She smiled as she listened and watched a flock of sparrows argue over the berries, despite her standing there; they were too busy fighting over easy food supplies.

Despite the stillness of the day Daisy felt uneasy. She was going to leave Grouse Hall tomorrow and live back at Mill Race by herself – a time she had looked forward to, in honesty. But still, something was holding her back from feeling happy. Perhaps it was the fact of leaving young Tobias behind. She had grown fond of the lad, but he knew he could visit her if he was ever in bother, and so far her sister had been playing the game with Daisy's monthly allowance for him. She looked at the penned-up fox cubs. They weren't cubs any more; they were fully grown and Tobias no longer played with them like puppies. Their teeth were like razors and they'd bitten the young lad a time or two, just enough for him to lose interest in them. She hoped the poor creatures could run fast enough to outwit the huntsmen and dogs. What Clifford had agreed to wasn't right; the cubs should have been killed along with their mother, rather than be ripped to pieces by the pack. She looked back at Grouse Hall. She'd hated it the first time she'd visited it and was no fonder of it now. It was an ugly house, like its owner – cold and grey. Clifford and it were well matched.

'What are you doing, Daisy?' Tobias ran up to her and smiled.

'I'm thinking, my love, that it's time to leave you. I'm going to my own home in the morning. But don't you fret, you'll be all right. Things are in place to make sure you're not treated as you were.'

Tobias cried and wailed. 'I don't want you to go, Daisy. He'll beat me and make me live under the table, like a dog again.'

'No, he won't, my love. I've paid Kitty to look after you, and if ever he touches a hair on your head, you come to me in Grisedale and tell me. Because Kitty won't get a penny more, if she doesn't look after you. But you keep this a secret – not a word; she mustn't know you know.'

Daisy kissed Tobias on his head and held him tightly against her. The poor lad, she'd miss him. But she had a life to live, and he was not part of it. From now on her life would be spent cooking for the Allens and living quietly until her wedding day. How things had changed for the better within a year. Yet still she felt something was waiting to happen just around the corner. Call it intuition. She couldn't put her finger on it, but something more was to happen, she was sure, although exactly what she didn't know.

24

Oversby and the Lunesdale Hunt came galloping at a pace up the roadway to Grouse Hall. The hounds bayed and sniffed, chasing whatever sport they detected on the dewy early-morning grass. The whipper-in blew his horn as they approached the garden and watched as the hounds went frantic at the smell of fox around the newly emptied cage.

Clifford came to the doorway as he heard the din outside. 'What the Devil . . . ? Why are you so early, man?' He tucked his nightshirt into his trousers and swore at his partner-in-crime as the hounds sniffed and licked at him, bashing his legs with their long, spotted tails.

'The early bird catches the worm, Middleton – or should I say "the fox" in this case? I see you've done the deed, so we should be in for a good day's sport, and my hounds will get their breakfast. Just look at them: keen as mustard, they can smell the foxes' blood already.' Oversby laughed cruelly.

'Keep your voice down. I don't want the lad to hear,

313

for he's fond of the bloody things.' Clifford pulled on his boots and laced them up as he sat on the garden wall.

'Going soft in your old age! It must be that pretty thing of a sister-in-law that's giving you manners. But I hear she's to marry the Allen lad. Now what's she doing that for, when there's the likes of me still single?'

'She'd want nowt with you, you old letch. You bat for the wrong side, for a start.' Clifford knew that Oversby preferred young men; it was well known, but nobody dared say anything out of turn. Even though it was illegal, Oversby held too much power in high places.

'Keep your voice down. I've always got a good eye for the ladies, and you don't know what you're talking about.'

'Aye, well, neither do you. What have you brought a spare horse for? It looks as jumpy as a box of frogs – you must only just have broken him in.' Clifford looked at the spirited gelding, which pawed the ground, wanting to be away from all the commotion of the hunt.

'I've brought him for you. You could hardly join us on that nag you've got; it's only fit for the knacker's yard. You'd be at the bottom of your field and we'd be halfway to Sedbergh. I'll not have you made the laughing stock of the hunt.' Oversby hit his leg with his riding crop as he watched Clifford pull on his waistcoat.

'I wasn't thinking of coming with you. I don't have the stomach for blood sports – there's nowt pleasant about seeing something live pulled apart by another animal.' Clifford had no time for the middle classes with

314

their so-called sport, and hunting had never appealed to him.

'Nonsense, man. It gets the pulses racing, to feel the horse under your thighs and chase the hounds when they know they are near the kill – there's nothing like it.' Oversby leaned down from his grey and whispered into Clifford's ear, 'Five guineas says I beat this miserable bunch to the kill; and if you do, I'll double it.' He leaned back in the saddle and watched Clifford look around him at the gathering hunt, weighing up whom he could outwit and outride. 'Aye, my gelding doesn't look a bad option now, so get yourself across its back. The hounds have found the trail.'

Clifford looked up towards the back of Grouse Hall. The hounds were baying in delight as they followed the foxes that had been sent up the gill edge and through the trees.

'Kitty, bring me my crop. I'm off with the hunt,' he yelled through the open kitchen door, before grabbing hold of the gelding's reins. Its eyes flashed and steam came out of its nostrils as Clifford tried to mount the frisky animal.

'Hold still, you bastard! You'll not master me – nobody does that.' Clifford led it to the mounting steps next to the barn and, with his injured arm holding the animal's mane and reins, pulled himself onto the back of the edgy horse. 'Now that I've got you, you'll do as I say.' He pulled back on the reins, making the bit unsettle the creature.

'Just be gentle with the bit, for he's soft-mouthed.

315

Don't damage him.' Oversby was a horse man and, while he wasn't above tearing fox cubs to pieces, being cruel to a horse was another matter.

Kitty came running out of the house with the crop in her hand. 'What are you doing on the back of that animal? You can't ride that with your bad arm. It looks like the Devil himself – just look at him flaring his nostrils. Come down, before you hurt yourself.' Kitty pulled on Clifford's boot, pleading with him not to be such an idiot.

'Out of my way, woman, there's a stake at risk.' Clifford snatched the crop from Kitty, brushing her aside, and horse and rider dashed out of the yard of Grouse Hall as if the Devil himself was chasing them. Oversby and the hunt followed, with a few stray hounds baying in their wake.

The horn could be heard loudly and clearly as the party made its way up the gill and over to neighbouring Uldale, with the hounds baying more and more as they got closer to their prey.

Kitty shivered in the sharp, frosty air of the morning; she was still in her nightdress with her shawl wrapped around her. The Devil take the man; he'd never listen to her when that fat, bloated Oversby was around. She looked up at the spare bedroom window. Through the dirty pane she could see Tobias looking at her. There were tears trickling down his face, for he knew all too well what had happened to his pet foxes. Damn Oversby; he brought nothing but bother whenever he visited.

*

316

Clifford trotted along with the rest of the hunt, next to Oversby and Reg Towler, the head huntsman. He didn't feel easy with the Lunesdale huntsmen, for they were all of better stock than him, and he had a feeling they were sneering at him having to be given a decent horse to join them. What did they know? They knew nowt about him, and there were some things he could tell them about their portly benefactor, Oversby.

Clifford decided to break away from the pack and put his horse into a canter as he followed the baying hounds, with their tails wagging and their noses down to the ground, hard on the trail of the foxes.

'Get yourself back here, Middleton,' Clifford could hear Oversby yelling at him as the hounds packed together at the first sighting of a fox's white brush.

The race was on to catch the fox, and Clifford was going to win it. He whipped his horse, urging it to go faster, jumping a thicket hedge and nearly making the petrified animal stumble as it landed awkwardly on the other side.

'Damn you, get up – we've to be first at the kill,' Clifford shouted in the horse's ear, as he smiled a wily grin and lay almost flat with the horse. It was galloping like the wind over the heather, through the sphagnum-moss peat bog and down into the pastures of Uldale. The fox darted in front of the pack, running for its life, its tongue red and dripping as it tried to outflank the hounds and rider. With a jubilant yell, both horse and hounds went in for the kill. Clifford looked behind him, realizing he was the first man there.

317

As he spotted his rival, Oversby, he pulled too hard on the reins, making the horse stop in its tracks with pain and fright. Clifford lost his footing in the stirrups, holding on for dear life as he flew over the horse's head and landed in front of it in a crumpled mess, his legs bent under him on the grassy slopes that led down to Cautley Spout. The horse bowed its head and sniffed at him. Sensing death, it whinnied loudly and then, dragging its harness, moved off to graze. The hounds sniffed and dribbled around Clifford, their saliva dripping onto his still body, the thrill of the fox gone, as the chase came to an end and the three lead hounds tore and argued over the few sinews that were left.

'Out of my way, you bloody things.' Oversby jumped off his horse and strode among the gathering hounds with his whip.

'Is he all right?' Reg Towler came running up behind him. 'He rode like a fool.'

'Aye, well, he'll not ride like a fool again. The silly bugger has broken his neck.' Oversby knelt down on one knee and gently closed Clifford's startled eyes. 'How the hell do we tell his wife?' He ran his fingers through his long, fine grey hair.

'Well, I'm not telling her, poor bitch. He was your friend, and he broke his neck on your horse, so it's your job.' The whipper-in spat and whistled for his dogs, as Oversby knelt with his head in his hands as he thought about what he had to tell Kitty.

'At least give me a hand with putting his body over

my horse. I'll walk him back over the fell top.' The rest of the hunt watched from their horses.

'Here, grab his arms and I'll carry his legs.'

Both men lifted the body of Clifford over the saddle of Oversby's grey mare and caught the skittish gelding that had been to blame for his untimely death.

'I wouldn't want to be in your shoes, mate. You heard her telling him not to go, and now you fetch him back dead.'

Oversby grabbed both horses' reins and started walking with a heavy heart back over the fell into Garsdale, with Clifford's body swaying on the back of his mare.

The rest of the hunt watched until Oversby and his burden were out of sight over the skyline, before sounding the horn to gather the hounds and trot back down the road to Sedbergh. It was still not yet lunchtime, but any appetite for the day had gone, with the death of Clifford. What fools the two men had been, and it had been no sport chasing a hand-reared fox, no sport at all.

Oversby made his way down the fellside following the gill, with two subdued horses and the body of Clifford. He rehearsed the words he was going to say to Kitty over and over again, and they still didn't convey the sentiment he wanted. He hadn't liked the man – in fact he had thought him a fool. A fool who was parted too easily from his money. But at the end of the day, he'd spent many a good night at Grouse Hall. His heart sank as he smelled the smoke from the fire burning at

Grouse Hall, and heard Kitty shouting for Tobias to come in for his dinner. He stood for a minute and looked around him. An hour or two earlier he was laughing at his hot-headed friend, and now he was bringing home his corpse. It was no day to die on; the sky was too blue, the air too sharp, too clear and cold, giving you a zest for life.

He watched as the autumn leaves fell silently to earth through the frost-filled air. They twisted and turned towards the ground, making a mottled carpet of yellow, russet and brown. He wished it was himself thrown over the back of his saddle. Yes, he had money, but he'd no wife to go home to and, most of all, no son. In fact if he was honest, fool or no fool, Clifford had been the one true friend who had always been there for him, and now he was gone. The bastard never did know when he was well off. Oversby smiled before whispering, 'Come on then, let's do it. You can't get out of this one, you old bastard.'

Oversby tied the two horses up outside the barn at Grouse Hall and knocked quietly on the half-open door of the kitchen. He gave a soft cough, and Kitty looked round to see who was standing in her doorway.

'So, you two idiots are back, then. I suppose you'll be wanting something to eat. Grown men chasing defenceless creatures – you should have more sense.' She went to the pan of potatoes that was boiling on the fire.

'Kitty, Kitty, I'm sorry. I've some bad news . . .'

'What, Clifford's lost his bet again. That's only to

be expected.' She banged two plates down on the kitchen table and picked up the pan of potatoes.

Oversby walked towards her and grabbed her arm, making young Tobias, who was sitting at the table, cower with fear.

'Listen to me, woman. I'm trying to tell you, your husband's dead.' Oversby realized that all his rehearsing had been in vain, as Kitty dropped the pan and screamed. 'I told him to go easy with it – but you know what he's like. Sit down, and gather your thoughts.' He placed his arm around Kitty's sobbing shoulders and guided her to the chair next to the fire.

'How did it happen?' she sobbed. 'Let me out, let me go and see him.' She stood up, her legs nearly buckling beneath her.

'Stay here and I'll carry his body into your parlour and lay him on the sofa. You'd better make the lad go upstairs; he'll not want to see him like he is.' Oversby nodded to Tobias, who hadn't moved from the table.

'Tobias, go upstairs! Go to your room.' Kitty nearly screamed the words at the frightened lad. Tobias ran out of the kitchen along the dark passage and up to the front bedroom, where he peered out of the window, watching Oversby struggling to carry his father's corpse into Grouse Hall.

'I didn't know he was going to be so daft on that horse of mine. It's frisky at the best of times, but he drove it too hard. The bloody thing has a mind of its own.'

Kitty sobbed over the body of her husband. Clifford

had been a bastard and a cad, but in her own way she had loved him. Now she was left on her own in the rambling, damp ruins of Grouse Hall, with his illegitimate son and no money in the bank.

Tobias crept down the stairs and stood quietly, half-hidden behind the parlour door. He peered at the body of his father lying lifeless on the sofa, and at Kitty wailing, while Oversby tried to comfort her. He didn't know whether to cry or not, for he'd always been treated like a dog by his father. But now the day he had dreamed of was here: his father had actually died, and he was free of the tyrant who had made his life a living hell.

Tobias stood for a moment, watching the scene, and then he ran; he ran as if he had wings on his feet. He had to tell Daisy, she had to know. This was important news and he had to share it with someone he loved.

'Tobias, what on earth's the matter? What are you doing here, and where's Kitty? Does she know you're here?' Daisy put down her darning and placed her arm around the red-faced and panting lad who had just burst into her home.

Tobias was bent double, trying to catch his breath, and coughing and sputtering as Daisy watched him. 'He's dead! Clifford, my father, is dead.' Tobias tried to catch his breath as he watched Daisy's face.

'Don't talk silly, Tobias; he'll not be dead. What makes you say that? You shouldn't say such things.' Daisy sat the young lad down and told him to get his breath.

'He's in our parlour on the sofa. He fell off a horse

and broke his neck this morning. Oversby and Kitty are with him now.'

'He can't be. You are wrong – you've heard wrong.' Daisy shook her head in disbelief.

'He is! The old sod's dead; he'll not hurt me again. It serves him right. He had my foxes killed.' Tobias realized what the death of Clifford actually meant to him: no longer would he clipped around the ear every five minutes, or shouted at and left hungry, for his persecutor was dead. And Tobias felt jubilant at his death.

Daisy sat down. She didn't know what to feel. She'd felt hatred towards Clifford for so long, and then she had to be grateful to him, for taking her in when she needed somewhere to go. But now, if Tobias was right, he was dead.

'Have they had the doctor?' asked Daisy.

'What do you need a doctor for, if he's dead?' Tobias asked.

'You just do, Tobias, to make sure he's dead.'

'He's dead all right. I saw him being carried into the house. Oversby had to drag him.' Tobias grinned. 'Oversby couldn't get his breath, and he dropped Clifford's head on the kitchen floor and he never yelled.'

'Come on, we'll have to go. My sister will need me.' Daisy picked up her shawl, wrapping it around her, and held out her hand for Tobias.

'I want to stop here. I don't want to go home.' Tobias sat and sulked.

'We are going to Grouse Hall. I'll be needed, and

323

they will wonder where you are. My sister has enough on her plate without worrying about you.'

'She'll not know I've gone, and she won't care.' Tobias folded his arms.

Daisy grabbed him and pulled him out of the house. 'I'm taking you home, and I need to comfort my sister. Now get yourself up that road.' The last thing she needed was a stroppy lad who didn't realize how the death of his father could affect him. Daisy felt a pang of sadness. She'd known Clifford all her life, and now he was gone. What would her sister do? Would Grouse Hall be safe, or had Clifford wagered it away? The world was going to change for Tobias and Kitty, but would it be for the better or for the worse?

25

Daisy fiddled with her gloves and watched as they carried Clifford's coffin out into the damp autumn air. A fine drizzle fell, making the moorland around Lunds chapel look bleak and grey. The flagstones were slippery with the wet weather, and one of the bearers nearly slipped as he lost his footing when turning the corner to the burial ground that overlooked the wild moorland. The fine raindrops hung like jewels on the long grass in the chapel churchyard, and a lonely sheep bleated a lament as Clifford was lowered into the ground.

'Thank you for coming, Sam.' Daisy squeezed his hand as he stood beside her.

'Nay, you needn't thank me. I wouldn't be much of a fiancé if I didn't pay my respects on a day like today.'

'No, but you needn't have come. Clifford didn't win many friends in his life, and those that he did are unsavoury.' Daisy looked around at the small group of mourners standing around the grave.

'And so we commit his body to the ground. Earth to earth, ashes to ashes . . .' The vicar stood pious and tall over the grave as he gave Clifford his last blessing.

Kitty was the only one weeping, and Daisy couldn't help but notice how supportive Oversby had become to her sister in the few days since Clifford's death. Even now he was offering his shoulder to cry on. She shook her head – knowing Joshua, he'd think he was in with a chance of buying Grouse Hall from the grieving widow. He probably owned half of it by now anyway, in outstanding money owed to him by Clifford.

Tobias stood by Kitty. It didn't look as if he'd grieved for one minute since his father had died. But who could blame him? For most of his life he'd been treated like nothing more than a dog by Clifford. It had been a miracle that he'd survived past his first birthday, the way he'd been treated.

'What will she do now?' Sam nodded towards Kitty.

'I don't know. She'll probably farm Grouse Hall on her own – plenty of women do farm without a man's help. At least she'll be clear of Clifford squandering all the money by his drinking and gambling. My father must be turning in his grave. He thought he'd set up Kitty for life, and instead he made her life a misery and turned her into an old woman.' Daisy couldn't believe that she had once been jealous of her sister.

'Talking of fathers, my father is working his hardest on my mother. He made some mince pies with your Christmas mincemeat and didn't say where the filling had come from. You should have heard her while she was eating them. It was amusing how quickly she backtracked, when she found out you supplied the mince-meat.'

'I don't know how to win her over. I can understand that she only wants the best for you – I would, if I had a son – but what can I do? I am what I am.' Daisy sighed.

'Be yourself, Daisy love – she'll come round. Here, look, scatter some earth on Clifford and let's put him to rest.'

The vicar offered Daisy a small box of heavy clay soil, so that she could take a handful and sprinkle it over the coffin. She thanked him, then went to the grave edge and threw her handful on the oak coffin lid. Buried in the ground with Clifford lay the secret of that terrible afternoon, and now she was free to live her life. No one else knew about her transgression, and now no one need ever know.

'I hope he's at peace.' Daisy looked at Sam. 'He never was in life.'

'Aye, and nobody else was when they were around him. Clifford was one of those that you knew shone too brightly and wouldn't last as long as most. He either ate you up or spat you out.' Sam winced at the thought of Clifford, as he wiped his gloves free of the soil.

'We aren't doing a bad job of talking ill of the dead, are we?' Daisy took Sam's hand. 'Come on, let's go home. We've seen him buried, and I'm not one for funeral teas.'

'Are you sure? Shouldn't you stay, for your sister and Tobias?'

327

'My sister seems to be otherwise engaged, and Tobias thinks it's the best day of his life. I don't think we will be missed at all.'

'No, happen not. Let's be away, lass, and have a bit of time together.'

It had only been a week since Clifford had been buried, but it seemed like a lifetime. Daisy had barely been at home, as she went back and forth to Grouse Hall to make sure her sister was all right. She needn't have worried because, without Clifford, both Tobias and Kitty had found a new spark of life. Kitty's only worry was that the solicitor had not written to her, as he had promised, after she'd enquired about Clifford's will, and she needed to know where she stood.

Daisy had pondered all week over whether to give her sister her full inheritance from her father, now that Clifford was dead, and she'd made up her mind that she would. With Clifford out of the way, there was no one to squander it, and Kitty would need it in the coming months. Daisy pulled her hat on and was about to start on her daily trek to Grouse Hall when there was a knock on the door.

She opened it to find a small boy standing on her doorstep.

'Letter for you, Mrs Lambert. I'm delivering it for Mr Winterskill, the solicitor in Hawes. He says can you read it and send your reply back with me.' The boy passed Daisy the letter and stood patiently on the doorstep, as she quickly opened it and read the few brief words instructing her to come to his offices on Tuesday next.

'You can tell Mr Winterskill that I'll be in his office at two o'clock on Tuesday, weather permitting.' Daisy was puzzled. Had he got muddled up between the sisters? Surely it was Kitty he wanted to see? She watched the young lad running back along the track out of Grisedale and then pulled on her hat. She'd explain to Kitty about her father's money, and see if she'd also received a letter from Mr Winterskill.

When Daisy reached Grouse Hall, the fire was burning brightly, and Tobias and the dog that had previously been kept outside in the shed were curled up on the rug in front of it.

'Well, somebody looks content.' Daisy took off her hat and stood and looked at the lad, as he tickled the dog's stomach while it tried to nip his hand.

'Kitty says I can bring Jip into the house now. It's to make up for what happened to my fox cubs. I know what happened to them, you know. I heard some men talking at the funeral.' Tobias hid his head in the dog's fur and stifled a sob.

'Aye, well, no good came of it. You shouldn't tame wild creatures, and nature has her way of getting back at you.' Daisy sat down at the table.

'Is that why my father died? Because nature knew he'd done wrong by the foxes?'

'Your father died because he was an idiot, who always thought he knew best and listened to nobody – that's why he died.' Kitty came into the room and answered, before Daisy could get a word in. 'Isn't that right, Daisy? I'm beginning to find out how much better off I am without him. We'll manage, won't we, Tobias? As long as I can keep food in our bellies and a roof over our heads.' She sat down next to Daisy and sighed while looking across at her sister. 'I thought you weren't coming today. You said you were catching up with the cooking?'

'Well, for one thing, I've a confession to make. Now promise you'll not get mad at me, Kitty, because I thought it was for the best while Clifford was alive.' Daisy put a bag up on the table and watched her sister's eyes. 'When our father died, the solicitor told me to give you his dresser and its contents. Well, like you and Clifford, I thought it held only his baking stuff, but when I looked inside the middle drawers, they all had a false back to them. That's when I found all this.' Daisy pushed the bag full of money towards Kitty. 'He never did trust a bank. I didn't give it to you before, because I knew Clifford would squander it.' Daisy paused. 'I hope you're not mad at me?'

Kitty started to count the money.

'There's hundreds here – there's more money than I've ever seen in my life! How can I be mad with you? You did right, for Clifford would have gone through it like a knife through butter. I don't know how to thank you.' Kitty's hands were shaking and her eyes filled up with tears. 'I was trying to put a brave face on it, but I was beginning to wonder how we'd survive winter. The back-end lambs didn't make much money, and I had to pay for the funeral . . . And then we've got to eat.'

'Shh! You're all right, Kitty. You are a little short, because that's how I've been paying you to look after Tobias. I couldn't have done it otherwise. But I'm just glad our father made us equal. You got the money, I got the house, and I'm sorry I didn't tell you earlier.' Daisy got up, walked round to her sister and hugged her.

'I'm sorry, too, that my words were sharp. We were always close when we were growing up. It was Clifford who drew us apart, and the fact that you left and went away. Talking of which, I nearly forgot to tell you that I found a letter. It's addressed to you. Clifford had hidden it in his bill box. He'd never have given it to you – he liked to keep us all under his control.' Kitty went to the kitchen drawer and came back with the letter, handing it to Daisy.

She looked at the handwriting. It was Jim's from Leeds, and she smiled and sighed. She'd thought she'd been forgotten, but she should have known better.

'I still can't believe I have all this money! I'm rich, and I don't have to worry. I'd better put it away. Are you not going to open your letter? It's been waiting for you long enough?' Kitty chuckled and took the bag of money off the table and placed it into the oak corner cupboard, locking it carefully.

'No, I'll read it at home – it'll pass a minute or two this evening.' Daisy smiled. She wanted to read it at her leisure, not when her sister was sneaking a look over

331

her shoulder. 'Did the solicitor get in touch with you today? His office lad gave me a letter saying that I should meet him on Tuesday at two. I thought he might have delivered a letter to you, too?'

'No, I've not heard anything. Tobias and I have been at home all day. Why would he want you?'

'That's the strange thing – I don't know. I wonder if the lad got the houses muddled up, but then again it was my name on the letter. I was certain the solicitor would have been in touch with you.' Daisy was puzzled; she'd no need of the solicitor when it came to Clifford. Anyway, she'd go to his office on Tuesday and tell him so.

'He perhaps wants you to be an executor, because Clifford probably didn't have a will. I can't remember him ever going to Winterskill's. In fact I'm sure that he hated the man.' Kitty poked the fire and added a peat log, while walking around the sleeping dog and Tobias.

'That must be it then. I never thought of that.' Daisy's mind was settled.

'Well, let's face it, our Daisy, I'm not expecting another windfall. I'll just be happy if I can stay here, and I should be all right. I remember Old Mr Winterskill coming round just after you'd gone wandering. He came to see Clifford's father – old Tobias – to amend his will, because he'd decided to change it. In fact our father was with him – he was a signatory – and I remember they were all in the parlour one afternoon when Clifford was away. When Winterskill and our father had gone, I spoke to old Tobias. You'll remember how difficult

332

that was, with him unable to speak and having to write everything down. And he just wrote on his slate 'house left to Bastard', so I know it's Clifford's. It's all old Tobias ever called him. He was ashamed of his son. I used to feel so sorry for him.'

'You'll be fine then, Kitty. Mr Winterskill must just want to check everything with a family member, to make sure it's done right. Anyway you seem very friendly with Joshua Oversby, I noticed. Be careful with that one. He's either got his eye on you and Grouse Hall or, God help me, Tobias. I don't like him one bit.' Daisy spoke her mind while she knew she could get away with it.

'He's decided he's played the bachelor too long. Clifford's death shook him up and made him realize that life's too short. He's been the greatest help to me since the funeral, so you be careful what you say. Besides, you can't talk – that Sam Allen's only after what he can get. Besides, Joshua owns Yore House and all the acres around it. He's worth a bob or two, and he's got servants.' Kitty folded her arms and waited for the response.

'Kitty, Clifford's hardly cold in his coffin and you have already weighed up your next man. Well, you just be careful. Keep Tobias out of his way, and don't be fooled; Joshua only uses women for one thing.'

Daisy was cross. Kitty was jumping out of the frying pan into the fire – had she no sense?

'I think you'd better go. Thank you for giving me my inheritance at long last. And I'll be waiting to see what Henry Winterskill says after your visit.' Kitty was furious. How dare her younger sister give her advice on men. Daisy was a fine one to talk.

'Right, I'm going. You know where I am, if you need me.' Daisy pulled on her hat briskly and left the warm kitchen, without even saying goodbye to Tobias. *Family*, she thought, *you're better off without them!*

Daisy sat quietly, reading her letter by the flickering candlelight. She smiled as she read the first line: *Dear Daisy petal*. She hadn't been called that since Leeds. She missed Jim, for he made her smile and feel sixteen again. Then she read the next line:

> *Susie's left me. She's run off with one of our salesmen. Big brother's saying that he told me so, and the Italian witch is loving every second. I don't half miss you – write soon.*
>   *All my love, Jim*

Daisy smiled, closed her eyes and thought of Jim. She missed him, too. He'd broken her heart when he'd become engaged to Susie, but now Susie had gone. She'd write back, just to cheer Jim up and see how things were. She was sure Sam would understand.

Tuesday was market day at Hawes and the street was packed with traders and farmers trying to sell their wares and animals. Daisy walked down the street, saying hello to the people she had come to know and trust. The gossip about her arrival had now been replaced by something else juicier, and the locals were beginning to accept her as Sam Allen's fiancée and as the lass who made jams for Luke. She waved as she passed the window of Luke Allen's busy shop. She could see him slicing some bacon, and Sam serving a customer. If she had time she'd call on them, once she had been to the solicitor's.

Daisy took a seat in the reception area and waited for the solicitor's office door to open. She felt uneasy; she still wasn't sure why she was here, and she'd not spoken to her sister since Kitty went into a huff over Daisy's advice about Joshua Oversby. The reception walls were painted in a sage green, with dark varnished doors and skirting. Along with the three chairs for waiting guests, there was a large walnut wall-clock marking time, which made Daisy feel more nervous with every minute. Why was she here? It didn't make sense.

The office door opened suddenly. 'Ah! Daisy, glad you're here. Please, do come through.' Henry Winterskill shook her hand and then prompted her into his office. 'Please take a seat. Are you warm enough? I'm afraid this old building is rather draughty, and there's a sneaky northerly wind today, blowing straight through these windows.' Winterskill smiled and then lowered his head to look at the papers in front of him.

'I'm fine, thank you.' Daisy felt even more nervous. She was sure Mr Winterskill was going to say something she wouldn't be happy about – she could just sense it.

'Now, the sudden death of Mr Clifford Middleton

335

has put us both in an awkward position, and I am going to try and handle it as sensitively as I can. If I upset you, and you want me to stop, please let me know.' Henry looked up from his papers and smiled at Daisy. 'Some time ago my father, whom I inherited the firm from, was requested to go and take a statement from, and make a will for, Clifford Middleton's father, Tobias. Also at this meeting was your father, Tom.' Henry leaned across the desk and stopped for a moment, watching Daisy's face. 'At that meeting Tobias, in his own way, told my father that Clifford Middleton had raped you and left you with child. I'm sorry to have to ask you, but is that correct?'

Daisy bowed her head and nodded, her eyes filling with tears.

'I'm sorry, but I have to continue.' Henry paused for a moment.

Daisy blew her nose and raised her head. 'I didn't realize what rape was then. But yes, he did.'

'Your father went on to say that you subsequently had the child and were told it was born dead.'

Daisy nodded. 'He's buried under the apple tree at Mill Race.' The tears poured forth. She could feel the years of grief, guilt and hurt flowing out of her.

'I'm sorry, Daisy, but what I'm about to say is going to be hard for you.' Henry paused again. 'Your father lied to you, because he thought it was for your own good. The child lived; your mother bathed him in warm water when she went downstairs, and what you thought to be a stillborn baby lived. However, your father couldn't

336

abide the sight of the child, so he took him to Clifford at Grouse Hall, where he's been living ever since. The child called Tobias is your son, Daisy; he's your baby that you thought dead.'

Henry leaned back in his chair and looked at the young woman. He tried to imagine what she must be thinking.

'No, he can't be – he's not mine. He didn't live . . . he's dead under the apple tree. It must be a lie.' Daisy pictured the lad whom she had befriended from the very first morning at Grouse Hall: the dark hair of his father; and those eyes, which she now knew looked like hers.

Her heart pounded. Tobias was a good lad, she knew he was; even though life had treated him poorly, he was still kind-hearted. And now she realized that Tobias was hers – her son. What was she going to do with a son? Did she want him or not, and could she cope with a boy she had believed to be dead?

The solicitor ploughed on with his duties while Daisy gathered her thoughts.

'This letter is signed by your father and by old Tobias Middleton, both swearing that the young lad is yours and was born out of wedlock because Clifford forced himself upon you. Now the reason they did this is because your father regretted treating you as he did. And although he tried to find you, he couldn't. He also realized that the child was being brought up by Clifford as little better than a dog. So he went to see Clifford's father and, although Tobias had suffered a stroke, he still had his wits about him. He protected your son's life by making him the heir to Grouse Hall, such that if Clifford hurt a hair on Tobias's head, he would have lost everything. As it is, Tobias hasn't had the best of childhoods, but at least he's alive. So, Daisy, I don't know if it's good news or not today, but you have a son you thought was dead, who is the heir to Grouse Hall.'

'What about my sister? Does she know?' Daisy was still putting everything together.

'She doesn't know anything, and I'm afraid the poor woman is left with nothing, apart from a lot of IOUs to Clifford's gambling friends. I have, however, drafted her a letter, because she will need to know where she stands. Please take a look at it and let me know what you think.' Henry passed the letter over.

Daisy had to read it at least twice. She handed it back to Henry.

'Is it to your satisfaction?'

She nodded.

'Then I'll have my boy deliver it.' Henry folded it and placed it in an envelope.

'No, I'll deliver it to her. She needs to know there was nothing between Clifford and me, and that I was young and stupid.' Daisy breathed in deeply and sighed, for her life had just been turned upside down.

'As you wish.' Henry smiled and passed her the letter.

'And Tobias?' Daisy's eyes filled with tears.

'Just take him home and love him. He's a lucky lad to have a caring mother, and a farm waiting for him when he grows up. It could be a good farm, could Grouse Hall, if it was looked after. Clifford's father made a good living from it, and that is why he had such a privileged life.' Henry Winterskill rose from his chair. 'There's paperwork to sign and various things to tie up, but I think you've been told enough for today. It must have come as a shock. And, Daisy, you must never feel guilty about what happened with Clifford Middleton. He was a cad, and I know you aren't the first young woman he has forced himself onto.'

Daisy smiled. She knew her eyes were red and swollen and that she probably looked a mess, but years of guilt had been lifted. Now she was going to get her son.

26

'You didn't need to give me that letter. As soon as you walked out of the door saying you'd been asked to go to the solicitor, I put two and two together. All these years I must have been bloody thick. My father talking to old Tobias, and then Tobias writing 'house left to Bastard' on his slate. That wasn't Clifford – it was your bastard son he was leaving it to.'

'I didn't know. I didn't know my son had lived, Kitty – they told me he was dead.' Daisy stood in the kitchen of Grouse Hall watching her sister pace back and forth as she read the letter.

'Clifford was always eyeing you up and, like a stupid puppy, you used to make eyes at him. I used to look at you and wish you dead. It's a pity I didn't get my wish.'

'Kitty, don't say that. I'm your sister. It wasn't my fault he raped me.'

'And then, when he died, you took pity on me and gave me some of our father's money. But how do I know you didn't keep half yourself?' Kitty looked with venom at her sister. In that moment she hated Daisy; and the way her father had always favoured her. Daisy was the clever one, the one who could bake and clean, the practical one; while she, Kitty, had been the pretty one that everyone admired, until life with Clifford put paid to all that. But Daisy was her sister and, no matter how much she thought she hated her, Kitty knew she always would be.

'I gave you it all. How much more do you think Father had? I don't know how he managed to save that amount. Listen to me, Kitty. Nothing's changed – you can still live here. Tobias is only young and doesn't need the farm yet.' Daisy was hurt by her sister's outburst. She knew the news was hard to bear, but she'd hoped that Kitty would understand.

'Shut your miserable, simpering mouth and take your bastard child with you out of my house. I never want to see either of you again.' Kitty grabbed Tobias by the scruff of his neck from where he was sitting and dragged him to the kitchen door. 'Go on, get out of my sight – neither of you is worth anything to me.' Kitty watched as Daisy ran after her son, making sure Tobias was all right.

'There's one thing you are forgetting, Kitty. If we are being brutally honest, then Grouse Hall belongs to Tobias. Which means it's mine until he reaches twenty-one, and you'd do well to remember that.' Daisy put her arm around Tobias. He was her son and no one was going to hurt him any more.

'There's just a few words that Clifford would have said, and that's "Ah, fuck off the lot of you." And this time he's right.' Kitty slammed the kitchen door, leaving Daisy and Tobias out in the cold night air.

'Come on, Tobias, you are coming to live with me. Now stop your crying – all's going to be fine. You'll have your own room, you can go to school and be well fed; and, most of all, you can call me "Mam" now.' Daisy's eyes filled with tears as she put her arm around the little body.

'What about my dog? I need Jip. I can't leave him there!' Tobias cried.

'We'll get another one. Now, how big should it be, and what colour? And what should we call him? He will be all yours to love, every day.' As they walked the two miles back to Grisedale, Daisy knew there were going to be hard days ahead for her and her son.

'Didn't I tell you that you want nowt to do with that lass. I knew she was trouble, the minute she walked over that threshold. There's no smoke without fire. Everybody in Hawes were talking about her, saying she'd been sleeping with her brother-in-law at Grouse Hall. Joshua Oversby says he saw them in bed together.' Mary Allen was lecturing Sam over the breakfast table. 'And now it turns out that the urchin-like lad was hers all along. Set your cap at someone else, lad, she's not the one for you.'

Sam was heartbroken. He'd gone to Mill Race to see Daisy, for his usual Sunday stroll with her, only to be confronted by the wild-looking Tobias, whom she was now calling her son. She'd sat Sam down and, with tears in her eyes, had told him what had happened, and said how sorry she was for misleading him, because of her shame. But Sam had doubted Daisy's story, as his mother's warnings rang in his ears, and now he felt cold and distant towards her. She'd lied when having that first tea with them, so what more was she hiding?

'Just leave it, Mother. I don't know what to think. Daisy says she was raped, and that she didn't know the lad had been born alive. My head is so full of folk telling me what to do, and what they think's good for me, that I don't know what to think.' Sam put his head in his hands. He loved Daisy with every inch of his heart, but why had she lied? Surely she must have realized the lad was hers.

'She's no good. And your father can just stop ordering stuff from her, because I want nowt of hers in our shop.' Mary Allen clattered the dirty breakfast dishes and glared at her son.

Luke smiled as he served his early-morning customer and passed her the change from a shilling. The raised voices from mother and son could be heard in the shop.

'Trouble brewing then?' enquired the old woman, who was a frequent customer.

'Aye, our lad's young woman has apparently got a bairn, and the father is her sister's dead husband.' Luke put his head down. He'd heard nothing else from his wife all night, and he was at his wits' end.

'Aye, it's all over Hawes. Some say she went with him freely, and some say he had his way with her and that's why she buggered off. Whatever she did, she's got

343

a bairn to raise that'll need a father. Not that she's short of a bob or two. I hear her lad was left Grouse Hall by his grandfather. The father must have been in the wrong, if old Tobias left it like that. I never could stand that Clifford – he was always a clever sod.' The old woman looked at Luke. 'Get yourself to Henry Winter skill's. He'll tell you right, then you'll know where you stand.' She had every sympathy for Luke. Mary was known as a nag who always thought herself better than anyone else, and she'd be hating the gossip.

'Aye, that's a thought. I'll make a point of seeing him – see what he says. He'll give me a right tale. I'm grateful to you for listening, Mrs Moore. Here, take two currant teacakes to toast for your tea, on the house!' Luke shoved two teacakes into a paper bag and dropped them into Mrs Moore's basket.

'They'll be grand. And just think on: she's not the only lass that had a baby out of wedlock, and she'll not be the last. I seem to remember your wedding was a bit sharpish. And I remember your mother denying the baby was yours, but by God Sam's the image of his father now. Right, I'll be off; thanks again for the teacakes.' Mrs Moore trudged out of the shop. She had a good memory for her age, and perhaps it had come into use today.

Daisy looked out of the doorway of Mill Race. It was wet, cold and the mist was hanging around the fells like a ghostly spectre. The weather matched her mood. She'd not slept for nights – not a wink since Sunday evening, when she had no option but to tell Sam her news. And now she knew that his mother would be drip-feeding him poisoned thoughts about her and Clifford and the conception of Tobias. She should have given Sam his engagement ring back there and then, for no wedding would ever take place now.

'Close the door, Mam,' called Tobias as he sat at the table trying to work out some sums that Daisy was trying to teach him. 'It's cold, and my paper keeps blowing in the draught.'

Daisy smiled. The word 'Mam' sounded alien to her, and she couldn't get used to the fact that she was a mother to this child. She was trying to teach him things to make him brighter. After Christmas she'd enrol him at school in Hawes, but at the moment it was best if they kept away from the place; tongues were bound to be wagging.

'Fresh air never did anybody any harm and, besides, we've a good fire. You'd be colder up at Grouse Hall if you were still there.'

Daisy leaned against the doorway and watched the mist banking over the fell end. It was then that she noticed the grey shape of a man climbing the path around the fellside, before disappearing down the ridge and coming into sight again. Who'd be daft enough to come visiting them on a day like today? It wasn't even fit for a dog to be out.

'We've a visitor, Tobias, but I can't make out who it is, apart from that it's a man and he's walking. He must be half-mad, coming out in this weather.'

'I hope it isn't Oversby. I don't like that man,' said Tobias.

'It'll not be him, my love, for he knows he'll never be welcome here.' Daisy peered at the man making his way towards them and waving, as if possessed, once he caught sight of her in the doorway. No . . . it couldn't be; surely not. He wouldn't be so mad as to come all the way to Grisedale! But it was indeed Jim, looking like a drenched rat.

'God, how can you live in this godforsaken place? I'm drenched, my feet are soaked, and you never told me how far away from the station you were. I'm knackered!' Jim stood in the doorway. 'Aren't you going to ask me in then?' His face lit up with a beaming smile. 'Or have I to turn back and catch the next train to Leeds?'

'Oh! I'm sorry. You were the last person I expected to see, tramping over the fell in weather like this. What on earth made you come? Why didn't you write and let me know?' Daisy ushered the sopping-wet Jim into her warm kitchen, where he stood next to the fire as the water dripped off him, making puddles on the floor.

'You sounded down in your letter, and I needed an ear to talk into. And the top and bottom of it, Daisy petal, is that I've missed you.' Jim looked dejected as Daisy closed the door on the inclement weather.

'Well, I am down – nothing's going right. But look at you! At least take your coat off; you're sodden. Tobias, run and get me a towel out of that drawer upstairs, and then Jim can dry himself.'

Tobias looked at the tall man who had invaded his mother's kitchen and stood still.

'It's all right, Tobias. This is Jim. I used to work for him when I lived in Leeds, and he's a good man, so you needn't worry. Now, go and get that towel.' Daisy smiled at her son, who was trying to figure out where Jim fitted into the picture.

'Now then, Tobias, your mother told me all about you in her letter to me. In fact I've brought something for you.' Jim reached into his pocket and pulled out a small box. 'I thought you might like these.' He smiled as he pressed the box into Tobias's hands.

'What are they?' Tobias looked at the box.

'It's a box of tin soldiers. I thought you'd like to play with them.' Jim smiled.

'Tobias, could you get the towel? You can look at the soldiers when you come back down. Jim, take your coat off, before you catch your death; in fact take your trousers and jacket off, for you are soaked to the bone.' Daisy pulled her airing rack down from over the fire. The pulley squeaked as she tugged on the ropes while lowering it to chest height. 'Come on, you needn't be shy. I'll not look.'

Jim peeled off his soaking coat and then, bashfully, his trousers and jacket, as Daisy turned the other way. He then placed them over the airing rack, before sitting down in the chair next to the fire, with the knitted throw from the sofa around him.

'By, lass, tha's a fast mover! Only just got into the

house and you've got my breeches off me.' Jim laughed as he dried his wet hair with the towel.

'There will be none of that. I'm in enough bother, without you adding to it. But it is good to see you. I'll put the kettle on.' She reached for the kettle from the side of the fire.

Jim dropped his towel and reached for her hand. 'I've missed you so much, Daisy. I didn't realize how I felt about you until you'd left. You always did have a way of making me smile. Not like Susie, who was only after one thing.'

He looked into her eyes and held her wrist as Daisy stood there, not knowing what to say. Her heart was beating fast; the man she had always wanted was in her kitchen, in nothing more than his underwear, telling her that he had feelings for her.

'Don't be daft. I'm engaged to be married. You want nothing to do with me.' Daisy pulled her arm away and filled the kettle, before putting it on the hearth to boil.

'But in your letter you said you'd fallen out – that your fiancé didn't want the lad?' Jim watched Daisy as she put three cups and saucers on the table and sliced three pieces of sandwich cake.

'Aye, well, he wanted some time to think about things. And you can't blame him. It came as a shock to me to find that I was Tobias's mother, so it must have been worse for Sam – God knows what he thinks of me. And he'll be listening to the whole of Hawes talking, and his mother will be adding her four penn'orth. He'll come back if, and when, he's ready.'

Daisy watched Tobias lining up his soldiers at the end of the table. She loved the lad; the truth was that she'd loved him from the first time she set eyes on him under the kitchen table. And no way was anyone going to hurt him again – not as long as she had breath in her body. She hoped Tobias hadn't heard that he wasn't wanted by Sam.

'Anyway, how's everyone in Leeds? And what happened between you and Susie?'

'Don't mention Susie to me. Once that witch Angelina cut me out of the new factory, her father and William bought back my shares in the firm, and then Susie wanted nothing to do with me. She's living with the sales manager they took on, when they moved to Roundhay Park. He's a swanky bastard who wears a sharply cut suit and charms the birds out of the trees.' Jim stared into the fire. 'The bastard!'

'You never told me you'd been cut out of the firm. What are you doing now? Are you still living above the shop?' Daisy couldn't believe her ears. So much had changed since she had left Leeds; Jim had been the one with his sights set on one of the new houses in Roundhay then, not William.

'Nope. I've no fixed abode, as they say. Daisy petal, I'm down on my luck: my family don't want me; my fiancée has dumped me; and I spent my last few bob on them tin soldiers and a train ticket to see you. How the mighty have fallen, eh! Daisy, Susie took me for every penny. Not like you – you seem to have gone from strength to strength. Is it two properties you own now?'

Daisy passed Jim his cup of tea and a slice of cake. What a fool she'd been, thinking that Jim cared for her. He was just escaping from his worries. And in her letter to him she had said how comfortable her new home was, and how much it was worth.

'Well, I'm sorry to hear of your hard times – you never put any of that in your letters. How did you get the letters, if you aren't living at the shop?' Daisy decided she'd be cool with Jim. He still might make her heart flutter with his winning smile, but his love of money had always got him into bother. Now that she looked back on her life at Leeds, she could see that Jim had only ever thought about money – and Susie.

'Freddie passed them on to me. But I shouldn't bother you with my hard times, Daisy petal.' Jim slurped his tea down and ate his slice of cake as if he'd never been fed before. 'You still make a good cake, lass.'

The afternoon went quickly as Jim told Daisy of his woes, along with his lack of money. 'What time's your train back?' Daisy looked at the clock ticking on the mantel. She knew the last train was around eight o'clock and the night was pulling in, as it was nearly four in the afternoon and darkness was soon going to fall, because of the weather.

'Back? I thought you'd ask me to stay a while, once you knew my plight.' Jim nearly choked over his second slice of cake.

350

'Jim, I've too much hanging in the balance in my life at the moment. I don't need the hassle of you living here, and having to explain to Sam and confuse poor Tobias. You are a dear friend – and always will be – and I'm sorry you've landed on hard times, but you'll bounce back, I know you will.' As soon as Daisy had said the words she felt a pang of guilt. They'd been so close, or so she'd thought, but when she looked back, she'd been like a puppy in love, hanging on Jim's every word. It had been William who had always been the gentleman in her life. 'As you are down on your luck, and because you were always good to me, I'll give you your train fare home, and some more besides. I don't want you sleeping on the streets, but I can't have you living here.'

Daisy stood up from her chair and looked at the crestfallen Jim, who stared into the fire, not saying a word. She walked through to the kitchen and climbed the stairs. Reaching under her bed, she stretched out for her cash tin and took twenty pounds out of it. It had taken her a long time to earn it, but she could do without it, for the sake of a friend. A pang of guilt overcame her: should she let him stay? She closed the tin and held the twenty pounds tightly as she walked down the stairs and into the kitchen.

Jim was already climbing back into his damp clothes.

'I'm sorry, Daisy, I shouldn't have presumed you would let me stay here. I was desperate – I'll go now.' For once he was reserved and quiet. He pulled his sodden

351

coat back on him and tussled Tobias's hair. 'You look after your mother, she's a good woman.'

'Jim, take this.' Daisy held the three months' savings out to him. 'I want you to have it. Go back to Leeds, rent yourself a room and make a new start. I can't send you out into this night with nothing.' She forced the notes into his hand and smiled. 'Call it an investment; you owe me, just for a change.' She bit her lip and fought back the tears.

'Daisy petal, I can't take all this. I didn't come for your money.' Jim's eyes belied his lips, and he knew it.

'I know, but you look after yourself. You'll bounce back; you can't keep a good man down.' Daisy opened the door on the gathering dusk outside. 'Now get back over the fellside and onto the road while it's light, or else you'll lose your way.'

Jim stopped and wrapped his arms tightly round Daisy. His wet coat rubbed against her warm clothes and he kissed her on the cheek. 'Thank you, Daisy. I'm sorry I disappointed you. I disappoint everyone.' He looked into her eyes and, in that moment, she realized just how much she loved him.

'You take care. And you are no disappointment.' She squeezed his hand and wiped a tear away from her eye as she saw Jim walking away from her. She watched him for as long as she could, before the mist and the darkness enfolded him. 'God bless you, Jim Mattinson. Perhaps next time around things will be different.'

27

'Well, are you satisfied now?' Luke Allen stood in front of Mary and Sam Allen. 'We had to know, so I thought I'd get it from the horse's mouth.'

Henry Winterskill stood in the front room of Luke's family house. He'd broken every rule in the book, but Luke had convinced him that it was in Daisy's best interests that his family knew the truth, and that the situation needed clearing up.

'She really had a hard life with her family. Her father regretted treating her like he did and, what with her rape by her brother-in-law, can you blame Daisy for papering over the truth?' Henry stood his ground for Daisy. She had always been true to her word with him, and she was always polite.

'Aye, but she's got a lad! Our Sam will have to raise him,' cried Mary.

'Your Sam will be the owner of Mill Race, if he marries Daisy. And while young Tobias is growing up, he will be able to put aside the rent from Grouse Hall. I think Daisy will come off worse financially than Sam.

After all, on her marriage everything automatically becomes her husband's, and I presume you'll want her to work for your business without pay?'

Henry watched Mary's hard face. She'd listened too much to the gossip of Hawes, instead of taking as she found.

'She's a grand lass, Mary, give her a chance.' Luke looked at his son. 'And you – you big lummox – get yourself up Grisedale and get a date set. She's waited long enough. I'm sick of seeing your sulking face around the shop. The lad's young enough to know only you as his father. He'll soon forget Clifford Middleton; he can't call him his father anyway.' Luke liked the lass, and that was all that mattered.

'I don't know, Father. Folk will talk.' Sam thought of all the sniggers and whispers he'd put up with over the last few weeks – he hadn't liked it.

'So what? Your mother was six months pregnant with you when we got married, and folk talked about us then, but they soon get over it. Something else comes along, and they forget.' Luke looked at his son.

'Father, you didn't have to tell him that!' Mary blushed in front of Henry Winterskill.

'If he loves her, he'll put up with the gossip and enjoy his life with her. It's no good if he's ashamed of her. He thought nowt of having his way with her on Moorcock Show day. Aye, you didn't think I knew. I wasn't born yesterday, lad. I know that twinkle in a young man's eye. It's what got me into bother.'

'If you'll excuse me, I think I'll go now. This is for

354

your family to sort out.' Henry Winterskill had heard enough of the Allen family secrets. It was time to leave.

'Well, thank you, Henry, I appreciate your time. I'll see you right. Would your good lady wife like a box of groceries? Sam will deliver them in the morning – no charge, of course. Let's say for services rendered?' Luke showed Henry out of the door.

'Well, why are you still sitting here? Get gone!' Luke flicked his apron at Sam and grinned.

Sam needed no further excuse. He'd missed Daisy so much. He knew he loved her – he loved her with every beat of his heart – and he was fed up with his mother making his ears burn every day with her constant nagging. He shot out of his chair like a rabbit out of a trap, with his mother shouting warnings behind him.

'Leave him be, Mother. You've a wedding to plan. We'll have to make the best wedding cake ever seen, because it's going to be a wedding of substance.'

Daisy watched Sam pacing back and forward in front of the lit fire. She had been surprised to see him standing on her doorstep, and now he seemed to be struggling with his words.

'Daisy . . .' He looked serious, and kept giving fleeting looks at young Tobias. 'You know that you are the centre of gossip in Hawes, but I won't listen to it. In fact none of my family will give the gossips the time of day, and we will stand your corner – we know you've been wronged.' Sam took a deep breath. 'You know how I feel about you, and that we are engaged to be married. Well, I was stupid when I said I needed time to think about it, especially when it comes to young Tobias there. I would be proud to make you my wife, and for Tobias to be brought up as our son.' He exhaled deeply, relieved that he'd said it as planned. 'Damn it, Daisy, I love every inch of you. Let's get married as soon as we can – and to hell with the rest of the world.' He grabbed her by the waist and kissed her, and kissed her again and again.

'Sam! There's Tobias.' Daisy smiled and struggled for breath.

'Come here, Tobias. I'm your new father, and I promise I will look after you for ever.'

Tobias ran to their side. 'Can I help myself to the toffees in your shop?' He grinned up at Sam.

'You can help yourself to a toffee every day, and have cake every day. And we'll make sure you have shoes and clothes when you want them. And that dog your mother was promising? Well, just go and have a look at what is tied up in the back of my cart.'

Tobias sprinted out of the door.

'Sam, you haven't?' Daisy watched from the doorway as Tobias got licked to death by an over-eager sheepdog puppy.

'I have. But what about you, Mrs Allen? When are we to be wed?' Sam held her tightly and kissed her neck. 'I know: how about Valentine's Day – the perfect date for perfect lovers?'

'That's lovely, Mr Allen. Time to read the banns, and for your mother to settle down to the thought of me entering your family.' Daisy had tears in her eyes as she kissed her man. All was perfect. She had her home, her man and her son. *Please God*, she thought, *let everything go to plan this time*.

The cold wind blew as Sam and Daisy entered the small chapel at Lunds at the head of Garsdale. It was a cold February day, but inside the chapel the love of the couple and their family warmed the very bones of everyone gathered there. Even Joshua Oversby and his fiancée, Kitty, beamed as Daisy and Sam kissed after the vicar's blessing.

'Excuse me, everyone. And behave yourself for a minute, my lad. Sorry, Vicar – you've said your bit, now I'll say mine.' Luke Allen stood in front of the congregation. 'I know some of you perhaps think these two shouldn't be married. But I knew from the minute I set eyes on Daisy that she was a grand lass. Now I just want her to know how much she means to me.' Luke fumbled in his pocket and pulled a full jam jar out of his pocket. 'In honour of my new daughter-in-law, here is "Daisy Allen's Lemon Cheese". I got the labels printed last week, as a surprise.' Luke grinned from ear to ear.

'Sit down, you silly old fool. There's more to life than lemon cheese.' Mary pulled at his jacket.

'Aye, lass, but she's going to make me a fortune.'

Luke winked as he watched his son and Daisy walk down the aisle, and whispered, 'Now that's what I call a good investment!'

Daisy's Little Book
of Everyday Recipes

Lemon Cheese

4 eggs
450g / 1lb caster sugar
100g / 4oz butter
Grated rind and juice of 4 lemons

Break the eggs into a basin. Beat slightly, then add the other ingredients and stir over a gentle heat in the basin, over a pan of simmering water, for about 20 minutes or until thick.

Pour into dry jam jars. When cold, cover securely and store in a cool, dry place.

Variation: Orange Cheese

Substitute 2 oranges for the 4 lemons, and add the juice of 1 lemon. Use just 50g / 2oz butter, melting it in a double saucepan or bowl, before adding it to the eggs, sugar, rind and juice.

Kiss-Me Cake

225g / 8oz self-raising flour
pinch of salt
50g / 2oz margarine
50g / 2oz lard
50g / 2oz sugar
1 medium egg, beaten
3 tbsp of milk, if required
raspberry jam
caster sugar for sprinkling

Preheat the oven to 180°C / 350°F / Gas Mark 4. Grease a baking tray.

Mix the flour and salt together. Rub in the margarine and lard and stir in the sugar. Mix to a stiff dough with the beaten egg, adding a little milk if necessary to get a good consistency.

Divide the mixture in half, then roll out both halves into thin rectangles. Place one rectangle on a baking tray and spread with the raspberry jam. Place the other rectangle on top and pinch the edges together.

Bake for 15–20 minutes until golden brown. When cool, cut into squares or triangles and sprinkle with caster sugar.

Onion Chutney

2 tbsp salt
1.4kg / 3lb coarse brown sugar
3.3 litres / 6 pints malt vinegar
3 dozen cooking apples, peeled and thinly sliced
5 medium Spanish onions, thinly sliced
100g / 4oz green ginger, thinly sliced
900g / 2lb sultanas
100g / 4oz bird's-eye chillies
40g / 1½ oz mustard seed
6 shallots, thinly sliced

Dissolve the salt and sugar in the vinegar, then strain and add to a preserving pan.

Add the apples, onions and ginger and the other ingredients, and cook gently until the apples and onions are quite tender.

Pour into small jars or wide-necked bottles. When cold, cover securely and store in a cool, dry place.

Christmas Mincemeat

3 large cooking apples, cored
3 large lemons
450g /1lb raisins
450g / 1lb currants
450g / 1lb suet
900g / 2lb soft light-brown sugar
50g / 2oz candied orange peel
30ml / 2 tbsp orange marmalade
250ml / 8fl oz brandy

Preheat the oven to 200°C / 400°F / Gas Mark 6.

Place the cored cooking apples in an ovenproof dish, cover tightly and bake for 50–60 minutes, until thoroughly tender. Leave to cool.

Grate and squeeze the lemons. Roughly chop the lemon shells, place in a saucepan and add cold water to cover. Bring to the boil, cover the pan and simmer for about 1 hour, until the shells are soft enough to chop very finely.

Scoop the apple flesh from the skins. Place in a large bowl. Stir in the lemon rind, juice and shell with all the remaining ingredients. Cover the bowl and leave for 2 days, stirring occasionally.

Pot into jars, pressing down the mincemeat well. Cover tightly and store for at least 2 weeks before using.

Victoria Sandwich Cake

Originally the Victoria sandwich cake was oblong, filled with jam or marmalade and then cut into fingers, or 'sandwiches'. Now the same basic mixture is used with many different fillings, and it is served as a single round cake.

fat for greasing
150g / 5oz butter
150g / 5oz caster sugar
3 eggs, beaten
150g / 5oz self-raising flour,
or plain flour with 1 tsp baking powder
pinch of salt
raspberry jam or other filling (such as lemon cheese)
caster sugar for sprinkling

Preheat the oven to 180°C / 350°F / Gas Mark 4. Line and grease two 18cm / 7-inch sandwich tins.

In a mixing bowl, cream the butter with the sugar until light and fluffy. Add the beaten eggs gradually, beating well after each addition.

Sift the flour and salt into a bowl, then stir into the creamed mixture, lightly but thoroughly, until evenly mixed.

Divide the mixture between the tins and bake for 25–30 minutes. Cool on a wire rack, then sandwich together with the jam or other filling. Sprinkle the top with caster sugar.

Westmorland Parkin

fat for greasing
200g / 7oz butter
450g / 1lb black treacle
450g / 1lb fine oatmeal
200g / 7oz plain flour
5ml / 1 tsp ground ginger
2.5ml / ½ tsp salt
10ml / 2 tsp baking powder
200g / 7oz Demerara sugar
100 ml / 3½fl oz milk
5 ml / 1 tsp bicarbonate of soda

Preheat the oven to 160°C / 325°F / Gas Mark 3. Line and grease two 20cm / 8-inch tins.

Heat the butter and treacle gently in a saucepan, stirring until the butter has melted. Mix together all the dry ingredients, except the bicarbonate of soda, in a mixing bowl, making a well in the centre.

Warm the milk in a saucepan over a low heat until hand-hot. Stir in the bicarbonate of soda until dissolved. Pour in the dry ingredients and mix well. Stir in the melted butter and treacle.

Spoon the mixture into the prepared tins and bake for about 1½ hours, until cooked through and firm to the touch. Cool in the tins and then cut into squares.

Farmhouse Pork and Rabbit Stew

Serve this delicious dish with jacket potatoes baked at the same time.

Serves 4
1 rabbit, jointed into portions
25g / 1oz flour, sprinkled with salt and pepper
1 head of celery, chopped
2 onions, chopped
225g / 8oz boneless pork, finely cubed
½ teaspoon sage
½ teaspoon thyme
275ml / 9fl oz milk
120ml / 4fl oz chicken stock

Preheat the oven to 160°C / 325°F / Gas Mark 3.

Coat the rabbit portions in the seasoned flour. Put half the celery and onion into a greased casserole dish. Arrange the rabbit on top and then the pork cubes. Sprinkle on the herbs. Cover with the remaining celery and onion.

Mix the milk and chicken stock together and pour over the ingredients in the dish. Cover and bake for 2½ hours. Serve with the baked potatoes to mop up the sauce.

Yorkshire Dream Cake

100g / 4oz butter
100g / 4oz plain flour
25g / 1oz soft brown sugar

Preheat the oven to 180°C / 350°F / Gas Mark 4. Grease a Swiss-roll tin.

Rub the fat into the flour and then add the sugar. Put into the tin, flatten out the mixture and bake for 20 minutes. Allow to cool in the tin.

225g / 8oz soft brown sugar
25g / 1oz plain flour
100g / 4oz chopped walnuts
75g / 3oz dessicated coconut
½ level tsp baking powder
pinch of salt
2 eggs, beaten

Mix all the dry ingredients together and then add the eggs. Combine well, spread on the top of the cooked mixture in the Swiss-roll tin and bake for a further 20 minutes. Do not overcook, as the cake will harden as it cools.

Sugar Apple Cake

100g / 4oz margarine
100g / 4oz sugar
2 eggs, beaten
100g / 4oz self-raising flour
grated rind of 1 lemon
milk for mixing
2 large cooking apples, peeled and sliced
2 tsp cinnamon and 2 tbsp of sugar, mixed together
25g / 1oz butter, cut into small pieces

Preheat the oven to 200°C / 400°F / Gas Mark 6. Grease a 20cm / 8-inch cake tin.

Beat the margarine and sugar to a cream, then add the beaten eggs, flour and lemon rind. Mix with enough milk to make a stiff consistency. Pour into the cake tin.

Place layers of apple slices on top. Sprinkle the cinnamon-and-sugar mixture over the apples and dot with butter. Bake for 35–40 minutes. When cold, serve with cream.

Author's Note

Although this book is a work of fiction, and most names have been changed and the events are completely fictitious, two Yorkshire families have influenced my writing. Here is a little history about these two great trading families.

ELIJAH ALLEN

This family-run business was started in 1860 by Thomas Allen, who was a farmer in Gayle, a tiny hamlet above Hawes in North Yorkshire. Thomas owned livery horses that he would hire out for use pulling carts, or for funerals and weddings. During the great railway-building era of the 1870s Thomas decided to diversify and had the good idea of filling a cart with food to sell to the hundreds of navvies working on the railway line at Ribblehead. Every week he filled his cart with provisions such as tea, sugar, eggs and tobacco, and the local butcher came along as well – with a shotgun under the seat, in case of trouble. Later Thomas's son, Elijah, and his wife Alice, a very resourceful lady, moved to larger premises in the centre of Hawes, where their shop can still be found today.

WILLIAM MOORHOUSE & SONS

The Moorhouse family hailed from The Bull at Broughton, near Skipton in North Yorkshire. William Moorhouse lived with his mother at The Bull, and moved to Skipton in 1851. He was William Stockdale's apprentice in a grocery shop on Sheep Street and, while there, visited outlying farms and was introduced by a Dales family to the delicacy they called 'lemon cheese'. In 1873 William married Angiolina Porri from Caroline Square, whose father owned a business in Sheep Street, Skipton, and the couple moved to Leeds and produced seventeen children. While working for his new employer – the grocer Ellison's – William produced lemon cheese, which he supplied to them and other grocers. It proved very popular, and in 1887 the family moved to Burley, where he started the Moorhouse business by making lemon cheese, orange marmalade and mincemeat; Moorhouse's became the first company to produce mincemeat on a commercial basis in April 1891. The Moorhouse business grew stronger year by year as William's sons joined the business, and it became a household name, known for its jams and spreads and especially for its Christmas puddings.

extracts reading groups

competitions books new

discounts extracts extracts

competitions discounts

books new books

events extracts

extracts new titles reading groups

interviews

events extracts

discounts

new books events

events new

discounts extracts discounts

www.panmacmillan.com

extracts events reading groups

competitions books extracts new

reading groups

events

books

reading groups